THE TIN
FACE
PARADE

JOLY BRAIME

For Popy

'Let us not be worms.'

ONE

—·—

A fellow once advised me that my overactive imagination would get my head popped open sooner or later. He was a rude man, and I considered his warning needlessly graphic, but it was kindly meant. Perhaps, as he delivered this dire prophecy, he had in mind the irregular manner in which his old friend Matthew Grayling had departed this earth.

Grayling was found in the early evening of October 31st, 1907, in his rented premises at the back of Shing's restaurant. The place was on Limehouse Causeway, within earshot of the great crashing and clanking of West India Docks. Set apart from the main building in an airless, blackened yard, Grayling's single-storey workshop was scarcely more than a shed, with decaying brickwork, one opaque window, and a soot-furred chimney pipe.

It was old Shing himself who made the discovery. Calling to collect the week's rent, he found the place in darkness, and was about to leave when he noticed the door was ajar. He ventured inside with the notion that burglars might have broken in, for he knew Grayling kept a valuable stock of sheet copper. There was no gas laid on in that humble place, and the small brick-built forge within had died back to ashes, but by the dull glow of his lamp, the landlord could discern well

1

enough that his tenant's lights were out in all senses of the phrase. A former seafaring man of granite demeanour, Shing had seen worse, but it was a gruesome sight all the same, and he sent a grandson to fetch the Metropolitan Police.

Grayling lay on the floor next to his deeply pitted wooden workbench. He was a large man of around forty years, with brawny forearms below his rolled shirt sleeves, and the soft, flabby bulk of one who in his younger days had been broad and strong. He had the long fingers of an artisan, but his hands were calloused by labour and discoloured by fire and chemicals. The back of one of them bore a faded regimental tattoo.

A rack on the wall above the bench held the departed workman's tools. Snips, stakes, hammers and files, each in its proper place, with two exceptions: a heavy iron hammer, and something known in the smithing trades as a candle mould stake. This latter item loosely resembled the head of a light, lopsided pickaxe, and was of solid steel – about as long as a man's arm and somewhat thicker than his thumb, with tapered ends. It had a specialised usage in the delicate working of fine sheet metal, but on this occasion it had been selected for its form rather than its function. The newspapers later described it simply as a 'mattock head', so as not to confuse the readership.

Another decision the newspapermen took on behalf of the public was to leave deliberately vague the manner in which hammer and stake had been combined to bring about the death of Matthew Grayling. Detail is a fine thing, but one can only pique the popular imagination so far. At any rate, most of Grayling's face had remained undamaged by the procedure, and strangely he did not appear to have been in pain in his final moments. His eyes were open, but not wide, and his mouth

2

was set in a beatific smirk that was quite at odds with the manner of his death.

More ghoulish by half, however, were the other faces present. For there were rows of them, lining both sides of the room, all gazing, expressionless, over the fallen man. Along one dim wall, the shelves held unpainted clay masks, spotted with soot from the forge. The faces were not sculpted, but had been cast from those of real men and women, only they were disfigured and ravaged – missing noses, eyes, chins and cheekbones, like Ancient Greek marbles used for musket practice by Ottoman invaders. Along the opposite wall there were more masks, but these were of intricately worked copper alloy, galvanised then painted with layers of enamel in pale flesh tones. These, too, were incomplete, but in this case it was because they had been designed to patch over only the damaged parts of the clay faces across from them. Noses and jaws were rebuilt; missing eyes and ears were replaced, the creations held in place by collars, straps and wire hooks.

Such was Grayling's remarkable profession. His employer, Fornasini by name, was a showman of note in less delicate circles, whose spectacle consisted of exhibiting on stage a string of unfortunates who at one time or another had survived the most grievous physical wounds. At the outset, these people would appear under the limelights as any other Tom, Dick or Harriet, but would then dramatically proceed – to the gasps of the crowd – to remove eyes, masks, wigs and even limbs, revealing shattered soldiers, jawless matchgirls, burned and broken veterans of a hundred calamities. To achieve such masterworks, Fornasini relied on craftsmen of great skill, and none were more accomplished than Matthew Grayling. Fornasini himself – originally a dental surgeon – handled the structural elements of the masks, but

3

it was Grayling who brought them so strikingly to life. Working from delicate sheets of copper, it was thus that he had fashioned an audience for his own killing.

Needless to say, the good fellows of the London press were in raptures over the whole affair. Men meet violent ends in shady districts all the time, and few enough of us pause to mark their passing, yet the particulars of Grayling's case – and his singular occupation – gave the illustrators plenty to work with.

Despite the protestations of the police that Grayling's demise was no more or less than a burglary gone awry, the next day – a Friday – found the Fleet Street hacks shrieking of intrigue. Was it organised crime? Shing was Chinese, after all. Or some deranged member of Fornasini's troupe gone rogue? In a short statement to a man from *The Evening News,* Giovanni Fornasini scoffed at such insinuations and professed himself bereft, but his grief was evidently not keen enough to prevent him from extending his performance schedule to accommodate a swell in audience numbers.

By early the following week, however, it had become clear that there were no more column inches to be had out of Matthew Grayling. The police maintained that they were looking for simple copper thieves, no further rumours were forthcoming, and the unlucky craftsman vanished back into the obscurity from which he had so briefly emerged.

....

At the time, I had no notion that the unconventional end of Matthew Grayling's life would have any bearing on the continuing matter of my own. I read of his discovery the following day, recounted exuberantly in one of the earthier newspapers that my club disdained

4

to stock. These were the rags I liked best, and I had picked up a copy from a boy on the way in.

My concentration that afternoon was fractured, and I skimmed the article with interest, then forgot it almost immediately as I moved on to a shameless piece of scuttle about a famously prim society beauty. The previous evening had been late and immoderate, and as I languished in a soft armchair in the Beech Lounge, I had at my elbow a glass of hock and soda water, in the hopes that Byron's trusted pick-me-up might prove effective for me too.

And here, before all that is to come, it might be as well to observe that some men go through life being the right fellow in the right place. I was not that sort of man, and before 1907 reached its close, a good number of people were to suffer and die for my inadequacies.

'Plans, Catcliffe?'

I looked up to see one of the neatest moustaches in London, attached to a shy-looking fellow who meant to relieve me of a great deal of money.

'I thought we might play a few hands,' he continued hopefully, picking at his collar.

'Rowland, I have no intention of indulging your mania for baccarat. It is a wretched game and I always lose. And anyway, yes, as it happens, I have made other arrangements for the evening.' I fished in my pocket and made a half-hearted show of checking my watch. 'Might we not have a drink instead? I have a few minutes before I must leave.'

Actually, I could have sat there for at least another hour, but Rowland Renwick's interruption seemed a good opportunity to detach myself from the scandals of the day. A night must begin somewhere, after all.

My own nights had a habit of beginning early, and for many years, my elders and betters had derived great pleasure from describing me in an age-appropriate succession of reproachful terms. I was twenty-nine years old, and as maturity tightened its grip, I had recently graduated from 'wastrel' to 'dissipated'. I do not recall being a 'brat' in early childhood, but I do remember being called 'wayward' at around twelve or thirteen, so perhaps that was when the rot set in.

In my defence, I was not completely without function. There was, in the East London factory of Catcliffe Steel, an office with the name 'Mr Harrison Catcliffe' engraved on a plate upon the door, and most days I did sit at my large polished oak desk for at least a few hours. Work was one way of making the time pass, and my optimistic father always made sure there was plenty of it available. This token contribution to the running of Catcliffe's could hardly be described as 'earning my keep', but it did give my existence some small justification, and more importantly it allowed me to tell people with suitable gravity that I was 'in business'. Mainly, though, I was in the business of amusing myself.

Somewhat crestfallen, Renwick declined my invitation for a drink, and withdrew with short, quick steps, continuing his search for someone to clean out at the card tables. I could never work out how he managed to win so often in a game with such a negligible amount of skill involved, but I felt certain that several men somewhere within that elegant Georgian building were in for an expensive night. At least they would probably deserve it.

Woodville's of St James's was far from the most exclusive of the London clubs, and while it was still possessed of enough snootiness to give it an air of grandeur, its unfussy membership policy was specially designed to accommodate oily-booted plutocrats like me. For my own part, I also appreciated the fact that its name was not a Latin or Greek word, or something relating to conscientious imperial service – especially since there was little enough conscience in that amenable place.

Stirring myself, I kicked my paper underneath the chair, then clambered out of its deep cushions without very much dignity and went downstairs to fetch my coat. The opulent and old-fashioned interior of Woodville's, decorated with dark oil portraits of great and anonymous men, belied the fact that it had only been there for fifteen years or so before I joined, and just as you didn't have to belong to a titled family to get past those burgundy doors, so also the matter of political affiliation was largely unimportant. It was a place that existed for pleasure and camaraderie rather than the opportunity to arrange advantageous marriages or discuss affairs of government.

That is not to say we did not have our fair share of politicians and blue blood. Several such men were drawn to Woodville's for exactly the same reasons I was, and Renwick's victims in the first-floor card room would likely include marquesses and ministers alike. Though he had never graced the tables, one such member was George Edlington, Lord Halsingham. I ran into him on his way out of the cloakroom, and he nodded graciously as I stood aside to let him pass. A baron in degree, though he manifested few of the ruthless and warlike Norman qualities that his title might evoke.

What little remained of his future was tangled together with mine, but until that afternoon I knew Halsingham only by sight. He was around the same age as me, perhaps a few years older, but we had never become friends. He was a regular at the club, rather quiet and reclusive, preferring his own company or that of a select few Etonian contemporaries who would sit in the more formal Pike Lounge (so

7

called because of a monstrous fish that hung in a glass case above the fireplace) and hold earnest discussions over strong coffee and cigars. His retiring nature was reflected in his looks, which – though he was tall and handsome in a lean, old-fashioned way – had a paleness and artificial fragility about them, as if he had issued from one of the gilt picture frames on the walls of Woodville's rather than from a human mother.

What everyone did know about Halsingham was that he was fabulously wealthy, and likely to stay that way since he avoided chancy investments and cards. He owned a vast swathe of Surrey countryside, with substantial properties in the north too, but during the week he lived in a mansion in Belgravia, returning to his estate each weekend. His wife was reputed to be a great beauty, but no-one I knew had ever met her. Beyond that, Halsingham had never seemed interesting enough to investigate further, and he was out of mind before my hat was in hand.

Two

—·—

Restored, to some extent, by the white wine and soda water, and by an hour or two slumped in a deep chair reading my grubby little paper, I emerged from Woodville's sometime after five. The clamour and clatter of Piccadilly a few streets away rang through the alleys, but the cobbled square on which I stood was quiet and chilly under the glow of the freshly kindled gaslights. I flipped the collar of my overcoat up briskly and inhaled a deep lungful of freezing cold air to jolt myself awake, tasting that unsavoury yet enticing London blend of coal fog, horse manure, sewage and carbolic, thick as cheap cigar smoke on my tongue. The night ahead seemed suddenly full of promise, yet turning in the direction of Regent Street, I came abruptly upon a scene that stopped me in my tracks.

Lord Halsingham, in evening dress and holding his cane low and inverted like a sabre, was engaged in a heated exchange with a most singular-looking man. Short in stature, this fellow was a bundle of bones in an oversized brown woollen coat, with a pointed face framed by heavy, grey-shot side-whiskers and a battered black bowler that might have been stolen from a banker some years previously. The mud-crusted cuffs of his trousers ended with two different-coloured shoes, and a second look revealed that, while the brown boot on his left foot was of cracked leather, the black shoe on his right was in fact simply painted onto the end of a shaped wooden leg.

'I have no idea what you are talking about!' cried Halsingham, his attempt to sound stern rather compromised by the speed with which he was backing away towards Woodville's. 'I warn you, if this is blackmail...'

'You're a liar!' raged the small man in return. 'I'm going to ask you again, and you mind how you answer.'

'How dare you! I'll not stand for this outrageous insolence!' and Halsingham drew back his cane with a swish as if to strike the other.

With unexpected agility, and strength beyond his size, the little savage sprang forward and cuffed Halsingham sharply under the eye, knocking him to the ground. He seized the cane from his prostrate adversary and commenced to beat him energetically about the body with it.

Up to this point, I had been considering how best to cross the road and ignore the whole incident. A course of action which was now unacceptable. As if to emphasise my obligations, Morris – the porter at Woodville's – came rushing past me in an effort to protect Halsingham and received for his troubles a vicious crack about the temple with the butt of the cane. The blow dropped him to his knees, and his smart bowler rolled drunkenly into the gutter.

'I'll have the truth out of you yet!' roared the man as he returned his attention to Halsingham.

As a fellow accustomed to the odd scrape, particularly when straying into the wrong parts of town while not fully in control of all his faculties, I was in those days a great advocate of a small palm pistol concealed about one's person. I flippantly believed my humble Remington Type II double-barrelled derringer capable of restoring peace far more effectively than any soothing word or gesture – a conviction in which I persisted right up until the night some months later when I shot someone with it. Over several years, I had produced it only three times, and had never discharged it, except rather inexpertly down a makeshift range in one of the furnace yards at Catcliffe's. A swede on a stick had sustained grievous injuries on my sixth cartridge.

I stepped forward and levelled my tiny weapon with what I considered an attitude of steely resolve.

'Leave him be, sir!'

The little man looked up at me contemptuously, but he did at least stop thrashing Halsingham with the cane. His expression changed abruptly to one of measured appreciation, and I could feel him gauging the likelihood that I would pull the trigger. He took in my fine clothes and hat, the comedic dimensions of my weapon and the amateurish way in which I brandished it, before lighting upon a couple of long and unsightly scars that adorned my face. There was a thin, pink channel along the flesh of my right cheek, and a thicker, paler one that disappeared into my hair above my left ear. They were unmistakably relics of past violence, and seemed to give him pause for concern.

Slowly, he lowered the cane, then snapped it abruptly over his knee and flung it aside. He loomed over Halsingham. His voice was hoarse, with a distinct Midlands accent.

'Thing is, I don't think your mate will shoot me, but you never know – he might find it in him. I haven't finished this, though. The truth's there and I'll get to it.'

Halsingham looked up at him, wide-eyed.

11

The little man shot me a look of practised malevolence, then turned tail and ran off down the street at some considerable speed, despite his limping gait. He disappeared into an alley and was gone.

As abruptly as I had come upon the incident, it was over, and I was pointing my derringer at empty cobbles. Releasing the hammer carefully, I placed it back in my coat pocket and stepped forward to offer Halsingham my arm, but trusty old Morris had already found his feet and was pulling the young peer upright. That slender, battered gentleman brushed himself down, fingered his bruised cheek, then gathered his wits and strode up to me, extending a hand.

'I am much obliged to you, sir. Halsingham is my name, and I am ashamed to say I do not know yours.'

'Harrison Catcliffe. Though you must call me Harry. Everyone does. Pleased to make your acquaintance.'

'In that case, please, call me George.' He flicked fretfully at a crust of manure adhering to his trouser leg. 'Your rescue was most timely, for I cannot say what injuries that ruffian might have inflicted upon me had you not produced your pistol just now. Do I take it you are an officer?'

I rubbed my pocket guiltily.

'Just a careful fellow.'

'Then your caution has been my good fortune. May I invite you to join me for a drink by way of thanks?'

It was back in the warmth of the Beech Lounge, with cigarettes lit and restorative brandies securely cradled in our hands, that Halsingham told me fully of his little drama. He remained entirely at a loss to explain it.

He had been headed to dine with an old friend of his father's, but he was a few minutes early so planned to walk to his evening appointment and take in some of the poisonous autumnal air. Scarcely had Halsingham set off along his way, however, when the roguish fellow with the wooden boot had stepped out of the very same side alley down which he later disappeared and begun to walk swiftly toward him.

'It sounds odd,' said Halsingham, 'but I fancy I could tell from the moment I saw him that he meant mischief. In no time at all he had blocked my way and called me by name.'

My new friend was not a natural storyteller, but he made a creditable (and faintly comical) attempt to convey the man's accent and manner.

'Lord Halsingham,' the little chap had said, with malice in his voice, 'you have been party to the murder of an old and dear friend of mine. I mean to have out of you the reason, and you'd best be straight with me.'

Replying that he did not like the man's tone, Halsingham had dismissed his allegations. He had added – rather unwisely – that the notion of him having dealings with any lowlife associate of such a fellow was frankly preposterous. This had not soothed his accuser's temper.

'He told me that he was not intimidated by my grand name, and that he had it on good authority that a man called Matthew Grayling had undertaken a confidential commission on my behalf not a few months back. The man had recently died, and he was convinced that the two things were connected.'

It took me a moment to place Matthew Grayling's name, but the newspaper article of earlier that afternoon quickly came back to my mind. I took a sip of brandy and looked at Halsingham encouragingly.

'Well, obviously the man might as well have been speaking in tongues for all the sense it made to me,' he said hastily, his face a picture of unimpeachable innocence.

After first protesting that it was a simple case of mistaken identity, Halsingham had lighted on the idea that perhaps he might be the victim of an elaborate blackmail scam. And it was at about this point that I had sauntered onto the scene, just in time to witness the waifish baron getting the shoeing of his adult life.

Halsingham's story was concluded, and all that remained for me was to rummage under the chair in which I had been sitting only twenty minutes previously, and to produce the news item on the death of Matthew Grayling. He read it with interest but was still none the wiser. He professed to never having met anyone by the name of Grayling, nor could he recall any occasion on which he had knowingly encountered Giovanni Fornasini or any of his associates. It was a perfect mystery, and one that even then piqued my curiosity.

We decided the episode was simply to be chalked up to the perilous nature of London life, and Halsingham vowed that he would think twice before walking the streets again on his own after dark, even in such an outwardly respectable district as St James's. I once again recommended a pocket pistol for just such occasions, and we both agreed that the incident had at least allowed us to make each other's acquaintance.

....

Over the weeks that followed, Lord Halsingham and I became friends of a sort. Despite his slightly skittish nature and sense of detachment, I found him to be an intelligent and articulate companion, quite kind even in his way. He was a man unacquainted with many of the rougher aspects of life, even compared to such as I, and this fact made his violent encounter outside Woodville's all the more incongruous.

We rarely alluded to the meeting with the one-legged man, for Halsingham was strangely embarrassed by it, and he requested that I did not disclose the matter to the other members of the club. In my mind, I did not associate this with deception, but rather with a reluctance to be in any way connected with the more sordid side of the city, and with a faint sense of shame that it had reached out of the fog and pawed at him. I had no reason to suspect that the story was anything more than one of mistaken identity, or perhaps, as he had suggested, an attempt to shock him into handing over money.

For his part, Halsingham made some splendid misjudgements about me, and I was far too delighted to consider disabusing him of them. He and his set knew little of industry, being in general more involved in either large-scale agriculture or politics, so over our occasional dinners I would talk expansively of the age of the machine. I would pepper my conversation with gauges of metal, die-setters and millwrights, deep drawing and pressing, safe in the knowledge that there was no-one around to pick holes in my chatter. This thin veneer of commercial wisdom, coupled with my mysterious scars and dainty firearm, led Halsingham to believe me something of a man of the world – a level-headed fellow who could be relied upon in a crisis.

It was this misapprehension, I now believe, that led him to approach me one early evening as I sat over sharpeners with some companions in the Beech Lounge. Drawing me aside, he asked if he might have a word in private.

'But of course, my good fellow,' I said. 'What is bothering you?'

'Nothing at all,' he replied with unusual joviality. 'Only that Lady Halsingham and I are holding a small party at my home in Surrey on Saturday – for it is the occasion of our wedding anniversary – and I wondered if you might agree to join us for the weekend. The party is really for my wife's benefit. She is apt to become a little low in spirits out in the relative isolation of the country, and I think she would be perfectly charmed to meet you – even if certain of your anecdotes might prove a little... vigorous for such a refined lady.'

His words might not have been entirely complimentary, but his meaning was generous enough, and despite the fact that I had no real desire to spend two nights marooned out in rural England, I accepted his invitation. Aside from my wish not to offend him, I had also some degree of curiosity about how Lord Halsingham might live, and what sort of woman he might be married to. I imagined them as a polite, reserved pair, with a couple of neat, pale children and a serene wolfhound plodding disinterestedly through oak-panelled hallways.

THREE

— · —

The saying goes that a shrewd man sees little difference between obstacle and opportunity and is able to turn both to his advantage. As a young veterinarian of some small means, my grandfather had decided that the heavy horses and towpath ponies which constituted his main livelihood did not feature prominently in a future where tireless iron beasts pulled with the strength of fifty Clydesdales.

Ferrous metals did not glitter like gold or diamonds, but old Jonas Catcliffe could see the glint of lucre behind their dull faces. He invested in a workshop, which after some years of relentless graft became a factory. By the time he died in 1905, this lone property had multiplied into three great oil-soaked steel mills, where hundreds of souls lived and died to feed the insatiable hunger of industry while Catcliffe men stalked the gantries above their heads.

Grandpa was a canny sort all right. When he lost his head for numbers and finally retired to a murderous twilight shooting half-blind at over-fed birds in the Yorkshire Dales, his sons took over the running of his little empire. The eldest, my father 'Young' Jonas, moved to London with his family to open the largest and most modern factory yet, and when I returned from my university studies in Leipzig, an office and a generous salary awaited. So you see, when it came to apportioning blame for the man I had become, Grandpa deserved his share.

By the time Friday came, I had long since gone off the idea of a weekend at Halsingham House. I had spent a fidgety morning hunched over my desk at Catcliffe's, trawling through bone-dry export paperwork as the presses boomed beneath me on the factory floor. The time had dragged abominably, and I was ready for a lengthy luncheon and several glasses of wine by the time I took up my coat, hat and case, and booted the office door closed behind me. Instead of the leisurely repast I so desired, I walked to a workmanlike dining room some few minutes from the factory. This establishment boasted what were undoubtedly the most uncomfortable seats in London – tall, narrow benches that one perched on perilously like a cat upon a windowsill – but the food was quick and excellent, and I hastily demolished a chop and a pint of good strong beer the colour of conker shells, before hailing a cab for Waterloo.

As usual, the station was a heaving bazaar of humanity at its most wretched – the chaos enhanced by the fact that the London and South Western Railway had been tearing up the whole area for as long as anyone could remember and seemed in no danger of ever finishing. Self-important businessmen with cases as heavy as their moustaches ploughed roughly through the crowds, sending ragged little families tumbling over each other like confused ducklings. Beggars propped their bent backs against the pillars, casting bare, scabrous legs out in front of them and pointing sorrowfully at their mouths in mute appeal. Passing the buffet, I caught a glimpse of an improbably elegant young woman in a braided coat and feathered hat seated at one of the tables, disappointment writ large across her face as she surveyed a cup of sour coffee and a dry, discarded shoe of a sandwich. A malignant fog of steam drifted damply through the cold air, and in the midst of the whole sordid carnival, a large black dog with a white chest sat morosely in everyone's way, wearing a collection box for the Railwaymen's Orphanage Fund.

Full to bursting with misanthropy, I eventually found a compartment to myself on what I hoped was the right train. It was not a busy service, and within a short time of pulling away from Waterloo, the smoking chimneystacks, peeling viaducts, ranks of blackened terraces and dingy hostelries gave way to the detached Georgian houses and long, thin gardens of genteel suburbia. Light began to filter more determinedly through the lingering gloom of the capital. I was reminded of a line from one of the great writers of our age, who described these areas as 'the monster tentacles which the giant city was throwing out into the country', yet soon I found myself beyond the limits of even these snaking tendrils. I changed trains at Guildford, from whence the tracks sliced eastward through the wide fields, clustered villages and outlying towns of south-eastern England. In a paddock by the railway line I saw a ragged Union Jack fluttering jauntily atop a gigantic pile of manure. No doubt the sentiment was more patriotic than the metaphor.

There was something about the English countryside – even in the gloom of a misty late autumn afternoon – that comforted the sooty soul of a city dweller. The bare trees, stubbly fields and herds of mud-spattered livestock standing immobile in the drizzle had a sort of cleanliness that seemed to strip away from one's heart the grime of the cobbles, and by the time I stepped onto the platform at Halsingham station, the misery of Waterloo was forgotten. I was self-aware enough to know that permanent residence in such a place would not be to my tastes, but at that moment a jaunt out of town felt like a grand thing to be doing, and I was glad I had not cancelled the trip on some thin excuse or other.

As the train lumbered out of the station, I paused on the deserted platform for a couple of minutes, looking out across the grey-green fields towards the huddled cottages of Halsingham village on the other side of the beck. Unaware that I was being watched, I closed my eyes and tasted for a moment the fresh air that still held a sniff of coal smoke. The place was so tiny it barely qualified as a station at all, and its existence was undoubtedly the result of some arrangement between an earlier Lord Halsingham and the railway company. Rural England was full of these odd little halts, where the landed gentry had granted permission to lay track across their estates in exchange for a convenient stop to facilitate their parties. I crossed over the rails and made my way out past the empty ticket office.

Halsingham's motor car, an ornate landaulette in dark green with gleaming brass details, was waiting for me outside. Next to the open-sided driver's compartment stood an affable, heavily built chauffeur, dressed in a spotless long coat and peaked hat. He had the physicality of a horseman about him, and I was willing to bet that he had started out as a groom in the days before engines came to Halsingham House. Even his vehicle appeared more like a carriage than a motor car.

'Mister Catcliffe, sir?'

'None other. Are you Halsingham's man?'

'That I am, sir. Rackley's the name. I'm to take you up to the house.' He reached out a hand for my luggage.

'Much obliged to you, Rackley. Is it far?'

'A quarter hour or so in this weather, sir. The lady is already in the back.' He gestured towards the enclosed rear section of the landaulette. 'Did you perhaps meet her on the train down?'

'I did not, but I am sure we will strike up an acquaintance soon enough.'

My interest piqued, I left him with my bag and clambered inside. Waiting for me in the spacious leather and velvet interior was the lady of whom Rackley had spoken. She was probably not more than twenty-four or five, wearing heavy woollen skirts above muddied boots, and a jacket of thick country tweed over an embroidered white flannel blouse, much in the fashion of a lady golfer. She had taken off her hat, and her chestnut hair was twisted and skewered into an elaborate pompadour arrangement, from which it was making a concerted attempt to escape.

I removed my hat and bowed to such an extent as the confines of the cabin would allow.

'Harrison Catcliffe.'

'Agnes Cleveley. Pleased to meet you, Mr Catcliffe.'

'Harry, please. Do I take it we were on the same train?'

'We were. My motor car is playing up – it's too tiresome. And if you are to be plain old Harry then I must be plain old Agnes. They told me to look out for you, though the man described to me did not seem the sort to be dawdling on a train platform with his eyes screwed shut and his nose in the air. Still, you have his scars, so you must be he.'

I laughed to conceal my faint displeasure. After all, no-one likes to be cast into a role they have not chosen. 'You have me at an advantage, for you seem to know all about me, and I have no clue who you are. I might venture to guess, but I fear I would be wide of the mark.'

'Why don't you venture to guess first?' She smiled one of those grand, warm smiles that are impossible to counterfeit, and I resolved to like her for the time being.

'All right, though you must not laugh too hard if I am wrong.'

I made a show of appraising her carefully, one finger upon my chin.

'Being young, expensively dressed and...' peering pointedly at her left hand, '...unmarried, I suspect you are probably related to one of the party. Your name is not Edlington, so are you perhaps a sibling of Lady Halsingham?'

'Blind luck! There's a whole crowd of guests attending this weekend and I could have been related to any one of them. However, you have me. My sister Henrietta is indeed Lady Halsingham, and I confess I can barely contain my excitement at seeing her after nearly seven months. Our father is Lord Kelverton, and I am obliged to spend most of my time at our home in Northumberland. Father's health has been rather poor this last year, and he is apt to fret when I go away – the lot of a favoured younger daughter, I'm afraid.'

Agnes was easy to take to, and the quarter hour in the back of the landaulette passed quickly. She told me she had two siblings – her older sister Henrietta, and a younger brother by the name of Richard – and that she had broken her long journey from the North East with a two-night stopover at her family's house in London. The previous morning, Lady Halsingham had informed her by letter that I too would be on the afternoon train from Waterloo. No doubt the older sister had hoped that the younger might enlist me as an escort, but I could see even from our brief acquaintance that Agnes Cleveley was untroubled by notions of her own vulnerability. I liked her all the better for it, along with the fact that she took even less trouble to feign interest in my work than I did.

....

Soon enough, we passed through a set of tall, partially gilded gates by a gatekeeper's lodge, and almost immediately a thin screen of oaks and copper beeches opened out into a long driveway descending to Halsingham House. Even in the failing light it was an impressive sight. The approach had evidently been meticulously landscaped by some latter-day Humphrey Repton, and it framed the house in a wide diorama of bold, natural colours, the palette of which had no doubt been carefully planned to vary dramatically and precisely depending on the season. More formal gardens lay behind the house, but leading down towards the gravel courtyard at the front were elegantly kept hedges and mature trees. To the west lay a wide man-made lake with a boathouse and a little pier at one edge.

The edifice itself was decidedly a castle rather than a house, but this was more due to its size than its style. Halsingham was imposing, of course, but its grandeur was not of the theatrical sort – especially when compared to the flamboyant mansions that we crass industrialists were fond of throwing up in the north. The only obvious concessions to bad taste were the man-size statues of rearing horses that stood on either side of the broad front door like gigantic chess pieces.

'It's a rum old place,' said Agnes as I gave her a hand down from the landaulette. 'Draughty as an old cowshed, but that's nothing out of the ordinary – our place is just the same. Halsingham just always feels a bit... well... stately.'

'Aren't all these great old houses stately? Isn't that the idea? Between you and me, I haven't been to all that many,' I admitted.

She took my arm with an attitude of reassurance, and we began to ascend the steps towards the front door together.

'I suppose it is, and I suppose they are. What I mean is, I can't really imagine anyone's ever played sardines at Halsingham.'

The butler, a mature fellow called Inman, was waiting in the doorway along with a couple of footmen, while two more unloaded the luggage. Halsingham was evidently not one to skimp on the staff, and it made me feel rather self-conscious about the single capricious maid in my own employ.

The inside of Halsingham House suited my impressions of its owner rather better than the exterior – with dark wood panelling, a wide staircase leading up from the hall, and murky oil paintings of former lords and ladies posing sternly with sighthounds and allegorical items. We were relieved of our coats, then Inman steered us through to a well-lit drawing room, where we were received by Lord and Lady Halsingham.

FOUR

—·—

O f course, it is easy to say with the enviable benefit of hindsight, but I feel certain that I sensed at once some trouble between Lord Halsingham and his wife. The pair stood further apart than two people ought to have done had they existed on friendly terms, and from the outset there seemed a distance between them beyond even that physical quantity of inches.

Though there was an evident family resemblance, Henrietta was in many ways strikingly different from her sister. Her beauty – the only real fact about her to have travelled up the railway line to London – was of the arresting sort that made men like me trip over our words, and there was a hesitancy about her that was at odds with her sibling's openness.

Tall and slender, with a long neck and flecked blue eyes, Lady Halsingham had a picturesque quality not unlike that of her husband. Where George belonged in the darkened, stately portraits of Woodville's, she was drawn from a different genre of fine art. Not a buxom Madonna or a smug allegorical representation of virtue, but rather a tragic heroine of Greek mythology, portrayed with alabaster skin, rosebud lips and resigned anguish.

'Mr Catcliffe, may I present my wife, Lady Halsingham,' announced Halsingham. 'Henrietta, this is Mr Harrison Catcliffe.'

She inclined her head gracefully, and I did the same. The press would later dub her 'the Bloody Baroness', but she was never that to me.

'Mr Catcliffe, I understand you were lately the instrument of my husband's salvation. I must thank you for your courage.'

'I assure you, Lady Halsingham, he has overstated my part.'

At that moment she spotted Agnes hovering slyly in the doorway behind me, and her whole bearing changed. The reserve in her smile melted away, and she rushed forward with a cry of delight.

'My dear sister, how I have missed you!' The pair embraced with the abandon of children – the older sister in her flowing, richly embroidered gown and the younger still in her bulky travelling clothes and boots. 'You have no idea how I've longed to see your face,' murmured Henrietta into a tweedy shoulder.

Recovering her composure, she disengaged herself and turned to me, the ripples of happiness still apparent in her demeanour.

'Please forgive my manners, Mr Catcliffe. I am so very fond of my sister, and I have not seen her since the spring.'

'I quite understand, Lady Halsingham. I don't doubt I would be just the same. And please, you must call me Harry.'

At this, Halsingham laughed nervously and stepped forward to kiss Agnes's hand, the familial intimacy of which he clearly found awkward.

'Come, you must sit down with us and have a drink. Tell us of your journeys.'

The drawing room was grand and not overly comfortable, with a slight excess of space that made me long for my own cluttered study, or the clusters of pillowy armchairs at Woodville's. The ladies perched on a settee and conversed excitedly, while Halsingham and I stood stiffly to one side. The last of the light was dying outside, and I could almost feel the cold country mist laying its fine frost on the outside of the large windows. I instinctively steered Halsingham towards the fire.

We discussed the journey from London, and I told him some tedious business anecdote in which he affected great interest. He began to mutter about a connection between my story and a recent session at the House of Lords, but much to my relief he was diverted by the arrival of more guests. I found him distracted, even more distant than usual.

For her part, Lady Halsingham looked much more at ease than when I arrived, and as the two sisters sat in conversation, it was as if Agnes's warmth had somehow carried through the evening air and breathed life into her sister.

The new guests were Lord and Lady Bowles, family friends of Halsingham's who had travelled down from Suffolk. Lord Bowles was a robust fellow with a majestic chestnut moustache, a decade or so older than Halsingham and me. Though familiar enough with the capital, he was a man who preferred his country pursuits over the diversions of the city, and he spoke with great relish of the sustained mass murder of God's lesser creatures. As with anyone who moved among the moneyed classes, I had a segment of my brain devoted to their taxonomy, and I classified Bowles with little difficulty as a hunting bore, making a mental note to avoid certain conversational triggers. Sportsmen are tedious enough of their own accord, and must

27

never be encouraged. His wife was a gauche yet likeable lady, displaying a provincial formality that clashed exquisitely with her frequent, vivid references to various digestive sensitivities present among her children.

This completed our party for the Friday night, the remainder of the weekend's guests having arranged to arrive on Saturday in time for the evening celebrations. Presently we went our separate ways to dress for dinner, and I was led upstairs to an expensively furnished room on the first floor. The curtains and bed linen were of a pleasing claret colour, with very small prints of fox hunts in thick gilded frames placed around the walls. A fire smouldered cheerfully in the polished grate, and the bed, as was often the case in old houses, was wide and short, as if it had been built for a corpulent child, or perhaps Queen Victoria. It was, in all, a much pleasanter room than those on the ground floor.

At home I was in the habit of dressing myself, but such a middle-class affectation would not do at all in the august surrounds of Halsingham. Bowles had brought his own man, while I was to share Halsingham's valet, a fellow by the name of Brown, who from the look of him had no doubt been the cause of more than a couple of amorous sighs below stairs. He was slim, with high cheekbones, a strong jaw, and deep lines at the corners of his eyes and mouth. His manner was confident and rather informal, and there was something about the way he carried himself that hinted at a tougher man behind the carefully pressed exterior.

As he went about his work, he chatted amiably, asking about my journey, my work and how I found London.

'If you don't mind my observing,' I gambled, as Brown busied himself with my bow tie, 'you strike me as a fellow who has not always been in service.'

He gave me a friendly grin which must have had paralysing effects on the kitchen maids. 'Am I making such a bad go of your tie, sir?'

'On the contrary, you are doing a capital job. It is just your manner, is all. Other valets of my acquaintance have been rather more... reserved.'

'A regular detective you are, sir. You're right – well, in a way at least. I was a batman – soldier-servant – in the British South Africa Police. Spent ten years or so over there. I returned just this February, and perhaps I'm still adjusting to domestic life.'

'Did you see much action?'

'After a fashion, sir, after a fashion. My first officer was lost in the Matabele war before I'd worked with him a year. God keep him, he wasn't much older than I was. Long time ago now, but I've done my share of fighting since under other men.'

'I'm sorry if I have forced you to speak of it, Brown. My curiosity sometimes gets the better of me.'

'Oh no, sir, it's quite all right. It wasn't a bad period of life. Of course, I've a good position here, but I still miss Africa sometimes.'

His conversation was a welcome diversion from the tension downstairs, and I considered idly that, had old Jonas Catcliffe's father not raised the money for his veterinary training, and had all the subsequent caprices of man and fortune not carried my own family on more profitable currents, then I might have ended up like Brown, making the most of the opportunities that life afforded. Self-deception is a delightful thing.

FIVE

—.—

Halsingham and Lord Bowles were taking a pre-dinner sherry in the drawing room when I descended, and Bowles was rhapsodising with cordite-scented delight about a necessary increase in the cull on his estate. Halsingham was subdued – more even than I had seen him before. He stared into his glass or the fire, and took almost no part in the conversation beyond the odd hum of assent, a level of participation which suited Bowles perfectly. As we waited for the ladies to come down, I began to fear that the night was going to be a long one indeed.

Thankfully, I had not reckoned on Agnes Cleveley, who breezed into the room alongside Lady Halsingham. Despite the older sister's poise, it was the younger who wrangled a room most adeptly into her own orbit, sweeping away as she did so the cobwebs of melancholy that Halsingham had been busily spinning across the ceiling. Making such entrances had no doubt formed part of their education, but it was no less impressive for that.

'Now, Lord Bowles, let us limit the hunting tales to no more than one every half hour. As you know, I enjoy the hunt myself, and between us we could swap stories all night, but you must own that it is hardly a subject for polite dinner table discussion.'

For all his bombast, Bowles was putty in the hands of the Cleveley girls. He returned Agnes's smile sheepishly, revealing an uneven jumble of yellow and brownish teeth.

'An eminently sensible suggestion, Miss Cleveley. Such simple and antique passions as ours are more suited to the open air than the dining table. Pray, of what shall we talk?'

To my surprise, it was Lady Halsingham, not Agnes, who turned suddenly to me, saying, 'I should love to hear of some of the pursuits of the city, Mr Catcliffe – Harry, I mean. It has been so long since I have enjoyed the pleasures of London. George stays there regularly, but for my own part I have a mother's lot, and rarely venture from home.'

'I have yet to meet your children, Lady Halsingham. Do I take it that the little Halsinghams are yet too young to be abroad at this hour?' With characteristic reserve, Halsingham had never spoken of his issue.

'There is only one. My darling Thomas is but five years old, and he is in bed now. He is not a well child, and he needs his rest, but we have high hopes that he will grow to be a strong young man. Is that not so, George?'

I realised that this was the first time I had heard either Lord or Lady Halsingham address one another directly, and Halsingham himself seemed uneasy with such an approach.

'Of course we do, my dear. And he will yet make a fine young man to follow his father and grandfather into the House of Lords.' Turning to the rest of us, he added, 'He is terribly bright, you know, though his health leaves him with so little energy. But my wife yearns to hear of London. Please, Harry, do tell her of your experiences. I am afraid that Mr Balfour asks a great deal of his representatives in the upper house, and I am afforded little time to enjoy the city as you do.'

31

....

The substance of dinner itself was excellent, for Lord and Lady Halsingham were not the sorts to cut corners in any point of correct entertaining. The servants bent their wine decanters glasswards with creditable liberality, though it seemed only Bowles and I were taking full advantage of this. In terms of discourse, it was, for the most part, an inoffensive affair. Until the arrival of the dessert trolley, at which point a nerve was unmistakeably pricked.

When Lady Bowles recounted a humorous story about one of her offspring – a murderous-sounding little snob of six years old by the name of Bartholomew – she could hardly have foreseen its effect upon the Halsinghams. It appeared that young Bartholomew was a restless sleeper, and would occasionally go on perambulations around the nursery while in a sort of trance, neither fully asleep nor fully awake. In such a state, he was apt to confuse real life with his dream world, and had only the previous week been discovered sitting in a darkened bedroom, holding a loud conversation with one of his sister's dolls on a shelf above in the mistaken apprehension that it was a wild duck in disguise. When his nurse attempted to return him gently to bed, he told her with absolute conviction that he was talking it out of its tree so he could wring its neck and eat it up for supper.

At this harmless anecdote, Lord Bowles snorted mirthfully into his wine glass, Agnes laughed politely, and the narrator herself let out a modest little titter, yet our host and hostess appeared suddenly stony-faced. We all noted this and returned pointedly to the bounty of the trolley, but Lady Bowles was not the sort to let a thought exist within the four walls of her own head when it could be spoken aloud.

'Forgive me, my dears! Something in my artless tale has obviously offended you. Perhaps you are not so partial to the hunt as we are?'

It was Halsingham who spoke, though hesitantly.

'Not at all, Lady Bowles. It is only that we have had... more regrettable experiences of this phenomenon, and we struggle to find it a subject for mirth.' He paused for a moment, avoiding his wife's eye, then continued, hurriedly, as if he might at any moment lose the courage to finish making his point. 'Indeed, what one might view as endearing and harmless in a child can be quite the opposite when carried to adulthood, and can make every night a torment for both the sleepwalker and those around them. One can reach the stage where even the simple motion of extinguishing the lamp before bed can become an act infused with the fear of what darkness and slumber will bring.'

He himself was visibly affected by this short speech, but not nearly so much so as Lady Halsingham, who interrupted him suddenly.

'George! I beg you not to make such insinuations in front of a table full of guests!'

'Henrietta...' he began, but she continued, her eyes bright with tears.

'A loving husband – one with even a shred of respect for the lady... shackled to him – would not denigrate her with these hurtful fictions! If you speak thus when I am in the room, I must be shamed to my very heart by the stories you tell when you are in town!'

As with most confirmed bachelors, I abhorred scenes of domestic discord, and I thought for a moment that Lady Halsingham was going to increase the awkwardness a hundredfold by fleeing the room in tears. Thankfully she did not. In fact, with a glance towards Agnes, who seemed almost equally moved in sympathy, she recovered herself a little. Her face took on an expression of tranquil despair that I felt certain I had seen before in a *Sacrifice of Polyxena* from the 1600s.

'Dear friends, I really must apologise. My husband and I are both very tired this evening, and it is perfectly beastly of us to argue in front of those who have come such a long way to enjoy good food and company.'

'Well said, Henrietta,' said Halsingham, with a hint of warmth returning to his tone. 'Please do forgive us. And, my dear, I am sorry to have upset you.'

There were several seconds of conciliatory silence, then Lord Bowles, who wielded conversation as if it were a circus strongman's hammer, launched into a story about a horse. On this occasion I think we were all grateful for his presence.

After dinner, both during brandy and cigars and thereafter in the drawing room, no mention was made of the episode. However, the taint of the earlier ill feeling nevertheless persisted, and most of the company made their excuses and retired to bed soon after we rejoined the ladies. For my part, I helped myself to a generous last tumbler from the decanter, borrowed a book from among the hefty volumes of Halsingham's library, and took myself upstairs.

The book was *The Arabian Nights*, though I noted with some mild disappointment that it was a modern version, and many of the lewder tales had been cleaned up or excised from the collection altogether. Nevertheless, the stories retained some of their exotic charm, and I sat leafing owlishly through the richly illustrated volume in an armchair by the fire until sleep dragged at my eyelids and I migrated into the fat child's bed.

....

It is an unavoidable side effect of two cups of coffee and a similar quantity of brandy taken shortly before bed that one awakes an hour or two later with an incipient urge to pass water. Far from being an annoyance, I have found this nightly waking to be a rather pleasant experience. One arises lazily, proceeds to effect delicious relief, then sinks back into the sheets, pausing a moment or two to savour the tranquillity of the early hours and the indulgence of going back to sleep without the least feeling of guilt. Throughout the act, one scarcely wakes up, and I suspect that on more than one occasion I have carried out the entire procedure in my sleep.

In the early hours of that Saturday morning – the last day of November – I awoke sprawled across the broad bed at Halsingham House, legs and arms flung wide apart like a pigeon blasted from the sky by Lord Bowles's shotgun. I slid off the edge of the bed, sleepily dragged the chamber pot from beneath, and commenced my business with it. As I listened to the soothing sound of the warm stream drumming upon the pan, I became suddenly aware of another sound in the background, something faint yet unmistakeably human. With the diminuendo of my own porcelain tinkling, the sound solidified into a voice, then two voices, one low, one higher, and both, though still scarcely audible, with the air of distress about them.

I considered for around a second and a half the possibility of returning to my bed, but curiosity easily conquered sloth, and I quickly donned a dressing gown and slipped out of my room into the darkened corridor.

I regretted almost instantly not bringing a candle. The dim moonlight which, coupled with the glow of embers from the fire, had served to illuminate my room after a fashion, barely penetrated the inky darkness of the long landing, and I had to feel my way along the walls towards the source of the sounds. The voices, one male and one female, were clearer now, and both seemed to be sobbing and crying out, shouting over the top of each other. It did not take long for my thoughts to return to the tiff over dinner between Lord and Lady Halsingham.

I will admit to feeling some small measure of guilt at snooping on the private affairs of a husband and wife who had treated me with nothing but kindness, but in my defence I can only say that curiosity is a characteristic of almost all humankind. As small boys in slums cluster round the corpse of a vagrant found frozen on a winter's morning, desperate to know his most private tragedies, so I crept down a black passage in the middle of the night in one of England's great country houses, keen to uncover the dramas within.

The thing about great country houses, though, is that they contain miles upon miles of corridors, landings and stairs, and if one is merely following a set of muffled sounds that could be issuing from any part of the building, filtering through servants' stairwells, chimneys or ventilation courses, it is almost impossible to find your way anywhere near them. This is doubly true when one is groping one's way along the wood panelling in the dark. After a while, during which time I must scarcely have covered twenty yards of Halsingham House (though I had turned a corner and gone down two steps without falling over), there was the sound of slamming doors and the house returned to silence.

I waited five seconds, straining my ears to catch another noise. Then ten seconds. Then there was a creak, much closer to me, and the shuffling sound of footsteps. It was not the step of someone going about their reasonable nightly business (say, a man rising from his bed to pass water), but a stealthy, sliding tread. The steps came closer and closer to me, and I was seized with a sudden fear that whoever this nocturnal prowler might be, there was a very real possibility that they might blunder straight into me. I pressed my back flat against the wall, my palms clammy against the panelling, my heels dug into the skirting board and my arms suddenly covered with gooseflesh that I could not attribute entirely to the winter air. The footsteps were almost upon me now, still quiet, still sneaking, but near enough that I could hear the way the bare feet peeled away from the wooden floor.

Then, in a moment, she passed me. Close enough that it was a miracle she did not see or touch me. My eyes were useless in the darkness (they may even have been closed, I could not honestly say), but in my mind was a vivid image of the woman slipping past me. I cannot tell you how I knew – what animal instincts enable us to distinguish a certain scent or way of moving from another – but I was almost certain that the woman who tiptoed past me at that moment was Agnes Cleveley.

I waited a long time, long enough until I could no longer hear even the most distant rustle of her feet upon the floor, then felt my way with infinite caution back to my room and the welcoming red glow of its dying fire. I slid the chamber pot back under the bed, then burrowed under the covers and slept a fitful sleep.

Six

— · —

I awoke to a gentle, almost apologetic knock at my bedroom door. Bleached-out slivers of winter light spilled through the curtains and across the foot of my bed. I called out sleepily, and Brown, the valet, strode smartly into my room.

'Shall I open the curtains, sir?'

I murmured my assent, and he parted the heavy velvet drapes, flooding the room with a bright, crisp country morning. He set a pot of coffee on my bedside table, as a very young housemaid stole in behind him with a coal scuttle and began coaxing the embers back to life. There was frost on the inside of the window, and the oily black coffee steamed ferociously as he poured it out.

'As requested, sir. I'm assured it's a strong brew. I'll return when you wish to get ready for breakfast.'

He left, and as I watched the girl blowing gently on the first flames, I remembered the bizarre parlour games of the previous evening. I was torn between curiosity and my desire for an easy, uncomplicated life, and I could not decide whether I would rather I had slept through. Eventually I consoled myself with the fact that, however cheerful the weather outside was, the climate within the walls of Halsingham

House that day was likely to be nothing short of glacial. A little intrigue to distract myself with could hardly be a bad thing.

Breakfast was, as predicted, a reserved affair, dominated (in my own mind at least) by my fascination at Agnes's acting prowess. She ate heartily, spreading the jam thickly on her toast in a manner that would have appalled the frugal men of my Yorkshire homelands, and with her hazel eyes as bright and mischievous as ever. She sparkled with good humour and levity, yet I knew – knew with even greater surety now I saw her again in the daylight – that it had been Agnes who passed me in the corridor in the dead of night. What did she see? And did she have any part in it? From her friendliness towards Lord Halsingham, I felt certain there was no tension between them.

She spotted me peering at her over my teacup and shot me a curious look, making me glance quickly away. She could not have known I had been concealed in the shadows as she returned to her room, so she had presumably taken my scrutiny as a sign of some unformed affection for her. Perhaps she was right. At any rate, I felt a sort of camaraderie with Agnes that stemmed from being the only two people in the house (servants excepted, of course) who appeared to take any interest in the world around them. Lord and Lady Bowles were like a pair of beagles fixated on the dual fascinations of blood sports and their own offspring, while Halsingham seemed to be drowning in a state of ever more chilly melancholy. He remained silent unless spoken to, and daylight brought out a sort of sickliness in him. Lady Halsingham had mercifully taken breakfast in bed.

Deciding that our complicity was a likely prospect, I made up my mind to speak with Agnes on her own if an occasion presented itself.

In the event, though, my first insight into the confusing goings-on at Halsingham came from the master of the house himself.

....

Despite the bustle of preparations for the evening's dinner party, the shadow of discord persisted indoors, and so I resolved to escape out into the sunshine at the earliest opportunity. I would have announced my intentions at breakfast, but for the fact that I thought Bowles might take it as an invitation to join me, and I hadn't the inclination to curdle the clear morning air with blood and powder. I therefore just asked Brown quietly if he would be so kind as to lay out my tweeds and stout shoes, and when the group rose from the breakfast table and dispersed, I padded quickly up to my room, in the hopes of seizing a quick hour of grass beneath my soles before anyone noticed I was missing.

As I descended again, however, I heard Halsingham call to me from the small room which served as his study. Upon entering, I found him busy with his correspondence, but attired like me in his outdoor clothes. He looked up and gave me a rare smile as he beheld my Norfolk jacket, knickerbockers and brogues.

'Do not be angry at Brown. He let slip that you were planning a little exercise, and I wondered if I might join you? It appears such a fine day outside.'

It was indeed a fine day, icy and clear, and as we set out, I reflected that perhaps Lord Halsingham and I were not so far removed from one another. At any rate, both of us clearly yearned that morning for open space and the sun on our faces.

'An interesting fellow, that valet of yours.'

'What? Brown? Most certainly. He has been a long-standing and faithful servant to our family.'

'Really? I was under the impression from speaking to him last night that he had only lately returned from long military service in Rhodesia.'

'You are quite correct. The officer he served for most of that time was my younger brother, Captain Robert Edlington. I daresay his life with Robert was rather more exciting than his existence here, but in many ways his transfer between brothers worked out rather well for everyone. Except perhaps Robert, though he was generous enough to bring the whole thing about, so he has only himself to blame. It was on account of Brown's wife.'

'His wife? He didn't strike me as the married type, if you know what I mean.'

Halsingham looked at me with hesitant disapproval, but it soon melted.

'He was married out in Africa. A terrible business, though not to start with. His wife was apparently quite the beauty, with a lively wit besides. Robert told me her father was a white tailor who made his uniforms. Not long after she and Brown were married she became terribly ill. A mortification of the flesh, I understand – something frightfully biblical. She was on a ship when she began to sicken, and by the time they could get her to port and a doctor, her affliction was greatly advanced.'

'She died, then?'

'No, not that. The physician was able to halt the progress of the disease, but she was left greatly disfigured. The capacity of her mind was not affected, and Brown says she remains as quick as ever, but her spirit was as ravaged as her body, and she could not bear to be in company. In these defensive little colonial outposts there is nowhere to hide, particularly for a soldier's wife, and in his kindness Robert suggested they move back here, to a place where relative peace and solitude might more easily be found.'

He gestured at the rolling chalk downs in the distance as we ambled down a wide field track towards the woods.

'He wrote to me and asked if I might find a situation for Brown. As it happened, our old butler was due to retire, so I asked Inman to become the new butler and house steward – we have another chap called Botham who manages the estate – and arranged for Brown to take over his duties as my personal valet. It was the least I could do after some of the stories Robert told me of his gallantry. I do believe my brother owed his life to Brown's actions.'

'So the wife lives here, then? At Halsingham?'

'Frances, she is called. Yes, on the far side of the estate. An old game-keeper's cottage that I let the Browns have on account of its isolation. Frances lives there, though people rarely see her, except sometimes hanging out her washing or working her vegetable garden. Even then, she wears a wide-brimmed hat and a heavy veil to conceal her face, with padded gloves to hide the deformities to her hands.'

'What a sad tale. You'd never know it to talk to Brown. He seems so chipper.'

'He puts a brave face on it. I know Robert was sad to lose him. Still, Robert's loss is my gain, and Frances has a happier life here than she could ever have managed in a Rhodesian barracks.'

We had reached a stile at the edge of the woods, and clambering over it we began to descend steeply into ancient deciduous woodland.

Huge sweet chestnuts and ash trees spread their twisting lattice of bare, gnarled branches high above us, and we scrunched through the thick carpet of rust-coloured leaves. At the bottom of the slope Halsingham paused, as though the intimate, protected atmosphere of the woods allowed him to speak more confidentially than he was able to out in the open.

'In fact, Harry, my joining you this morning was no mere desire for fresh air – though I will own I am finding it most fortifying. I wanted to speak to you more privately about another matter than the histories of my servants. You cannot have failed to notice that affairs in my home are not... as one might hope.'

I began to protest unconvincingly that I had observed nothing of the sort, but he interrupted with uncharacteristic brusqueness.

'No, Harry, I know you are just trying to be kind, but you were there at the dinner table last night. I know it might not seem as tragic as the story of the Browns, and I don't doubt that their sense of stoicism is much greater than ours, but my wife and I have been beset by the most wretched misery for some time now. I wanted to explain it to you.'

'There's really no need, if you'd prefer not to,' I interjected, hoping sincerely that he would ignore me.

'No, I need to tell someone. I value your good opinion, and also perhaps I am selfishly hoping for some advice. The only other person I can talk to is my brother, and he returns from Africa only every few years. There are the makings of a small scandal in there somewhere too, which renders many of my usual confidantes out of the question, and...'

He paused for a moment, but I did not need him to finish his sentence. He was alluding to the indefinite matter of my status in the social pecking order – moneyed enough to be approachable yet without the pedigree and connections to be a threat.

'Don't worry, George. I won't sell you out to the gossips.'

Mere words as they were, this reassurance seemed to relax him a shade. Halsingham turned and began walking deeper into the wood, scuffing his feet through the fallen leaves as I followed.

....

'Henrietta comes from a very distinguished family, and it is not a husband's conceit to say that she is a woman of considerable beauty. I was advised to pay her court by my aunt, Lady Carleston – my own parents having both passed away by the time I turned twenty – and the families on both sides could see what an excellent match it was.

'We were married seven years ago, not long after Henrietta's nineteenth birthday. At that time, she was not such a mournful creature – no, do not protest, let us speak frankly. She was bright and warm, a woman any husband would have been proud to call his own. I look back to those early days now, trying to see more clearly where I might have been at fault, but without success. We did not know each other well when we were first married, but we became gradually better acquainted with each other's ways, and were content, I thought.

'After less than a year, though, she began to seem distant. Never quite unkind, but somehow almost... disdainful. Nothing I could define clearly enough to reproach her for, but something. When she discovered she was with child, her spirits seemed considerably lifted, and I had hopes that the birth of our son would restore our happiness, but in fact it accomplished the opposite. Thomas has never been a well child, and as an infant, death nearly took him from us several times. A child's suffering is painful for any parent, but where I reconciled myself to the possibility of his loss, I fear Henrietta became consumed by her fear for him.

'She attended constantly at his bedside, waiting up all night, watching him by lamplight, listening to his breath, and nothing I could say or do would persuade her to take care of herself. She barely ate, and reduced herself to such a state of exhaustion that one day she collapsed, and it took two weeks of care in one of London's finest clinics before she was able to come home. She never entirely recovered, and though Thomas grows slowly stronger with age, my wife has ever since been an increasingly dim reflection of that lovely girl I wed. Her health is terribly fragile, and she must adhere to a strict regime of medicated baths, strong tonics at morning and evening, and abstinence from rich food and drink. Though it manifests itself in physical infirmity, the doctors are adamant that hers is an affliction of the mind.

'All this, though a great sadness to me, I could have lived with, but the latest manifestation of her deteriorating nervous state is a leap into the intolerable, even for me.

'In early spring of this year – through most of March and April – I took Henrietta, Thomas, and the majority of my household, and leased a chateau in the south of France for a month. Henrietta wished to modernise some parts of Halsingham House, and while the work was going on, she thought some time in a warmer climate would be beneficial to our son's health as well as her own. And indeed, it did seem as if she might have been right. While we were there, Thomas's breathing seemed easier, his body more robust, and Henrietta's mood was correspondingly brighter. I fancied that the very notion of France was a greater tonic to her than anything prescribed by the doctor, for she began to improve even in the weeks leading up to our departure.

She graced me with occasional, unbidden smiles, even when there was no-one present for whom to put on a show, and I began to hope for the future.

'Upon our return, though, she began to have the most violent disruptions to her sleeping hours. I gather that her sleepwalking was well known in the family when she was younger, and during our... nights together, she was occasionally a little disturbed. Talking nonsense, getting up and shutting herself in the wardrobe, that sort of thing. But what took hold of her this year was a wholly different malady. It began slowly at first, perhaps a single episode every few weeks, yet it quickly escalated, and in more recent months it has been occurring most weekends when I am home from town. You will have noticed how shaken I appeared last night when poor Lady Bowles told that story about her son, but the truth of it is that when Henrietta sleepwalks it is unbearably sinister. She appears as if awake, yet not herself. A savage, animal creature which has little in common with my wife save her face. I have awoken in the night to find her leaning over me in her nightgown, teeth bared, yet the moment I open my eyes she flees my chamber, flying back to her own room.

'I have taken to turning the keys in the locks before retiring – our bedrooms have an adjoining door as well as sharing a corridor – only to awake in the night to the sounds of slow, deliberate scratching at one door or the other, punctuated by the occasional heart-stopping thump against the wood. Truly, Harry, these nocturnal assaults sound harmless, but to go to bed each evening in terror of what shock awaits you in the night... that is no way to live. I am worn out, and I can scarcely bring myself to lay my head down in my own home.

'Worst of all, she remembers nothing afterwards. We find her in her bed, disorientated and still half asleep but convinced that she has never left her room. She rants and rails at me – at the servants who I have called to me – cursing us as liars; claiming that it is an elaborate fiction on my part. But it is no fiction. I have pleaded with her to consult a trusted doctor specialising in disturbances of the mind – a fellow called Rochester, at whose clinic she has been treated on several occasions – yet she resists. I have suggested a compromise of allowing an impartial observer to confirm it to her by standing watch outside her bedroom door, but even this she refuses completely. Her spite towards me is now so undisguised that in my more uncharitable moments I wonder whether the whole thing is some deliberate scheme of hers to drive me to distraction.'

....

Halsingham was so agitated that for a moment I thought there was a genuine risk he might dissolve into tears, but thankfully both of us were spared this mortification. He paused, took a moment to compose himself, then finished weakly, 'I am utterly at a loss.'

This, then, was the bitter reward for my curiosity, and no sooner had he finished his tale than I wished it untold. Apart from resolving there and then to put a chair against my door before I went to bed that night, I felt the crushing sensation of having little to offer my friend by way of help or advice. I opened my cigarette case and lit one for Halsingham as I considered his dilemma.

Bachelors are uniquely unqualified to start evaluating other people's domestic arrangements. All the same, I could not help feeling that much of Halsingham's story seemed simply to describe the creeping unhappiness and disdain of an isolated young wife not very much

47

in love. As for her illness during young Thomas's troubled infancy, there was nothing odd in a mother fraying her nerves to ribbons at the possibility of losing her only child. Years of worry and loneliness could take their toll on a person's spirit, and I felt sorry for Henrietta, with her restrictive medical regime and her occasional stays at the clinic.

When it came to the immediate problem, though, I could see no explanation or solution. Like Halsingham, I had never heard of anything like it. I had encountered plenty of sleepwalkers and talkers before – English boarding schools are full of them – but they had mainly been comedic, and had only ever come close to calamity once when a boy called Henderson had nearly tossed himself down the stairs. It was hardly comparable.

'The simplest answer would just be for Lady Halsingham to go and see your specialist doctor,' I thought out loud, lighting my own cigarette. 'Surely there's nothing to be gained by simply ignoring it?'

'But you see, Harry, that's just it. She claims I'm making the whole thing up. She is completely paranoid that I am somehow trying to write her off as a madwoman. If only someone else could witness her actions. The servants have always retired to their quarters by the time anything occurs, and it is not proper to ask them to spy on their mistress.'

I saw now what it was he actually wanted me to do, and I wondered how much longer it would take before he came straight out with it. For it was not my advice he was after. The Right Honourable Lord Halsingham was a hereditary peer, a gentleman and a pillar of the establishment. He was, in all things, a man of the utmost propriety. Harrison Catcliffe, on the other hand, was a scar-faced social climber with a pistol in his pocket. Surely such as he would see no harm in a little skulking around a stately home in the dead of night?

Halsingham was a deplorable actor, and his expression of surprise when I made the suggestion would have made a Drury Lane pantomime dame wince.

'Do you think it would work, Harry?'

'I'm not sure, but at least if I catch her in the act then perhaps I can talk to her about it. She'll be displeased with me, of course, and if she's paranoid enough to think you're making it up then there's no saying she'll believe me either. Still, there's a chance if I swear I've seen her sleepwalking too that she might agree to see a doctor about it. Surely – if only for that reason – it's worth a try.'

In truth, I was far from sure it was worth a try at all, and more to the point I felt thoroughly rotten about agreeing to spy on a woman who had welcomed me into her home. But it was Hobson's choice. Either way, I stood to disappoint one of my hosts, and as we walked on, Halsingham's mood much improved, I silently cursed my friend for making me his creature in this.

There was another complication, too, and one which I hadn't the will to consider fully just at that moment. I was now reasonably certain I knew what Agnes Cleveley had been doing after dark the previous night. Just as Halsingham had recruited me as his agent, so his wife had most probably enlisted her sister to prove her own story. Which meant there would be two of us creeping through the corridors that evening.

....

Halsingham announced with regret that he had affairs to attend to back at the house, but I had no business to draw me indoors, and no wish to inflict upon myself that dreadful tedium which besets any big house on the morning of a party. I watched my host depart through the trees, then turned on my heel and stalked deeper into the woods, my steps dogged by ill-humour. The track was broad enough to drive a carriage down, and the hysterical clucking of game birds rang out through the trees, together with the horrid scraping screams of the jays. Crows in fancy coats, I thought, and felt more generously towards them after that. I left the path for no better reason than that I was tired of it, and struck up a steep bank through a swathe of rhododendron thickets, heading for a fence at the top of the hill which marked the edge of the wood. The ragged remnants of a downed pheasant hung limply in the branches above me.

Reaching the fence, I clambered over it, then paused on the other side to catch my breath and empty the leaf litter from my damp shoes. Before me, a soggy field stretched out towards a copse at the far end. A cottage nestled by a wide gate at the edge of the trees, and I could see a parallel pair of high hedgerows running past it, presumably concealing a road. I resolved to cross the pasture and see if that lane might return me somehow to Halsingham House, for retracing my steps always held the tang of cowardice about it. The ground was a good deal churned up by hooves, but there was no sign of any cattle for the time being, and I tottered unsteadily over the muddy, uneven ground towards the gate.

It was only as I neared the cottage – a modest yet attractive affair with wood smoke drifting thinly from the chimney and the faded, dried-out blooms of the summer's hydrangeas peeping over its low hawthorn hedge – that I noticed a woman standing very still in the little garden. She was inexpensively but tidily attired, with a wide hat and a thick veil of the sort favoured by motorists. She made no move to acknowledge my presence, but it seemed to me that she could not have failed to notice me. In the spirit of friendliness I called out hallo and waved across at her. This seemed to register, and a single gloved hand was raised hesitantly in return.

Thinking that perhaps she was simply wary of strangers, I turned my steps towards the woman, intending to put her mind at ease as to my identity and my reason for passing so close to her home, but as I drew closer she began to shrink away in the strangest manner, like a cornered creature. It was only then that, through the translucent curtain of her veil and beneath the heavy shadow of her hat brim, I glimpsed the outline of her face, and realised with a start that I was in the presence of Frances Brown, the valet's wife.

In that brief moment alone did I behold in some small part the extent of her terrible injuries, for even obscured as it was, the face before me was ravaged beyond all semblance of what it might once have been. She must still have been young, and yet I fancied I could discern great folds of pale skin hanging beneath her sad eyes, and other parts where the flesh seemed altogether absent. Her nose appeared bulbous and misshapen like an old drunk, her lip twisted. All this I saw just for an instant, and to my most wretched discredit it must have shown in my own countenance, for that unfortunate woman turned tail and fled, wordlessly, back into her cottage.

Seven

—·—

With Halsingham House deep in the throes of party preparation, luncheon was a mercifully brief and functional affair, which suited me just fine. Halsingham's confidences had left me in low spirits – not to mention my sense of shame at having embarrassed Mrs Brown so witlessly as I passed – and I hadn't much inclination either to make conversation or to endure it. After lunch, I sought the solitude of a corner seat and the *Spectator*. As usual, the paper's querulous journalists seemed to concern themselves principally with railing against the Germans, though I was cheered to read a short item stating that Shackleton and the *Nimrod* had reached New Zealand. At least someone was engaged in an enterprise with a whiff of nobility about it.

Given that making an ally of Agnes was now completely out of the question, it was somehow inevitable that as I sat flicking through the newspaper, she and her sister should drop lightly into a couple of nearby chairs. Henrietta and Agnes were not to know that they were the last two people in the world I wished to converse with just then, and they gravitated towards me in much the same way that a cat stalks unerringly for the lap of the one person in a room who does not want it there.

Worse luck, they had been together all morning, and Agnes had once again polished up her sister into an altogether brighter button than the one I had seen at dinner last night. Henrietta's mood was almost jovial, and this friendliness did nothing to lessen my guilt.

'Tell us, Harry, have you ever been to Northumberland?' she asked me. 'Our family home is there, and it is ever so long since I visited. I do miss it so.'

'I'm afraid not – my family are Yorkshire people. I may have passed through your county on my way to Scotland as a boy, but I could not swear to it.'

'I daresay it wouldn't be all that memorable if you had,' smiled Agnes. 'It's grey and cold for nine months out of every twelve, and I long for escapes like these. My sister has the romantic memory of an exile. She remembers only the good parts and nothing of the bad.'

Agnes nudged Henrietta affectionately with her elbow, and her sibling unconsciously linked her own arm through it.

'Perhaps, Agnes, but it is home. You'll see soon enough, once you marry and someone takes you too far away for too long. Home is the place you grew into – like a set of clothes that were tailored to you without you ever realising it. Wherever you go in the world, every-where else sits wrong in some small way or other.

'Don't you pine for your own home now and then, Harry? I think we northern creatures are not built for the south.'

She smiled, with a wry melancholy that transformed her seven-teenth-century features briefly into something more Pre-Raphaelite.

'I feel like I ought to agree with you, if only because you put it so poetically – but I'm afraid in my own case it wouldn't be true.'

I grinned, shuddering inside as I flattered her. Judas Catcliffe.

53

'Maybe it's just that home never fitted me very well,' I went on. 'Second-rate tailoring at best. We lived in the city rather than the countryside, and I grew up between worlds. The factory workers were wary of us and the well-to-do thought us rather rough.'

'I would hardly call you rough,' said Agnes. 'Brash, perhaps.'

I was grateful to be teased, and I rose to it, running a finger mutely along one of my long scars.

'Never mind those. I bet they have an innocent explanation. A pet budgie caught you with her beak.'

'I may tell you one day.'

'But not just now,' she said, widening her eyes with mock shock, 'for you wish us to think you *disreputable*.'

'My great-grandfather was a gravedigger.'

'Ours was a slaver.'

Agnes looked at me expectantly, but I was outgunned. Henrietta glanced from one to the other, then rescued me.

'Rough or not, you seem to fit tolerably well in my drawing room.'

'I was shipped off to boarding school pretty quickly. Places like that do a roaring trade in scrubbing the oil stains out of industrialists' sons.'

My guilty conscience was making me confessional.

'Then I suppose university in Leipzig and my travels on the continent more or less finished the job. What I mean is that I have no great attachment to Yorkshire, at least not now.'

I hastily moved the subject on before I could recall too keenly how much I had pined for the familiar accents and sooty brickwork of home during those first years among the braying little savages at prep school. One of my earliest memories was of a wiry old chargehand careering around the cobbled factory yard with me hoisted on his shoulders pretending to be a jockey. Strangely, it was a reminiscence that always made the grown-up Harrison Catcliffe feel like a bit of a fraud.

'I expect the most important thing is where your family are,' I continued. 'Mine are mostly in London. I see far too much of them. It's only natural that you would miss your own people when you live so far away from them.'

'It's true, I do. And here in this house I haven't the diversions of London to distract me.'

'Though there's Thomas, of course,' interjected Agnes hastily. 'He must be a great comfort to you when you are missing us.' I noticed she did not mention Lord Halsingham. It seemed rather a pointed omission.

'Oh indeed, Thomas is my greatest joy. Such a bright boy, and his health improves year on year.'

'I'm delighted to hear it,' I said. 'I still haven't had the pleasure of making his acquaintance, though I presume we shall run into each other at some point before the weekend is out.'

As it happened, I was just making conversation, but I saw her light up with pride and realised that an encounter was now not only inevitable but imminent.

'You must! I shall fetch him here at once.'

'On the contrary, it would be the height of rudeness to tear him away from important nursery business. Might we not seek him out and distract him only for a few moments?'

I yearned to do something, anything, to extricate myself from my corner, and Lady Halsingham gladly acquiesced. Making our excuses to her husband, she led me out, followed by Agnes, who smiled encouragingly at me when no-one was looking, as if to congratulate me on what a good job I was doing of cheering her unhappy sister. My treachery knew no shame, and I smiled back.

....

It will sound ungenerous to say that I was not anticipating much from little Thomas Edlington. In my defence, all I can say is that I had encountered his like on many other occasions. The spoiled and sickly little dictator, his self-esteem relentlessly nurtured and his weaknesses concealed from him – these indulgences no doubt bestowed in the spirit of kindness and love, yet bearing the ultimate fruit of a tiny yet fully formed boor, old and cantankerous before his time. English society produces legions of these gouty homunculi, and one runs into them as adults – frail and tyrannical as ever yet frequently in positions of great power.

Such were my expectations, but in Thomas's case I was substantially wide of the mark.

We found him marshalling a rag-tag skirmish line of lead soldiers as they assaulted a much more numerous and well-formed square of adversaries, their muskets levelled. As we approached, he laid one of his bold attackers solemnly on its side, presumably to denote a fatality.

'Thomas,' said his mother as he looked up, 'I've brought someone for you to meet. This is Mr Catcliffe, a friend of Father's from London.'

She began to kneel down next to him, but he stood up and turned to us.

His fragile health was immediately evident from his slight build, his pallor, and the way his flesh did not bulge ripely from his bones the way it usually does in a boy of such an age. There was a lot more of his father than his mother in him, and I thought it curious that Lady Halsingham could so adore and dislike that same face upon its different masters.

Young Thomas's porcelain appearance was further accentuated by his clothing. As was the fashion, he was dressed in a voluminous, bottle-green velvet outfit with a high collar and short trousers – the sort of thing that might have passed as a fancy-dress costume two hundred years earlier at a Venetian court ball. I had never quite worked out whether the parents of our age dressed their children like their dolls or the dolls like the children, but at any rate, with his wide, glassy eyes and unnaturally white skin, Thomas Edlington would not have appeared out of place in the Gamages Christmas catalogue.

His smile, though, was broad and unselfconscious, and he extended a small hand towards my own in a considered gesture which, in other children, might have been pompous or comical.

'I am very pleased to meet you, Mr Catcliffe,' he said.

'And I you, Thomas. Tell me, what's happening with your soldiers? It appears it will not end well for this small band over here.'

He looked down at them then back at me.

'They're mounting a rescue. Look, here are their friends.' He pointed to a line of toy soldiers with the same colour jackets behind the superior force. 'Some of them will die, but they will win eventually, and they shall all be heroes on account of the rescue.'

'Why don't you give them more men, Thomas?' asked Agnes. 'You've lots more of them in the box.'

I answered for him.

'It would be no fun if they were assured of winning. Thomas knows they're going to win, but they don't. Am I correct?'

He smiled and nodded, then an idea caught him.

'Mr Catcliffe, would you like to see some magic?' he asked suddenly.

Both his mother and Agnes looked surprised, but before they could say anything, I accepted his offer with a nod. Thomas adopted a severe and dramatic air, picked up a soldier from the box, held it up to me, then made it vanish. The disappearance was accomplished with a goodly amount of struggling with his sleeves, but was exceptionally well done for such a young lad. Having waggled his hands carefully at me to prove the soldier had vanished, he then plunged one of them into my jacket pocket and withdrew it triumphantly, clutching the missing toy.

We applauded enthusiastically, while I considered how fortunate it was that we had not been in the city, else he might have provided an even greater eye-opener for all present by withdrawing a .41-calibre Remington Type II derringer instead.

'A wonderfully executed trick, young sir. How on earth did you do it?'

He looked at me solemnly. 'A magician never reveals his methods.'

'But where did you learn it, Thomas?' asked Lady Halsingham.

'Robbie, cook's boy taught me, Mother,' he admitted. 'He knows a few, but he won't teach me the others. You are supposed to use a penny.'

'Robbie, the cook's boy...' parroted his mother curiously. 'I wonder who in his family is an amateur conjurer?'

'Not cook, I think.' Thomas allowed a shy smile to break through his showman's persona.

'Well I thought it was a simply marvellous trick,' said Agnes. 'You must bend young Robbie's ear to teach you more.'

'I will, Aunt Agnes,' promised Thomas, glancing sidelong at the soldiers as if he was keen to get back to the action.

'All right, Thomas, we'll leave you to your toys,' said his mother. 'Though you do know the ones in the red coats are supposed to be the good ones.'

'Yes, I know that, Mother. But I still like the blue coats better.'

As we left, I watched him take a little metal cannon out of the toy box and place it ominously on the carpet.

....

Throughout the afternoon, various guests began to arrive for Lord and Lady Halsingham's party, and by the time we sat down to dinner in our tails and gowns, there were sixteen of us around the table.

The Earl and Countess of Wrenleigh were the most high-ranking personages in attendance, though far from the oldest, and Lord Wrenleigh cannot have been above thirty-five, with his wife considerably younger. Lacking a discernible jaw of his own, he had counterfeited one with a beard, yet despite displaying the physiognomy of his selective breeding, I found him thoughtful and broad-minded company. His wife I scarcely noticed, and I suspect she will have judged the evening a success in that regard, for during our one brief conversation before dinner I found her skittish and unfriendly, much more inclined to the society of the other married ladies.

Lord and Lady Oakwood, meanwhile, were a polite couple at opposite ends of their fifties, with two daughters a little younger than Agnes. The younger, Jeanne, was an argumentative girl whom the senior Oakwoods evidently regarded as being highly troublesome, though in their position I should have been far more concerned by the elder, Amelia, whose shy smile and darting glances were as practised as they were disarming. These were directed principally towards the three unmarried men of the company, who apart from me were Rowland Renwick and Albert Grieve.

Renwick, of course, I knew from Woodville's, and I liked him well enough when he was not trying to inveigle me into a game of baccarat. A Scot by birth, though the only time I ever heard his accent give him away was on the word 'poem', which he pronounced 'poime'. The son of someone or other semi-important in the government, Renwick was extraordinarily fussy in matters of appearance. His pomaded hair was parted dead centre, and he had an unconscious habit of rolling the tightly waxed points of his immaculately groomed moustache. Despite his rather dashing name, he was a careful, nervous man, devilishly lucky at cards and harmless in every other regard.

Grieve, by comparison, was a strutting little barnyard rooster. I had never met him before, but his background was not unlike my own, if you were to swap steel for textiles and my meandering continental education for a furiously ambitious ascent through the societies at Oxford. It had been impressed upon all of us at school that an educated young man should be 'elegantly competitive' in his endeavours, but some, like Albert Grieve, were hungrier in that regard than others. He had distanced himself emphatically from his industrial origins by embarking upon a promising career in the city, and was in general one of those fellows who views every man he meets as either an opportunity to be exploited or a threat to be put down with extreme prejudice.

As another tomcat at the table, I fell squarely into the latter category, and Grieve took an instant dislike to me. Fortunately, Rowland

Renwick presented an easier target, and Grieve spent much of the meal loudly belittling him, while the older Miss Oakwood tittered, the younger scowled, and Agnes deftly ignored him except when his remarks were aimed unavoidably in her direction.

I fancied that I discerned in Grieve's behaviour towards Agnes a heightened degree of cartoonish gallantry, and this neatly illustrated the towering scale of his vanity. It was true, of course, that American millionaires occasionally managed to marry their dollar princess into particularly hard-up blue bloodlines, but the likes of Agnes Cleveley – Lady Agnes if we were being proper – remained unassailably top-drawer. When Lord Kelverton's younger daughter made a match, it would most certainly not be with the Albert Grieves or Harrison Catcliffes of this world – a fact once summed up by a tipsy young lady at a coming-out party who told me 'You're ever so droll, Harry, but you must see you're not a *prospect*'. Grieve evidently perceived no such hurdles, and perhaps, swirled in with my more general dislike, there may have been a modicum of jealousy.

Halsingham's acquaintances were nothing if not varied, and our party was completed by the Fletchers, who owned the neighbouring estate of Endsleigh and were friends of my father. From an unglamorous start as an apprentice clerk in a shipping firm fifty or so years earlier, Dick Fletcher had risen to become the principal owner of a substantial steamship company, and his fortune, though possibly fragile, was immense. He was an extraordinary fellow – rough and canny, with an underlying sense of unflappable calm borne of a life which had seen vast gains and catastrophic losses incurred as he gambled his fortune again and again upon the whims of the sea. Some considered him rather unpatriotic on account of the innumerable tonnes of Canadian grain that his steamers regularly hauled across the Atlantic, driving down the price of our domestic crops, but Dick Fletcher had no time for such sentimentality. He was a black-eyed old magpie, hollow-cheeked and fierce-eyed, his shallow breath bubbling wetly in his lungs.

Oddly enough, he got on famously with Bowles, while Mrs Fletcher – a bright lady with the hardness of her younger years etched deeply but not unkindly upon her face – steered his conversation expertly towards subjects considered acceptable at a baron's table.

It was an enjoyable meal, and the talk was sufficiently lively that I almost forgot my misgivings about the night ahead. Even Halsingham took wine enough to regale us all with details of an interesting pamphlet he had lately studied, entitled *The Decline of the Turk*. I was seated next to Agnes, and once I had overcome my urge to tell her everything (which I recognised as that automatic compulsion to confess to a pretty face that has been getting foolish men into trouble for millennia), I settled into her company well enough.

'Why *do* you insist on everyone calling you Harry, rather than Mr Catcliffe?' she asked, as the servants cleared the fish course.

'I have been wondering the same thing,' interjected Lord Wrenleigh with good humour. 'Of course, a man may go by whatever pleases him, but all the same, it is rather irregular.'

Sidelong glances from other diners made it clear that he was not alone in this opinion. Members of the aristocracy were frequently discombobulated when I insisted so gauchely upon first-name terms, and I liked to think it was because they had evolved an elaborate system of titles, etiquette and military service to solve a similar problem to the one encountered at my family firm.

'I fear, Agnes, that the answer will be rather less interesting than you anticipate. It's simply that there are ten Mr Catcliffes working across our three factories, and four of them occupy offices within a hundred yards of my own. The confusion is never-ending, and the less said about our incoming correspondence, the better. We thus go universally by our Christian names, so my father is Mr Jonas, my middle brother is Mr Gregory, and I am Mr Harrison.'

'So shall I not call you Harrison? It's rather more distinguished than plain Harry.'

'Outside of the factory, only my mother calls me Harrison, and then only when she is very displeased indeed.'

'Capital!' chuckled Wrenleigh, twitching his finger at his half-empty glass as Inman passed with the decanter.

The highlight of my own evening undoubtedly came when Albert Grieve sought to show up Rowland Renwick and me by recounting a confrontation with a fellow student at Oxford. Allegedly the man had attacked him, and he had in return been roundly thrashed. Grieve was not a big man, nor powerfully built, and I could not help wondering as to the particulars of his opponent.

'Of course,' Grieve drawled, 'I daresay there are few men around this table who have had to settle an argument with their fists, however regrettable it may be.' Renwick pinched the tip of his moustache between finger and thumb, fixing his gaze submissively upon the quivering remnants of his set raspberry cream, and Grieve looked pointedly at me as he added, 'Assuming, Mr Catcliffe, that those marks on your face are ceremonial in nature.'

He was more or less correct, both about my peaceable nature and the source of my scars – but before I could reply, Grieve was robbed of his impending triumph by the husky tones and estuary vowels of old Dick Fletcher.

'Have I ever! First man I knocked out in my day was my own father, drunken sot!'

He chuckled, or coughed – I couldn't tell which.

'And I'll own that settling up with your knuckles is no way to do business, but sometimes you've got to make a point. Had this captain once, resourceful but greedy. I kept dismissing men in his crew for stealing before I caught him red-handed flogging my goods off to a competitor. Knocked him all over the wharf. Then there was a group of lads who cornered me and one other on our way to the bank when I was a fresh-faced eighteen-year-old working at Mulligan's. I'd have been out on my ear if I'd lost the day's takings...'

He was drowned out momentarily by a roar of honking laughter from Lord Bowles, and Mrs Fletcher took the opportunity to side-track him deftly into a debate about the disestablishment of the East India Company (some fifty or so years earlier, yet still much talked of round tables such as these, where people pined for what they still insisted were Britain's most glorious days). But his work was done, and Grieve sank quietly back into his chair, his Oxford punch-up exposed for the schoolyard tussle it doubtless was. Even the younger Miss Oakwood could not resist a broad smile.

As we milled around in the drawing room after dinner, I reflected to myself how much more hazardous it might be to make my way undetected across a house that was now full of people, especially younger men who could not be relied on to retire early and absolutely. All except the Fletchers were staying, and who was to say what might occur after bedtime in the corridors of Halsingham House?

Eight

— . —

In my bedchamber, I put my nightshirt on, extinguished the light, and sat nervously in bed, the room illuminated only by the glow of the fire. I listened like a hunter – or perhaps the hunted – to the sounds of activity gradually subsiding in the corridors of the old house, suddenly more aware than ever before of every bump and creak. I felt like I was back at school again, preparing for some illegal night-time sortie to plunder the kitchens or scale the chapel roof, only without the gleeful anticipation that used to temper my anxiety.

There was a period of five minutes or so during which the house was silent (or at least as silent as any such draughty pile can be on a windswept autumnal night), yet I still could not bring myself to leave the warmth of my bed. Venturing from my room represented a sort of crossing of the Rubicon, and I had almost convinced myself that no good could come of meddling in other people's affairs, when I realised that I was simply allowing the coward in me to gain the upper hand. Pressing my bare feet to the cold boards, I cracked the door, peered out cautiously into the darkness, and crept into the corridor. At least the household kept no dog indoors. If I bumped into anyone I would just tell them I was off to empty my chamber pot over Albert Grieve as he slept. It might raise eyebrows, but surely no-one would object.

Halsingham House was a labyrinthine place, with an unreasonable number of creaky doors linking its network of rooms, landings and passageways. The right combination of turns and doors would lead me to the family wing, but the wrong one might send me tumbling down a servants' staircase or into bed with Lord and Lady Bowles. During a time of quiet in the late afternoon, I had taken the opportunity to familiarise myself with the layout of the corridors, yet as I shuffled quietly through the blackness, stopping every few seconds to strain my ears and eyes ahead of me, I quickly began to doubt myself. Was it two steps down, or three? Then a left or a right? I took the left, then the right which I thought followed it, only to bump softly into a wall with my outstretched hands. Retracing my steps, I took a different course, which seemed more promising. Finally, without any further wrong turns, I reached the corner round which I was almost certain Lord and Lady Halsingham's rooms lay.

The master and mistress of the household occupied a string of interconnected rooms lining one side of the corridor in the south wing. Furthest from me, at the far end, was Halsingham's dressing room. Next to it was his own bedroom, and then that of his wife, no doubt with a securely locked door between the two. Lady Halsingham's bedroom, in turn, opened into her private bathroom, and finally the corner of the corridor concealed a tiny landing, with narrow spiral stairs reaching right up from the kitchens to the maids' rooms at the top of the house. The servants used the staircase to bring hot water up, and it had doors leading both directly into the bathroom and out into the corridor.

Here, I was presented with a different manner of problem, since the corridor along which the Halsinghams' rooms were arranged ended in a large window. It was a mercifully murky night outside, and the moon was not bright, but even so, this stretch of passageway was not plunged into the same abyssal blackness as the rest of my route. If I lurked there, then anyone else abroad would be certain to spot me. Darting a quick glance around the corner, I noticed the black shape of what looked like a large, free-standing wooden cupboard situated between me and Lady Halsingham's room. It would obscure my view of the two bedroom doors, but if I flattened myself against the shaded side of the wardrobe then it would camouflage me beautifully. Stealthily, I took up my position.

From then on, it became a waiting game, and though I tried to mark the quarter hours by the distant chiming of a carriage clock somewhere below, I quickly lost track of time. It was freezing cold, and I vacillated between cursing myself for not thinking to bring a blanket, and wondering whether I would fall over if my feet went numb. I had not even worn a dressing gown. Fatigue made my eyelids sore, but I did not dare close them in case I fell asleep standing up. I had been hoping the night would pass uneventfully, but I now dreaded the possibility of an extended spell leant against my tall wooden cabinet.

The wind sighed and whistled across the windowpanes. Somewhere, I heard the sound of a door opening and closing, and a little later a faint knock and the distant hiss of hushed voices. There was a scraping noise that I supposed might have been the dragging of a chair or a chamber pot, and the creak of a heavy foot on a floorboard somewhere alarmingly close by. Did these people not sleep? At least my host and hostess slumbered on silently. I rested my eyes for a few moments.

Suddenly, there was a disturbance, not of sound, but of air, and I opened my eyelids just as a cold body pressed itself up against mine then immediately recoiled in alarm at finding me concealed in the shadowy hiding place which it had itself presumably intended to occupy. As the body stepped back with a sharp intake of breath into the patch of dark grey light from the window, it materialised into Agnes Cleveley, dressed in her nightgown and with her light brown hair woven into a plait which hung down over one shoulder, reaching to just below her ribs. Her eyes were wide and white in their sockets, and I quickly stepped out into what little light there was to show her my face. I placed my finger over my lips, but there was no need, for she made no sound.

Her shoulders sagged slightly with relief, but she reached up and took hold of my side-whiskers with icy fingers, dragging my head down to her own height.

'What are you doing?' she breathed into my ear, almost silently, yet with unmistakeable irritation on her warm breath. I could smell her tooth powder.

'The same as you,' I whispered back. It took her a few seconds to unfurl in her mind the chain of events that must have brought me to this stretch of dingy passageway, but as her grasp of my transgressions grew firmer, so too did that of her fingers on the side of my face. She twisted my whiskers pointedly.

'To think we were so nice to you,' hissed Agnes, almost audibly this time, 'when you were his agent all along!'

'I wasn't,' I tried to protest in an undertone. 'Only since this morning. He didn't give me much of a choice. Trapped me into it.'

'Then you must be an even bigger idiot than you look. Go back to bed!'

'No! I'm staying. We'll know the truth of it soon enough.'

She paused, then with a sort of sigh she relaxed her grip, allowing me to straighten my neck a little, and stood on her toes to bring herself up to my ear again.

'The truth of it,' she whispered testily, 'is that George is a liar who wants to have my sister locked up as a madwoman just because she doesn't love him. He's not an imaginative man, and I suppose he thinks what worked with Lady Mordaunt thirty years ago ought to do the trick for Henrietta too.

'But maybe you're right. You can't do any harm here, and I might as well have some company.'

I pushed myself into the corner made by the wall and the cupboard, and Agnes shuffled up next to me.

'Let me share your hiding place. Henrietta told me this would be the best spot to conceal myself.'

After that she didn't say a word, and I could tell she wasn't looking at me. Her shoulder was squashed against my upper arm, and though such proximity would have felt highly inappropriate in the daylight, somehow the darkness and the fact of our nightclothes made it seem less awkward, as if we might have been two children crammed together during Halsingham House's first ever game of sardines. Apart from anything else, the warmth of another human was a blessed relief in the perishing corridor.

As we stood there in silence, I wondered what she had observed the previous night. Had she witnessed anything at all? Clearly not enough to banish all doubt, anyway. Should I tell her I had seen her? Perhaps it was best to save that particular card in case I needed to play it later.

'Harry?' Agnes whispered, turning her head to me. Wordlessly I inclined my ear towards her face.

'When you see that George is lying... will you tell the truth?'

'Of course,' I whispered, and I meant it too. 'If he isn't, will you?'

'She's my sister.' And she lapsed back into silence.

I could not say how long we were there before Agnes tensed suddenly at my side. For a moment I could not tell why, then I heard it too: the almost imperceptible sound of bare feet on the wooden floor. But the footsteps were not coming from the Halsinghams' rooms. They came from round the corner, the same passageway that I had crept down a couple of hours and what felt like a thousand years earlier. Surely no-one else could be coming to spy on Lord and Lady Halsingham. For starters, there was no more space behind the cupboard.

But when the figure rounded the corner, I felt Agnes freeze. For our visitor was Lady Halsingham herself.

....

She was dressed in her nightgown, with her hair tied in a plait like Agnes's, and there was something terribly odd about her manner. She did not move like the lady of the house, but in a drifting, catlike way, placing her feet deliberately and lightly, and stopping to poke whimsically at the corner of a picture frame in the dim light from the window at the end of the corridor. Her eyes, normally such a watery blue, were shadowy sockets, and her pale skin showed up like white marble against the black wood panelling.

Where had she been all night? Had her room been empty all the time we had been lurking outside it?

Lady Halsingham tiptoed slowly, casting around herself without really seeming to see anything, but even so I was convinced that she must come upon us in our hiding place. My nightshirt was of a dark blue, but Agnes's gown was of white, and even in the shade of the cabinet it now seemed to me that she would show up at least as a ghostly and foreign shape in the darkness. My neck was so whip-taut that an aching sensation began to stretch from the base of my skull to my crown. But Henrietta meandered past us without incident. For maybe half a minute we could hear her considered footsteps in the passageway behind the wardrobe, out of our view, the eerie scratching of a fingernail along the timber panelling. Then there was the quiet opening and closing of a bedroom door.

We were left in silence.

With Henrietta's departure, I relaxed ever so slightly. Agnes did not. She remained a statue, cold as the grave. Then I heard her turn her face to me. I felt something touch the back of my hand lightly, and applying my finger to it, I felt a wetness that could only have been a tear, fallen from her raised chin. I could not see the wretched appeal in her eyes, but I could imagine it, and my heart sank with the awfulness of the decision I was about to be faced with. She was going to ask me to lie. Foolish Harry, I thought, how have you found yourself here?

In light of what followed, it does me little credit that I wished fervently for a way out. For affairs to take any direction in which I would not be forced to damn myself by telling a truth or a falsehood. But the rational part of me has, I suppose, always known that whatever went through my mind had no bearing on the events that were now merely a matter of seconds away.

71

There was the sudden bang of a door being flung wide and re-bounding back off the wall; the rush of footsteps running towards us; the thump of someone bouncing off the other side of the cupboard, and the slam of Lady Halsingham's door. A scuffling inside the bed-room, then silence. Three, perhaps four seconds, no more than that. And then a whimper.

Agnes was even faster round the cabinet than I was. She flung the door to her sister's room wide open, and as we barrelled through it, we were greeted with a harrowing vision.

In the weak moonlight, Henrietta lay across her bed, flat on her back like a drunkard. She was drowsy but conscious, and the faint cry we had heard was her. The front of her nightdress was streaked with thick gouts of dark liquid. It was smeared up her neck and face, and her hands and forearms were bathed in it. In the darkness it looked like tar, but the smell was wrong.

I fumbled to light the bedside lamp with a match from the silver vesta case that lay next to it, and as I turned back, the warm light sprang across the bed to illuminate Lady Halsingham. The clean parts of her nightdress went from grey to white, the oily blood turned wet and red, and those horrifying, cavernous eye sockets that we had beheld only minutes earlier returned to the pale blue of the tragic heroine, wide with confusion and terror.

'Henrietta!' cried Agnes, already stained with blood herself, her hands all over her sister, frantically searching for the wound. 'What have you done? Where are you hurt? Harry, get help! Please! She's bleeding!'

'I... I...' slurred Henrietta, looking down at her gory clothing with tears suddenly pooling in her eyes. 'What's...? Please, help me!'

Agnes kissed her forehead feverishly, then went back to seeking the injury with panic in her eyes, turning her over roughly to find the nightdress on her sister's back still almost pristine white.

'Where is it?' she wept at me in desperation. 'Where is she hurt? She'll die if we don't find it!'

But I knew. The blood was not Henrietta's.

I was out of the door as quickly as I'd come through it. I took the lamp, plunging the sobbing sisters ungallantly back into darkness, but I needed to see what was next door.

In the novels, they always notice the details. Had I been a more sanguine fellow, and a rather better narrator, I might have observed all manner of useful things. But I did not, for as I stood in the open doorway to Lord Halsingham's bedchamber, holding my lamp aloft, I saw only one thing.

'Oh, George.'

NINE

—·—

Oddly, one of the things that struck me most about that night was how terribly funny everyone looked padding around the corridors in their nightgowns. Coupled with the disorientation and hysteria that afflicted most of our strange little party, a casual observer could have been forgiven for thinking Halsingham House one of those hellish Victorian asylums for the mentally unsound, albeit one with expensive paintings and four-poster beds.

My memory of those first minutes in Lord Halsingham's bedchamber is not the clearest, at least in terms of the time involved. I have, for example, little idea how long I stood over his body like a man hypnotised, staring at his massacred throat, opened as wide as his staring eyes. I must have touched him, because later there was blood on my hands. After what could have been seconds or minutes, I heard Agnes rushing into the room behind me. She pushed past, then recoiled with a sound somewhere between a gasp and a cry, seizing my arm to steady herself (not that I was the perfect rock myself). Next door, presumably still in the dark that I had left her in, Henrietta began screaming.

It was Rowland Renwick who found us first. Poor Renwick. Possibly the least useful person who could have stumbled upon the scene. But the others were close behind him, and fortunately Lord Wrenleigh found it in himself to take control, getting the lamps lit, summoning the servants and sending Rackley the chauffeur out in the car to fetch the police and the doctor. There was a lot of howling and crying, as one might imagine. At some stage I found myself led dreamily out of the room by Bowles, who bore up pretty well himself under the circumstances. I realised Agnes was still clinging to my arm, like a piece of driftwood, apparently unaware that it was connected to another human at the shoulder. I glanced at her sister's door. It was closed, and Inman, the butler, stood outside. He was in his nightshirt too, only for some reason he had seen fit to pull on a smart black jacket over the top, which made him appear even more absurd.

An older maid, still half asleep and shaking with what might have been dread or just cold, steered us downstairs to the drawing room, where the housemaid I had seen that morning was trying to revive the evening's fire as a footman fiddled with the lamps. Somehow, all the light, and the warmth which presently began to seep from the fireplace, made me feel better, as if the monstrosity I had found in the darkness was receding. Only I knew it was still there, upstairs.

Agnes had detached herself from me, and had perched, shivering, on the edge of a chaise longue. I found a decanter of brandy and a glass, poured out a stiff one and offered it to her. She did not acknowledge it, so I drank it down myself, then sat next to her, sniffing absent-mindedly at the fumes from the empty glass.

....

The village bobby – who arrived a half hour or so later alongside the local doctor – was a blustering fellow, full of his own importance and wildly out of his depth. He sent the poor chauffeur straight out again to retrieve two more constables from neighbouring hamlets, and upon their arrival, he promptly despatched one of these to get a message to London.

'It's one for the Yard, there's no question about that,' he decreed sagely, as if this had somehow been even remotely in doubt.

This policeman, Woods by name, ordered his colleague to find him some tea, before commencing to interrogate Agnes and me clumsily in front of more or less the entire household. I mumbled the bare bones of my tale; Agnes said not a word, staring miserably into the fire. Constable Woods attempted to press her, at which point Lord Wrenleigh, who had henceforth been the soul of restraint, exploded in a fit of pique and threatened to leave right there and then with the chauffeur (unhappy man must have spent half the night at the wheel) to fetch a superior officer, however far afield he might need to venture. Woods relented sourly and allowed us to retire for what few hours remained until morning. I daresay few of us slept.

....

The first train of the morning brought not only a stern detachment from Scotland Yard, but also the newspapermen who no doubt had been the first to be discreetly notified by the desk sergeant. These latter were given short shrift and escorted off the estate by an exhausted Inman and his staff, while the Yard men applied themselves firstly to interviewing Constable Woods, and secondly to inspecting the scene of the killing, which had remained locked shut once the doctor had confirmed the death and the enervating bobby had satisfied his curiosity the previous evening. The third step, of course, was to question the witnesses.

It was Brown who entered my room with the news that the detectives wished to speak with me. He found me still in bed, sat upright with my knees hugged to my chest and my red eyes fixed sightlessly on the window.

'They're a persistent lot, sir. Probably wouldn't do to keep them waiting too long,' he added apologetically.

I did my best to buck up a little and put on a braver face.

'I didn't see you in all the confusion last night, Brown. Did you witness the... room yourself?'

'Indeed not, sir, for I'd retired to my cottage for the night, and it's some way distant from the main house. I've no wish to see inside that room, either. I've witnessed my share of bloodshed – I was assistant to a regimental surgeon for a spell, and I've a fair strong constitution for that sort of thing – but there's a difference between what you see in war and the likes of this.'

I had always imagined the sight of butchery was harrowing enough wherever it was encountered. I took a deep breath and swung my legs over the side of the bed, recalling as I did so how cold it had been when my feet touched the floor the previous evening.

'A bad business anyway, sir. Terrible business. I liked Lord Halsingham very much.' He busied himself picking out some clothes for me, and it struck me that he would not have presumed to do this unless I had seemed to him visibly incapable of making such decisions for myself. It was a kindness, both in saving me the embarrassment of my confusion, and also in tacitly letting me know that I needed to pull myself together before I was ready for Scotland Yard.

I was the first to be questioned, partly in my capacity as first on the scene, and also maybe because even hard-bitten officers of the law were reluctant to disturb such a collection of lords and ladies until they were ready to be interviewed of their own accord. I had little appetite for breakfast, but I took my coffee to the drawing room and was introduced to a detective called Inspector Oughton. A craggy personage in middle age, he was surrounded by a powerful miasma of tobacco and was rather carelessly presented – despite having once been a sergeant in the British Army, as I later discovered. He was terse, but not unpleasant, and he let me tell my whole sorry tale without interruption, before picking apart almost every detail of it. Occasionally he would jab his pipe stem meaningfully at a sandy-haired constable who sat quietly to one side, recording everything in his notebook. In common with all policemen, Oughton aroused in me a crippling feeling of guilt, and I had several times to remind myself inwardly that it was not I who had murdered Lord Halsingham.

I withheld nothing, including my brief sortie on the first evening in Halsingham House, but I did not identify Agnes as the person who had passed me in the corridor. I justified this to myself on the basis that I could not prove it had been her, but really I suppose I hoped to spare her the discomfort of incriminating her sister further by recounting anything she had witnessed that night. Surely poor Henrietta was utterly condemned by the testimony I had already given, and Agnes would have no choice but to confirm it. At least I hoped she would, and I felt a sudden chill at the possibility that she might be driven by loyalty to cast doubt on my version of events. I wished only to be gone from Halsingham House without delay, to return to London, and to distract myself with as imaginative a combination of vices as was necessary.

When my questioning was done, I begged leave to return to the city (citing reasons of commerce rather than those above, though I am sure my desires were clear enough). Inspector Oughton had full details of my lodgings and place of employment, and he saw no reason why I needed to remain.

'I shall contact you for further statements as necessary, Mr Catcliffe. May I ask, were you previously acquainted with any of the guests other than Lord Halsingham?'

'My father is a friend of Mr Fletcher's, and I've dined with them on occasion. And there's Mr Renwick, though our familiarity is only slight. I know him from my club.'

'Very good. Thank you, Mr Catcliffe.' He allowed himself a brief sigh as he packed a fresh fill of tobacco into his pipe with a yellowed thumb. 'I suppose I must question the sister now. Don't relish the prospect. Already tried to talk to Lady Halsingham, but God knows I got no sense out of her. A bad business,' he mumbled, echoing the same understatement Brown had made earlier on. He looked up at me again, with a faintly accusing look, as if he had forgotten my presence and had now caught me eavesdropping. 'You can go.'

I asked Brown to pack my bags immediately, but the next train from Halsingham station was not for a couple of hours, so I pulled on my overcoat and hat and set off for a walk in the drizzle. Needless to say, I studiously avoided the route I had taken with Lord Halsingham the previous day. I felt a little queasy as the thought occurred to me that he would never again stroll in these fields. He had seemed to enjoy walking in the fresh air.

It came to me how little I had really known of George's character. How striking our conversation had been the day before in the context of a man who I had credited with very few inner workings. Now that he was gone, I began to feel a peculiar sensation that he might never have existed; it was as if he had only ever been a portrait in Woodville's, brought to life without very much depth by the incomplete imaginings of my own mind, then hastily imbued with the potential for unrealised complexities in almost his final scene on the stage. The nonsense of grief.

....

Returning to the house, I could see a great deal of movement in the rooms both downstairs and upstairs. I could imagine them all huddled together, some shocked, some grim, some attempting to claim a greater role in the drama than they had in fact played; whispering, speculating, voicing suspicions, mournfully fleshing out the unassuming image of Lord Halsingham with those crude, exaggerated brushstrokes in which people always seek to depict the dead. I had little inclination to join them, and resolved to slip away quietly. It was not at all the done thing, but I cared not a bean.

Nosing round the front door, I prevailed upon a footman to fetch Inman (who appeared not nearly so haggard or shaken as I had expected). He expressed no disapproval, nor in fact an opinion of any kind at my deliberate faux pas, but merely sent a boy to summon Rackley, and another to see about my luggage. I perched on the steps, sitting on the long tails of my overcoat, and smoked as I waited.

I did not hear Agnes coming until she sat down softly on the step, a couple of feet from me. She looked wretched, though I did not think it necessary to tell her so.

'I've just finished being questioned,' she said, looking out absently over the drive. A cock pheasant stood motionless on the gravel, apparently having run out of things to do until someone shot it.

'It wasn't so bad, I suppose. Not as bad as I feared it would be. I hope that's it, and I never have to tell anyone again.' She rubbed the corner of her eye with her index finger. 'Only it won't be, will it? I am going to have to tell this story over and over for the rest of my life.'

I hesitated for a moment, before asking what she knew must be on my mind.

'What did you tell them? The same... I mean, the same as me?'

'I don't know,' she said, sighing. 'I don't know what you told them. The inspector didn't say. He was probably trying to play us off against each other. But I told them the truth, if that's what you mean. Did you tell the truth? You must have. I knew you would sink me if I tried making anything else up.'

'I did. I had to.'

'I know you did.' She fell silent for an uncomfortably long time.

'Harry, I don't know what to say to you.' I didn't know either, so I stayed quiet. Together we watched the pheasant take two tentative steps, then pause to consider its next move.

'I'm going to try and take Thomas back to London with me, for now. He's still in the nursery, playing with his soldiers. He knows something is going on, but no-one has been brave enough to tell him what. I imagine it will have to be me. Bless him, I don't suppose it will mean anything to him that he is now Lord Halsingham.

'They won't let me see Henrietta. My poor sister. The one thing she must need more than anything else is a friendly face. She didn't mean to do it. It wasn't even really her. We're not ourselves in our dreams, are we?'

The silence lasted much longer this time, and was interrupted only by the noise of Rackley appearing with the landaulette. The excitement was more than the cock pheasant could endure, and it flapped off in a panic, clucking frantically.

I stood, as Brown passed us coming down the steps with my case.

'Sneaking off?' she asked me, in a tone so inscrutable that it might have expressed amusement or disappointment. I nodded.

'I can't face them all.' I looked at her with undisguised pity. 'I wish you didn't have to either.'

She took a deep breath.

'But I do. Goodbye, Harry,' she said simply. She attempted a small smile, which ended up being an abominable approximation of one, then turned quickly and walked back into the house.

There was nothing more to do. I got into the back of the landaulette and gazed out at Halsingham House. Inside, people had obviously heard the approach of the motor car, and I could see mousey little Lady Wrenleigh closest to one of the downstairs windows, looking at me with bewilderment. I averted my eyes quickly. As we drew away, Brown stood smartly on the steps. I nodded at him and he shot me a reassuring grin. It was inappropriate, but it was welcome.

My involvement with the events surrounding Lord Halsingham's murder might have ended then and there, and I cannot make up my mind whether that would have been a good thing. Dawoojee and Liza Dukanwalla would certainly have preferred it that way, and so might Agnes, if she knew the truth. In my defence, though, I never chose to take the matter any further. Rather, I was railroaded into it by a retired marine of His Majesty's Royal Navy, by the name of Jabez Potter.

TEN

— · —

As one might have anticipated, poor George's nightmarish end was the stuff of dreams for one particular group of London professionals. I should imagine many a pint pot was raised to Henrietta's horrendous deed in the pubs of Fleet Street, and there was scarcely a paper of any degree that did not carry the story for some days afterwards. Newspapermen are ever prone to sensationalism, yet in truth the murder was so extraordinary as to be almost without the need for embellishment.

There was, however, rampant speculation as to motive. To anyone who was not there, the notion of a wife butchering her husband with his own razor (for it was this implement that she had employed) while apparently sleepwalking was utterly unbelievable. There were mutterings of affairs and narcotic habits on both sides. One enterprising amateur historian discovered that the Edlingtons and the Cleveleys had clashed in battle during the Wars of the Roses, and several papers devoted a column or two to this ancient blood feud.

What the newspapers were demonstrably light on was anything about what had happened next – particularly to Lady Halsingham. Rowland Renwick's impeccable moustache was nowhere to be seen at the club, and the rest of Halsingham's set were far too delicate to talk about the matter, if indeed they knew any more than I did. I supposed I should find out soon enough, for a black-edged card had arrived in the post. George's funeral was set for the Saturday following his death – December 7th – and I planned to return to Surrey and pay my respects.

It was on the Wednesday afternoon, however, as I was leaving Woodville's, that I was deftly hooked back into the drama from which I had earnestly been hoping to exit stage left. Though the clock had not yet struck four, it was already on the point of darkness, and a pervasive December drizzle hung in the air. Recent events had rather taken the savour out of the city – for the time being, at least – and I was making my way home to dine alone. Even at the club, eyes followed me from room to room as if I were a domestic suspected of pocketing the best silver. It was just poorly disguised curiosity – for my name had been mentioned in the papers as a guest as Halsingham House – but I disliked it all the same.

'Catcliffe? Harrison Catcliffe?'

I considered ignoring the voice and striding off towards Piccadilly, but I did not, for there was something familiar in it that made my hackles rise.

I checked myself on the steps outside Woodville's and turned to see him limping quickly towards me, his wooden foot clunking on the cobbles like a horse's hoof. The black bowler was pulled low over his eyes, and his face looked even more rat-like than the last time I had seen him, framed by his bushy side-whiskers.

For indeed it was he, George's assailant of less than a month earlier, appearing as disreputable and dangerous as ever. I drew myself up as tall as I could – glancing behind me at the club doors in case I needed to make a run for it – but he stopped a couple of yards short of me and did not appear about to pounce.

'Doesn't feel right, though, does it?' he said simply and loudly with his wide Midlands vowels. He stank of baccy and horses.

'I'm sorry?' Then I had a thought. 'How do you know who I am?'

'Followed you around for a bit, didn't I. Weeks ago. Wanted to see who you were. If you were involved. But you aren't one of his lot. Not really.

'So?' he added impatiently.

'So what?'

He looked exasperated, as though he'd just spent hours explaining something to me in great detail, rather than barking six or seven clipped sentences.

'So my mate Matthew Grayling does a job for your mate Lord Halsingham, all on the quiet. Won't say a word about what he's been doing. Then four months later, old Matthew – tough as you like – gets done over in some run-of-the-mill blag, dies just like that. "Not suspicious," says your mate who hired him in secret. Your mate says he never knew him, but I say he did. Next thing, your mate gets his throat slit by his missus while she's having a bad dream. You believe that?'

'Not that it's any of your business,' I snapped, 'but I do. I saw it.' He paid no heed to my brusqueness. In fact, I fancied I saw a glint of a smile.

'Did you, though? Are you really absolutely certain that the man's wife just sleepwalked into his room and did him in right under your nose without remembering a thing afterwards? I mean, maybe she did, but maybe she didn't. Got to be worth a thought, hasn't it?'

I began to open my mouth, but I couldn't think of a thing to say. Probably because he was right. Something in me did want to believe there was more to George's tragedy than the simple facts as I had witnessed them.

'Oh, you and your fancy words. Quite the talker,' he said. 'Tell you what, I propose to you that you come to a pub with me and you tell me what you know and I tell you what I know.'

I hesitated.

'I'll be honest with you, mate,' he said. 'I need your help. And you need mine, though you don't know it yet. But you will.'

His confidence was so absolute that if he had been selling miracle clap cures I would have bought one on the spot. As it was, a drink did not seem such an imposition, and I had more or less persuaded myself that he meant me no immediate harm.

'So? Are you going to come and have a pint, or is that little ladies' gun of yours going to show me her snubby nose again?'

....

The White Bear was close enough for convenience but far enough from both Woodville's and home that no-one would know me. Steering my companion into the carbolic-scented saloon bar, I furnished us with a couple of stoneware pint mugs and took a deep pull at mine.

'I find my conversation is much improved if I know to whom I am talking.'

He made no apology for his manners. As I got to know him better, I would realise that contrition was not in his nature.

'Jabez Potter.'

'And your profession, Mr Potter?'

'Well that depends. These days I'm a drayman for the Vauxhall Brewery. But they say once you've done enough soldiering you're never truly anything else.'

His pint remained untouched while he rummaged in the bulging pockets of his coat, producing a stubby pipe with its bowl apparently carved into some sort of squat human figurine. He opened up a Barlow knife and commenced to carve himself a generous fill from a tarry hunk of twist.

'You were in the army?'

'Navy, mate. Royal Marine Light Infantry. Fifteen years. Time of my life, at least till the Boxers did for my leg at Langfang.'

'I am sorry to hear it,' I mumbled disingenuously, as if I had somehow failed to notice his absurd wooden boot. 'I imagine you consider your background in delivering beer and fighting means you are almost certain to discover facts missed by the police.'

'Now, now, Catcliffe. Don't get snippy with me. I just want to get to the bottom of things, is all.' A match flared in his spatulate fingertips, and he sucked the smoky yellow flame lovingly into the blackened bowl of his pipe.

'But I *am* at the bottom of things. I saw everything.'

Swallowing my misgivings, I proceeded to sketch for him, in hushed tones, the events of the previous weekend at Halsingham House. I glossed lightly over some more personal aspects of the Halsinghams' unhappy marriage, but I recounted the murder in detail, finishing with my questioning by Inspector Oughton and my abrupt departure.

'I suppose I shall have to face them all again this weekend. The funeral is on Saturday.'

'No word of what happened to the lady?'

'None, I regret to say. And now I have told you my side. Perhaps you would tell me yours.'

During the course of my story he had finished his pipe, scraped the ash and dottle out onto the floor with his pocket knife, and sipped lightly at his tankard. He now proceeded to lubricate his ravaged voice box with an enormous gulp of beer.

'First of all,' he began, pausing to belch, 'I suppose I should tell you about Matthew, since to you he's just a name in a newspaper article. But to me he was a good mate. The best. He was a marine too, see, and we fought and sailed the world together through our best years. After that right royal cock-up with Seymour in China, I got invalided out – what with my leg and all – and Matthew decided he'd had his fill, so he left the marines not long after I did.

'Simple as I can put it, Matthew had a bit of magic about him. If you ask me, that's why he got into working for Fornasini. There was those among our mates thought he did it out of some grand desire to repair hacked-up old soldiers like me, but I reckon it was the illusion – the trick of it – that he loved most. He was always a one for a swindle, right from when I first knew him. He used to rinse the new lads of their money on the ships by betting them he could push his bayonet through six-inch timbers, or turn a bag full of cartridges into bent old forks from the galley. All done with the most wondrous sleight of hand. More than once was the time some sore loser called him a cheat and went for him, but Matthew and me could always handle ourselves below decks.

'He was full of talents, Matthew – good with his hands and fiendish clever. His old man was a coppersmith with a little shop. Did all the usual stuff patching pots and kettles and the like, with a sideline turning out fancier pieces. Matthew learned the trade as a lad and took on the fine embossing and chasing work when the booze got a hold of his dad. Finally, when he was twenty or so, the business disappeared in the bottom of a bottle, the old man followed it, and Matthew ran away to sea.

'Fifteen years later he comes home from the navy to find that artisan smithing is the new thing in London. His dad was just unlucky – wrong time and place. So Matthew rents a room off a mate of ours who runs a pub down Limehouse way, buys himself some tools, and starts cranking out dainty little bits for the arts and crafts crowd. Match safes, tea trays, cig boxes – that sort of thing. Then one evening he goes for a night out at the varieties and comes across Giovanni Fornasini and his troupe of poor patchwork buggers. Pompous sod. If he's Italian, I'm the king of Siam.'

He rubbed a rough finger over his knuckles, and I noticed they were scabbed and bruised. Potter had left the navy behind him, but it seemed like his life was never far from a fight.

'Anyway, Matthew's having a pint in the pub down the street after the show, and who should walk in but Fornasini himself looking to wet his whistle. Matthew tells him how he loved the show, the two of them get talking. It soon comes up in conversation that the stuff Fornasini's using for his masks – some sort of plaster, I think – is too bulky, and doesn't last. So Matthew says he can use thin sheet metal to work up a better one, and Fornasini takes a chance on him.

'That was six years back – more or less – and though I hate to say it, that bugger Fornasini did all right by Matthew. Saw his talent, paid him decently, helped get him set up with his workshop at Shing's, eventually made him his right-hand man. Matthew's masks were so good that people even started calling Fornasini's act the "Tin Face Parade". He won't have liked that.'

Potter paused to waggle his empty pint pot at the barman. He did it with the casual presumption of old acquaintance, though it was entirely possible he had never been in the White Bear in his life.

'Then earlier on this year, Matthew starts taking occasional trips out into the country – four or five of them in late February and early March. See, there's two strands to Fornasini's business. The stage show is a regular earner, but he also provides masks, limbs, eyes and other... you know... accessories, as private commissions. Sad truth is that most people who need them can't afford them, but even the rich have accidents. Every now and again some Dragoons officer gets shipped home in pieces or an automobile comes off the road with a pretty young deb in the back seat.

'Matthew was all very cagey about where he'd been. When I pushed him, he said he'd been out in Surrey working on a commission for someone called Halsingham, but he wouldn't say any more than that. If I'd had any inkling what was in store then I'd have got it out of him, but like I say, it wasn't unusual. He travelled for special jobs sometimes, and the clients paid him well to be discreet.

'All this is back in early May. After that, Matthew's in London right through to October, until one day he winds up dead in his workshop.'

The barman set down a couple more pints on the table, and Jabez conveyed with an efficient twitch of the head that I would be paying for them.

'I suppose you read about it. After that thing in the street with your mate?'

'Before, actually. There wasn't much detail, but the suggestion was that the police thought it a burglary gone wrong.'

Potter glowered over the lip of his pint pot.

'Limehouse coppers,' he pronounced savagely, as if that were an explanation in itself.

'Work-shy bunch of bent bastards. It's true that his stash of sheet metal was gone, and that it would have been worth a bit, but there's too much that's just not right.'

He began counting each item off on tobacco-stained fingers.

'First, it's rough enough round there, but Matthew and old Shing both paid their dues to the right people. Second, Matthew was a lot to take head-on, and anyone who knew the workshop was worth robbing would know that. Why not wait until he was out? And I'll tell you the clincher: there's a mate of mine hears every little whisper of what goes on in that district, and no-one's talking. If it was a local job, someone would know, and they don't.

'I imagine your pal Halsingham has half of Scotland Yard sniffing round his corpse, but an old marine in Limehouse isn't worth the time. They've questioned a few of the usuals and they've got people looking out for the stolen metal, but that's it. Tried to have a talk with them about bucking their ideas up. Nearly ended up in a cell.'

I pictured to myself with some small amusement what Jabez Potter might mean by 'having a talk'. I had a feeling I had witnessed it back on the street outside Woodville's.

'They did let one thing slip though. He was drugged up, they reckoned. They didn't say what with, but I bought a couple of pints for a constable down the pub and he said it was the only way they could see to account for his dopey face and the fact he didn't look to have put up a fight. Copper reckoned Matthew had taken it himself – old war-dog chasing his devils away and so forth. But Matthew wasn't into all that. Didn't even drink much.

'And honestly now I've gone as far as I can without help.'

He gave me a pained look.

'The only thing I can see that's out of the ordinary is this work he did for your mate Halsingham. And Lordy was so cagey about it. Makes me all the more convinced it matters. Then Halsingham himself goes the way of all flesh and you can see the way my thoughts are running.'

'But even if he did work for Lord Halsingham and you haven't got the wrong end of the stick, it was nearly six months between the work and your friend's death,' I pointed out. 'Hardly the perfect crime if they were trying to cover up something he knew.'

'I know that,' admitted Potter. 'But would you just try and help me? Find out whatever you can, if there's anything?'

For such a generally abrasive man his look was genuinely beseeching.

'Here's the thing. I can't be the man who could have done more and didn't, do you see? And aren't you even slightly curious about your mate? Don't you want to know for sure?'

'I do,' I admitted, 'but I also wonder whether it isn't better to let dead men rest in peace. Whatever we uncover, if anything, it's not going to bring either fellow back. And I very much doubt we will find out anything they would be proud of.'

The shame welled up in me almost as soon as I had finished speaking. Let sleeping dogs lie: that tired yet compelling argument, used for centuries to justify simple apathy. The truth was that I felt that same impulse which, on the occasion of my last encounter with Jabez Potter, had tempted me to cross the road and leave Lord Halsingham to his beating.

But Potter did not harangue me for my cowardice as he might have done. Instead, he searched around in his pocket.

'Now listen here, Catcliffe. How much do you know about what happened with Seymour in China?' he said, changing the subject abruptly.

'Not much. It was seven or so years ago, wasn't it? And please stop calling me Catcliffe – we're not at boarding school. I suppose you should call me Harry like everyone else. As far as I remember, Seymour gravely underestimated the Boxers during the rebellion and tried to march on Beijing without nearly enough men. He suffered heavy losses at the battle of Langfang and during the long retreat, but survived by stumbling across an arms depot.'

'That's about it. Couple of thousand of us, mostly our lot and a fearsome gang of Germans. Some Russians, Italians, Frenchies and Americans in there too. Fleas seemed to like the Frenchies best, couldn't say why.

'I told you I lost my leg at Langfang, but that's not quite right. Surgeon didn't take it until after. You've never seen fighters like the Boxers. They were something else, charging straight at us, screaming and swinging these bloody big swords and spears. Bang them full of bullets and they just kept coming. The one that got me was playing dead. I stepped over him and he popped right up, hamstrung me with his knife from behind before one of the lads could get a bayonet into him.

'I got through the battle, but I was in a bad way. Lucky I didn't bleed out. Couldn't walk on my own, barely even conscious half of the retreat. Old Matthew got my arm around his shoulder, and he dragged me along that riverbank for five days, Boxers hammering us all the way. By the end my rifle was gone, and Matthew was down to a handful of cartridges, but he wouldn't leave me even when I told him it was all right. Eventually, like you say, there was this mad bloody stroke of luck and we found a fort stacked high with ammunition at Xigu. We held out till the boys from Tianjin could get out to rescue us, and finally they got us back to safety.

'It was a week or so later, after they'd had the rotten leg off and just before they shipped me home, that Matthew turned up to visit me in the hospital. "Take care of yourself, Jabez," he said. "I've whittled you some company for the voyage back."'

Potter laid his pipe on the table in front of me. It was not of briar, but appeared something more akin to cherry wood, much tarnished with dirt and use. The charred, heavily caked bowl was carved with some skill into a cartoonish depiction of a pouting woman's face, surmounting two bulbous breasts which the smoker's forefinger would naturally cradle as he puffed away. It was a truly obscene little object.

The rat-faced old marine smiled crookedly.

'Now do you see why I can't just leave it be?'

Eleven

—•—

G iovanni Fornasini had absolutely refused to speak to Potter, on the grounds that he did not associate with the rougher sort except from the vantage point of a stage. If we were to discover more about Matthew Grayling's mysterious commission at Halsingham House, however, Fornasini seemed a sensible place to start, so it fell to me to see if he might be friendlier towards a man in a more expensive coat.

Parting from Potter at the White Bear, I promptly abandoned my plans for a quiet night. I bought a baked potato from a sooty cart outside the pub, then burned my mouth wolfing it down in the cab home. Changing with great haste, I rushed back downstairs and picked up a fresh cab for the Mile End music hall where the Tin Face Parade was to be found that evening. Remarkably, as I found myself with a function to carry out – however nebulous it might be – the malaise that had dogged me for the previous few days dispersed into thin air. The same damp spray of rain that had so depressed my spirits just a few hours earlier now felt cleansing and invigorating in the cold night air.

Potter had furnished me with the details of the public house in which Fornasini was liable to be found after the show, but I elected to go and see the spectacle all the same, for I was deeply partial to the theatre. London at that time offered an enticingly rich gamut of stage entertainment. Quite apart from the swagger and snap of the ubiquitous musical comedies, in high-class West End playhouses one could witness drawing-room dramas contrived around geriatric actor-managers, or profound social parables scrawled by randy playwrights in tribute to their fragrant leading ladies.

At the other end of the scale lay the venue at which Fornasini and company were performing that night. It was a music hall of my favourite sort: a dated, crude and colourful temple of entertainment, at which Londoners worshipped with a zeal outstripping any the church had seen in centuries. There would be no sober one-act plays or family-friendly quips here. From the outside, the coloured glass and gleaming brass of the theatre door glinted invitingly, and as an extravagantly dressed young couple in front of me breezed inside, I caught a glimpse of the gaudy plasterwork of the interior and a savoury whiff of that intoxicating scent of the stage – the robust combination of aromatic tobacco, cheap perfume, spilt booze and greasepaint. It was a peephole into a London of decades earlier, a rough edge sanded off the city in more upmarket districts by the march of modernity.

Making my way through the hubbub by way of a drinks kiosk, I found myself a reasonable seat near the end of a row. I settled back with a cloudy glass of rough brandy just as a lithe girl with a good deal of black paint around her eyes swept onto the stage in a dress that made my drink seem positively opaque, proclaiming that she was Queen Cleopatra of the Egyptians. Judging by their prominence on the playbills, Giovanni Fornasini and his Tin Face Parade promised to be the highlight. And indeed they did not disappoint.

To begin with, Fornasini took the stage alone, in order to heighten the anticipation with a minute or two of suitably dramatic exposition. He was scrupulously clean-shaven, his thick, jet-black hair plastered to his skull with lashings of pomade, and dark eyes under a single heavy brow slung grandly between his temples. His teeth were over-large yet astonishingly white and even, and he flashed them liberally at the audience. He was by no means a tall man, yet in his wine-coloured velvet jacket and with his mirrored black shoes glinting under the lights, he affected a massive stage presence. His voice, with its strong Italian accent, was deep and resonant, and it boomed across the hall above the commotion of London at leisure. A dental surgeon he may have been in another life, but in this place he was a showman to his fingertips.

Somehow I think I had not quite believed that Grayling's masks, or the accoutrements provided by the other craftsmen in Fornasini's employ, would stand up under the uncompromising glare of the lime-light, and I was expecting some manner of awkward, macabre comedy. Yet I was greatly mistaken.

The first man out was, as anticipated, an ex-soldier. A great bear of a fellow in shirt sleeves and waistcoat, his thick, furred forearms folded, his eyes narrowed, and his broad chin thrust defiantly out below a squashed boxer's nose. His hair was receding, but his greying side-whiskers and moustache were exuberant. Everything about him spoke of strength and robustness.

'May I introduce you, ladies and gentlemen, to Sergeant Alf Mc-Carthy, who I humbly suggest might serve as a commendable example of courage to us all. This bold man fought with great valour for his country over the course of many years, until the terrible events of which I shall presently give account. But first, let yourselves be transported to the exotic plains of the Transvaal, home to the mighty lion, king of beasts. For it was there, five years ago, that Sergeant McCarthy met with unthinkable suffering under the hot African sun...'

As Fornasini's voice effortlessly cut through the hubbub of excited whispering, I found myself playing the same game as the rest of the crowd. It seemed to me that McCarthy's steely eyes caught the light in different ways, and that only his left one blinked. Was the right made of glass, perhaps? A broad scar ran up his neck, vanishing abruptly at the corner of his mouth. Was its further progress yet to be revealed? Was there something beneath his heavy moustache? And that smart, stiff way in which he had walked forth to centre stage before pivoting sharply on his heel. Was it military habit or physical necessity? This was Fornasini's formula: the anticipation; the speculation; and the reveal.

Judging by the way the gasps around me echoed my own, I was not the only one who had failed to notice that McCarthy's arms had remained folded for the duration, and it gave me quite a turn when he removed the left one at the shoulder, leaving his rolled-up sleeve dangling slack. The fingers had been sculpted so they fitted around the bicep opposite with absolute realism, and even the hair upon the arm had appeared as genuine as that of its authentic counterpart. Concerning the right eye, my instincts had been correct, but my imagination had been lacking, for not only was the eye itself a counterfeit, but so was a good portion of the cheek, the bridge of the nose, the ear and the side-whiskers. The moustache, it seemed, was entirely McCarthy's own. The horrendous injuries were long-healed, but Matthew Grayling's painted copper had accomplished more than any surgeon could.

Five consecutive survivors demonstrated Fornasini's miracles, while the man himself recounted their harrowing tales, shrewdly reminding the audience from time to time that those among them who chose to return on a different night would be introduced to further members of the Tin Face Parade. There was a railwayman crushed by a runaway goods wagon, a cabman kicked in by his horse, and a fellow from Chelsea whose house had burned down. Less graphic but more dramatic than some of the others was a young woman called Elsie who had lost part of her jaw to white phosphorous poisoning in the match factories.

Somewhere along the way, I began to feel very strange inside, and to understand something of why Fornasini's show was so popular. It was just too much. There was an element of voyeurism about it, but it was more than that – it was a form of classical tragedy, with a dash of the Roman arena. As flies to wanton boys were these poor souls to the gods, and we all knew it.

In my school days, as I butchered Greek unseens from Euripides or Sophocles, I had pondered why the ancient Athenians would choose to sit for whole days at a time in their open-air theatres, watching dramas in which entire families and nations were buried beneath avalanches of murder and suicide, betrayal, guilt and vengeance, without a grain of hope anywhere to be found. The crushing misfortunes of Antigone or Medea were never-ending, and those ancient audiences must have cried themselves out until there was nothing left, yet somehow enjoyed the process.

There was the same sensation in Callaghan's Music Hall as pretty Elsie took off her mask.

....

After the show, I headed two streets down to the King William Tavern and sat in the saloon bar with a pint and a small meat pie, awaiting my quarry. I regarded the powdery pastry and its anonymous greyish filling with curiosity. Fox, perhaps, tenderised beneath the wheels of a passing train. It tasted most savoury.

Potter's information, no doubt obtained by stalking the poor man's shadow relentlessly like the grim reaper in a bowler hat, was entirely accurate, and I was not kept long before Giovanni breezed self-consciously into the bar. He had changed his clothes to rather drearier city attire, and though he had wiped off much of his greasepaint, a substantial amount still remained around his eyes and at the edges of his mouth, giving him the look of a prostitute in disguise.

He was obviously a regular sight in the King William, for despite his evident wish to be greeted on entry, few patrons in the busy saloon bar looked up. I sidled up to him at the bar, counterfeiting surprise.

'Surely it cannot be? Mr Fornasini? I have just this evening been watching your Tin Face Parade at Callaghan's Music Hall. A most magnificent spectacle that quite lived up to its reputation! Would you allow me to stand you a drink, sir?'

As I spoke, I could feel him appraising me, his gaze lighting appreciatively on my fine clothes and my elegant hat. With the march of fashion and custom, my insistence on wearing a top hat about town bordered increasingly on affectation, but it was a very handsome hat, and Fornasini was evidently a man who shared my preference for theatricality over practicality. He flashed his enormous white teeth.

'You are too kind, good sir,' he simpered richly, his accent far less pronounced than during the show, but still noticeable enough that I wondered whether it might be authentic. 'I am indeed Giovanni

Fornasini, and it is most gratifying to garner praise from a fellow of such evident discernment as your good self. Though I will own that modesty prevents me from revealing the many kind compliments that I have received concerning my unusual little entertainment. I was just this morning speaking with a well-known theatrical agent – who you will understand I am unable to name for reasons of discretion – about the possibility of bringing it to a rather larger theatre in the new year. The crowd there clamour for my art, but I feel such loyalty to my patrons at Callaghan's that it will take quite the offer to tempt me away.'

He smiled again widely, then deferentially asked for a glass of port.

'This place is fine as they go, of course,' he confided in a low tone, his sonorous voice barely above a rumble, 'but they have none of the new drinks.'

We sat down and he lit a cigar, watching lazily as the dense, yellowish smoke curled up towards the tiled ceiling. I produced one of my own, searching in my pocket for my match case.

'I thank you, sir,' he said, raising his glass. 'May I ask your name?'

'Of course, Mr Fornasini. I am Harrison Catcliffe.'

'A pleasure to meet you, Mr Catcliffe. Tell me, did you have a favourite among my performers?' he boomed. 'Wait, do not tell me, it was Miss Elsie. You have the look of a gentleman about you, and there is something about a damaged little thing like Elsie that tugs at our protective impulses.'

He was right, but something about the way he put it made me feel seedy, so I lied.

'The elegant workmanship of Elsie's mask was indeed a wonder. But I confess to being interested more by the engineering than the appearance. The way Mr Langtry the railwayman capered about so on those legs of his was quite remarkable.'

Fornasini's approval was evident.

'A fellow of intellect over sentiment, Mr Catcliffe? Very good! I know my man who built the limbs, Earnshaw, would be most gratified to hear your praise. Indeed, the appearance of the masks, though they capture the imagination so, is only a very small part of our work. The real marvel of the object is not apparent to the spectator, for there is function behind the form. Were Elsie sat at this table with us, you might not find her painted copper face quite so convincing close up, but the structure of the thing would allow her to take a drink and even to speak to you, after a fashion.'

I recalled from the newspapers that this function of which Fornasini spoke was his own speciality, though it was no less impressive for his lack of modesty.

'I notice that none of your performers accompany you this evening?'

'Ah, no indeed. Several of them are rather shy of their fellow man. Of those you saw tonight, only McCarthy regularly enjoys a jar in a public house, but I ask of him – and the few other drinkers in the company – that he does not frequent those hostelries in the immediate proximity of wherever we are performing.'

He took on a slightly pained expression, picking his words with care.

'You must understand, our famous "tin faces" are exceptionally lifelike, but the effect is considerably heightened by lighting, stance and perspective. It is better if the punters do not have too much of a chance to examine them at close quarters afterwards.'

'I understand, Mr Fornasini. You are a medical man, but you are also a showman. I am certain your companions recognise that.' I wondered if they did. For my part, I would not have liked to start telling that burly sergeant where he could and could not drink.

He filled his cheeks meditatively with smoke from the cigar.

'For a medical man, I have ended up in a strange place, it is true. I daresay there are few enough dentists finding themselves holding forth upon the London stage. But would you believe me if I told you that, at the outset, I had no thought to put my patients under the limelights? My object was only to help those for whom surgery had reached the limits of its powers. A man can be healed, but afterwards he must be rebuilt, and it was in this endeavour that I hoped to distinguish myself.'

'Most commendable, Mr Fornasini. Though a curious specialism, if you do not mind my observing.'

'I'll say.' He scraped a little grease paint from the corner of his nostril with a fingernail. 'As a dental surgeon, I was used to a certain degree of artifice, but it was a chance encounter in 1898 that set me on my path. Have you heard, perhaps, of a man called William Veale?'

'Indeed I have not, but please do go on.' I had the impression it was a well-rehearsed tale.

'Well, Mr Veale was a miner, from Cornwall originally. Sometime in the middle of the last decade he was working in Africa, and he made a catastrophic mistake with some dynamite. The explosion took most of his face, including his eyes, nose, his upper lip and his cheeks, along with a good portion of his jaw. The man was a dreadful mess, yet somehow he survived. He hid behind a veil and could scarce eat or drink.

'But it was not this wretched fellow that I met. The Veale who I took a drink with three years after his accident wore dark glasses to hide his missing eyes, but he could speak, eat – even smoke – and to the casual observer he appeared no more remarkable than you or I might. Though of course he was much more remarkable than us. A London dental surgeon of great skill had taken wax casts of his injuries and had manufactured a gold plate which fitted into the gap in his jaw, restoring function. An artist had then created a face mask of fine silver, painted to match Veale's own skin. Working somewhere in the uncharted territory between medicine and art, these fellows had restored a man to working order in the most marvellous fashion, and on meeting him, I resolved there and then that this would be my field.

'The unfortunate truth, however, was that I could not make a living at it. My work is unavoidably expensive, and most of the people with a need for it are destitute. I thought to offer my services to the army, but they would have none of it. The performers of the Tin Face Parade, or "Fornasini's Medical Marvels" as they were at the start, were a sort of shop window – projects accomplished at my own expense to demonstrate my skills and bring them to a wider audience. It took a long time for the commissions to pick up, but the crowds came in great numbers right from the start.'

I saw my chance.

'Do you get many? Commissions, I mean?'

'More and more these days, as it happens.'

'What sorts, if it is not too bold of me to ask?'

He had seemed to see no harm in the first question, but the second set him distinctly on edge.

'Oh, all sorts. You understand I cannot say more. Many of my clients are very wealthy and place considerable value on discretion. Newspapermen are always trying to wheedle stories out of me, you know. Not a newspaperman, are you, Mr Catcliffe?'

His tone was not as jovial as it might have been, and I had the feeling of having overreached myself. I changed the subject hastily.

'Indeed not. My family runs a heavy engineering firm.'

'Aha! A craftsman yourself, then.'

I laughed.

'Assuredly not, Mr Fornasini! Craftsmen there may be at Catcliffe's, but I cannot count myself among them.'

But he was pleased with his parallel, and his momentary animosity faded as quickly as it had appeared. He went on.

'The secret is in the fit, you see. It always displeases me when people talk about the men and women of my troupe as "patched up". Patching implies roughness, mismatch. Many cheap limbs are just that – patches: approximations aimed at covering over something that is missing. My work is more akin to darning. There is foreign material there, for certain, but its function is to knit together the ragged edges, to restore utility, and to blend in.'

I could not help thinking that whoever made Jabez's leg had not taken quite so much pride in their work.

'I shall be sure to remember your ethos when I am recounting the marvels of the evening to my friends,' I assured him. Then, because his weakness had been so gloriously easy to distinguish and I had enjoyed a couple of drinks, I added, 'There is a former military fellow of my acquaintance who I think might take great interest in your work, for he himself has laboured with a most inferior limb these past seven years.'

His little eyes narrowed gleefully through the smoke as he made all the wrong assumptions.

'Most certainly. You must tell that most discerning officer – if it should arise in conversation, naturally – that a Fornasini limb is an objet d'art in itself, but that both function and aesthetic can be tailored almost infinitely to the slightest desires of the wearer.'

'I shall be sure to do so. I daresay he will perhaps have heard tell of your name, for I recall there was that dreadful matter of your mask-maker that I read of in the papers.' I saw his eyes suddenly turn dark and indignant. 'Though perhaps I am mistaken, and it was a different fellow for whom the craftsman in question worked?' I added hastily.

His expression softened, and his whole persona shifted slightly. He sipped at his port and gazed at the pitted surface of the table.

'No, you are right, sir.' He looked genuinely melancholy. 'Poor Matthew was a great loss to me. Dare I say it, a great loss to the world of medical artifice in general. I have struggled to replace him. He was a talented man, and terribly discreet, though he could be persistent when he wanted to be. The first time I met him was in a public house in Lambeth, back in the days when my star was not as emphatically in its ascendancy as now.

'Initially I thought he might be a beggar of some sort, or a common vagabond, particularly since he introduced himself to me by stealing a shilling from me in a coin trick – always terribly fond of a coin trick, he was. But lord knows, where Matthew was unrefined without a doubt, the man was keen. I gave him short shrift to start with, but when he undertook to provide me with a lifelike mask of his own face – and at his own expense – as an indication of his skill, I felt I had nothing to lose. He was waiting outside the theatre the following week, and so convincing was his appearance under the gaslights and the shadow of his hat brim, that I did not at first realise he was wearing the mask in question. It was vastly superior to the ones my performers wore.'

'Remarkable.'

'Quite, and never let it be said that Giovanni Fornasini is guilty of prejudice in the matter of social class. Where true gems are concerned,' he opined, 'one must be prepared to excavate the dingiest of mines, and the matter of talent is no different. Matthew was certainly a rough stone on the outside, yet the quality of his substance was unquestionable. I hired him at once, and the relationship was most profitable for both of us over the course of half a decade. By the end, he was my most trusted man in the whole company, overseeing a good deal of work on my behalf.'

'I recall in the papers there was some talk of foul play.'

He scowled.

'There was, but those grubby little rags will print anything in search of the sensationalist's coin. Sometimes I own I am at pains to tell the difference between certain elements of our popular press and the penny dreadfuls of Queen Victoria's era.' He looked skyward and puffed at his cigar to emphasise his modernity, as if the venerable old bird had turned her toes up in the distant days of yore, rather than half a dozen years earlier.

'So you do not hold with such talk, then?'

'I certainly do not. Matthew's death was a tragedy. A waste of life all too common in our wretched city. But simple robbery it can only have been. And I shall tell you why.' He jabbed the end of his cigar at me. 'There was simply no-one who would want Matthew Grayling dead.

He was a quiet man. A gentle man, even, notwithstanding his violent past in His Majesty's Royal Navy.'

'You do not think, then, that it might have borne any relation to his employment?'

'Do I take it you are suggesting one of my performers might have done it?' he asked with evident surprise. 'To be sure, there are those among them whose sensibilities are somewhat... fractured... by the dreadful events of their past, but any deranged enough to murder wantonly?'

He let the question hang rhetorically.

'No, Mr Catcliffe. Certain members of the Tin Face Parade are periodically a danger to themselves, if you catch my meaning, but none are a threat to others. And even if they were, it would be a brave fellow indeed who would seek any sort of physical confrontation with a man like Matthew. McCarthy alone, perhaps, might be in with a chance of handling him, but the two liked each other well enough.'

'And in the course of his private commissions, perhaps? Could there have been a wealthier client nervous of his discretion in a personal matter?'

His demeanour sharpened again perceptibly, as if I had stepped on his tail.

'Do you know, Mr Catcliffe, I find this line of conversation most irregular. I wonder if you are not perhaps an agent of the Metropolitan Police with such an interest.' His teeth smiled, but his eyes did not, and I fancied his Italian accent became decidedly more Cockney for a moment.

'Forgive me. I have a horrid compulsion towards prurient specu-lation,' I said, laughing, in what I hoped was a successful attempt to cover up my sudden panic. 'I read a column in the newspaper and all at once I believe myself a member of Scotland Yard. It is a dreadful habit – I do hope you will forgive me.'

'Not at all, Mr Catcliffe,' he replied, apparently accepting my admission. 'Mr Conan Doyle and his imitators have made consulting detectives of the whole nation. We are all wont to theorise in such cases as these. I must own I have given the matter similar thought myself, but in this instance I think we may both restore our hand lenses to our desk drawers. Poor Matthew's death was a terrible crime of the lowest sort. Nothing more nor less.'

This was clearly his last word on the subject, and I masked my disappointment for the next fifteen minutes or so while I listened politely to Giovanni's unflattering appraisal of the theatre manager at Callaghan's (who was not called Callaghan) through a fug of cigar smoke. Eventually, having finished my drink, I took my leave on the pretext that a card table awaited me at my club, and with suitable promises to recommend his art to my distinguished military friend, I turned up my collar and marched out into the darkness.

I was far from convinced by Fornasini's sincerity, and my instinct – that most capricious of faculties – whispered to me that his account was incomplete, though it could simply have been that there was nothing more to tell. Now I had been set upon the path, I felt certain that there was something to be unravelled, but so far my only basis for supposing this was the unsubstantiated paranoia of an angry little drayman.

TWELVE

The funeral was a bleak, uncharacteristically simple affair, in a cramped, icy-cold village church. The tenants and estate workers shivered in a respectful crowd outside while the newspapermen peered in frustration through a stiff line of police constables at the edge of the churchyard.

The sermon was lengthy, more akin to a theological lecture on the concept of an immanent God, with abundant quotation of scripture and almost no mention of the man whose expensive coffin sat below the pulpit, save for one passing reference to 'the tragic nature of Lord Halsingham's passing'. In this instance, I could not blame the beleaguered country parson for resorting to obfuscation. God had not, after all, dealt very generously with George at the end.

The church was full, but Halsingham's friends were few in number. Most of the congregation were distant relations, family friends or others bonded to the Edlington family through arm's-length allegiances. From my vantage point on the end of the back row I could see a line of gentlemen from the club, one of whom kept pinching the points of his moustache in a familiar manner. Rowland Renwick had emerged from wherever he had been hiding, and next to him stood Albert Grieve, looking bullish even in such a sombre setting. As I arrived at the church, I had spotted the two of them apparently deep in conversation, which was something of a surprise, since they had given no indication of any acquaintance at dinner the previous week.

There were other familiar faces too, like the Bowleses, the Wrenleighs, and old Mr and Mrs Fletcher. Inspector Oughton of Scotland Yard stood not far from me, an incomplete quantity of the stubble scraped from his jaw in concession to the formality of the occasion, yet otherwise as shabby as ever, his eyes flicking endlessly back and forth among the assembled company.

Lady Halsingham, needless to say, was missing, but little Thomas sat on the front row, looking more ghostly than ever in his mourning clothes and clinging solemnly to Agnes's arm.

As the service ended and the congregation filed out row by row, beginning at the front, I saw Agnes and Thomas walking up the aisle towards me. Both had their lowered eyes fixed on the iron grate in front of them with such earnest concentration that I wondered if it was a tactic they had agreed upon before the start of the service in order to avoid meeting anyone's eye. I tried to give them what I hoped was a reassuring smile as they passed, but neither one looked up.

In one respect, this was something of a relief to me. I had promised Potter – highly unimpressed by my lack of success with Giovanni – that I would use the funeral to try and ascertain whether or not Matthew Grayling had been at Halsingham House earlier in the year, or even perhaps to lay the foundations for an audience with Lady Halsingham. But in the event, I hadn't the stomach for it. My conscience rebelled at the notion of intruding upon the ashen little boy's grief, and I was glad of their averted eyes.

As one of the last men out of the church, I paused to look around. Without the coffin, the mourners, and the hundreds of yards of black crape festooning dresses, hats and armbands, it was a much more cheerful sort of a place. The bright, cold winter light seemed to gain a degree of warmth as it filtered through the stained glass and fell across the hewn wooden pews and the mediaeval stone font. I turned and followed the sombre train out past an untidy stack of hymn books on the table by the door.

....

My family's move to London some years earlier had suited me rather well. As my parents prepared to up sticks for the big city, I was concluding my university studies in Saxony, these having been directly preceded by a year touring Greece, Italy and Turkey (and other countries in which tortoises roam free). It had already begun to occur to me that after so long sampling the diversions of the continent, a return to my flinty northern hometown would, paradoxically, be the cruellest exile.

London, I was sure, was the only place for me, and fate played generously into my hands. The poverty and wretchedness of the city were not hidden from me, but for an unencumbered young man with money in his pocket and adventures on his mind, London was a playground.

I had quickly escaped the new family home out in Blackheath, installing myself instead in a comfortable set of rooms on the upper levels of a terrace off Great Portland Street. My landlord and lady lived on the first floor and ran the draper's shop underneath, and they were well-disposed toward me on account of my employing their youngest and most unmanageable daughter, Edie, as a general maid.

A sparrow of a girl with a voice like a sergeant major, she breezed in at unpredictable hours of the day to prepare my meals and to relieve me grudgingly of any domestic chores, but otherwise I lived alone and kept whatever irregular hours and habits I cared to. As they were fond of saying up in Yorkshire, my whole household was under my hat brim, and this suited me just fine.

On Monday lunchtime, when I returned from my modest day's work at Catcliffe's, I discovered a note left for me with Edie. She had cast it upon the hall floor, presumably so as not to impede her dusting of the side table.

Dear Harry,

Please forgive me for ignoring you on Saturday. You were almost the only friendly face in that whole sombre crowd and I felt rotten about it afterwards, but I had given Thomas my word we would escape the scene without being drawn into conversation.

I am writing to let you know that Thomas and I arrived early this morning in London. We are staying at my family's house in Kensington (address above). I simply had to get us away from Halsingham House, if only for a short time. Also, we are closer to Henrietta this way, and I have hopes that we may be able to see her soon. My father's current ill health leaves him and my mother unable to make the journey from Kelverton, so I am Henrietta's only ally for the time being.

You are welcome to call upon us if you wish. We could do with a little brightness in days like these, and I have no doubt you are the man for the job.

I hope this note finds you well,

Agnes

I shared her certainty that I was the man for the job, and my natural pleasure at the thought was compounded by the pleasing realisation that I might even be able to fulfil the mission in which I had failed so completely two days earlier. Jabez Potter and I had an arrangement that I would contact him by leaving a message with the landlord at the White Bear – a hulking chap with a broad, guileless smile and a downy moustache – but I had left no such note, on the grounds that I was not yet ready to endure his scorn at my lack of success. However, it was only a matter of time before he turned up skulking outside Woodville's, and I welcomed the opportunity to make some progress before the antagonistic little drayman sought me out.

I called on Agnes and Thomas later that same afternoon. The house was one of those grand, pillared affairs which abound in South Kensington. Emblems of the divide between the affluent west and the squalid east.

A severe-looking footman, like an ancient bald vulture in a black coat, answered the door suspiciously, but he was eventually persuaded to admit me to the sitting room. There the lady of the house awaited.

'I fear I was not myself the last time we spoke,' Agnes said hesitantly, after we had seated ourselves.

I too had worried that our meeting might be awkward, or cold, on account of the detached way we had been with each other on the steps outside Halsingham House that Sunday morning. Of course, we had been utterly overwrought, but for my part at least, I was regaining my equilibrium well enough.

Of Agnes I was less sure. The blow had come a lot closer for her. She seemed more like herself again, but there was something wilful about her lightness – forced, even. Good for her, I thought. People are always obsessed with trying to see through a brave face, and I have never understood why.

'I wasn't much better myself. Why don't we put it out of mind, if we can?'

'No, I have a little more to say,' she said, amiably yet firmly. 'You see, I have a feeling I left you with the idea that I blamed you for telling the truth. Maybe I did, but I don't know what else I expected you to do. It was madness to expect you to perjure yourself so recklessly in front of Scotland Yard when you didn't even want to be there in the first place. I didn't either, actually, not that it matters now. Anyway, I wanted to say that before we go further. Otherwise it will sit between us and we'll never really be friends again.'

'Well then, it's said, and we can be friends again.'

'I hope so,' she said, smiling.

'Actually, you are my second friend today. Mr Albert Grieve visited just earlier. He wished to enquire whether there was any way in which he might be of service to me – and Thomas, of course – during this difficult time.'

I fancied there was a touch of mirth about the corners of her mouth.

'Very solicitous, Mr Grieve,' I offered in as non-committal a tone as I could manage.

'Yes, solicitous, that's it.' Agnes avoided my eye by looking at the carriage clock. 'He only left half an hour ago. I suppose you will be sorry to have missed him.'

This was wicked, and she knew it.

'I don't think Drew much approves of all these gentleman callers,' she went on, nodding her head towards the hall door. 'Though he must surely realise that I am on borrowed time as it is.'

'Your footman? No, he didn't seem very pleased to find me on the doorstep.'

'He won't have been. If it's any consolation, he isn't very pleased to be in London at all. He hates it here. In the normal course of things he is under-butler at Kelverton – which is just the way he likes it – but Father insists that he comes down whenever I am in residence. I imagine the idea is for him to keep a weather eye on me, vet any gentlemen who turn up and report back to Father. He's a kind-hearted fellow really.'

'He could have fooled me. Did Grieve get the same reception?'

'Not quite so frosty, I think. Mr Grieve is so sincere, it lends him a little more dignity.'

Tea came, and we talked of her intentions while she was in London, all the while knowing that the conversation must inevitably light upon Lady Halsingham before too long. It was almost with relief that Agnes eventually found her way to the subject.

'Henrietta is in an institution,' she explained. 'It's not a prison, but she is secure. She is locked in her room and no-one has been allowed to see her yet except the doctors and the police. We're assured she is being very well cared for, and her physicians are evaluating the state of her mind. Doctor Rochester is one of the most pre-eminent scientists of the human brain in the country. He has treated her several times over the past five years or so, at this same clinic, and is uniquely placed to assess her disturbed state. If he can persuade a court that what happened to George was a genuine unconscious episode, beyond my sister's control, then perhaps she may not... well, you know.'

Perhaps she may not hang was what she meant. It had not occurred to me until then that Lady Halsingham might face the gallows. The fact was that she had killed her husband, and if a court decided that she had acted with intention then she would swing for it. I had a horrid glimpse, through the lens of my imagination, of the coarse rope being tightened around that pale, slender neck.

'She won't,' I attempted to reassure her. 'We both saw her, and there was no waking soul behind those eyes. The police have my statement, but of course I'll tell it to a court too if I have to.'

I drained the dregs of my tea, playing for time.

'Actually, Agnes, there's something I need to come clean about, if you will allow me.'

Agnes looked up, suddenly on guard.

'Of course. Should I be worried? Will I have to throw you out?'

'Something and nothing, perhaps. On the night before... it all happened, I found myself abroad in the house after dark. I heard noises and went out into the corridor to investigate. The sounds ceased not long after I emerged from my bedchamber, but in the darkness a figure passed me. I'm almost certain it was you, Agnes. What did you see? I'm loath to bring it up, and you may rest assured I won't change my story, but I must know, for myself. Did it have any bearing on what happened the following evening?'

I had delivered my confession nervously, yet Agnes did not appear annoyed at being spied on, accidentally or otherwise. She merely hung her shoulders in resignation.

'So that's why you were odd around me that next day. I did wonder. Alas, you'll be disappointed, Harry. Like you, I heard raised voices in the night. I suspect everyone in the house did, though only you and I were impertinent enough to poke our noses in. My excuse is that one of the voices was my sister's. What's yours?'

I remained mute. Her point made, she continued.

'When I got closer, I realised it was an argument between Henrietta and George. They were in Henrietta's bedroom. My sister was crying, slurring her words, like she'd just woken from a deep sleep, but George's fury was... uncharacteristic.'

'Doesn't sound like old George.'

'It wasn't. Not like him at all. He railed at her for tormenting him in the night. From what he was saying, it sounded as though just a few minutes earlier she had rushed into his bedchamber in a frightening aspect.'

She saw the way I was looking at her.

'But the only proof was his own word – and *he* was the one who sounded unhinged. How was I to know? Who was to say he hadn't dreamed it all then crashed in upon her room and woken her from her slumber?'

'You were not to know. And you mustn't ever think it. Not ever, Agnes.'

'Honestly, the violence in him that night. You knew George. He was many things, but not a man of temper or passion.'

'He wasn't himself that weekend. There was a point during our morning walk when I thought he might cry.'

Her eyes widened.

'I always thought him so steady. Yet there he was right on the edge of desperation.'

I thought back to that night in the cold of the corridor. The distant voices and the ghost of Agnes passing me in the dark.

'So you weren't there at Henrietta's request?'

'Not that night. Her maid called me to her room the next morning – you'll recall that she hid up there rather than taking her breakfast downstairs with the rest of us. That was when she asked me to wait in the corridor after lights-out.

'She was absolutely adamant that she hadn't acted as George described. She swore she'd never left her bed.'

'What did she think was going on?'

'She was convinced that he had some plan to have her committed – detach himself from their loveless marriage and take another wife. I know, it sounds insane to say it out loud, but I believed her when she told me. Let the rest of the world doubt my sister, I thought, but not me. Now I wonder if her paranoia might have been another symptom of her condition. Honestly, Harry, I don't know what to think.'

I considered her words.

'If anything, this only bears out what happened the following evening. It seems to me that these night terrors of Henrietta's were a genuinely unconscious thing. Surely she cannot be blamed for events committed while she was not of her own mind, however appalling.'

Agnes looked gloomy.

'I don't suppose many of George's compatriots will feel that way.'

'I don't suppose that matters. They weren't there.'

She took a deep breath, bringing herself back to practical things.

'For the time being all our hopes must lie with Doctor Rochester's observations. I shall attempt to see Henrietta tomorrow. I have been in regular communication with the doctor since last week, and I met with him as soon as we arrived.'

I looked at her expectantly, and she touched the tip of her tongue unconsciously to her upper front teeth in a manner that signified she was picking her words carefully.

'He's a bit... prickly, not the most sympathetic. But I don't doubt his competence, and that's Hen's best chance. He says she is in a very distressed state of mind, apt to become frantic when she contemplates the reality of what she's done and the future she's lost. They've had to sedate her heavily during the nights.

'I asked if I might be allowed to see her – in fact I tried every approach in my repertoire. Flattery, flirtation and everything in between. Eventually the waterworks did the trick – he conceded that I might visit the hospital first thing tomorrow morning and see if she is in a condition to receive me. He emphasised that he couldn't guarantee anything. Actually, I think he quite enjoyed emphasising it.'

'Will you take Thomas?'

'Not yet, no. Poor lamb has been bereft without her, but I won't have him see her like that. He has a rich imagination, and where Henrietta can find sleep at night through tranquilisers, I don't suppose they'll let me use them on a child.'

The corner of her mouth twitched.

'At any rate, I want to see how the land lies before I try taking Thomas to see his mother.'

'How much does he know?'

Agnes sighed, the world-weary heave of a much older woman.

'As much as I can get him to understand. I'm sure my parents will disapprove, but I decided that trying to keep secrets from him now will only end in complications later. He knows from me that his father is dead. He knows that it was a terrible accident, and that his mother did it without meaning to. And he knows that he's Lord Halsingham now. What he really understands of these facts is anyone's guess. I don't know if he comprehends what death actually means, or whether he expects his father to reappear at some point. I'm dreading his reaction when he first sees Robert.'

'You mean George's younger brother, Robert? Why?'

'Did George never tell you?' Agnes looked surprised for a moment. 'No, I suppose he mustn't have. How very like George,' she said sadly. 'He always talked about his brother as if he were much younger, but in fact George is – I mean was – the senior only by a matter of ten minutes.'

I have never been the sharpest tool in the box, and the incomprehension on my face must have been comical, for she almost laughed at me when I finally got there.

'They are twins?'

'Identical. At least in looks. That's why I'm worried what Thomas will think when he sees Robert. He hasn't seen his uncle since he was a babe in arms, and will not remember him when Robert arrives from Africa – as he is almost certain to do within the next month. It was George's wish that Robert would act both as executor of his will and as Thomas's guardian, with full control over his affairs until he's old enough. Robert is hastening back from his posting to fulfil his responsibilities, and I can only hope that Thomas will see how different his personality is. In terms of character at least, the Edlington brothers were chalk and cheese.'

'You know Robert too, then?'

'Oh yes. We used to go and stay with the Edlingtons when George was paying court to Henrietta, before Robert went abroad. It's funny,

Robert and I both teased Hen dreadfully about her sleepwalking – it was well known in the family. But George never did. It's as if even then he knew...' She stopped for a moment, then shook off the thought and continued.

'The age difference between us seemed greater then. I wasn't yet seventeen when my sister and George were married, but I remember Robert well. Though I've only come across him once since those days. He doesn't come back from Africa much. He's roguish, energetic, quite different from his brother. George always said darkest Africa was the best place for him. I'm quite certain that even in his most unguarded conversations he doesn't reveal the half of his goings-on. In fact...' She hesitated.

'Go on?'

'...He reminds me a little bit of you, Harry. In our private conversations at Halsingham House, Henrietta and I wondered if George's liking for you might have stemmed in some small part from your reminding him of his distant twin.'

'It's always possible, I suppose. Would he have skilfully manipulated his brother into stalking the corridors of Halsingham House after dark and spying on his wife?'

'Unlikely. Robert still has some sense of right and wrong.'

....

I persuaded Agnes, during the course of our conversation, to let me go with her to the Rochester Clinic where Henrietta was being treated. This being accomplished so easily that I felt she must be glad of the offer of an escort. The more I thought about it, the more I began to suspect that I had received her card that morning with this very end in mind.

Before I left, I went with her upstairs as she looked in on Thomas. He was to be found, as on the occasion of our previous meeting, sat on the floor playing with his soldiers, in a bedroom that had been hastily adapted into a nursery. But there was a listlessness about him that had not been there before. His little eyes were sunken, and his smile as he stood was half-hearted at best.

'Good afternoon, Mr Catcliffe.'

I recalled what Agnes had said earlier. But I saw now she was wrong to question Thomas's comprehension of events. The lad knew exactly what death meant.

THIRTEEN

— · —

I knew something was amiss before we had even crossed the threshold of the Rochester Clinic. Dr Rochester's establishment was housed in a large former mansion at the end of a smart cul-de-sac just off Hampstead Hill, with high gates standing wide open, a short drive and comparatively modest but well-presented gardens to the front. The trees and flowerbeds were bare for the winter, but the leaves had been fastidiously swept, and over by the east wall a couple of frost-dusted benches sat beneath the naked branches of a small orchard.

It was early in the morning, not much past half eight when we drew up in Agnes's motor car – a magnificent imported machine of which she was justifiably rather proud, with a long, cylindrical radiator and a folding top. As we passed the gates, we could not help but notice two police constables huddled in their double-breasted greatcoats at one side of the broad front door, stamping their booted feet in the cold and talking in hushed tones. They looked up as we approached.

'Can we help you, sir? I'm afraid the clinic is closed this morning.' The man had a wispy moustache and his cheeks and chin were scoured with pockmarks.

It was Agnes who replied.

'I am sorry to hear that. My name is Miss Cleveley, and at the very least I would like to speak to Dr Rochester. I am here to visit my sister, Lady Halsingham.' I pondered whether Henrietta was technically a dowager now. I would have to consult Debrett's.

The policemen glanced at each other, then the one with the marked face opened the door and led us into the entrance hall. It was an airy, bright room, with wooden floors, tall windows to the front and a staircase to one side. The sounds of muffled voices and brisk footsteps echoed around the white walls, and there was a smell of food masking that faint chemical odour characteristic of the medical establishment. Next to the staircase was a desk where a middle-aged woman sat poring over a sheaf of papers. The constable did not enter the hallway himself, but clicked his fingers at the woman and said curtly, 'They're here to visit Lady Halsingham.'

She looked up, then abruptly back down again, as if afraid her eyes might betray something they were not supposed to.

'Good morning, sir, madam. Please follow me.'

She led us wordlessly down a corridor to a waiting room outside an office, then knocked discreetly at the door and popped her head round. There was a lengthy, whispered exchange, before she opened the door fully and ushered us in with a nervous smile.

Our first shock was to see Inspector Oughton of Scotland Yard sitting on one side of the desk. As his eyes lighted on me, his brows twitched ever so slightly in surprise. Opposite him, in an expensive armchair, sat a harassed-looking little man in his thirties, with a full moustache and pinched features. His bald pate shone in the bright light from the window, and what hair remained round the sides and back was dark and cropped short. One elbow was on the desk, and his forehead rested wearily on his outstretched thumb and forefinger. He peered at us sidelong, without moving, then blinked long and hard, and stood up.

'Miss Cleveley,' he said briskly. 'Good to see you again. Forgive me, sir, but we have not met before.'

I was about to introduce myself, but Oughton piped up from his seat.

'This is Mr Harrison Catcliffe. Another guest at the unfortunate party at Halsingham House. Apparently he is escorting Miss Cleveley to her appointment today.' I felt his piercing gaze on me and recalled telling him confidently that I had no connection to any of the other guests that weekend, save my father's friendship with Dick Fletcher and a passing acquaintance with Rowland Renwick. I could see how my turning up with the only other witness might prick his suspicions.

'Quite right, Inspector,' replied Agnes, making a bad fist of concealing her alarm at his own presence. 'Mr Catcliffe called yesterday to enquire as to Henrietta and Thomas's wellbeing, and I invited him to accompany me.'

Rochester seemed barely to notice me. He waved us both, with a hint of impatience, to the two chairs which a constable was pulling up next to Oughton.

'Forgive the inspector's attendance, but we've had a rather dramatic night. In fact, your arrival is timely enough, since I was going to have to to send for you anyway.

'The nub of the matter, Miss Cleveley, is that Lady Halsingham has vanished. She was sound asleep at three o'clock this morning when the night nurse looked in on her, but when her daytime nurse did her rounds at seven, she was gone.

'The door to her room was locked, but her window had been levered open from the inside with some sort of flat object – the inspector judges that it was something along the lines of a chisel. I really don't know how I can even begin to apologise for this. Nothing like it has ever happened in this clinic before.'

Agnes looked aghast, but as the first of her questions took shape in her mouth, Oughton spoke.

'I have just been talking with the good doctor about the... unorthodox step of keeping a murder suspect in a ground-floor room with no bars on the windows. When my betters agreed to the family's request that she be kept here while her state of mind was fully investigated, it was on the understanding that she would be securely contained.'

'Oh for goodness sake,' snapped Rochester, 'she has been observed all week, and I am well acquainted with her history. I have treated her on several occasions before. Lady Halsingham is a danger to no-one while she is conscious. She is a complicated case, certainly, but in the years I have known her she has never shown the slightest hint of violence – nothing whatsoever to point towards the deed of which she stands accused. And anyway, she was heavily sedated. She should have been deep asleep until she was woken this morning. Even then she would have remained sluggish until lunchtime.

'Apart from anything else,' the doctor continued warmly, 'you yourself confided in me that there is the significant possibility Lady Halsingham is no more a murderer than you or I!'

Silence fell abruptly over the room.

'The crucial word there,' began Oughton, rubbing his greying collar with evident discomfort, 'was "confided". Which I think you would agree, Doctor Rochester, implies a degree of discretion when in the presence of bodies directly connected to the affair.'

Rochester took a breath, as if considering how best to dig himself out of the gaping hole that had just opened up beneath him, but he thought better of it and fell silent. Agnes, however, would not be quieted so easily.

'What is it, Inspector? Is there some fact you've neglected to tell us?'

'The facts of the case, Miss Cleveley, are, as they have always been, a matter for detectives,' replied Oughton obtusely, avoiding her sharp eye. But he had misjudged her. Agnes Cleveley was no longer the disorientated, exhausted woman he had interviewed the morning after George's murder.

'How dare you.' She spoke quietly, enunciating each word in a tone so chillingly imperious that I felt certain she had been equipped with it at her Swiss finishing school. 'Do you really mean to tell me that you have concealed evidence that might suggest Henrietta's innocence? That you have left me to believe my own dear sister a murderess? Do you have the faintest conception of your own cruelty, Inspector? You will explain yourself this instant.'

If Oughton was wounded by this, he did not show it. He was not an expressive fellow, though from the way he hung his shoulders I almost believed he might have felt a degree of shame at whatever had made him keep his information to himself. No doubt it was professional, but it was callous too.

'Lady Halsingham is by no means cleared of this crime,' he said sullenly. 'But it would appear there may be other factors at play. Last weekend your sister's maid discovered that the jewel box in her bedroom was almost empty. The theft was not immediately obvious because the box was of a split-level construction, with the jewels that Lady Halsingham wore most regularly in the tray on the top. Most of these items remained, concealing the fact that the larger compartment beneath had been completely emptied.'

'And you neglected to mention this why?'

'Not that it's any of your concern, Miss Cleveley,' he answered sniffily, 'but I have kept it quiet for two reasons. Firstly, because the two incidents may not be connected. The jewel theft could have been a crime of opportunity in a household thrown into turbulence. Secondly, because whether or not there is a connection, the best way to find the thief is to wait until the stolen goods show up somewhere. No-one is going to start pawning jewels that they know everyone is looking for, and I would prefer to let them think the deed remains undiscovered, at least for now.'

I watched as Agnes's arctic demeanour gave way to hope.

'But if the two crimes *are* connected, then it could mean someone else stole the jewels and killed George in his room next door, just as Henrietta sleepwalked in on them. The shock might have awoken her abruptly and sent her rushing back to the safety of her own room in the disorientated state we found her in.'

'It's conceivable,' said Rochester thoughtfully. 'Sleepwalking can usually only be sustained in tranquil, undisturbed surroundings. Too much outside disturbance can produce a violent effect upon the sleepwalker as they awake, and they may not later be able to recall the circumstances surrounding their return to consciousness. I don't mean to be dramatic, Inspector, but Henrietta may even have looked upon the murderer's face yet be incapable of retrieving it from her own memory.'

I had remained virtually mute since entering Dr Rochester's office, but I now ventured to make an observation.

'The strange thing, gentlemen, is that I was concealed in that corridor for a long time before Agnes joined me, and I could swear no-one came in or out of those rooms. Meaning Lady Halsingham must already have been roaming the passageways and any intruder must already have been in George's room – for poor George had not been long dead when we found him, and the deed could not have been done earlier. But then...'

'...There is the servants' staircase at the end,' Agnes interjected, following my train of thought. 'All four rooms are connected to each other, and that little staircase links them directly to every floor in the building. In her trance, Henrietta could have drifted up or down a level via the stairs, then returned to her room by her habitual route. And whoever killed George could have got in – and out – the same way.'

It was a stretch and she knew it. Oughton did not actually snort, but he might as well have done.

'Miss Cleveley, you will tie yourself in knots if you start looking for every conceivable way in which your sister could be innocent,' he pointed out impatiently. 'Quite apart from the fantastical implausibility of it, several witnesses – including Mr Catcliffe here – have stated that Lord Halsingham was in the habit of keeping his bedroom door locked, which sinks your theory completely.

'Those jewels could have been taken at any time either before or after the murder, and could even have been hidden somewhere else by your sister herself as part of a larger scheme. After all, spiriting herself out of this clinic is hardly the act of an innocent woman. No, Lady Halsingham must remain my principal suspect.'

Agnes looked downcast, but I could tell that the possibilities and explanations were boiling away within her all the same. A thread of hope is not so easily discarded.

'And we have still to ascertain how she got her hands on something to pry the window,' Oughton continued, returning abruptly to the present. 'The doctor here is adamant that no such object could have fallen into Lady Halsingham's possession during her stay here.'

'Not to be indelicate, but we aren't in the habit of leaving sharp metal objects lying around when our establishment is full of the mentally unstable, the hysterical and the suicidal,' said Rochester, glowering at him. 'You keep implying that my staff have been negligent, and I won't stand for it.'

'Not necessarily *negligent*,' Oughton responded quietly but pointedly. 'If everything was as you say, then she couldn't have managed to escape without an accomplice. And since her window was forced from the inside of the room...'

His implication was not lost on the prickly doctor, but Agnes, buoyed by the possibility of her sister's innocence, would have none of it. The studied calm of the preceding minutes was lost in sudden nervous energy.

'But this is ridiculous! All of it!' she cried. 'Why would Henrietta break out of here? It makes no sense at all. She's not going to go on the run! What would that accomplish? And where would she run to? She barely knows London, and she has few enough allies in town – most of her acquaintances are friends of George's.

'She is alone, Inspector, with nowhere to flee to. The sad truth is that Henrietta doesn't have anyone in her life who would risk themselves like this to help her.' At the thought of her sibling's loneliness, her eyes glistened.

Oughton withdrew his pipe from his pocket, then observing the doctor drawing breath to chide him, he replaced it resignedly. He waited for Agnes to finish, then said simply and with devastating insensitivity, 'Forgive me for speaking my mind, Miss Cleveley. But there's you, isn't there?'

....

My own alibi was rather weak. I imagine such is the case with most people between the hours of three and seven in the morning, but Oughton made no allowances for that. By the time he had finished with me, I was half-convinced that I myself had popped Henrietta's window open and spirited her away. I rather wished I had stayed up carousing all night, disgracing myself publicly in front of scores of onlookers and perhaps ending up in a police cell for good measure.

With a marked lack of chivalry, I regretted having accompanied Agnes that morning. Had I not turned up unexpectedly by her side then Inspector Oughton would not have given me a second thought, and I might still have been at my breakfast table, contemplating popping to Catcliffe's to swank about a bit on the gantry before taking a long lunch.

The inspector's questioning was as thorough and unsettling as ever. Rochester defended his staff ferociously, vowing that he would trust the life of his infant daughter to each and every one of them. I could not make up my mind whether his indignation was on behalf of his employees or because his own judgement as an employer was being called into question – but his arguments seemed sound enough. There were, among his small and experienced staff, only two who had not worked for him for a period of more than two years. Of those, one was the gardener's boy and the other a scullery maid. Both were apparently of good character, went home at night, and should not in their daily business have come into contact with the patients anyway.

Amid all his sharpness, Doctor Rochester's repeated apologies to Agnes did at least seem heartfelt. I suspect he realised that Henrietta's escape was partly due to his own hubris. In his enthusiasm and sympathy for her case, not to mention his supreme confidence in his own assessment of the danger she posed, he had – as Oughton had so critically observed – been woefully cavalier about the security of a potential murderer.

As for Agnes, she displayed a marked lack of indignation at Oughton's insinuations. After her brief outburst she had regained her composure, remaining articulate during his further questions. She focused her full attention doggedly on the inspector, as if Rochester, the constables and I were simply not there. There was something unsettling about her coolness. It was a façade – of that much I was certain – but whether it concealed distress or guilt I could not say. I did not especially like Inspector Oughton, with his searching eyes and his loaded statements, but his reasoning was compelling.

If anyone in London were likely to come to the aid of the friendless Lady Halsingham, it must surely be Agnes Cleveley. I would never have admitted, even to myself, that I suspected her of any involvement in her sister's flight, but yet it is remarkable how quickly the seeds of suspicion can germinate. If pushed I would certainly not have staked my life on her innocence.

Whatever the truth, I was aware of a gnawing sensation that I had once again been played into a game I wished to have no part in – whether through human hand or simple bad luck. If it was the former, then I decided miserably that the human hand in question was quite possibly my own.

....

Henrietta's disappearance, however, was not the worst surprise that lay in wait for us that cold December day. When we stepped out of the coach onto the broad pavements of South Kensington, Drew, the footman, opened the front door before we even had chance to climb the steps. He was a stiff, unflappable old fellow, but even his monumental composure seemed ruffled.

'Miss Agnes, please come in quickly. There has been a terrible... incident.'

Together with the footman, we rushed into the hallway, where two maids were comforting Thomas's nanny as she sat weeping on the stairs. She looked up into Agnes's frantic face and gulped between sobs, 'Thomas. Thomas is gone.'

Fourteen

— • —

'Mark my words, Catcliffe, if they're on a ship anywhere in London, I know the man to find 'em.'

After Lady Halsingham's escape and Thomas's disappearance, I had not altogether welcomed yet another of Jabez Potter's ambushes. On this occasion, he had pounced on me as I attempted to enter my own home late the following afternoon, pursuing me through the front door and up the stairs into the sitting room. Edie was flicking a feather duster accusingly at the mantelpiece and had cast about in alarm for something to use as a weapon before I put her at her ease.

Initially, he was truculent at my recent silence, but I managed to placate him with a cup of tea from a still-dubious maid and a seat in my favourite armchair. With one of my best cigars screwed between his teeth, Jabez's mood improved still further. For the first time since our peculiar acquaintance had begun, he was even persuaded to remove his cavernous overcoat and hat, revealing stiff, bristly hair that absolutely refused to lie down when freed from its felted prison. As we warmed ourselves by the fire in my small sitting room, I recounted to him all that had happened since we had last spoken. He snorted derisively at my unproductive encounter with Giovanni, blowing an expensive jet of smoke from his nostrils, but his ears pricked up behind his bushy sideburns at the news of Henrietta's flight and Thomas's subsequent abduction.

For abduction it simply had to be. I had called for Agnes early on that dramatic morning, before Thomas was up, and we had already been well on our way to the Rochester Clinic before the boy's nanny had entered his bedroom to find him missing. There were no signs of a struggle, and it appeared almost as though the child had left of his own volition. And yet, when Oughton and his constables made a thorough inspection of the house, a door backing onto the garden from the drawing room was found to have been forced, and there were traces of mud on the carpet consistent with someone entering from outside.

It was generally agreed by the servants that, in the dead of night at least, an intruder could conceivably have got from the drawing room door to the child's bedroom without disturbing the inhabitants of the house. The only occupied bedchamber such a nocturnal visitor would be obliged to pass would have been Agnes's. When she realised this, my friend sat on the stairs and pressed her head in her hands as if she intended to crush it. Someone had walked right by her door as she slept and had taken her nephew. When I saw her devastated by this irrational guilt, I felt rottenly ashamed that I had ever doubted her, even for a moment.

Oughton, of course, was already on the trail of the fugitives. Descriptions of Henrietta and Thomas had immediately been despatched to police constables monitoring all the rail stations and the major road routes out of the city. It seemed a futile exercise to me, given the enormous potential for anonymity in London's seething human anthill, but the inspector did not share my cynicism. For once reassuring rather than accusatory, he explained to Agnes, 'Remember how conspicuous they will be. Lady Halsingham has never before travelled by public transport. She has no money, no belongings, and no experience in navigating the city, save by private coach or car. She and the boy will stick out like a sore thumb. Believe you me, we'll have them before the day is out.'

But his optimism had been ill-founded. As Potter and I looked out at the gaslight glowing through my sitting room window, nearly two full days had passed since Henrietta's escape had been discovered. Agnes, in flagrant disobedience of Oughton's edict to remain at the house and await word from the police, had spent the intervening hours combing London in her motor car, sometimes visiting spots she knew Henrietta was familiar with, sometimes aimlessly scanning the crowds at St Pancras station. I didn't know her well enough to say whether this stemmed from determination or desperation.

I had stopped at the house that morning, but Agnes was not there, though my visit had regrettably coincided with a similar call on the part of Albert Grieve. I found him even more unfriendly and territorial than usual, and I would not have been surprised to discover that he had taken the time to wet the neighbourhood lampposts on his way in.

There was also a permanent watch on the Halsingham mansion in Belgravia. When the police first visited, they had discovered the valet, Brown, already on the premises, together with a small staff engaged in sorting through George's belongings and preparing the residence for the anticipated arrival of his brother, Captain Robert Edlington. There was no sign of Henrietta, but Brown and the rest of the staff had promised to remain vigilant in case she risked returning to the family home.

'Look at it like this,' Potter went on, as I refilled his teacup, 'the coppers have got the roads and the rails pretty much tied up. I'm not what you might call a great admirer of their work, but a rich young murderess like her on the lam with a little lad in tow – they'll throw everything they can at it.

'Now, not to say Lady Halsingham thinks like me, but just suppose she's a mite more resourceful than everyone reckons. She seems to have been so far, right? Well, if I was going to try and get out of London on the quiet, there's no way better than by boat. So many hiding places, so much coming and going down by the wharves – you smuggle yourself onto a ship and so long as the crew don't rat you out, the police will never catch you. You could even wrongfoot them completely and take the canals inland.'

'Shouldn't I be passing this insight on to Inspector Oughton?'

'Don't be soft, lad,' scoffed Potter through the steam from his tea. 'Haven't you heard anything I've just said? Coppers don't know the docks and wharves. Sure, your Inspector Oughton can send some constables over to ask around, but who's going to tell them anything? Plenty of the boys down there have got something or other to hide, and nobody wants the police snooping about, whatever the reason. Word gets out they're searching boats and half the port will take to the waters like a flock of ducks with a dog sniffing around, probably with your Lady Halsingham on board.

'What you need is inside knowledge. The right connections, and the right way of framing the question to the right people. And there's a man I know who can do just that.'

It felt thoroughly futile and hopeless, but if nothing else, Potter's plan might distract me from my overwhelming sense of uselessness. The notion of sitting around doing nothing when everyone else was out on the hunt seemed unbearable, and perhaps that was how Agnes felt too. Twice now I had been in the right place and yet looked on helplessly as events ran away with themselves in front of me. Now there was an opportunity, however slim, to have some kind of influence upon the story in which I had so far been a mere bystander.

Naturally, I had long since lost sight of the fact that none of this was any of my business.

....

I had never been to Limehouse before. In my mind's eye, it evoked a terrifying tableau of London in the bad old days, when street lighting was non-existent and cut-throat razors or worse lurked in the choking miasma of the pea-soupers. The reality of it was not nearly so nightmarish, but it wasn't exactly salubrious either.

My chief impression as I picked my way along a street just behind Dundee Wharf, with Potter stamping impatiently in front, was of the great bustle surrounding me. A stream of men and women from all corners of the globe pushed past in either direction, occasionally smart, occasionally ragged, often carrying bundles and baskets of one sort or another. Emaciated draught horses toiled in their harnesses, lugging great wagons piled high with sacks and barrels. A great din of creaking, crashing and yelling carried through from the wharves, mingling with an overpowering smell of bilge water, sour unwashed bodies, effluent, horses, strong baccy and old booze. Through the open front doors, clerks and agents peered out of cluttered offices and shops, many with Chinese or Jewish names on their peeling signs. On the upper floors men smoked out of the windows and called down to their friends and enemies. The shouted conversations taking place around me over the barking of dogs and the hooting of steamship horns from the river were a Babel babble of a thousand tongues, scarcely half of which I could place.

At Potter's suggestion, I had sought out a millwright at Catcliffe's – a discreet fellow of roughly my own size – and had offered to pay him well for a set of his old clothes. I had told him a half-truth about wanting to visit a livelier district without drawing undue attention, but this precaution was unnecessary, since the man was sensibly much more interested in the money than the reason. Thus modestly attired, I felt much more secure and anonymous than I might have done in my customary finery. Spying my reflection in a shop window, I noticed with satisfaction that the cold air was adding to the effect by making my scars appear rather more livid.

Presently we turned down a narrow alley running south off Rope-makers Fields, following it round the back of the buildings to a small courtyard where, despite the fact that it was not yet past ten in the morning, a group of sailors sat drinking mugs of beer on rickety wooden stools and chatting gruffly in a Slavic language. Behind them, a set of wide double doors stood open, a painted sign above depicting a hook-nosed man in a white turban with a ruby pin. No legend accompanied the image, but unless I was very much mistaken, we had arrived at the Saracen's Head.

Inside, the tavern was spacious and rather empty, with stained wood floors, green and yellow tiled walls and a rough-hewn bar shielding a stack of long shelves groaning with bottles and glasses. There was no divide between public and saloon bar, and I supposed the patrons of the Saracen's Head cared little about such niceties so long as the liquor was cheap. Even indoors there was a heady, malty scent from the sprawling Barley Mow brewery a couple of streets away.

As we entered, an elderly and very ugly white bull terrier rose stiffly from a ragged blanket by the bar and trotted over to Potter, its claws clacking on the wooden boards. He extended the back of his hairy hand, which it licked affectionately.

'Hello boy,' he cooed in a voice with all the sweetness of a file scraping across rotted timber, before turning his attention to the barmaid. She was aged around nine or ten, with tousled black hair, dark eyes and olive skin, and she gave him a broad, gappy grin from where she stood on a box behind the bar. Her voice, when she spoke, was a high-pitched Cockney sing-song.

'Hello, Uncle Jabez! You looking for Dad? He's out talking to some fellas at one of the docks. Don't know when he's back.'

Two or three out of the handful of punters looked up momentarily. Most remained gazing vacantly into their pints. Potter reached over the bar and ruffled her hair.

'Thanks, Maggie. Your old dear about?'

'She's not out of bed yet. Says it's us bloody kids and this bloody pub worn her out,' parroted Maggie. 'Sorry,' she added. 'Do you want me to tell 'em you looked in?'

'It's all right thanks, love, we'll wait till one or other of them turns up.'

We took a seat in the corner, and Maggie disappeared from her stool and emerged a moment later with a couple of bottles of bitter. She scampered back out through a flimsy door behind the bar, and we heard her footsteps clattering up the stairs. Potter and I sat in silence

141

drinking our beer. There was another spate of banging on the stairs, as if someone had tipped a basket of cannonballs down them, and the door behind the bar opened a crack to reveal two pairs of inquisitive brown eyes. They were scruffy little boys of around the same age, a deal younger than Maggie, yet unmistakeably of the same exotic stock, with their dark hair and tanned complexions.

'All right lads. How you doing?' called Potter, but the door shut abruptly and there was more commotion on the stairs as they went back up.

We sat in silence again. At a nearby table, two hungover whores were swapping stories that the sailors outside might have paid good money to hear.

Finally, when we were halfway through our bottles of beer, there was a more sedate step on the stairs, and the door opened once more to reveal a youngish woman with red-blonde hair, deep dimples at the corners of her mouth and a dark-skinned toddler clinging solemnly to her hand. She gave Potter a sleepy smirk.

'Jabez. Sorry, love, late night. Always seems to be a late night in this bloody place. Useless husband never about when you need him.' Her disposition, though abrupt, was milder than her words, and she kissed Potter on the cheek then sat down, placing the child on her lap. She reached out her hand to me across the table.

'Liza Dukanwalla.'

'Harry Catcliffe. Pleased to meet you, Mrs Dukanwalla.'

'I suppose you're a part of whatever business Jabez has got with Duke?'

'It's Harry's business, not mine,' interjected Jabez. 'I'm just the go-between.'

'Truth be told, it's not really my business either,' I added nervously.

'Whose business is it then?' she asked with just a hint of caution in her fleeting smile. 'Not that it matters, of course. If it pays, Duke'll do it. Sometimes does it if it doesn't pay, silly bloody man. He'll do near anything to save getting behind the bar and putting in a bit of graft.'

'Don't worry, Mrs Dukanwalla, I promise I can pay for your husband's time,' I reassured her.

'Sorry, love, I don't mean to be crabby. Really I don't. I'm sure you're a square enough bloke.' The toddler squirmed in her lap and she rubbed the back of its neck soothingly.

'How's his arm?' asked Jabez. I thought he was talking about the child, but by the way Liza answered, I understood he meant her husband.

'Oh, you know what he's like. Says it's right as rain, but his grip ain't what it was, if the broken glasses I keep finding behind the bar are anything to go by.'

'He'll mend. Always does.'

'Always does,' repeated Liza without any great conviction. She turned to me. 'Tell me then, what is it we can help you with?'

It was Jabez who spoke.

'We need to find someone. Two people, actually. And it's an easy job. This pair will stick out like anything.'

He outlined the background briefly, then I gave her detailed descriptions of Henrietta and Thomas. Liza listened carefully.

'You weren't joking. If they've come through any of the docks or wharves round here, I've no doubt Duke's already heard while he's been pissing about doing whatever he's been doing. If they've gone through a different bit of the port it might take him a day or two. I'll pass the message on anyway. You still living in the same place, Jabez?'

Potter gave her his address again, just to make sure, then we finished our beer and set off back out into the alleyway.

'Good to see you, boys. Sure that bloody waste of space will be in touch soon.'

....

Liza Dukanwalla was a woman of her word, and it was scarcely twenty-four hours before I received a note from Potter as I sat pretending to work at my desk at Catcliffe's. The commissionaire brought it in, informing me that it had been delivered by a disreputable-looking boy who had impressed upon him the great urgency of its contents then demanded payment from the recipient. Potter's writing was every bit as atrocious as I might have expected.

Duke says six tonit at the Sarasen. JP

I did not enjoy making my way to the Saracen's Head without an escort, particularly since Limehouse was a substantially different place after nightfall. It appeared no less busy, but the commotion was of an altogether more perilous sort, and I felt glad of my shabby clothes. Also, I will own that I have always been nervous of sailors, particularly those who have recently stepped ashore. A man who has been effectively imprisoned for a month and a half in a 150-foot wooden or steel tube, along with over a hundred other souls, is unlikely to make for the most predictable and even-tempered of fellows. Despite the chill there were many such mariners abroad that night, all of them highly inebriated, and I did my damnedest to remain as unremarkable as possible as I wound my way through the night to the pub courtyard. Gaunt mongrels hurled themselves at me out of the shadows, spitting

144

and snarling then slinking swiftly back into the darkness as I turned to face them.

Potter was already at the Saracen's Head, seated at the same table in the corner of the now-heaving hostelry, and he was obviously enjoying himself since he had removed his hat. Seeing me, he touched his forefinger lazily to his hairline in salute, as his companion rose and extended a hand to me warmly.

Dawoojee 'Duke' Dukanwalla was tall and lean, without an ounce of fat on him. The sleeves of his collarless shirt were rolled, and as he held out his right hand, every sinew and muscle on his forearm stood out under his taut skin. His grin was yellowish, his hair was thick and unruly, and his nose had been broken badly at least once. An old, healed scar twisted the corner of one eye. More than his physical appearance, though, I was struck by his energy, for there was a sense of momentum about him which seemed to carry one along with it, as if one could never be around Dawoojee Dukanwalla and not be making progress in some way or other.

'You must be Harry. Mr Catcliffe. I'm Dawoojee. Good to meet you, mate.' His accent was impossible to pin down, and with each phrase he spoke, I was convinced I could pick up a different regional lilt. By turns he sounded Cockney, Indian, Bristolian or even Caribbean. The truth of it was that he had learned his English while working alongside men from all corners of the empire, and his dialect was a spectacular mongrel parlance.

Drawing back my chair to sit down, I unintentionally dislodged the aged bull terrier from under the table. The beast backed away awkwardly, raising its egg-shaped head to regard me with benign curiosity, then relocated itself beneath Dawoojee's seat.

'Sorry about Cap. Old brute's always in the way. Don't know why we keep him around,' said Dawoojee, laughing. 'Hands down the worst bloody pit dog you'll ever see. Never won a fight in his life. Survived some right brutal maulings, mind, but could they ever get him to attack? Lost so much cash on him that it seemed cheaper just to buy him.' Almost as an afterthought, he added, 'Plus it was only a matter of time before they fed him to the ones who made more money.'

Dawoojee Dukanwalla was a lascar, which is to say he was an Indian who had gone to sea when he was scarcely past boyhood and had spent more than twenty years crewing British ships the world over. In terms of their predisposition for villainy, the press considered lascars more brutish but less innately diabolical than the Chinese, and the likes of Dawoojee had furnished some of our nation's most celebrated writers with memorable creative inspiration, usually connected to the opium trade.

Somewhere along the way, during a period of shore leave in London, Dukanwalla had charmed his way into the arms of a rather acerbic redheaded barmaid called Eliza Madden. The liaison was a brief one, but to his surprise, whatever subsequent companionship he sought in the course of his peregrinations around the globe, the Madden girl remained the one he dreamed of during the roughest nights on the wildest seas. Eventually, after some years, he found the resolve and the opportunity to reacquaint himself with his old flame, and was astonished to discover that the four-year-old girl at her knee bore an unmistakably Dukanwallan aspect. Duke was not a man who placed much stock in fate, but even he had to admit that the signs all pointed in one direction.

Having built up some small savings, he had promptly married Liza, purchasing a run-down yet popular tavern in Limehouse and installing her as landlady. The decision to put down his roots in London was not a difficult one, for after two decades on the water, his native city of Surat in India's Gujarat region had long since ceased to feel like home.

He sat, now, with his long legs stretched languidly out under the pub table, and pushed across a little pack of Capstan Navy Cut cigarettes by way of welcome. Striking a vesta, he lit first Jabez's then mine, then twiddled the dwindling match in his fingers, contemplating it playfully for a moment with his own cigarette dangling unlit from his lip.

'Don't, mate,' said Jabez sharply.

Duke looked at him levelly, then raised the match, sucked the last flickerings of flame up into the end of the cigarette and blew a cloud of smoke across the table. Potter uttered an unrepeatable word, and the Indian smiled.

'Jabez believes it's bad luck to light three cigs from the same match.' He dropped the spent vesta in a pool of spilt beer on the table top. 'Old soldiers' witchcraft. Thinks it means I'll get my head shot in by a sniper. Fortunately, the only rifle in the Saracen's is up in my bedroom.'

Apart from fulfilling Dawoojee Dukanwalla's family commitments, the Saracen's Head in Limehouse had also provided the ideal base of operations for his more discreet and lucrative business, and it was with good reason that he was so rarely to be found behind the bar. For many years, even as he plied the oceans aboard sailing ships and screw steamers, Dawoojee had been running additional errands on the

147

side, all the while filling his agile memory with a wealth of information on every port and ship he came across.

It had begun, in predictable fashion, with a little small-scale smuggling, but the important distinction between Dawoojee and the thousands of other sailors who dabbled in such illicit trade was that his research was always meticulous. He went out of his way to discover which officials could be bribed, where the fences could be found on any given night, or which pubs had hidden means of ingress from the waterfronts. At the seamen's boxing matches where he had been bloodied in his younger days, he forged allegiances with sailors of other nations and gained access to vessels and dockyards which his peers found off-limits. His natural charisma and apparently open nature were of great help to him in this. He learned the habits of the maritime authorities, right down to which shifts the most apathetic customs men were on duty. He got pally with the nightwatchmen at the enclosed docks and cultivated friendships with the shipping clerks who could tell him every boat that went in and out of the port on a given day. Sometimes the goods he had been commissioned to move did not even touch the shore between boats, being transferred by means of tugboat skippers, harbour pilots or lightermen.

Eventually, Dawoojee had found himself in the happy situation of achieving more money for less risk. His chief assets, after all, were his vast knowledge and his connections, and by judiciously allowing people to pay him for access to these things, he could let others take on the lion's share of the danger while still netting himself a tidy profit.

And so it was that – through romantic accident and professional convenience – he had eventually confined himself to a single port, albeit one of the largest and busiest in the world. He had familiarised himself completely with its inner workings, cultivating his networks of contacts and gaining access to the various repositories of information, both official and otherwise, that recorded its goings-on. He spent his days out and about, striding across the waterfronts of London at an energetic clip, watching, talking, eliciting confidences, pursuing whatever snippets of information men cared to pay him for. He would track down boats, cargo or people; could give you access to whatever timetables or rosters you desired, and could arrange all manner of introductions. No dockyard, however secure, was off-limits to Dawoojee Dukanwalla. Liza complained archly that after five years half the punters in the Saracen's Head seemed to drink for free in return for some favour or other, and her husband would only say that such men were paying far more for their beer than ever they knew.

It was unsurprising that he had not encountered any great difficulties sniffing out our fugitives.

'They sailed in the early afternoon two days ago out of one of the wharves on the south bank at Rotherhithe. Little steamer called the *Tyne Lass*. Arrived in a four-wheeler three quarters of an hour before the ship cast off.'

'What? The very day of Lady Halsingham's escape? Unbelievable!' I could not contain my amazement that Henrietta had found her way onto a ship only a matter of hours after she had abducted Thomas.

'Resourceful lady, or so it seems. I reckon even my Liza would have a time getting herself onto a boat at such short notice.'

Potter gave me a meaningful look, verging on self-satisfied, which I did my best to ignore.

'Where did she go?'

'Calais. At least that's what she paid for. There were a few stops before that, so I can't know for sure until the ship gets back in a week or so. Though if I was you, I might take another avenue if I wanted to find her.'

'Oh?' With the flair of a natural storyteller, he was enjoying holding something back.

'Lady had help. A bloke brought them down. Find him and I'd wager you'll find your way to her soon after. Shouldn't be all that difficult. He's a paid fixer with connections to the family or he's a friend willing to risk his life for her. Not too many men in either group, I'd have thought.'

'I see your point, Mr Dukanwalla. Any idea what he looks like?'

'Nothing much. Average height, dark hair, beard – probably fake so no-one can recognise his face – decent clothes but nothing flash. Could be half of bloody London. What my lads did say though was that he seemed like he was in charge of things. Like he knew what he was doing. You want my opinion then I reckon when that ship gets back the captain will tell me the lady's passage was booked in advance by that same man.'

'You mean, before she even escaped from hospital?'

'Exactly. He gets her passage on a ship then breaks her out the morning she's due to sail. They stop by to get the little lad then he brings her straight down here and loads her onto the ship. No hanging around in London, no chance of getting spotted by your copper friends. Must have known they'd turn the city upside down looking for her.'

Potter, who had been rather taciturn for a man ordinarily so forward with his opinions, peered at Dukanwalla through the smoke from his little carved pipe.

'Sounds like a paid hand to me,' he said. 'Knows his way round the wharves and can move fast when the pressure's on him. He broke into two houses in a single morning then spirited them out of the city pretty much instantly. How's a lady like her going to get herself acquainted with a bloke like that?'

Dukanwalla shrugged, then leaned in, laying his elbow across the sticky table top.

'There's another thing too. Man carried the little boy from the hansom onto the ship. He was fast asleep the whole time.'

'Doped?' hazarded Potter.

'Doped.'

FIFTEEN

— · —

I thought Inspector Oughton's ire at my enquiries most unwarranted. Far from being delighted at Dawoojee Dukanwalla's findings, he berated me roundly for taking matters into my own hands.

'I suppose, Mr Catcliffe, you think yourself awfully clever for handing your money over to some waterfront thug in return for a pack of nonsense. I should be obliged if you would give me his name immediately and I shall send my constables to retrieve what is yours.'

'I'll do no such thing,' I retorted testily, attempting to cover my nervousness with feigned ill-humour. 'I promised that he should remain anonymous, and so he shall. My man has committed no crime, and in any case the sum was a most trifling one.'

There had in fact been no fee at all for Dukanwalla's services. When I attempted to broach the subject of reward, he had refused rather gruffly.

'Jabez says this might have something to do with Matthew,' he had said, 'and I wouldn't feel right taking payment for that. I'll only ask that you give the impression you forked out handsomely if the missus asks.'

I had not until that point, I think, understood that the Limehouse pub in which Matthew Grayling had rented a room when he first

152

returned to England was none other than the Saracen's Head. Dukan-walla, Potter and Grayling had a long history, though how the two marines had found their way into Duke's orbit was anyone's guess. Probably crime or violence, undertaken in some far-flung port for reasons that would make no sense to one of life's innocents such as Harrison Catcliffe. Whatever the case, the three men had been firm friends, and if Potter believed that Grayling's death was more than simple misadventure then Duke did too.

Oughton glowered at me.

'Are you refusing to disclose information to an inspector of Scotland Yard?' he bristled, but I did not have a chance to reply.

'I must confess myself surprised at you, Inspector.'

This was delivered in the same bitingly icy tone that Agnes had deployed during her last encounter with Oughton.

'You yourself have fared deplorably in the search for my sister. Yet when Mr Catcliffe comes to you with insights that could conceivably be of aid, you reject his information out of hand since it wasn't obtained by your own methods. If I'm not very much mistaken, you are allowing simple professional vanity to obstruct the business in hand.'

Had I ventured to voice such an opinion, I have little doubt that the inspector would have found a reason to throw me in a cell, or simply had me beaten unconscious by a couple of obliging constables, but Agnes Cleveley in a sour mood was a much more formidable opponent. I congratulated myself inwardly that I had taken my findings to her first. If you must find someone in life to hide behind, I can highly recommend picking someone who has been to finishing school.

Inevitably, as I had told her my fanciful and convoluted tale of retired Royal Marines and murdered mask-makers earlier that after-

153

noon, Agnes's incredulity and impatience had been ill-disguised, despite her attempts to be polite. Her attention had improved markedly, however, when my story reached the point of Dukanwalla's discovery. Whether or not she believed the rest of it, she had immediately latched onto to the reported sighting of her sister as the only tangible lead in a mire of supposition.

Oughton's eyes burned with indignation, but he recognised that further argument was futile. This was the second time he had encountered Agnes in disagreeable aspect, and he appeared ill-equipped to deal with her.

'Very well, Miss Cleveley. I will send some officers to the wharves to investigate these claims further, though I can't promise you that they will discover anything to corroborate Mr Catcliffe's information.'

He glared at me as he continued.

'In the meantime, I must discourage both of you most strenuously from pursuing further enquiries of your own. You possess neither the full set of facts nor any experience in the field, and in meddling in police business you may well obstruct the progress of our investigation. Notwithstanding the very real possibility that you may put yourselves in danger or lay yourselves open to exploitation by unscrupulous characters – as I regret it is highly likely that Mr Catcliffe already has.'

As I perceived it, this constituted a resounding defeat for the policeman, however much he might have tried to dress it up. I did not wish to cause further aggravation by crowing over him, so I apologised for my presumption, adding (a trifle recklessly) that I hoped there would nevertheless turn out to be some value in my information. I reassured him falsely that I would take no further part in the investigation, at which point he turned expectantly to Agnes, who gave him no such guarantees. She merely stood and thanked him frostily for his continued efforts to find her missing sister and nephew.

'Insufferable man!' she pronounced with venomous dislike as we emerged from the station and made a beeline for her motor car. 'He knows he's been caught out, and rather than accept it with good grace he tries to have your informant arrested.'

Her driver hastily tossed his cigarette end under the hooves of a passing cart horse and opened the door smartly as we approached.

'Home, Miss Cleveley?'

'Anywhere but here will do,' she replied curtly.

Agnes did not stew for long, however, and as the car juddered away along Victoria Embankment, leaving Scotland Yard and the disgruntled Inspector Oughton in our wake, she left her ill-humour behind with them. She turned abruptly in her seat, her eyes fixed expectantly on mine.

'So, then. I think I know what we need to do next.'

....

Another trip to Halsingham House had not been high on my list of aspirations for the December of 1907, yet once again I found myself stepping from the Waterloo train to behold Rackley waiting with the Halsingham landaulette. It was Sunday – a fortnight since I had fled the scene of the crime that bleak day. These jaunts to the country were becoming a weekly occurrence. The afternoon was a clear one with the low winter sun casting a feeble warmth upon the air, and magpies hopped and chacked on the station roof like clockwork birds.

'Good afternoon, Mr Catcliffe,' said Rackley, nodding to me. 'Miss Cleveley. Will you be staying long?'

'Only overnight,' replied Agnes breezily. 'I require some papers from my sister's bureau, and Mr Catcliffe has been good enough to accompany me for the journey. He has business with Mr Fletcher at Endsleigh, as luck would have it.'

Rackley was far too well-brought-up to raise an eyebrow, though I wondered what rumours might be abroad below stairs before the afternoon was out. Then again, after recent events at Halsingham House, the servants perhaps had better gossip to play with.

Though Agnes's appearance at the house was more or less acceptable under the circumstances, it would have been inconceivable for me to stay at Halsingham House in the absence of an invitation from Captain Edlington (who was, by all accounts, still at sea as he undertook the lengthy return journey from Rhodesia). The notion of business with Fletcher, however, was a plausible one, so long as one ignored the fact that Dick Fletcher's London offices were within walking distance of my own, and I could simply have found him there on Monday morning.

Still, the old man had seemed most amenable to helping us in our efforts. I had telegraphed him the previous afternoon, outlining in the briefest terms my need to visit Halsingham House to make 'unofficial' enquiries and asking if perhaps we might together cook up some excuse for me to impose upon him. His reply had been immediate and enthusiastic.

I climbed into Fletcher's carriage – drawn by a pair of glossy Cleveland bays with dappled flanks – and watched the Halsingham motor car chug away toward the mournful old house. Agnes's evening was going to be a gloomy and solitary one, but if there was anything useful lurking among Henrietta's papers, she would find it.

We had been careful not to start spinning theories together, but we both knew what Agnes would be looking for as she rifled through the remnants of her sister's closeted existence. Henrietta had known the man who got her out of London. Was he a professional whose services she had enlisted, or was he something else? It seemed inconceivable to me that the timorous Lady Halsingham could have kept a lover, but Agnes had said nothing to indicate that she shared this opinion. Indeed, I could not help noticing how careful she had been not to deny the possibility.

Whatever the manner of Henrietta's acquaintance with this enigmatic fellow, it had almost certainly pre-dated Lord Halsingham's murder. Since that night, she had come into contact with no-one except medical staff and police. Neither of whom were incorruptible, of course, but it was a stretch. So if she hadn't managed to turn a copper or a nurse, how had the escape been arranged? And if she had paid the man, then what had she paid him with? She had no money. Whatever Potter believed, it seemed increasingly likely to me that Lady Halsingham's mysterious accomplice was a personal ally rather than a paid hand.

....

I spent an enjoyable enough night with the Fletchers, partaking of their excellent cellar and appraising them of all that had gone on thus far, from the morning of the escape to Inspector Oughton's ire at my adventures in Limehouse. The grizzled shipping king smirked when he heard about that.

'Dukanwalla still operating out of the Saracen's, then? Thought someone would have put his inquisitive eyes out years ago,' he wheezed ghoulishly. 'I wonder what he could tell me about my own business that I don't already know. Plenty, I should think.'

He was a savage old cove, but as we came to talk of the events of that terrible weekend – as was always inevitable – I fancied there was an odd sadness in him. He listened as I recounted my conversation in the woods with Halsingham, and my glimpse of Frances Brown up by her cottage.

He nodded, pushing a finger down his collar as if it were pinching the baggy skin of his stringy neck.

'Poor little sparrow. I hate to see a pretty thing like that ruined by a stroke of fate. I sometimes run into her down by the woods where my land meets Halsingham's. There's a pool there where I like to sit and have a smoke sometimes, and maybe she likes it too. Never comes close, like, but she'll raise a hand to me from the trees.'

The long sentences were a struggle for his ailing chest, and he took a moment to get his breath back.

'You know, I think old George in his big house and little Frances Brown in her cottage were as lonely as each other. George spent so much time trying to do the right thing by that wife of his, but for all the years we were neighbours they never seemed like friends. You always felt…' he paused, maybe to relieve his lungs or maybe just to try and articulate it, '…like they'd just met a week or two ago and were still working each other out, rather than being seven years past the altar. Well-mannered as the day is long, but I don't remember them ever swapping a smile. Anyway, I won't speak ill of him. Whatever else Halsingham was, he always struck me as a good and honest man – and I've known enough of the other sort to see them plain as day.'

Fletcher was a man who valued discretion, and his opinion of the police did not seem terribly high. When I left the next morning it was with the promise that I would call upon him if ever he could be of help to me. Though it was not spoken out loud, I had the distinct impression that the arrangement was intended to be reciprocal, and I wondered whether at some juncture down the line I would be asked to put my acquaintance with Dawoojee Dukanwalla to use on old Fletcher's behalf.

Fletcher himself left first thing in the morning for London, but he was good enough to put his coach at my disposal, for I had elected to take a later train back to the city. Agnes would only have one opportunity to nose around Henrietta's belongings without arousing suspicion at Halsingham, and I wanted to give her as much time as possible.

Arriving to pick her up from Halsingham House, I found her waiting for me in the drawing room, already attired in her coat and hat for the journey. She was visibly dejected.

'Nothing. Or at least nothing which will help us,' she said.

'So you found something, then?' I intuited tentatively.

'Something... and nothing. There were papers pertaining to my sister's private life a long time ago. Perhaps I'll tell you about them sometime, but they are of no relevance just now.' She sighed. 'Come on, Harry. I've had a miserable night in this dreary old house. Let's go back to London.'

Brown, who had returned from his work preparing the house in London, loaded Agnes's bag into the Fletchers' carriage, helped by a small boy who carried her hat box. The valet greeted me warmly as I came out of the house.

'Good morning, sir. Been visiting the Fletchers?'

'Indeed, I had affairs of business to discuss with Mr Fletcher,' I lied cheerfully. 'Are you well, Brown?'

'Tolerably, sir. Tolerably.' He glanced at Agnes as she descended the steps, then at me, and the faintest hint of a smile played upon his full lips, but he said nothing.

As the carriage pulled away, I gazed out at the grand house for what I hoped would be the last time. Brown raised his hand in salute, Inman nodded formally from where he stood by the door. The small boy did not look up at us, but fiddled with his sleeves.

Suddenly, I sat bolt upright. The child's gesture was one that I had seen before.

'Agnes, who's that lad?'

She looked dreamily out of the window, then replied, 'Oh, just a little servant boy. I think he belongs to the cook.'

I pushed the door open abruptly and shouted out for Fletcher's driver to pull up the horses, leaping with a marked lack of grace onto the gravel drive before we had even reached a standstill. I did not look back at Agnes, but I should imagine she appeared almost as confused as the three servants, who were in the process of re-entering the house when they saw me running back towards them.

'Forgotten something important, sir?' asked Brown good-naturedly.

'I'm sorry, no, I wished to speak briefly to the boy,' I gasped breathlessly, scarcely glancing at the valet.

The child looked up at me fearfully as I knelt down in front of him. He was not a thing of great beauty, with moist nostrils and wide-set eyes under a shock of auburn hair, but he seemed sharp enough.

'Don't worry, my boy,' I said, 'you aren't in trouble. I just want to know a couple of things, and there's a shilling in it for you if the answers are to my liking.' He smiled at me nervously.

'Yes, sir?'

'You see, I have a keen interest in magic and conjuring, and when I spoke to young Thomas some weeks ago, he showed me a trick that he said you had taught him.'

'Oh, *that* one,' said the boy proudly. 'It's all right, I suppose, but it's an easy trick. Would you like me to show you a better one?'

'Maybe later, young man. Maybe later. What I'd like to know just now is where you learned the tricks from? I know a magician doesn't reveal his sources, but I would very much like to find out.'

'From the man who came in the spring,' he replied without hesitation. 'The big friendly one with the tattoos. He had his dinner with us in the servants' hall while the house was quiet. He taught me lots of tricks.'

'What man is he talking about?' I asked, looking up at Inman and Brown and fishing in my pocket for a coin. I could hear Agnes striding up behind me. She laid a hand on my arm.

'Harry? What's going on?'

'I think, sir, that he's talking about earlier in the year, while the family were away in France,' said Inman, looking confused. 'Lady Halsingham wanted three of the bedrooms modernising and took the opportunity to have the work done while the family was from home. The man might have been one of the carpenters.'

'Can I ask why it is of interest, sir?' Brown interjected. 'Perhaps it's something we can help you with?'

'Maybe, Brown,' I said, dispensing the promised shilling into the lad's clammy palm. 'When I first met Lord Halsingham, it was through an encounter with a man who believed a friend of his had visited Halsingham House at around that time – this friend being a big fellow with tattoos and a fondness for magic tricks. But he was no carpenter. Rather he specialised in reconstructing damaged faces through artifices of enamelled copper...' I ought to have made the connection earlier, but even as it sprang to my mind, Brown himself voiced it.

'Surely, sir, the only reason such a man could have for coming here would be to do something for my own dear Frances. I have heard of such marvellous devices, but I can assure you they are well beyond our means.'

'It's not possible, then, that the Halsinghams could have paid his bill without your knowledge? Perhaps as an act of kindness for your long loyalty to Lord Halsingham's brother?'

Brown shook his head.

'I'm afraid not, sir. It's the sort of thing one or other of them might have thought to arrange, for they were kind people to us, but surely it would have required a personal consultation with my Frances. There are no secrets between us and she would have told me. Believe me, if there had been a better way to conceal her injuries than her hat and veil, she would have spoken of nothing else for the rest of the year.'

I rubbed my temple, perplexed.

'I confess myself at a loss. The boy's description of the man he met is too similar to be a coincidence, yet why was he here if not to do his job?'

'I'm sorry, sir,' said Inman. 'We both accompanied the family on their trip, along with most of the household. We left only a small number of servants behind to look after the house.'

The little witness had been distracted by my bright shilling, but he looked up as Brown laid a firm hand on his shoulder.

'Robbie, will you go and bring your mother? All haste, there's a good lad.'

It was a smart notion, and when the cook arrived she recalled the man well enough but could shed no light on his purpose or his name. She had seen him only once, the day after the family left for France. He had taken his lunch in the servants' hall along with the gang of carpenters employed on Lady Halsingham's renovations, and cook had assumed by his bag of tools that he was another tradesman. He had kept himself apart from the others, sitting at the far end of the table and amusing the boy with coin tricks.

The frustration was overwhelming, and Agnes's expectant glances did nothing to soothe it.

'Perhaps the man was simply one of the carpenters after all,' I said, sighing. 'If only anyone could remember a name. That at least would confirm whether or not your fellow and mine are one and the same.'

It was then that Inman's face brightened with a thought. 'Maybe we can find it out. If the man was not with the other workmen then he will have been paid separately by the housekeeper, Mrs Etchells. Her book-keeping is impeccable, and if payment was made then you can be sure she will have a record in her ledger. If there is no separate entry then we will know he was with the carpentry firm, and you can ask there.'

'Could you take a look, please, Inman?' asked Agnes, sensing the importance of the matter without understanding it fully.

'I'm sorry, ma'am,' cut in Brown apologetically. 'We'd love to help – truly we would – but Mrs Etchells' books are part of the late Lord Halsingham's affairs. We can't hand over those sorts of papers without the consent of Captain Edlington, in his capacity as guardian to young Thomas. Even to such friends as yourselves. My apologies, but you must understand.'

His loyalty to the Edlington brothers was admirable, but obstructive, and I looked to Inman for support.

'I'm afraid Brown makes a good point, Mr Catcliffe, sir. We could lose our places here if we were found to have revealed private matters pertaining to the running of the household without the captain's consent. Can it wait until he arrives? We expect him within the next two weeks, all being well. I am certain he will be happy to oblige.'

'Listen,' I said quietly. 'What if I told you that the name on that invoice could be a vital clue in discovering the whereabouts of Lady Halsingham?'

Inman looked from me to Agnes, then across to Brown, the cook and the boy, before lowering his eyes deferentially and regretfully. With conscious formality, he replied, 'If that is the case, then I will gladly provide any papers necessary to a representative of the police. Mr Catcliffe, you must understand my responsibilities, and I hope you will bear us no ill will.'

The butler's mind was made up, and I could see we would make no further headway with him. On some level, I was rather touched that he and Brown should cleave to their masters, both old and new, with such fidelity, though this feeling was at that moment entirely swamped by a tide of exasperation. I could not go to Oughton, and Mrs Etchells' books would remain beyond my grasp, however confident I was of the name that would be printed upon her ledger.

I thanked the bewildered domestics and returned thoughtfully to the carriage, with Agnes walking patiently a couple of steps behind me, awaiting an explanation.

Proof or no proof, Jabez Potter was right. Matthew Grayling had been at Halsingham House.

Sixteen

—·—

P otter possessed many excellent characteristics (however few of these he might routinely have displayed), and yet humility and sensitivity were not among them. At least not when he considered himself to have been proved correct. Discovering himself vindicated in the matter of Matthew Grayling's link to Halsingham House, his pomposity bordered on the insufferable.

'Mark my words, we're onto it now!' he cackled, jabbing his pipe stem at me from his customary perch in my most comfortable arm-chair. His mood was so buoyant that he had not only removed his coat and hat, but he had even ventured to roll up his soot-speckled sleeves, revealing a smudgy, bluish tattoo of a curved sword that he had almost certainly applied himself.

'Are we, Mr Potter?' asked Agnes, from a straight-backed seat by the fire. She had said very little since Potter had arrived, confining herself to sipping thoughtfully at her tea and measuring my peculiar friend over the rim of her teacup with undisguised intrigue. Their acquaintance was a quarter of an hour old, and the meeting of worlds was a glorious thing to behold. He now grinned across at her, in a gruesome manner which no doubt he considered winning. She returned his smile politely, then asked tentatively, 'What... exactly, I mean... are we on to?'

Potter shot me a withering look, as if her perceived slowness were my fault rather than her own.

'If Matthew was working at the big house then you can be sure there's a secret that goes with it. I guarantee it.'

'And I don't doubt you. But how will this help us find Henrietta?' enquired Agnes.

'It won't, but it might help us get to the bottom of some other questions, which in their turn might put us on the right track to finding her. Where there's one mystery, there's another, see?' he explained with exaggerated patience. 'If Matthew was there then it means someone in that old pile was getting something made by Giovanni's workshop, but none of them are talking about it. It might not necessarily have been a face – Matthew was a bloke Giovanni could rely on, and he sometimes went places as his agent, taking casts and measurements or doing fittings. Was it one of the family, I wonder? The boy?'

'Wait a moment.' I held my finger up. 'I don't think it could have been. Remember the Halsinghams had just gone away when your friend Grayling took lunch in the servants' hall.'

'Ah, but if the cook met him in the middle of March then it would have been his last visit,' countered Potter. 'The family were at home for all his earlier trips. He might just have been dropping off the finished work.'

'You're grasping, Jabez.'

'Oh, we're all grasping,' he said irritably. 'You're grasping, the police are grasping. I tell you what no-one's grasping at – the collar of that runaway murderess. "The Bloody Baroness" they're calling her down the Bear.'

'She didn't kill him deliberately,' said Agnes stiffly. At Potter's throwaway remark, curiosity had turned sharply to animosity, and her sudden dislike was palpable. I was increasingly coming to see that, for all her charm, Agnes Cleveley did not like to be disagreed with.

'No-one is saying that...' I interjected hastily, but Potter cut me off with gleeful bluntness.

'Yes they are. I am. I know it's not the explanation you want to hear, young lady, but the simplest answer is that your sister faked her sleepwalking and did for him herself.'

I began to wish I had not let Agnes meet such a consummate bull-baiter as Jabez Potter. He continued, 'Think it through. She knew you were waiting outside the room to see what happened. She puts on a bit of a show for Lordy a few times, convinces him she's got a problem and makes sure some other people know it too, then she sets you up as a witness, strolls past you all dreamy like and slits his throat with you right there to vouch for her. "I was unconscious, your honour."'

There was a loud clank as Agnes slammed her teacup down abruptly and glared at him with undisguised bile.

'How dare you paint her in such a manner? You don't know anything about her! Not the tiniest thing! I grew up with Henrietta!'

'Maybe, but she does seem to have been doing one or two things out of character lately, doesn't she?' Potter went on blithely. 'If I'd asked you a month ago, would you have told me she could break out of a secure hospital, drug and kidnap her own son and enlist the help of some resourceful scoundrel to spirit her and the boy out of the city right under the nose of a hundred police officers?'

'Mr Potter, if you are intent on proving to all and sundry that Henrietta effected some... some diabolical plot to murder her husband and make her own dear sister into an unwitting accomplice, then you and I had better part ways this very instant. I shall continue my own investigation, and you may do whatever you wish.' She was quivering with fury.

Finally perceiving the powder magazine of rage that was about to detonate spectacularly in the seat opposite, Jabez relented in his merciless needling and continued in a gentler vein.

'Steady on, girl. Look, I'm not saying that's the answer. Chances are it could just as easily be something else. I'm only saying it's a thought, and we should consider it. Whatever the explanation, there were secrets in that house. Surely you won't deny that?'

He stopped talking, and an uncomfortable silence descended upon the room. A chunk of wood popped in the fire, spitting out a glowing ember onto the hearth. Potter's method was crude, but if he had spoken out of turn then he had also accomplished a necessary evil. There was no way we could continue our enquiries while clinging doggedly to an absolute belief in Lady Halsingham's innocence, against all reason and appearance. Finally, Agnes spoke.

'Forgive my temper, Mr Potter. You're a rude little man, but you're right, there were secrets. I discovered one just last night when I was going through Henrietta's papers, and perhaps it's making me especially sensitive to my sister's cause this afternoon.'

We both waited for her to continue.

'I'd known for years that love had left the marriage, but it was more than that. I don't think Henrietta ever truly loved George. What we all took for infatuation in those first days of courtship, I now believe to have been love for another.'

She rose, crossing the room to the coat rack by the door of my little sitting room and retrieving an envelope from her coat pocket. She tossed it miserably on the coffee table and sat back down.

'This is a short letter from Robert, George's brother. It reads like the last correspondence of a longer exchange. In it he says that they can never be together. That she must marry George, and that he is leaving for Rhodesia. That he will not see her for many years. It's a sad, curt letter, full of things left unsaid.

'Perhaps it has no relevance to the questions at hand. Perhaps it does. All I would ask is that this knowledge goes no further than these four walls. Harry, I know I can rely on your discretion. Mr Potter, we have only just met, but where your manners could do with some polish, I venture to hope your morals are true enough.'

Visibly drained, she picked up her teacup again, realised it was empty, and set it back on the side table. I took the paper and read it through. She was right, it was a blunt letter, and the sparse wording and jagged hand betrayed the heart of a young man in anguish.

I passed it to Jabez, who scanned it briefly. He proffered it back to Agnes, who shook her head slightly. At this, he tossed the paper into the fire, then sat back and watched the edges blacken and curl. A puff of flame turned it to grey ash that quivered like the wing of a desiccated moth.

'It's the guilt that makes me short-tempered,' said Agnes quietly. 'I think of Henrietta, cornered into marrying the wrong man right from the start, unhappy and alone all those years. I wonder why she didn't tell me until the weekend of the party, but then I think back to our conversations and I see she sometimes tried to. Only my head was too full of motor cars and parties. Of appearing the faithful daughter to my father, and trivial local affairs at Kelverton, and when I might escape back to London again, and a hundred other things.'

She sighed.

'Half the time, if I'm honest, I didn't think about Henrietta at all. I could have been such a better sister.'

Jabez scratched his stubble and looked at his feet.

'When it comes to it, I can't help thinking if I'd kept a better eye on my mate he might still be here. He'd have never let it happen to me.'

By the time the little blaze of the letter had died back into the glowing embers, no trace remained in the room of the enmity that had flared up between my two friends.

I opened my mouth for the first time since their heated exchange had begun.

'You can trust us, Agnes. And I thank you for telling us about Robert Edlington's letter. If we three can at least be open between us, and open-minded in our pursuit of the truth, then perhaps we'll stand a chance of getting to the bottom of all this.'

I addressed myself to both of them, but I held her gaze as I spoke, choosing my words with more care than I was accustomed to. She said nothing, but I fancied I could read acceptance of a sort in her face. There was nothing to be gained by making her admit the possibility of Henrietta's guilt out loud.

'As to our next move, may I make a suggestion? I suspect we won't get access to Halsingham House again until Captain Edlington is back, by which time it may be too late to find out what Matthew Grayling was doing there. We don't even know whether he was hired by Lord Halsingham, his wife, or some other. Since we can discover neither the customer nor the commission from the Halsingham House end, perhaps there's a man in London who might give up the information if we can apply the right pressure.'

An expression of blank incomprehension fell across Agnes's face. Jabez, restored once more to good humour, smiled slyly.

'This man. Italian, by any chance?'

'The answer to that question, I fear, is truly beyond us.'

....

I suppose every fellow must live somewhere, yet of the residences my imagination might have furnished for Giovanni Fornasini, none could have been as extraordinary as his true abode. For the larger-than-life showman, who spent his evenings presenting marvels of medical engineering to the masses of urban London, lived in a most unremarkable, respectable, semi-detached house on a quiet back street not far from Finsbury Park.

With its smart front door and separate tradesman's entrance on the lower ground floor, it was the sort of well-appointed suburban home that might have appealed to a modestly affluent senior clerk and his family. Indeed, as I mounted the three steps in the murky darkness of early evening and rapped at the front door, I half expected to have got the wrong house, and to come face to face with a real-life Charles Pooter, clutching a tin of red enamel paint. The address had come from Jabez – obtained, no doubt, by chasing the unwitting entertainer home from the theatre in his wagon full of ale barrels. It seemed remarkable to me that Jabez Potter's employers continued to subsidise an existence which contained so little in the way of beer delivery and such a great deal of stalking round London in pursuit of personal matters.

A maid answered – a wary, truculent creature – but on beholding first my handsome hat, then Agnes standing immaculately turned out behind me, and finally the extravagant French motor car drawn up at the side of the road, she softened and invited us into the hallway. She disappeared through the first doorway on the right, closing it behind her, then after a short, whispered conversation with some unseen personage, she showed us into a smart, if slightly dated, front room. It was warm with a small fire and the glow of wall-mounted gaslights, and heavy with the scent of patchouli. A slender woman in her thirties, with dark hair and even darker eyes, rose from her chair as we entered.

'Lucilla Fornasini. You are looking for my husband?' Her voice was low, and like Giovanni, she had a slight accent. Her manner was not welcoming.

'We are. I am Mr Harrison Catcliffe and this is Miss Cleveley. We're sorry to come unannounced, but the matter is of the utmost urgency.'

'I am sorry, but Giovanni is out tonight.'

'Please forgive us. We hoped we might just have caught him before he left for the theatre…'

'My husband works hard. He is not often to be found at home, and this late in the afternoon is hardly the time to be making house calls.'

'Again, forgive us. We're sorry to have disturbed you. Might you be able to tell us at which theatre your husband can be found this evening? I understand Callaghan's is closed tonight, so perhaps it's another establishment?'

She drew breath to respond, but at that moment a great clattering and shouting arose from the next room. One of the voices had the unmistakeably rich quality of Giovanni Fornasini. I rushed through the adjoining door into a small dining room, much simpler in its furnishings than the showy front room, to discover Fornasini and Jabez Potter grappling violently with one another. Both men were powerful for their size, but Potter's movements were quicker and crueller, and he already appeared to be getting the upper hand.

'I shall summon the police!' screamed Lucilla, but as she turned to rush from the room her husband managed to get half to his feet, gasping in broad Cockney,

'No, Lucilla! Don't!'

This momentary distraction was all the opportunity Potter needed, and in an instant the Italian – if indeed that he was – was on the floor again with Jabez's elbow in his neck. This time he submitted and lay still, which was more than could be said for his wife.

'What is the meaning of this?' she raged, though whether at us or her husband it was impossible to tell.

'What have you done?'

She brandished a small china clock in one hand, and it would only be a matter of moments before she brained one or other of us with it.

'It'll be all right,' croaked Fornasini weakly, his thickly pomaded hair hanging untidily across his eyes in stout, oily ribbons.

'Please, Lucilla, go up to your bedroom and wait for me there. I need a moment to talk to these people alone.'

'No. Why? Who are they?'

'My dear, please, listen to me. This is merely a misunderstanding. These gentlemen – and this lady, whoever she may be – and I have only to explain ourselves to one another and the matter will be at an end. But it is of a confidential nature. Please, Lucilla.'

His wife said nothing, but flounced angrily out into the hallway, dragging with her the inquisitive maid, who had bustled in at the time of the commotion. She still held the clock in her other hand. Jabez grudgingly allowed his opponent to rise, and together the four of us moved slowly through to the front room. Fornasini looked at Potter with unconcealed rancour, his eyes flicking contemptuously down towards the drayman's inferior wooden limb.

'How did you sniff me out back there?'

'It wasn't hard. These two thought to leave me in the back of the motor car, but I fancied making my way down the side of the house and having a peek through some windows. And who should I spot in this back room but your own good self, hiding from Harry here. So I snuck in through the scullery and thought we might have a little talk.'

'Damned maid never draws the curtains properly,' sighed Fornasini melodiously, attempting to restore some semblance of smartness to his dishevelled hair.

We seated ourselves, and I introduced Agnes, without mentioning her connection to the Halsinghams. A snob to his core, his face lit up as he appraised her deportment and clothing, discerning her status with a practised eye.

'Enchanted, I'm sure, madam. I only wish our meeting had been more dignified.'

He glowered at Potter, who was sprawled in a large armchair, rummaging in his overcoat pocket for his pipe.

'And I apologise for our intrusion,' replied Agnes graciously. 'It was not our intention to assault you like this. But we need to know the truth about an important matter, and from what I can gather you were not entirely frank with Mr Catcliffe when you last spoke.'

'As I recall, Mr Catcliffe did not ask me any direct questions,' he ventured cautiously. 'Merely probed my opinions on a few minor matters.'

'See?' grunted Potter. 'I knew you pussy-footed around him too much.'

Fornasini bristled.

'Indeed,' he spat back sarcastically. 'Far better to stick your nose in my face on a street corner and threaten me with violence. A lot of good that did you.'

'Please, Mr Fornasini,' interrupted Agnes. 'If Mr Catcliffe could just ask you those direct questions now, then our regrettable foray into your Monday evening can be at an end.'

'Very well, my lady.'

'Thank you,' I began. 'First, I just need the specifics of the job that Matthew Grayling undertook at Halsingham House earlier this year.'

'I am afraid I can't give you that. A job there was, and I regret I didn't admit it before, but I provided only the introduction. Lady Halsingham had heard of Matthew's skill somehow. I doubt she had personally been to see the Tin Face Parade, but we've occasionally worked with people of her milieu, so perhaps he came recommended through a friend. It's very irregular for people to want to deal privately with one of my craftsmen, but it does happen – usually when the commission is of an especially sensitive nature.'

'Bit of brass makes a body paranoid, in my experience,' offered Potter helpfully from his cloud of pipe smoke.

Fornasini disregarded him.

'Of course, I prefer to oversee all our work myself, and in many cases my surgical expertise is essential to the process. But business on the customer's terms is better than no business at all. In these instances I take a modest fee for the introduction. I swear I don't know what the job was.'

I glanced across at Agnes.

'Are you absolutely certain that the client was Lady Halsingham? Not her husband?'

'Oh, I've no doubt that he paid for it and knew about it. Perhaps he was responsible ultimately, but the man who came enquiring implied that it was on the lady's behalf.'

'The man?'

'Well, it might surprise you to know that it wasn't Lady Halsingham herself who sought me out at a variety hall in Lambeth on a Friday night,' he said, a trifle archly. 'It was one of her servants. Nondescript fellow, middle age, I imagine. Said the lady was looking for some very specific expertise, and that only Matthew would do. That it was a private matter and I was to give Matthew the time he needed to complete the job without asking him any questions. The money for my own small part was generous, so I took it, made the introduction, and that was that.'

'Except it wasn't, was it, Mr Fornasini?'

Intimidation was not something which came naturally to me, but I tried to be as stern as I could.

'I may not have asked you direct questions last time, but I gave you plenty of opportunity to be evasive, and you were. Then you tried to hide from us today. What has this man got over you?'

'Nothing,' he urged. 'Look, they just paid me an extra sum to keep it to myself if anyone came enquiring. Like I say, it was probably just the nature of the job that they wanted to keep quiet. Our work can be very personal. The particulars of private commissions are none of my business, but the client's privacy is. I just take the money and fob off any questions from people like you.'

'Can you believe the gall of this bag of guts?' barked Potter from the chair. 'You knew someone killed Matthew over this, and you stayed quiet for a few shillings? How many pieces of silver were there, wretched Judas?'

Giovanni looked exasperated.

'Listen!' he said, 'There is absolutely no link between the work Matthew did at Halsingham House and his death, or that of Lord Halsingham. How could there be? Matthew made masks for injured people. Sometimes other fine items like hands or fingers. I don't know – maybe she wanted fancy copperwork of an altogether different sort? He was a skilled man in his field, but he didn't make the Bloody Baroness sleepwalk into her husband's room with a straight razor!'

Agnes's countenance was glacial.

....

'That's all we need,' mumbled Potter dejectedly, turning his hat in his hands and staring absent-mindedly at its greasy interior as Agnes's motor car rumbled back through central London. 'Another man with no distinguishing features. At least this one wasn't wearing a costume beard. Is he the same one who put your sister on the boat, I wonder, or is the whole of London made up of entirely average and identical men going about their business with perfect anonymity?'

178

'Take heart, Mr Potter,' Agnes rejoined brightly, 'for I do believe our pool of suspects isn't as great as it might appear. There is, to my knowledge, only one middle-aged man in employment at Halsingham House, and he has lately wilfully obstructed our investigation.'

'You mean Inman, the butler?' I asked. 'But he was all for letting us see the household papers until Brown piped up.'

'So it appeared, I will grant you. But perhaps he was confident that the valet would raise such an objection, being a man of loyalty. He lets Brown object so that it doesn't look like it was his idea to deny us access to the papers.'

'It seems a bold gamble.'

'Well perhaps he is a bold man,' she cut in, a mite impatiently. 'And evasiveness doesn't necessarily make him a traitor. He may be concealing the truth through loyalty to either George or Henrietta. Besides, I don't see who else it could be. The footmen are all younger, and it certainly can't have been Brown, who is neither middle-aged nor... unremarkable.'

Clearly Brown's good looks turned heads above stairs as well as below.

'Well, assuming it was him, what good is this knowledge to us?' I asked, thinking out loud. 'He's incorruptible, and he's made his position clear that he won't answer any more questions unless he's ordered to by the police or his new master.'

Agnes sighed. 'If only Robert were back, how much easier this would all be. How long can it take to get back to London from Africa? Surely in such circumstances as these someone else can be found at short notice to command his men.'

'He army then?' piped up Potter.

'Rhodesian Police,' I replied. 'British South Africa Company.'

He grunted derisively. 'Mercenary buggers. Never trust those boys.'

Agnes pulled her fur stole closer about her in the cold of the back seat.

'Robert is an adventurous soul, Mr Potter, but he is an honourable one, you can count on that. His men administer the protectorate on behalf of the Crown, and he's just as much a British soldier as you were.'

Potter did not respond. He evidently felt no great love for the late Cecil Rhodes's private army, and perhaps his view was not without some justification. I could not help but remember that it was a raid by this same body of men that had precipitated our war with the Boers.

'I think perhaps there's a way to get the information we need,' I suggested. 'Are you as confident as you seem that Captain Edlington will be sympathetic to our cause? Even taking into account what we now know about his history with your sister?'

'I am. This matter with Henrietta must of course remain unspoken, but if anything, I can only think it will strengthen his resolve to discover the truth.'

'Then perhaps in his absence we might venture to trust his right-hand man. My instinct tells me that Brown is a fellow who can be relied on, and since neither of the men so far described to us fits his singular description, it's safe to assume that he's no part of this affair. I'll visit him tomorrow afternoon. Perhaps he can discover what we cannot.'

'Suppose I'll just cool my heels then, shall I?'

'I think that would be prudent, Mr Potter.'

Seventeen

—·—

J abez and I elected to be dropped outside the White Bear. I fancied
that, as Agnes said goodnight, her tone held a pang of regret that
she could not join us. It would have been the height of impropriety,
but truthfully it did seem rather unfair to leave her out.

'I'm sorry you cannot come in with us,' I said.

'It looks ever so nice. I can see inside through that broken window.'

'I say, Agnes, when I go to Limehouse, I wear a set of old clothes I
bought from a man at the factory. A sort of disguise. If you dressed as
a prostitute or a fishwife, you could drink gin in the pub with us to
your heart's content.'

'What a good idea. Maybe not a prostitute though.'

The cold out on the street was perishing, and a few half-hearted
flecks of snow settled on the smart black car as it drew away.

In truth there was little more to discuss, but the encounter with
Fornasini had been a tense one, and when Jabez grunted 'Bear?' I had
welcomed the opportunity to settle my nerves. The landlord served a
toffee-tasting Burton ale strong enough to take the legs from under a
shire horse, and I ordered a couple of pints of the stuff once we had
taken our seats in the warmth of the public bar.

'Prickly lass,' cackled Jabez, suckling at his pipe. 'Doesn't seem to like me very much.'

'Indeed, I can't think why, Jabez, for you have gone out of your way to make yourself so agreeable.'

He bared his teeth in what I took as a comradely smile but could also have been a gesture of open aggression.

'Sarcasm doesn't suit you, mate.'

'Perhaps not. Anyway, Agnes is all right. She's just used to people saying and doing what she wants them to.'

'People like you, you mean.'

I nodded resignedly.

'People like me.'

Presently, Jabez announced in colourful fashion his need to pass water, and went in search of a lavatory. I turned round on my stool, intending to watch the comings and goings of the busy public house, and to my surprise I found myself face to face with none other than Albert Grieve.

'Hello, Mr Grieve. Fancy seeing you here. Are you well? I would not have thought this was your sort of place.'

I was not especially pleased to see him, but at least I made some small attempt to hide my feelings. For his part he regarded me with unconcealed disdain.

'It's not my sort of place, Catcliffe. But I can't say I'm surprised to discover you patronising such an establishment.'

I was rather taken aback by such open hostility.

'I say, old boy, there's no need for that. If you don't like me or the pub then it's easy enough to take yourself elsewhere.'

'But you see, Catcliffe, the fact of the matter is that I'm here to see you.'

There was something in the way he articulated my surname that irked me. The effect was that of talking down to a younger boy at public school, and perhaps such was his intention.

'To see me? I can't think what we have to talk about, Mr Grieve. And how did you find me? Surely Woodville's would have been a surer bet than here? One of your Oxford chums could have got you in.'

'Discussions of this nature are not for such institutions as Woodville's. As for tracking you down, I don't mind admitting that I followed you. I have, in fact, been following you all evening.'

'My goodness. You've had a long drive, then.'

He ignored me.

'I shall get right to the point. I wish to ask what you mean by hanging around Miss Agnes Cleveley in such a persistent manner?'

Though I understood the implication of his words well enough, it was not a question to which I could readily formulate an answer, so he continued uninterrupted.

'I mean to say, I find you have been dragging that most noble young lady all over London, to the most obscure locations and in the most insalubrious of company.'

He looked pointedly at Jabez's empty stool.

'Only the other day I learned from her footman that you had not only been entertaining her within your own rooms – in the company of a common drayman, no less – but that you had been on a mysterious trip to the country together. Are you actively trying to destroy her reputation? As one with a genuine concern for the lady's wellbeing, I demand an explanation.'

'Demand all you like, Mr Grieve, you won't get one. And there has been nothing improper in my conduct towards Miss Cleveley.'

'Surely you are not so blinkered as to believe that. My own high regard for the lady prohibits me from thinking ill of her, but others may not be so charitable in their opinions when they find she has been keeping company with a man of such low repute and sordid habits.'

His insults were water off a duck's back, but truthfully I had not considered the effect my society might have on Agnes's social standing. She was perfectly capable of choosing her own friends, and I was not so vain as to believe that our current closeness was anything more than a necessity of circumstance. All the same, I felt a shade uncomfortable, and wondered if I were truly a bad influence. I reflected that a few minutes earlier I had been recommending she dressed up as a whore so she could come and drink rough liquor in down-at-heel boozers.

Not that I was going to give Grieve the satisfaction of observing this.

'I don't wish to hurry you, Mr Grieve, but if you might tell me what it is you actually want?'

'I think I have made myself clear enough, Catcliffe.'

He probably had, but in the event, he was distracted for a moment by Jabez's return. My companion hopped back up onto his stool, and in doing so, his wooden leg caught on Grieve's cane. The stick slipped from his hand and clattered loudly to the floor. Grieve inhaled sharply through his teeth in a show of pique.

In Potter's position, another man might have apologised or picked up the cane, and yet another might have taken umbrage at the un-necessary petulance of the response. But Jabez did neither. He simply glanced wearily over at Grieve as if he were the most tedious creature that had ever lived (I was familiar with the expression, since he frequently employed it upon me), then went back to his pint.

'Someone's written a right funny poem on the bog door, Harry,' he began. 'Whoever did it had better hope word doesn't get back to his missus.' He began to recount the contents of this bawdy verse, when Grieve abruptly interrupted him. However, he elected to play Jabez at his own game, addressing his remarks to me and ignoring my companion entirely.

'I seem to recall you never did admit whether or not you had ever been forced to fight a man, Catcliffe. You won't mind if I make the assumption that you haven't? In that case, allow me to give you a bit of advice. The key to winning a fight, from my own experience, is in the element of surprise. You have to strike without warning. It might not be the most honourable way, but when it comes down to it, combat between men is about winning above all else.'

Perhaps he had more to say. From what little I knew of the man, he almost certainly did, but his chance had passed, for within moments of delivering his thinly veiled threat, Albert Grieve found himself on his back among the cigarette ends on the muddy floorboards of the White Bear. He rolled and retched, clutching his middle where his belly met his ribcage.

'Good advice, that,' observed Jabez, getting back up on to his stool. He sniffed appreciatively at the fragrant, rusty brown contents of his pint pot, and took a contented pull. He shot me a quick backward glance, and the violence in that little man crawled uncomfortably round the base of my neck. Grieve's too, no doubt.

'Just a half pint next time eh!' called out some wag with a strong northern accent as the young man writhed on the floor.

Even a chap as deluded as Grieve must have realised his catastrophic misjudgement. Threatening an unknown man in a rough pub was fantastic idiocy, whoever you were, and he made no further efforts to press his point home. He picked himself up, followed by his fallen cane and hat, then departed with as much wounded dignity as he could muster, given the rumble of murmuring and snickering that followed him out of the door. He paused only to address me one last time, wiping a spider-web string of spittle from his chin.

'I hope we understand each other, Catcliffe.'

As it turned out, we did not. Not at all.

Eighteen

— · —

December had well and truly set in. In London, the overnight snow had merely dusted the city, all but vanishing away before the first clerks skated awkwardly across the icy pavements in the darkness of the early morning. In the Surrey countryside, though, it had fallen in greater quantities and had settled on the wide, stubbly fields. It had softened their barrenness and lent a Dickensian Yuletide feel to the scene, despite the fact that festivities were still a good week hence.

Looking across the marzipan pastures from my train window, I saw smoke drifting cheerfully from the chimneys of isolated stone farmhouses, and I imagined rosy-cheeked children sopping up bowls of hearty soup with fresh-baked bread. In fact, they were probably gnawed through with cold and hunger (scarcely a year went by without some outcry at the impoverished state of our rural communities) but they did not help themselves by living in such inviting-looking homes.

It was well into the evening when I set out from Halsingham village, for the confidential nature of my visit meant that I desired to catch Brown at home rather than showing myself at the big house. It was only a half hour's walk from my room at the Edlington Arms, and I had come prepared with a warm overcoat, stout boots and my heavy walking stick. The whiteness of the snow-crusted hedgerows lining the narrow country lanes showed up brightly in the darkness as I passed.

Of course, I had seen the Browns' cottage before, on the occasion of my encounter with Mrs Brown (and indeed I hoped fervently that the young lady bore me no ill will over that episode). However, the place appeared quite differently when approached from the road in the snow and the dark. Set in a remote corner of the estate, it backed onto a small patch of ancient, deciduous woodland and neglected coppice. In the gloom beyond the hedge bordering the little dwelling I could see wild stools of hazel, their dense, gnarled poles twisting upwards towards the bare branches of the tall trees above. Outlined against the waxing moon, the delicate, fanned canopy of slender twigs like musicians' fingers suggested that these sleeping giants might be beech, that most ladylike of trees. There was lamplight in the cottage window, and as my footsteps crunched down the path, I could see Brown himself peering through the curtain.

As I approached the door, Brown opened it, dressed in flannel trousers and a thick, high-necked woollen jumper of the sort worn by sailors. His expression was one of mild surprise, but I sensed that he was not a man easily discomposed.

'Mr Catcliffe, sir. An unexpected pleasure to see you. Please, do come in. I'm intrigued to discover what brings you to my door at this hour of a winter's night.'

'Thank you, Brown. I promise I won't detain you long. I do hope I'm not disturbing you – or your wife – unduly.'

I followed him inside. There was no hallway, and the ground floor of his cottage consisted of one simple room with a small range fire-place, sparsely furnished with a table and chairs and a couple of comfortable armchairs. At the opposite side of the room to the range, an open wooden staircase led to the upper floor. It was spartan, but clean and warm, lit by a brass spirit lamp on the table and with a cheering smell of wood smoke about the place.

He gestured towards one of the armchairs, then took a seat himself.

'Don't concern yourself on my account, Mr Catcliffe. As for my wife, I regret that she is not currently living here with me.'

'Indeed? I'm sorry to hear it, Brown. I do hope Mrs Brown isn't unwell.'

'Sadly, yes. Her condition – perhaps you've heard – is mainly physical, but it affects the mind too. I thought the isolation here would help, but it seems to have done the opposite. She needed sympathetic company and conversation, and I had my responsibilities up at the house. Just wasn't here enough. My Frances got terribly lonely.

'She's got a maiden aunt at Tunbridge Wells, and she's gone to live there for a bit. See if it might buck her spirits up a bit. I'll visit her when I can, and I daresay Lord Robert may allow me some indulgence in the matter. You'll recall we were old comrades in Rhodesia.'

'I do hope she improves quickly. Such a separation cannot be easy for either of you.'

'None of it's easy, Mr Catcliffe,' he said, smiling thinly, 'though Frances and I always seem to manage somehow. But please, sir, I'm keen to discover your purpose. It's a rather unconventional visit, if you'll forgive me saying.'

As he prepared a pot of tea, I filled him in on the events that had lately overtaken us. He already knew all about my movements and what I had seen on the evening of Lord Halsingham's death, and he had been fully appraised of Henrietta's subsequent escape from the

189

Rochester Clinic. He listened carefully, however, as I narrated the course of my own investigation, my unlikely alliance with Jabez Potter, the links between Halsingham House and Matthew Grayling, and Dawoojee Dukanwalla's discoveries concerning Lady Halsingham's flight from London. I finished by recounting the previous evening's encounter with Giovanni Fornasini.

Brown took a gulp of tea. 'So, sir, if I understand you rightly, you've come to me because you feel that Mr Inman may somehow be involved in this affair?'

'Exactly. Though we can't be sure of his motives, it seems likely that he was the man who first approached Mr Fornasini. If only I could get that wretched dentist to tell me the whole truth. I'm convinced he's keeping something from us.'

'I think I may put your mind at rest about Mr Inman's motives at least. He's worked in this household since he was a lad, long before Lord Halsingham – the former Lord Halsingham, I mean, God rest his soul – ever succeeded to the title. His devotion to the family is absolutely beyond question, sir. If he is hiding something about this man Grayling, then he'll be doing it for the family.'

'I wish he would exercise his judgement rather than his loyalty.'

'I don't know, sir.' Brown looked torn. 'I can see why he wouldn't wish to reveal things about the family to outsiders, even ones like yourself and Miss Cleveley. If you discovered anything, you might take it to the police and he wouldn't have any way of stopping you. Privacy isn't easy to get back once you give it up.'

There was a slight firmness of manner that made me wonder whether I might have misjudged him. Perhaps, for Brown too, faithfulness to the Halsinghams trumped reason.

'And what about you, Brown? Where do you stand on all this?'

'Oh, I'm just as loyal as he is, Mr Catcliffe. Except my own loyalty is to Lord Robert above all others. He and I were thick as thieves out in Africa, and along the way we've come to owe each other a great deal.'

He finished the last of his tea and licked a stray fleck of leaf from his top lip.

'I do also wonder, sir – and forgive me if I'm speaking out of turn – but it does sound as if you've been focusing all your attentions on the family, when there was a full house of people there that weekend.'

'Go on, Brown.' He was right, of course.

'It's only that I've seen too much of the world to believe in coincidence, Mr Catcliffe. Lord and Lady Halsingham had their problems, and all of us in the house knew it, but they slept in adjacent rooms every weekend, and neither came to any real harm until the night there were twelve guests in the house. The same night a whole pile of jewellery disappeared off the premises too. What I'm saying is, I've a very high opinion of Mr Inman, and I'd hesitate to lay anything at his door until I'd had a good think about all the others.'

Thoughtfully, I put down my own empty cup.

'Perhaps you're right. If I promise to consider the other guests, will you perhaps agree to look into Mr Inman's involvement for me?'

'I'll try, sir. But can you not wait until Lord Robert arrives? I'm sure he'll be as keen as you or Miss Cleveley to discover the truth. Granted, he and his brother were very different men, but still frightful close when all was said and done. And he was always very fond of Lady Halsingham.'

I had, naturally, omitted from my narrative any mention of the letter that Agnes had uncovered, but I still could not help wondering how Robert Edlington's approach to the situation would be coloured by his former passions for the murderess.

'I'm afraid time is of the essence, Brown. Lady Halsingham is still in flight, and the boy's still missing. They aren't safe, and we must pursue any clue as to their whereabouts as quickly as we can, before any harm befalls them.'

He raised an eyebrow at me.

'Harm may befall the lady all the same, if she's hanged for murder.'

....

I spent the night at the inn in Halsingham village, returning to London by the first train the following morning. As I sat in an empty compartment, looking out at the grimy snow heaped at the edges of the track, I considered my meeting with the valet. I wondered whether I had been successful in my endeavour or not.

Certainly, before we parted, he had eventually promised to make his own quiet enquiries into Matthew Grayling's work at Halsingham House, both by attempting to track down the man's invoices, and through discreet enquiries among the servants and estate workers. He had a notion that the carpenters who had carried out Lady Halsingham's renovations might have been a well-known Guildford firm, and he would seek to verify this. Furthermore, he also undertook to press Inman, as subtly as possible, for whatever information he might be able to draw out of him.

For all this, I was by no means certain that Brown would in fact apply himself to any of the above tasks. I sensed that his loyalty was of a rather more nuanced sort than Inman's blind devotion, but I also understood that after I had left he would have sat and deliberated awhile with his conscience. Placating me with promises did not mean he would fulfil them. Still, the most important thing was that he had listened to a full account of the facts and now stood in a better position to understand the difference he could make.

And then there was his gentle reproach at my having so carelessly put the other guests out of mind. I thought of Rowland Renwick, that odd, whiskery little catfish. Pretending not to know Grieve at the party despite their apparent friendliness at the funeral. I tried to remember how quickly he had appeared on the scene after Halsingham's murder. Then there was Grieve himself, trailing us so bizarrely all over London. Was he warning me off Agnes, or seeking to end our enquiries together?

Arriving back in London, however, I was forced to put Brown, Renwick and even Grieve from my mind, for as I walked through my front door, I discovered a note that Edie had left for me on the floor in my small entrance hall. The ghastly penmanship was instantly familiar, and I tore open Jabez's missive.

Duke has news. Come with all hast to the Sarasen. DO NOT TELL HER LADDYSHIP. JP

I considered changing into my street clothes, but the time on the note was nine o'clock in the morning, and it was already approaching eleven, so I turned straight on my heel and set out again for Portland Road station without having so much as removed my coat and hat.

....

When I found Jabez Potter and Duke Dukanwalla, they were both in a state of great excitement, which in Potter's case had certainly been helped on its way by two pints of Liza Dukanwalla's best ale consumed before lunch. But their enthusiasm was natural enough, for it appeared that Dawoojee had tracked down the elusive Lady Halsingham.

He had, after some delay, managed to talk to the captain of the *Tyne Lass*, the cargo steamer upon which a lady matching Henrietta's description had fled London a week earlier. The captain had missed Duke's message in Calais, but his return run had brought him back into London at the weekend, where he quickly discovered that Dawoojee Dukanwalla at the Saracen required the particulars of a mother and son who had lately travelled upon his vessel. It wasn't the sort of summons any sensible fellow would ignore.

Their passage had been booked the day before the *Tyne Lass* was due to sail by a well-spoken, bearded man in his thirties who appeared good-natured but cagey. The price he offered was far above the going rate for the rather basic cabins normally occupied by travellers of comparatively modest means, so the captain had accepted without hesitation. It was this same bearded man who had conveyed the lady to the ship the following day, together with her child, in a standard London four-wheeler. He had carried the child aboard, waved them off from the quayside, then vanished.

The crossing had been a rough one, and she had kept to herself for the duration, conversing neither with the crew, nor with the handful of other passengers on board. Few enough people ventured on deck during winter voyages anyway, but the lady had pointedly shunned all human contact, taking her meals in the small cabin for which she had paid so handsomely. Of the child, nothing was seen from the moment he was conveyed on board in London, to the occasion of their disembarkation in Calais, where he had been carried from the cabin, similarly insensible, by his mother. The captain of the *Tyne Lass* had been led to believe by the bearded fellow that the lad was an invalid, and that they were headed to warmer climes in the interests of his health. The captain was no fool, but by that same token he also knew not to ask questions when the money was good.

Most intriguingly of all, before the odd couple had left the port in a carriage, the mother had undertaken some business with another captain. They had not been seen since.

'But I thought you said you had found her?' I asked, confused.

'That's the best bit,' said Duke, winking. 'Let's go for a little walk, shall we?'

As we rose to make for the door, Liza called out sharply from behind the bar.

'Oi! What do you think you're doing? Catch your bloody death!'

She held up a balled scarf and flung it across the room at Dawoojee.

'There's things in this world'll kill me quicker than the cold,' he retorted mildly, but he wrapped the scarf around his exposed neck all the same. Liza turned away abruptly to conceal a triumphant smile, and busied herself needlessly rearranging the bottles on the shelf.

Captain, the bull terrier, wriggled to his feet and made half-heartedly for his master's heel, but Duke flapped his hand affectionately at the arthritic creature.

'Stay, boy. Stay.'

I followed him out into the front courtyard of the Saracen's Head, where Jabez paused to pass water noisily into an obliging drain. Our breath steamed in the cold afternoon air.

'Much better,' said Potter, grinning. 'Wouldn't do to go chasing through town on a full bladder, would it?'

'Chasing?' I asked, rather slow to make the inevitable deduction. 'She's here?'

'Might be,' replied Dukanwalla slyly. 'The captain of the *Tyne Lass* said that before the Bloody Baroness left the port at Calais last Wednesday, she asked about passages back to London. Mate of mine at Calais docks says she booked onto a steamer called the *Jeanne*, which was hanging around in port for a few days after a long run before heading across to London this week. Told the captain that the passenger would turn up on the day. Implied it wasn't her, but I can't see who else it would be.'

'So was it? Her, I mean.'

Duke smiled. 'Now, it wouldn't be any fun if I had all the answers. We'll find out soon enough. The ship is due in with the afternoon tide in an hour or so.'

If it was Henrietta, I wondered what might have possessed her to return to the city that she had only lately fled, and who this man was that had been her creature in London. I could make neither head nor tail of it.

The *Jeanne* was operated by one of the smaller steamship outfits a little way upriver at Wapping, so we stepped out with some haste. By that time the huge commercial docks were all boxed-in and off-limits to the public, but the scruffy independent wharves and warehouses – crammed along the banks in the eastern part of the city – still had the buccaneering spirit of a bygone era about them. We perched on a heap of cocoa bean sacks destined for some Quaker chocolate factory or other, and smoked while we watched the lightermen jostling with one another out on the water in their little flat-topped barges. Jabez was as restless as I, but Dukanwalla appeared in playful mood. He amused himself by setting his teeth in a grimace, flaring his nostrils grotesquely and exhaling cigarette smoke through his nose in a passable imitation of a vividly painted Chinese dragon on a nearby shop sign.

'You know,' he ruminated, turning his attention to the churning muddy expanse of the Thames as the first boats began to trickle in on the tide, 'my father told me ships would be the end of me. He was a shopkeeper back in Surat. A good, stable bloke, dependable as you like. Never set foot on a boat in all his days. Thought floating yourself out on the sea was a sure way to find yourself rotting at the bottom of it. He never could understand why I didn't want to be a good lad and take over the shop.'

'I shouldn't worry, mate,' observed Jabez, teeth clamped around his pipe. 'I doubt you've ever been in any danger of being a good lad.'

'You don't know that,' said Duke, sniffing and adjusting his scarf. 'I might have made a very respectable Gujarati shopkeeper. In an earlier time, before there were big old ships to bring the world so close together, I'd have taken the life without a second thought. Wouldn't have been a bad one either. There would have been a lot less hanging around stinking wharves in the freezing depths of winter.'

Jabez shot me a knowing look. Duke loved loitering around the water's edge, whatever the weather. I noticed that a small but significant number of the passers-by gave him a respectful nod or a friendly smirk, while others studiously avoided his eye as they hurried past.

In fact, we did not have to wait long for the *Jeanne* to arrive. She was a Dutch steamer, rather past her prime, her paintwork blistered with rust and salt. As her crew lowered the gangway and prepared to unload the cargo, we watched from a safe distance as the small number of passengers disembarked.

It took a moment or two before I spotted my mark, and I gave Dukanwalla a sidelong glance, pointing discreetly with the smouldering tip of my cigarette. He raised his eyebrows at me quizzically, and for that I could not blame him, since at first even I had not recognised Henrietta.

The former lady of Halsingham House had undergone a drastic transformation. Her fair hair was cropped short, and what remained of it was stuffed under a cloth cap. She wore a mass-produced jacket and trousers not dissimilar to the street clothes I had acquired from my obliging millwright, and her womanly form was obscured within the folds of an oversized light brown overcoat. To any casual eye, she was simply a young man of slight build coming ashore after a short voyage.

But it was more than simply her costume, for Henrietta had what could only be termed a swagger about her. The nervous, fragile air that had hung about her at Halsingham House was long gone, and it struck me that she looked far more charismatic as a murderess in men's clothing than she ever had as a refined society lady. There was something else about her too, but I could not quite put my finger on what.

What immediately became apparent, though, was the fact that we had made a grave tactical error. Or rather, that I had. For just as the strutting young rover formerly known as Lady Halsingham blended effortlessly into the milieu of the Wapping waterfront on a Wednesday afternoon, so Harrison Catcliffe, in his fine cloth-top boots, his morning coat and his handsome top hat, stuck out like a gaudy popinjay as he attempted to lounge nonchalantly among the wharf workers. Her gaze alighted on me in an instant, and recognition sprung into her eyes.

Dukanwalla was fastest off the mark, and as she bolted for the warren of tortuous alleyways that tangled backwards from the wharves, he whipped after her, jinking and weaving right and left through the crowd like a rangy old lurcher. Flinging down my cigarette, I raced as nimbly as I could in his wake, with Jabez at my heels.

Henrietta, though, was fast and displayed surprising stamina. Not only that, but she had an unerring instinct for throwing off pursuit. I might have been rather impressed, were I not trying so hard to catch my breath as I dashed down ammonia-scented ginnels and across busy thoroughfares, narrowly avoiding collisions with road traffic and other pedestrians. Jabez had fallen behind, but Duke was ahead of me, and for all Henrietta's craftiness and her head start, he was nearly upon her. I saw him lay one big paw upon her shoulder, at which point she spun at him, and I glimpsed the glint of metal in her hand. He tried to twist away but lost his feet, and both of them went down, barrelling into a mud-spattered shopfront along with a couple of street dogs that had joined in the chase.

In a moment I had caught them up, but Henrietta was already on her feet again, her left side slick with filth. She sprang out into the road without a backward glance, darting round the front of a great grey cart horse. I had but a moment to make my decision, and I watched her disappear behind the flow of traffic as I turned back to Duke. He was panting hard, and blood was spreading across his slashed shirt front. He looked up at me, coughed, then managed a grin.

....

Set beneath Dawoojee Dukanwalla's ample quantity of wiry black chest hair, and intersecting a blurred tapestry of tattoos from long-forgotten ports, several ugly scars bore testimony to previous encounters with edged weapons. Notwithstanding this, he declared that Henrietta's blade had inflicted a 'right stinger'. She had torn a wide rent in his flesh, from the crest of his right collarbone across to his left nipple, and Liza was almost as livid as the wound itself.

'And when it turns rotten and you die shivering and raving, stinking like the bloody grave, will it still be a right stinger then?'

'Don't worry, girl, it'll be fine. The blade was sharp and clean. Actually, I think it was a barber's razor. Woman had class.'

Liza looked at him sourly as she daubed rubbing alcohol on his chest, none-too-gently. We were sat around in the upstairs room of the Saracen's Head, with one of the two little boys peering wide-eyed at us round the half-open door. His brother was probably serving behind the bar.

'There's nothing classy about any girl who carries a steel,' she pronounced acidly, before turning her attention to me and Jabez. 'And as for you two, do you have any idea what I'd have done to you if you'd brought my Duke home in a bloody box? Sure enough, he's got more lives in him than a cat, but one day they'll run out, mark my words.'

She was worked up, of course – and rightfully so – but as with our previous meeting, I perceived that her manner was not as severe as her language. I supposed there was no way to be married to a man like Dawoojee without accepting to some extent that untoward happenings would intrude upon one's life. For all her bluster, the way she gripped his arm reminded me of the way my grandmother had clung to crabby old Jonas Catcliffe in the weeks leading up to his passing. I think perhaps I saw most clearly at that moment what it must be like to be Liza Dukanwalla.

There was the sound of footsteps on the stair, and little Maggie bounced into the room, followed by a tanned man with a huge moustache, pouchy eyes and a Gladstone bag.

'I found him, Ma!' she chirruped. The fellow looked weary.

'Damn you, Duke, lad,' he grumbled. 'Three months at sea and a man just tries to have a quiet drink.'

'Now, Fred, don't be so dour,' winced Dawoojee as the man prodded around the wound with a broad finger. 'You know how a favour begets a favour, and would you rather have a favour from any other man in this fine establishment?'

Maggie skipped off to pull the pints downstairs, and we caught the door and took our leave. As we departed, Duke called after us, 'Don't worry, boys. Once Fred's sewn me back together again I'll track her down. You just watch me run that spunky lass to ground.'

Liza followed us out, and at the bottom of the stairs she laid a hand on my arm.

'Word in your ear, Mr Catcliffe, if I may?'

Her voice was steady, but I felt apprehensive all the same. Jabez had already gone through into the bar.

'You seem like a reasonable sort. Or at least you've more reason in you than those two. Jabez and my Duke would march merrily through the front gates of Hell if it would get them out of an honest day's work.'

It was dark and close in the stairwell, and the clamour of the pub poured through the flimsy wooden door from the bar, together with a humid wave of dirty shirts, tobacco and spilled beer. A shaft of light picked out a stripe of red hair and a weary green eye.

'Listen, he's on a bad run. April of this year, two men walked in here one morning, blades out, looking to rob the place. Out-of-towners – didn't know who Duke was. Wasn't much cash behind the bar, but Duke wouldn't hand it over. Cracked a glass and went at it. We put what was left of those boys in the river late that same night, but they cut his left arm to the bone. He was lucky he didn't lose it.

'November last year he was down by the wharves and a man warned him off with a pistol. Duke thought he was too quick for that. Bloke finished up doing as he was told, but Duke spent an evening on that table up there while another half-cut ship's surgeon like Fred fished lead out of him. And now there's this girl with her razor. Any one of them could have been the end of him. Next one might be.

'What I'm saying to you, Mr Catcliffe, is that there'll be no running that girl to ground like he says. Duke's part in this is over. He thinks he's the same twenty-year-old rover without a care in the world, but he's just not fast enough any more.'

'Understood, Mrs Dukanwalla. I will not call on him again in the matter.'

She softened a touch.

'Thanks love. Appreciate it. And I'm sorry. The thing is, Duke's never belonged anywhere – in Surat they think he's too English, and in London they think he's too Indian. But he belongs in this pub, with us. I'd like it if he could grow older here, maybe even put in a couple of shifts behind the bar before his days are out.'

'I understand. He's already done more than enough. And I wouldn't worry too much – he was pretty fast on his feet this afternoon.'

Opening the door for me, Liza shot me a charitable half-smile, showing the deep creases in her cheeks.

'Just seems that way to you, love.'

NINETEEN

— · —

T he trickiest aspect of possessing a piece of information, as I was rapidly coming to realise, was knowing what to do with it. It is widely acknowledged that a secret is of no consequence without the possibility of its being told, but my last encounter with Inspector Oughton had taught me that honesty was not always the best policy.

I considered briefly whether it would be better to keep Agnes in the dark for the time being, but I just couldn't imagine lying to her – which was odd, given how appallingly I would end up betraying her less than a fortnight later. I knew she would be extraordinarily displeased to learn of Henrietta's arrival after the fact, but equally I understood why my confederates had kept her from the wharves that afternoon. Had we been successful in detaining Lady Halsingham as she disembarked, any attempts to question her (or even simply to restrain her) would have been hopelessly compromised by Agnes's presence. Given the choice between the truth or Henrietta's liberty, I had no doubt where Agnes's instinct would point her.

Still, she would not see it that way, and I could only pray that she might be placated to some degree by being allowed to decide whether or not the fact of her sister's reappearance should be taken to Inspector Oughton of Scotland Yard. I knew, in truth, that we could not possibly justify keeping such a development from him, but I would let Agnes be the one to declare it.

I also hoped she might be distracted by the opportunity to get the first look at a clue which no-one else had yet inspected. And thus it was that Agnes's aquiline footman answered the front door in the early evening to find me red-faced and jacketless, dragging a large brown trunk up the steps from where my obliging cabman had deposited it on the pavement.

....

As feared, Agnes's rancour bordered on incandescence.

'You *absolute* rodent! You trot out these grand words about trusting each other, Harry, but while I must apparently disclose everything, you and your friend Rumpelstiltskin are free to pick and choose what you tell me! How is that remotely fair? She's *my* sister, not yours, and you presume to judge what is best for her on the strength of a single weekend spent in her company?'

She had risen from her chair during my mumbled account, so as to pour down her condemnation of my treachery from an elevated position.

'Or is it my own reactions that you think you can prophesy so accurately? Just how well do you believe you know me, Mr Catcliffe? That persistent man Grieve never tires of cautioning me against you on his frequent visits, yet I fear he may have overestimated your merits.'

I felt wretchedly small.

'Please, Agnes, I've said I am sorry, and I'll say it as many times more as is necessary. However, to provide some punctuation amid my pleas for forgiveness, do you think we might inspect your sister's luggage?'

'That,' she declared, indicating the scruffy leather trunk, 'is not Henrietta's. Look at the state of it!'

'The captain of the *Jeanne* swore that it was what he had been instructed to unload from her cabin, and when she did not return for it, I thought it only right to convey it over here as a peace offering.'

She regarded me with narrowed eyes and a mouth that might have been fashioned from a piece of folded wire.

'Aha. So that's it, is it? You imagine that by allowing me to investigate this insignificant artefact you'll somehow absolve yourself of your sins. Not so, Harrison Catcliffe. I'm not a child or a dog, to be distracted with a trifle. We will open the trunk, but consider your behaviour neither forgotten nor forgiven.'

I did my best to appear remorseful, but rather spoiled the effect by picking up the poker from the marble hearth and swinging it back and forth in my hand. Agnes's indignation briefly gave way to confusion, and I pointed the poker mutely at the heart-shaped brass padlock on the trunk.

'Have you done this before?' she asked sceptically.

I didn't answer, because I hadn't, and I went on to make a mess of it. It took me upwards of ten blows – several of which missed the lock altogether – to get it open. By the time I lifted the lid, the footman had knocked at the door to check that everything was all right.

Inside was a motley assortment of both masculine and feminine clothes, of varying sizes and universally low quality save one outfit of a vastly superior cut. This dress, with high neck, puffed sleeves and lace trimmings, was very grubby, but was unmistakeably of a different grade to the rest of the garments. In fact, it was almost identical to the dress which Agnes wore at that very moment.

'Is this Henrietta's?' I asked.

'I don't know. I haven't seen it before, but it's the sort of thing she might conceivably wear of an ordinary day. Though she wouldn't venture outside in such a dress without a coat, hat and gloves – especially not in weather like this.'

'She wore a coat when we saw her, but it was rather over-large, and tailored for a man.'

Further down in the trunk we found a selection of oddments. Tooth powder and brush, a box of vestas, a lambfoot pocket knife with a cracked horn handle, and well-thumbed editions of three novels. Agnes glanced at the spine of one, and seemed surprised.

'She spoke passable German, but I didn't think she had any interest in reading it.'

I flicked through them, for my own German was quite fluent after my time at university there.

'Even if she did, she'd have had trouble reading these. The language isn't German. I think it's Dutch. I wonder if she got them from someone on the ship? It was a Dutch vessel.'

The trunk revealed little, and save the single out-of-place dress, it could quite conceivably have been the luggage of a relatively poor migrant couple, making their way across the channel to start a new life in London's great wilderness. Agnes was unimpressed.

'None of this makes the slightest bit of sense. It's all just so completely out of character. Henrietta doesn't have a violent bone in her body, so to hear of her got up as a man, slicing your pub landlord open with a straight razor... it's preposterous, Harry.'

I drew breath to remark that Agnes's sister had lately utilised a similar razor to horrifying effect on her late husband, but I thought better of it and remained silent.

'Well,' she continued, 'I suppose you must go immediately to Scotland Yard and tell them everything. And no, Harry, I'm not coming with you. Apparently you're quite capable of handling things on your own.'

....

My third dressing-down of the day, after Liza Dukanwalla and Miss Agnes Cleveley, proved to be something of a relief, perhaps because on this occasion I answered Oughton's questions so meekly and comprehensively that I gave him little need for gruffness. It served no purpose now to conceal Dukanwalla's identity, and though I doubted that my agent in the Port of London would thank me for bringing him to the attention of the unkempt police inspector, I had the distinct impression that after our previous meeting Oughton had already been making some enquiries of his own. The particulars of my informant did not seem news to him.

Since my Church of England upbringing had denied me the pleasures of purgative absolution in the confessional, I decided that I might as well make Oughton my padre, and I spewed forth a torrent of guilty narrative. Not only did I regale him with the details of our adventures at the wharves, but also the whole tale of Matthew Grayling and our interviews with Fornasini. I imagine the inspector was quite exhausted by the end of it all.

'Mr Catcliffe,' he began, with the testy air of a schoolmaster attempting to explain something simple to a very backward child, 'it seems to me that, convinced of your own misapprehensions about

Lord Halsingham's death, you have fallen under the spell of a man yet more deluded than yourself. I must caution you in the strongest terms against further associations with this fellow Potter. He has committed no crime for which I may reasonably arrest him, but mark my words: unchecked, this man will lead you into harm's way.'

He paused to draw at his pipe. There was a quantity of spittle in the stem, and it made a gurgling noise as he sucked on it.

'As for the Indian, there at least I may venture to take action. It may surprise you to know that before I became a policeman, I spent some years in the army as an NCO, and I met his like a thousand times over in Egypt and the Sudan. They're not to be trusted, Mr Catcliffe. I shall instruct a pair of constables to visit him at the Saracen's Head and command him in the strictest of terms not to pursue this matter any further. The man will be feeling vengeful, I shouldn't wonder, but it is for the law – and the law alone – to mete out whatever justice is necessary in this case.'

He let me off with a modest scolding for having gone to such lengths on my own, but after once again making me promise disingenuously to mind my own business, he allowed me to go home rather than flinging me in a cell. It was by now well into the evening, and it seemed about a thousand years since I had awoken that morning in one of the well-appointed rooms at the Edlington Arms. I dined alone at a nearby restaurant before retiring to my fireside with a cigar and the swashbuckling escapism of Baroness Orczy's new Pimpernel novel, neither of which I managed to enjoy.

TWENTY

— · —

The British South Africa Company was a sort of latter-day East India Company, formed by that most celebrated of British colonials, Cecil Rhodes. The great man himself had, only a few years earlier, shuffled off this dreary mortal coil at a relatively unripe age – but then when a fellow has managed to grow as rich as a god, raise his own private army, bring entire nations more or less under his personal rule and get a country named after him by the age of forty-eight, it is probably as well for the rest of mankind that he does not survive too long.

To my discredit, the affairs of sub-Saharan Africa had never really been of great interest to me, however much their fauna had delighted me since a bewitching boyhood encounter with a giraffe at Regent's Park Zoo. But even I understood that 'protectorate' was a slippery term. British as these colonies may have been in name, the truth was that they belonged to Rhodes, his cronies and their mining concerns.

To maintain order without large numbers of British Army troops, Rhodes's company had formed the British South Africa Police, more commonly known as the Rhodesian Police. Calling them 'police' was another bit of trickery, designed to lend a reassuring familiarity to what was in essence a mercenary army. They had shown their teeth in the

Matabele Wars and the Boer War, with some commentators accusing them of having started this latter conflict.

They were a bold and adventurous bunch, with a whiff of entrepreneurial amorality about them – and I could see why men such as Robert Edlington and Brown the former soldier-servant might have ended up among their ranks. For the likes of Edlington – whose older brother was going to walk away with both the family estate and the woman he loved – Rhodes's colonies must have presented an appealing opportunity to forge a life for himself in a new world, free of much of the baggage that weighed down the old one.

In his absence, Robert Edlington intrigued me. Partly it was his colourful professional life, but also I wondered how he might have come over the years to reconcile his frustrated love for Henrietta with that strong bond of affection which Agnes said had existed between the two brothers – and more recently with the terrible reality of the deed that George's wife had committed. Robert's words in the letter that Jabez Potter had tossed into my fireplace were raw and rancorous, but they were the writings of a younger man, and the heartsick twenty-five-year-old lieutenant was now a seasoned captain of nearly thirty-three. There was a lot of water under the bridge.

Also, and possibly on account of his delayed entry into our drama, I will admit that in my fanciful mind he had become a sort of Richard the Lionheart character. An upright chap who was going to help us straighten everything out when he returned from his interminable foreign wars. It was thus with some interest that I read a note from Agnes as I prepared to make my way to Catcliffe's the following morning.

Dear Harry,

Robert is finally home. I received a card from him this morning, so perhaps we can finally get the answers we are looking for. He is staying at his family's London house before heading to Halsingham at the weekend, so I have arranged that he will call on me for tea at three o'clock this afternoon. Will you join us?

Yours,

Agnes

P.S. Your treachery is not forgotten.

....

I knew, of course, that Robert Edlington and his poor departed brother were identical twins, but even so, there was something profoundly unsettling about entering the drawing room at the Cleveley family's South Kensington mansion to see the shade of my friend George rising from the table to greet me. I have met other sets of twins where the resemblance has faded as separate lives have etched their own tracks onto once similar faces, but save for the slightly leathered complexion of years in the hot African sun, this Edlington brother was the mirror image of the other. Until the face smiled, at which point it became that of an entirely different man.

'Harry, this is Captain Robert Edlington. Robert, this is Mr Harrison Catcliffe.'

He shook my hand warmly.

'Mr Catcliffe, it's a pleasure to meet you. I'm only sorry that our first encounter is in such circumstances.'

'I'm sorry too, Captain Edlington. Please accept my deepest sympathies. I was very fond of George – he was a good fellow.'

The smile faded, and he nodded gratefully.

'He was. A very mild and a gentle man. It was not the way anyone expected him to go.'

Agnes bade us both sit down, and Drew brought in the tea tray. The butler's manners were markedly improved compared to my previous visits.

'You must call me Robert, Mr Catcliffe. Agnes speaks highly of you, and I know you were a friend to my brother, so let us be friends too.'

'Harry, then.'

Agnes interjected.

'Only his mother calls him Harrison, and only when she's very cross. I've considered adopting the habit myself.'

Robert smiled automatically, but something in his glance at Agnes told me he had noted the informality.

When I turned up, Agnes had been in the midst of setting out a full account of that grim evening at Halsingham House. Once the pleasantries had been observed and tea had been poured, she returned to her story. The telegrams Captain Edlington had received in Rhodesia had been cursory at best, and his first act on arriving in London the previous night had been to seek out the Earl of Wrenleigh at his club. Wrenleigh had told him all he could, but admitted he had come on the scene late. For a fuller tale, he recommended that Robert should speak to Agnes or a guest by the name of Catcliffe.

And so Agnes Cleveley told him what it was we had seen, heard and found in a dark corridor nearly three weeks earlier. Afternoon tea in the Cleveley family household was a generous affair, but the sandwiches and sweet dainties languished untouched on their china platters. Agnes swallowed down her horror and narrated the tale as clearly as she could, while Robert strove to hide his grief as the grisly revelations piled up. Two people so close to those involved ought to have amplified each other's emotions, but strangely they did not, and the encounter was marked by a level of briskness and control.

When Agnes had finished, the captain closed his eyes and gripped the bridge of his nose between his finger and thumb.

'Poor, wretched George. Forgive me, Agnes, Harry, it's just the pity of it all. And Henrietta! Poor, dear Henrietta – she doesn't have it in her heart to hurt any creature. What terrible illness, what delusion drove her to this? The guilt she must feel! They say she's fled? And taken little Thomas?'

Agnes nodded.

'She was a patient at the Rochester Clinic – where George sent her before, do you remember? Dr Rochester was trying to prove what you and I already know – that she couldn't have committed conscious and deliberate murder. She was supposed to be secure there, but she wasn't. It seems likely that she had an accomplice in her escape, but I can't think who. She took Thomas from the house as we slept and hasn't been seen in London since.

'And Robert, there is something else. I know nothing we can do will bring George back, but there might be more to all this...'

I knew we would have to take Robert Edlington into our confidence, especially if he was going to help us answer those urgent questions surrounding Matthew Grayling's work at Halsingham House. Even so, it seemed to me that Agnes was putting a lot of trust in him at a very early stage. Had there been time to confer beforehand, I might have suggested giving him an abridged version – not just to keep certain cards close to our chests for the time being, but also to spare a bereaved man some portion of that false hope that Agnes herself had found so very difficult to approach in a spirit of rationality.

I recalled how warmly Agnes had spoken of him before, and, seeing the earnest way she looked at him now, I wondered all of a sudden whether there might not be more to her feelings for the returned soldier than the simple bond of in-laws. On Robert's side, of course, he had once been passionately in love with the older sister, but that had been a secret. Now in my mind's eye I saw the younger girl in the background. Sixteen years old when she met him, unfinished and impressionable. Had she seen George paying his attentions to Henrietta and wondered whether this charismatic spare might settle his gaze on a lesser prize?

I was surprised to find these suspicions accompanied by a sharp twist of melancholy deep inside me, and I did my best to shake it off. Somewhere in the whirl of blood and excitement I had forgotten the unspoken limits of my friendship with Agnes, but I remembered them now.

'Harry has been at the heart of it all, so I'll let him tell you himself,' explained Agnes, turning to me.

And tell him I did. From the first encounter with Jabez Potter outside Woodville's to the reappearance of Henrietta down at the wharves the previous afternoon. I left nothing out, channelling that sting of irrational jealousy into honesty. I persuaded myself that if the case affected anyone beyond the unhappy couple themselves and young Thomas Edlington, then surely it was the fellow sat in front of me. He could not hope to be much of a guardian without a boy to guard, and I was convinced that we were his best chance of finding Thomas.

He remained quiet as I spoke, then once I had finished, he began thoughtfully, 'Not the story I expected to hear today. Not even close. Henrietta at liberty in London as a cross-dressing buccaneer, slicing up lascars? It's unimaginable.'

'So was what we saw that night at Halsingham House,' said Agnes quietly. 'But we saw it all the same.'

'She was always so gentle. So set apart from anything rough or desperate.'

For a moment, the shade of a private love hung in the air, and he could not have known we understood it.

'As to this fellow, Grayling,' he said, shutting a door on the past, 'there may still be nothing in it. But we should set it to rest one way or the other. I'm custodian of Halsingham House now, and I can get answers where you couldn't. If there is truth in any of it, we owe it to both George and Henrietta that it comes out.

'You were right to trust Brown – though I'll admit to a little bit of pride that you had difficulty getting him to co-operate without my consent. He and I have been through the mill together at one time or another, and he's as faithful to me as I am to him.'

He smiled crookedly at the memory.

'I'll talk to him as soon as I get back to Halsingham. If there's something to be gleaned from that house then he'll sniff it out. He's always been dependable like that.

'As for Inman, I don't know him well. I haven't lived at Halsingham since he became butler, and in his earlier days as a valet he always worked with my father or George. However, he has served at Halsing-ham for his entire working life, and I'm confident that the only reason he would conceal anything is through loyalty to my family. Trust me, if there's anything to be told, he will tell me.'

He stood and turned to Agnes.

'And now, I regret, I must take my leave. There's a lot to do before I can pretend to take control of affairs at Halsingham House.'

He took her hand and kissed it with the easy dash of a cavalryman.

'Life was certainly much simpler in my camp in Rhodesia. I'm afraid I've forgotten what little I ever knew about London society. I daresay someone will tell me what clubs I should join, and I suppose I'll have to develop a taste for musical theatre.'

I took his lead to make my own exit, and rose to shake his hand.

'Or you can just read the reviews and pretend. If in doubt, tell people how very much you enjoyed *Merry Widow*. I think it's the best of the lot. Diplomatic intrigues and fortune-hunting, and a Parisian brothel called Maxim's. As for the rest, I wouldn't worry too much. Given the circumstances, people ought to give you a bit of leeway.'

'Harry, you have no idea,' said Agnes, smiling thinly. 'They're a sharp-eyed bunch of hawks, waiting to pounce on the most trifling mistake. *Merry Widow* is the perfect example. Don't you know it's most unpatriotic to wax lyrical about a German operetta, even if it *is* the best? You only get away with this sort of thing because you've no breeding, just bags of money. No-one expects you to behave properly.'

'*Merry Widow* is Austrian, not German,' I said with a hint of annoyance. Her tone was light, but her meaning was not especially kind, and I could not think what I had done to deserve it.

'Tall whippet, small greyhound,' she replied tartly, daring me to try and have the last word.

217

'It sounds like you have the best of both worlds, Harry,' broke in Edlington airily, surprised by this sudden sourness and seeking to soothe it. He took his coat and hat from the footman. 'I don't suppose you have any jobs going, do you? I'm afraid I don't know a thing about industry.'

I tweaked the brim of my topper to set it straight upon my head, then gave him what I hoped was a reassuring smile.

'Nor do I. No-one ever seems to notice.'

As we were saying our farewells, there was an apologetic knock at the door. A servant I had not seen before entered and whispered something to old Drew.

'Miss Agnes,' announced the old crow, 'it would appear that there is a constable at the door wishing to speak with you urgently.'

I saw hope and fear leap into her eyes.

'Certainly, Drew. Please show him in at once.'

Robert and I remained standing with our hats and coats on, yet with unspoken accord we made no move to depart as the tall, sandy-haired officer was ushered in. He bore an unfortunate resemblance to a shameless pederast from my prep school, and I recalled him as the fellow who had been taking notes when Inspector Oughton had first interviewed me that bleak morning at Halsingham House. The man nodded at me in recognition.

'Mr Catcliffe.' He turned to Agnes. 'Miss Cleveley. I am Constable Jessop. Inspector Oughton requests your presence at the earliest opportunity. Mr Catcliffe, the inspector has sent another officer to seek you at your factory, but finding you here, might I request your presence also?'

'Is the lady to be left in the dark until it suits your inspector?' asked Robert pointedly.

'My apologies, sir. May I know to whom I am speaking besides Miss Cleveley and Mr Catcliffe?'

'Captain Robert Edlington. Brother to the late Lord Halsingham and guardian to his son.'

'In that case, sir, you'd best come too.'

'For heaven's sake, man!' urged Robert. 'You're not on the stage. Spit it out.'

'It's one of the other guests from the party at Halsingham House, sir. A Mr Grieve. He's been found dead. Looks like he may have done himself in.'

TWENTY-ONE

— · —

I did not understand why I too was required at Scotland Yard until I saw the unattended dray half-blocking the road outside. The scruffy cart had no barrels on it – and was in such a deplorable state that it might easily have belonged to a rag and bone man – but a barely discernible patch of peeling paint on the side proclaimed it the property of the Vauxhall Brewery. A bad-tempered draught horse was tied haphazardly to a lamppost, munching on a nosebag, and he stamped his mud-matted fetlocks as we passed.

Sure enough, Jabez Potter sat sullenly in an uncomfortable-looking chair outside Oughton's office, scratching at the tidemarks of London filth on the shins of his trousers. He raised his bushy eyebrows at me as I entered. It seemed the inspector had heard tell of our disagreement in the White Bear and was making sure alibis were in order.

In fact, when the particulars of Albert Grieve's demise were revealed to us, it seemed a rather redundant step to have been looking for culprits, but perhaps after being so conspicuously undercut by Duke's investigations, Inspector Oughton simply wanted to impress upon us what a thorough fellow he was.

Grieve kept a substantial flat off Piccadilly, on the ground floor of a very grand mansion block with enclosed gardens to the rear. At around six o'clock that morning, his manservant had heard a shot fired, and on entering his master's bedchamber, he had discovered Grieve slumped at his dressing table, missing a portion of his head, and with a pistol in his limp hand.

Tragic as this was, of principal interest to Oughton was the table top in front of the deceased, which contained a goodly amount of jewellery. Even beneath the lacquering of dried blood, this was unmistakeably both expensive and feminine.

Lady Halsingham's former maid had been sent for, in order that she might positively identify the gems as belonging to Henrietta. The unlucky woman was in a precarious position as a lady's maid in a house with no ladies, but she had remained in residence at Halsingham until Robert arrived to make a decision about her future.

'Perhaps I can help in the meantime?' ventured Agnes. 'I can't pretend to recognise all my sister's jewellery, but perhaps there will be some familiar pieces?'

Reasoning that it could do no harm, Oughton sent Jessop to the safe to fetch the items, and the constable returned bearing a bundle of dirty sacking about the size of a dead pigeon. The inspector laid this sorry-looking item on his desk, and with some ceremony he unwrapped it to reveal the treasures within.

And treasures they really were. Gold, silver and gemstones of many colours – precious heirlooms that had found their way down to a woman who was mistress of one great family and eldest daughter of another. I shuddered to think what they might be worth.

It was a clear enough indication of Agnes's exalted background that her gaze did not linger acquisitively over the glittering pile of trinkets like my own or those of the policemen. Rather, her eye alighted immediately upon one particular piece. Reaching out, she withdrew a star-shaped brooch. It was not a large object, fitting comfortably into Agnes's palm, but even a philistine like me could see that it was an exquisite item. Mounted in gleaming silver, there must have been upwards of fifty tiny diamonds set into twelve points surrounding a brilliant central stone.

'This one!' said Agnes, excitedly. 'I know there are many like it in rich ladies' jewellery boxes, but I'd recognise this star brooch anywhere. It was my grandmother's. She died about ten years ago, and it went to Henrietta. She loved it – said it always reminded her of Granny when she wore it.'

Oughton nodded in acknowledgement.

'Thank you, Miss Cleveley. This bears out our suspicions, though of course we'll ask the lady's maid to confirm it when she arrives. If you would be so good as to return it for the time being.'

Agnes replaced the brooch with some small degree of reticence, and Jessop withdrew to secure Henrietta's jewels once more within the fireproof safe somewhere in the bowels of the building. I was wondering idly what else might be squirrelled away in there, when Oughton returned me abruptly to reality.

'I gather, Mr Catcliffe,' said the inspector in businesslike fashion, 'that there was an encounter between yourself and Mr Grieve in a public house on Monday night, during which blows were struck. May I ask the cause of the argument?'

I glanced guiltily across at Agnes. There was no sense dancing round it.

'Mr Grieve disapproved of my friendly association with Miss Cleveley. It was my understanding that he followed me to the White

Bear on the night in question in order to warn me off.' I heard a stern intake of breath from Agnes but kept my eyes resolutely on Oughton.

'However, that wasn't what caused the scuffle you've heard about. That was a simple misjudgement on poor Grieve's part. He was in a belligerent frame of mind, and he threatened Mr Potter, who responded more robustly than he anticipated. No-one was badly hurt, and to my mind no harm was done.'

'That's as may be, Mr Catcliffe,' said Oughton darkly, 'but for the man to have taken his own life within the week, you'll agree there is the appearance of a connection. Wouldn't be the first or last time a murder has been dressed up as a suicide. Grieve's room was on the ground floor, and there was an open French door leading out onto the gardens behind the building. I very much doubt you've got it in you, but can we be certain of Mr Potter? I knew little lads like him in the army. In my experience, they were always the ones to watch.'

Jabez himself was still waiting outside the office.

'I think I can put your mind at rest, Inspector. Jabez is a fierce fellow when his blood's up, but this tussle with Albert Grieve meant nothing to him. Grieve threatened him and was briskly seen off. Job done. I suspect he barely remembers it.'

Inspector Oughton appeared satisfied with this, at least until Jabez's whereabouts that morning could be vouched for. He turned his attention to Agnes and Robert, his manner becoming more deferential.

'I'll be in touch when Lady Halsingham's maid has had a chance to check the jewels. In the meantime, I would caution most strenuously against any further amateur detective work, much as I know you are fond of it, Miss Cleveley.'

He evidently saw no need to caution me after our interview the day before.

'Even if the jewellery does indeed turn out to be from Halsingham House – as seems to be the case – it doesn't mean Mr Grieve had any hand in the murder. He may just have taken the opportunity to pinch the jewels during the confusion.'

I hadn't liked Grieve, but I was still sad at the way he had left this life. I wondered what it was that had driven a man I had thought so cocksure to such a desperate act. Guilt, perhaps? Surely not about the theft. Even if he had later regretted stealing Henrietta's jewellery, it wasn't nearly worth ending himself over. Had he been involved in something more? I did not recall seeing him anywhere abroad on the night of George's murder – either before or after the event. The more I thought about it, the more his presence at Halsingham that weekend just didn't fit.

'Honestly, Harry,' murmured Agnes caustically as, together with Robert, we made our way onto the gas-lit street, 'brawling over my honour in that seedy Oxford Street drinking den. How perfectly absurd.'

There was something about the way she said this that made me dislike her for it. It was the implication that Grieve and I were the same – that I had somehow made myself ridiculous by forgetting my place, just as he had. Perhaps what really needled me was that she had said it in front of Robert.

Agnes realised as the words left her lips that it did not do to speak ill of the dead, and she added hastily, 'Poor Mr Grieve. He may not have been the most sympathetic of men, but I always thought him harmless.

I wonder what he had got himself into? Surely he was not involved in George's death.'

'After the things I've heard today, I'm not sure anything is off the table,' said Robert solemnly, helping her into the back of her car. 'Do you believe Albert Grieve any less capable of the act than Henrietta?'

'I suppose not, when you put it like that.'

He closed the door of the motor car, and the two of us stood back to watch it depart. It was just then that I had a thought, and I stepped quickly up to her window.

'Agnes, I wonder, can you remember what brought Albert Grieve to Halsingham House that weekend? Was he a school chum of George's?'

'No, I don't think so. Actually, I don't believe he knew George very well at all. He was a friend of Rowland Renwick's. You remember, the nervous little fellow with the moustache? Grieve was visiting elsewhere in the area, and Renwick asked George if he could join us for the evening.'

I was reminded of the evident familiarity between Grieve and Renwick during George's funeral service, and it unsettled me. If they were truly friends, then why would they have concealed it? Grieve had made such a point of demonstrating his disdain for Renwick during the meal, while for his own part the fastidious little man had uttered not a word in reply. It occurred to me again that while Grieve had been nowhere to be found on that terrible night, Renwick had arrived on the scene almost too quickly. I knew little enough of either fellow, but Renwick was a card player of some note, and a handful of Lady Halsingham's jewellery would go a long way towards dispersing the most crippling of gambling debts. I resolved to pay a visit to the card lounge at Woodville's before too long.

Agnes's conveyance moved away a few feet, then it suddenly halted, and I heard her call my name. I jogged over, took my hat off and put my head through the open window. Her eyes were fixed on the road ahead, and her hands fidgeted in her lap.

'I still think you're not the worst friend, all things considered,' she said softly from the dim interior, without looking at me. 'I've been mean to you today and I'm sorry. If I forgive you and we agree not to quarrel any more, will you promise to trust me in future?'

'All right, Agnes.'

'All right then. Best remove your head from the car unless you want me to take it to Kensington.'

I put my hat back on and watched her driver deftly negotiate the disreputable old drayman's cart that still obstructed the road. Jabez remained inside the police station, no doubt enjoying the full effect of Oughton's interrogation style and perhaps thanking his lucky stars that he had fought with the marines in China rather than under Sergeant Oughton in the Sudan. My own rooms were within walking distance, but I strolled down to the Victoria Embankment with Robert, as he hunted for a cab to return him to the Belgravia house that until lately had belonged to his brother.

'So Rowland Renwick is still about, then?' he said.

'You know him?'

'From Eton. He was in our year, but more George's friend than mine. Used to come to the house sometimes in the holidays. Pleasant enough chap – wouldn't say boo to a goose. Jolly fine moustache. You're acquainted with him also, I take it?'

'He's a member at Woodville's, my club. A demon at the baccarat table.'

'Baccarat?' He grinned. 'And they call it a gentlemen's club?'

'If it's good enough for the King, it's good enough for his humble subjects.'

The sovereign's weakness for the game was legendary. It had once nearly cost him his throne.

'One has to admire our monarch,' said Robert thoughtfully. 'He lets convention bend to him rather than the other way round. If he wants to play disreputable card games, avail himself of other men's wives or alter the cut of the frock coat to flatter his paunch, he just goes ahead and does it. The rest of the world must simply follow.'

'Portly old coot is the spirit of the age.'

Robert hailed a passing cab, and we said our farewells.

'I return to Halsingham House tomorrow, but I'll write to Agnes with whatever I can discover about your Mr Grayling.'

We shook hands.

'Thank you, Harry. It's good to know someone's been holding the fort while I've been so far away.'

TWENTY-TWO

— · —

W e did not have to wait long to hear back from Robert, and on the following Monday – the day before Christmas Eve – I was summoned to lunch with Agnes in the lavish dining room at the Cordovan Hotel. It was an unabashedly ostentatious place, with a whiff of Regency grandeur about the rich crimson carpets and pink marble-effect pillars. The high ceilings were heavy with ornate plaster-work and electric chandeliers, while the tall, round-topped windows overlooked the north end of Green Park. I could not work out why Agnes had picked it, not least because to my mind it was uncomfortably close to the scene of Albert Grieve's end.

My dining companion requested sole lightly fried in butter, with potted fowl to follow. She let me pick the wine, despite the fact that she herself would undoubtedly have made a better choice, and told me so once the man had departed.

Agnes's spirits seemed disordered somehow. She sported a most inappropriately exuberant hat, its shoulder-width brim piled high with dyed black tulle and ostrich plumes. Yet her face in its shadow was pensive. She made occasional attempts at lightness, but they had the feeling of token gestures, and I was reminded that nothing had been heard of her sister and nephew since Henrietta had cut up rough with Duke down at the wharves five days earlier. At that moment she reminded me of sad little Elsie from the Tin Face Parade. Her mask was a fine piece of work but it wasn't quite so convincing close up.

'Do I take it you've had word from Robert?' I asked her, as the waiter departed with our order.

'I have. I received a long letter this morning. Shall I read it to you?'

'Don't you think this is rather a public place for that?'

'I think, Harry, that you give our fellow men and women too much credit. Most of them aren't the least bit curious about anything at all.'

She inclined her head towards a solemn-looking gentleman at the next table, dabbing sauce primly from his moustache with the corner of a serviette. Over the clink of cutlery, his wife's querulous voice was clearly audible, passing banal comment on the slapdash working practices of someone else's gardener.

'I guarantee that the people in this sort of place are far more interested in their own lives than ours.'

'Very well. Please, do tell me what the captain has to say.'

'I am afraid you'll be disappointed.'

'That was always inevitable.'

She unfolded the letter.

'"My dearest Agnes," he begins, followed by a paragraph or two about how strange he finds it being back at Halsingham House. I shouldn't wonder, after all that's happened there. He goes on: "I must first inform you that Henrietta's maid has verified that the jewels found on the dressing table of the unfortunate Mr Grieve were indeed your sister's property. That good lady has further stated that, while the items did belong to Henrietta, they constitute only a small portion of those jewels that were missing, and the least valuable parts of the collection at that. Even the star brooch you so cleverly recognised, though of great sentimental import, was not comparable to many of the other pieces in monetary terms.

"'I have spoken to that frustrating fellow Oughton, who refuses to express any point of view whatsoever, but when pushed he suggests that Grieve may already have sold the bulk of the gems. The inspector never commits himself to anything. I can see why you and Harry were driven to undertake your own investigations.'"

Agnes gave me a sour look, presumably intended to express her own opinion of Inspector Oughton.

"'You may inform Mr Catcliffe that first Brown, and now I, have been making enquiries surrounding the possibility that his man Grayling may have performed some service at Halsingham House, and I must ask you – can you be certain of this Italian? Our housekeeper has no record of any payment either to Grayling or Fornasini, nor does the land agent. Apart from the cook and her boy, no-one else in the house recalls Harry's tattooed man, or can account for his presence on that or any other occasion.'"

I had feared a revelation of this sort. For my part, I was in no doubt that Matthew Grayling had been there. Robert was right to doubt Fornasini's information – which was all the more unreliable for having been obtained in part through violence – but the first clue connecting Potter's old friend to Halsingham House had come from the lips of Grayling himself. There had been no reason for Jabez to doubt his friend's word, and I in turn had no reason to doubt Jabez. All the same, Jabez was vastly disreputable. I trusted him, but I could not expect Robert or even Agnes to do the same.

Agnes continued to read from the slim sheets of paper on the table in front of her.

'"Furthermore, I have spoken to Inman, and the man swears he has never heard of either Matthew Grayling or, for that matter, Giovanni Fornasini. I am inclined to believe him, for he has always seemed an honest enough sort. Though he might conceivably have kept certain facts from you on that earlier occasion, he would certainly have told them to me, for unless I am grossly deceived, his loyalty to my family is as unshakeable as I had suspected."'

She lowered the paper and beheld me with a sort of pity in her eyes.

'I'm sorry, Harry, really I am. I wanted to believe this as much as you did. Though perhaps there's an answer to this Matthew Grayling business after all. He continues: "There were a good number of workmen at the house during the family's absence, but the only sums noted in the housekeeper's ledger were those paid to a well-respected carpentry firm in Guildford called Ainscough and Son, who oversaw the renovations. I wrote to them, and while their reply stated that none of their workmen matched the description of Harry's chap, they admitted to taking on men from other local firms in order to meet Henrietta's ambitious schedule of works.

'"I know it will not please you to hear it, my dear Agnes, but the most likely answer is that Matthew Grayling and the tattooed man at the table were two separate fellows – the latter a Surrey labourer casually employed by Ainscough's. As you are aware, most of the staff were abroad with the family at the time, but Brown continues to make wider enquiries among the estate workers. If he discovers anything more, I will of course notify you immediately, though I must confess myself of the mind that the solution above seems both reasonable and likely."'

I must have looked a picture of dejection, judging by Agnes's face. Her smile was consoling and hopelessly forced.

'This is all most frustrating,' I said simply, and a trifle petulantly, as the sole arrived.

'Does he say anything else?'

'Of course, but nothing more about Matthew Grayling. Of course, he's keen to find Henrietta, and asks permission to speak directly with Mr Dukanwalla. He's plainly fed up with Inspector Oughton's prevarication and has already cabled the police in Calais to check on their search for Thomas. And he asks if he may call upon me tomorrow. Things being in order at Halsingham, he's returning to town to take a more active part in the hunt.'

She paused for a moment to contemplate her forkful of flaked white fish, glistening in its buttery coating, before popping it into her mouth without any great relish. I tried a piece of my own. The sole was doubtless excellent, but the bitterness of disappointment made it taste like dead wasps on my tongue.

'To business, then, Harry,' said Agnes abruptly, as if to lift us up from our dreariness. 'We must tell Robert the address at which Mr Dukanwalla is to be found. You can give me the details and I shall pass them on.'

'I am afraid I've promised Mrs Dukanwalla not to ask any more of Dawoojee. He's given us a good deal of help and has been badly hurt in the process. Besides, his link to the case was through Matthew Grayling. Without him, Duke has no reason to want to help us further.'

'Well, perhaps it will be a question of changing his role from that of an interested party to a paid adviser. And I daresay we can put Mrs Dukanwalla's mind at ease about her husband's safety. Robert will see to it. He's used to taking the lead in these sorts of affairs.'

'I'd really rather remain the point of contact, if it's all the same to you.'

She stopped eating her fish and peered at me incisively.

'Harry Catcliffe, I do believe you feel threatened by Robert.'

I did, of course, but I was damned if I was going to admit it.

'No I don't,' I replied stiffly. 'I think he seems like a fine chap.'

'Of course you think he's a fine chap, but you don't want to let him take over from you, and I can't think why. If Robert wants to take a more active part in looking into his brother's killing, then he has every right to do so. Far more right than you – far more right than me, even.'

Her tone was not unkind. In fact, it was infuriatingly rational.

'You've lectured me in the past on the need to be sensible about all this. Now it's my turn. Robert is an officer and a leader, resourceful and experienced, and we should leave it to him – however much we want to continue playing our part. Remember, Harry, the most important thing now is finding Henrietta and Thomas. We can't help the dead, but we must do our utmost to help the living, and Robert is best placed to do that. He's Thomas's guardian. It's his job.

'You have been wonderful these last weeks. Really quite remarkable, especially given how brief your friendship with George was. I'm enormously grateful to you for giving me help and hope when I needed it so badly.'

Agnes's words were heartfelt, but despite her gentleness I felt wounded. I saw plainly that I was being dismissed.

Yet I did not quibble further, for how could I? She was right, of course, and it does not do to become possessive over something so abstract as a murder investigation. I was taciturn for the rest of the meal, and despite my best efforts, I must have appeared deflated, for as we left the Cordovan, she stealthily took my gloved hand and gave it a reassuring squeeze.

'Please, Harry, don't be upset. Not over this. You've done more than anyone could have asked of you. Robert will keep us both informed of any developments, and you and I can still see each other. Except now we will perhaps be able to talk of happier matters.'

....

Among several things left unsaid at that luncheon was the relief that Agnes would doubtless feel knowing that – along with my own retirement from active participation – these latest developments in the case of the Halsingham House murder would also signal the end of her acquaintance with Jabez Potter.

I, on the other hand, was certain that he would not see matters that way, and it was with a heavy heart and a sense of foreboding that I left a note for him with the landlord at the White Bear, arranging to meet there in the early evening.

If Potter were a terrier – a form to which I indeed suspected he might revert during full moons and solstices – he would have been one of those diabolical little farmyard curs that will shake a dirty old pigeon to rags rather than eating a perfectly palatable bowl of fresh meat from the butcher's shop laid next to it. His tenacity was admirable at times but he was utterly single-minded in his fixation on a single idea, to the exclusion of all reason.

'Doesn't explain anything, as far as I can see!' he barked at me, spraying a combination of spittle, Watney's ale and tobacco juice across the table. 'And what about all the questions we still haven't answered? Who doped Matthew? Why did they pay Fornasini to keep quiet about Matthew's involvement if he wasn't even there?'

'Fornasini isn't a trustworthy witness. We intimidated him into talking and he would have said anything to get us out of his house.'

'Well I believe him. Don't you?'

'I suppose I probably do, on balance.'

'And what about me? Do you believe me? Just bought you a pint, didn't I?'

I sighed.

'What do you expect me to do, Jabez?'

He looked at me with vast incredulity in his eyes.

'What do I expect you to do? I expect you to finish what you started, mate. Get to the bottom of it. Find the woman; find the lad; find Matthew's killer. Wind it all up.' He stopped. Even he must have realised that his expectations of me had been hopelessly high.

'Look, I've no right to be a participant in this investigation any more. While Robert Edlington was abroad it made sense for me to look into things, but now that he has returned, my part in it is ended.' I could hear the regret in my own voice, and I wondered why it was there.

'You brought me into this because I could help you, but now Robert is better placed to do that. Go to him instead. He is much more competent than I am.'

'Except he's not going to listen to me, is he? Because he's already sacked off the possibility that the murder has anything to do with

Matthew. He just wants to find the girl. Lord knows what he'll do once he tracks her down. Send her to the hangman or marry her, it's anyone's guess. But he won't believe that Matthew's murder and Halsingham's are connected. You do.'

'And perhaps I don't any more,' I replied sharply.

'You don't mean that, mate.' He looked suddenly crestfallen. It was not an attitude he had ever displayed before, and I instantly regretted my words.

'No, you're right, I don't. But that makes no difference to the way things are. I cannot be involved in all this any more. And I'm sorry. But your best chance is to push your agenda on Robert through Duke. He's planning to hire him to track down Henrietta and probably Thomas as well. If you want to lead him back towards Matthew again, that's how you can do it.' I read reluctant acceptance in his face.

'I still think you're bloody soft backing off, but I suppose I should be grateful for all your help,' he muttered. He didn't say he was, just that he ought to be. I smiled wryly.

'Cheers, Jabez. I'll see you.' I finished my pint and left, glancing back at the peculiar, dogged little fellow sucking moodily on his pipe in the corner. He, at least, would see things through, unless he died first.

Stepping gloomily out into the drizzle, I felt rudderless. I leant against the front of the pub and lit a cigarette without much enthusiasm. Across the road from the White Bear, Broxton's the butcher had a lavish Christmas window display of poultry, game and fruit. I stood looking at the long wires strung along the front of the building, festooned with damp geese, turkeys, chickens and rabbits all dangling by their hind legs, interspersed with holly wreaths and sooty sprays of mistletoe. There must have been a hundred dead beasts up there.

In the doorway a burly fellow – presumably Broxton himself – stood proudly, arms folded, wearing a long jacket and fob watch with his butcher's apron.

I had no desire to go home for the night, but all of a sudden I had nothing to do. And then it came to me that there still remained one question which I alone was in a position to get to the bottom of.

TWENTY-THREE

—.—

D ismissed as I may have been, I had a lead that was beyond
the reach of Inspector Oughton, Robert Edlington, Agnes
Cleveley, Jabez Potter and even Dawoojee Dukanwalla, since none of
them were members at Woodville's. And I could be almost certain that
at that very moment, this particular lead would be sitting in the card
lounge on the first floor, busily cleaning out the great and the good
around a baccarat table. If Albert Grieve had been up to anything at
Halsingham House that weekend – whether it was murder or simple
opportunistic theft – I felt sure that Rowland Renwick was in on the
secret. I returned swiftly home to change into my evening clothes, then
bent my steps towards those familiar burgundy double doors.

It had always surprised me that an exceptional card player like
Renwick – who once told me that as a boy he had excelled at whist,
cribbage and bezique – found himself captivated by such a crude,
unsophisticated pastime as *chemin de fer*. Among games based on
the intricate understanding of mathematical odds and psychology,
baccarat was the equivalent of taking oneself to the races and wagering
arbitrary amounts of money on any old nag. Even I could play it.
Proponents of the game tried to claim that there was some measure
of skill in deciding whether or not to take a third card, yet most of

the time there were simple rules of convention which dictated this choice. The rules were designed in such a way that the most paralytic drunk could play on into the small hours, and in fact only the chaotic influence of strong drink ever really made it interesting.

Nevertheless, not only did Renwick play with a dedication bordering on mania, but he also invariably seemed to come out on top at the end of the evening. How he managed this, I could not say, but perhaps there was more sophistication in the choice of that one card than I cared to believe. Or maybe he was a good deal craftier with his sleeves than the cook's boy at Halsingham House.

By the time I arrived at the card lounge, Renwick's game was in full swing. I waited until there was space at the table and was then obliged to shed a goodly amount of Grandpa Catcliffe's steel money before Renwick decided to take a break. I played one more round, before excusing myself and seeking him out where he sat digesting his success with a glass of whisky in the Pike Lounge. As I approached, he was peering at the back of his highly polished cigarette case, presumably to check his moustache was still in order.

He regarded me with some small measure of suspicion as I dropped into the armchair opposite and took a sip at my own glass.

'Hello, Catcliffe. Haven't seen you round the table for a while.'

He was quite correct. While never a big gambler, I had been partial to a few hands in the old days. I realised now that I hadn't ventured anywhere near a pack of cards since before the party at Halsingham House. Perhaps it had only been boredom that had ever drawn me to the tables in the first place.

'I've been busy, Renwick. This business with Halsingham. And now it turns out Grieve was involved too.'

'Was he indeed?' Renwick asked, rather disingenuously. 'What makes you say that? Poor man. It's not right to speak ill of the dead, you know.'

'Surely you must have heard. He was found with some of Lady Halsingham's jewellery.'

Renwick had evidently not been privy to this information, and a look of horror stole across his face.

'I won't believe it!' he said abruptly. 'You're tricking me, Catcliffe, and I don't know why. What do you want from me?'

'I promise you, it's the truth. I only want to know what Grieve was doing there that night at Halsingham, and I think you can tell me.'

He looked affronted.

'And why would you think that? What have I to do with Albert Grieve? I scarcely knew the chap.'

I took out my cigarettes and matches and offered them across to Renwick. He shook his head mutely. Lighting one for myself, I sat back.

'Listen to me, Renwick. I know he was at Halsingham House that night because you were friends. Because he happened to be in the area, and you asked if he could come. But the thing is – and you'll forgive me for speaking plainly – I don't believe for a moment that Grieve just happened to be in the vicinity of Halsingham. He was a town mouse like me. What would he have been doing out in the Surrey countryside? No, he wanted an invitation to that party, and you arranged it for him.'

Renwick's discomfort was palpable, but he didn't have the gall to deny it. He fiddled with his moustache and looked absent-mindedly across at the great pike mounted in its glass case above the fireplace.

'Fine. You're right. I did fix for Albert to be there that night, but honestly, thieving was the last thing on his mind.'

'But the jewels...'

'Oh come on, Catcliffe. I can see you don't know the Grieve family. They're rich as Croesus. What would he need with ladies' trinkets, except to buy them for women with expensive tastes? However those jewels found their way into Albert's rooms, I can't believe he would have taken them. He was... I mean, he could be...' He paused, evidently looking for the courage to come out with something damning. 'What I mean is that he could be an arrogant brute, but he was no thief.'

'So why was he there?'

Renwick gave me a mournful little smile.

'Remarkable that it has not occurred to you. Particularly since he felt you were such a threat, but perhaps his level of ambition was so foreign to you that you couldn't see it. I suspect if I were to ask the others sat around the table that evening, few of them would have missed the fact that he was there for Miss Cleveley.'

'Agnes? What has she got to do with it?' I knew, of course, but rather stupidly I needed it spelling out. Renwick acknowledged my obtuseness with an impatient sigh.

'Albert asked me to arrange an invitation to Halsingham's party so he could contrive an introduction to Miss Agnes Cleveley. He had identified her as what he regarded to be a suitable match – being a younger daughter of a prestigious family – but he needed an excuse to begin calling upon her. The weekend at Halsingham House was to provide just such a thing. That's why he was there. I don't know why he was found with Lady Halsingham's jewels, but you can be sure he didn't take them. His mind was firmly fixed on a different prize.'

So there it was. Grieve was not a thief, nor was he a murderer. I thought back to how reluctant Agnes had been to believe in his guilt. Had she discerned his purpose all along but been too modest to reveal it? I felt oddly sad for him. Had he genuinely felt affection for her, I wondered? Or had he just been seduced by the ways in which her personality and status could enhance his own? Whatever the case, there was no crime in any of it.

There was another consideration too, which was that if the jewels had been found in Grieve's rooms then some outside force must have put them there, making his death begin to look increasingly like murder. Someone had tried to make him appear responsible for the theft and perhaps even George's killing, and at the back of my mind was the uncomfortable fact that Albert Grieve's demise had coincided with Henrietta's return to London.

I had learned what I needed to from Rowland Renwick, but one thing still troubled me.

'Tell me, why did you do it?' I asked, screwing the end of my cigarette out in the embossed silver ashtray.

'Do what, Catcliffe?' He looked alarmed. 'Those jewels had nothing to do with me.'

'Not the jewels. Why did you do what Grieve asked of you? Agree to talk to Halsingham on his behalf, I mean – get him an invitation? He was a beast to you across the table that night, doing you down in front of the ladies at every opportunity. I didn't even realise you were friends.'

'We weren't.'

'Which makes me even more curious about why you would do him a favour.'

'I've had it in my power to do him favours from time to time over the years. When I can, I do, that's all.'

'But why?'

Renwick looked at me guiltily, saying nothing.

'What is it, Renwick? What did he have over you?'

He took a deep breath, as if hoping I might go away in the meantime, then in hushed tones he began.

'We were up at Oxford together, at Keble. They were... lively days.'

'And?'

'And one night, when I had been unforgivably immoderate in my indulgence of wine and brandy...'

'Yes?' I felt sure he was on the verge of recounting some chaste yet mortifying homosexual misunderstanding.

'...I ended up... with a lady of the night!' he gabbled, mortified.

A good deal of my brandy went down the wrong way, and I found myself racked by a fit of coughing.

'You had your way with a prostitute, Renwick?' I gasped through my tears.

'Quiet, please!' he urged. 'And I didn't "have my way" with her. If you must know, I fell insensible very early on in the proceedings.'

I swallowed hard and wiped my eyes.

'You mean to say,' I hissed, 'that Albert Grieve has been blackmailing you for the better part of a decade because you hired a prostitute once when you were at Oxford, then fell asleep before you got anywhere?'

'I beg of you, the shame is too great.'

'Renwick, you are the noblest fellow at Woodville's.' I drained my glass and stood up. 'Back to your baccarat table with you. I'm tired, and I've followed this investigation just about as far as I care to. I'm going home.'

....

Back in my rooms, I was on the point of taking myself to bed, when my doorbell jangled. After descending the stairs – for Edie refused stridently to answer the bell at night, reasoning that only those of the most villainous sort made house calls at such an hour – I opened the street door to the most unexpected and unwelcome sight of Inspector Oughton, a man who I had hoped I might never see again. His expression was sombre, and he was not smoking, both of which alarmed me. Behind him, a stiff-looking constable peered disinterestedly at the rolls of fabric in the draper's window.

'Mr Catcliffe, I'm sorry to disturb you at this time of night,' he grunted. 'But we think we've found Lady Halsingham. Would you be so kind as to come with us?'

I must have appeared as confused as I felt, for he added brusquely, 'Someone needs to identify the body, and we would rather not ask the sister, if it's all the same to you.'

TWENTY-FOUR

— • —

W hoever had killed Henrietta had gone to little trouble to conceal the crime. The young man – for so she had appeared – had been in a busy public house just north of the Strand, in that shady hinterland of theatres, brothels and boozers that never quite seemed to be dragged up by the smarter districts that bordered it. No-one could remember quite what time the youth had arrived, or who he had been sitting with, but one or two punters recalled seeing his face at some point or other during the evening.

Henrietta had been discovered at closing time in the deserted yard behind the inn – a patch of waste ground where the proprietor kept decaying old furniture, empty beer barrels and various other oddments – and it was as she had fallen that she was presented to me for identification. She lay on her back, her overcoat still bearing traces of Limehouse mud down one flank, and with her half-open razor lying a couple of yards from the body. The drizzle hung heavy in the night air, and she was soaked through, her short hair snaking in dank, wet strings across her cheek. Some more sensitive soul – later revealed to have been the publican – had pulled the coat closed across her. Even in the frozen dead of winter, there was still the distinct smell of sewage characteristic of the area, and in combination with the pungent dark

Virginia from Oughton's pipe, this mercifully concealed from me any odour of blood, though I could plainly see that the coat was saturated with it. Henrietta's head was thrown back, a handkerchief stuffed in her open mouth, her eyes staring. It was not a dignified end for a society lady so far from home, and above my powerful nausea I felt overwhelming sadness. Whatever terrible things she had or had not done, she had merited better than this.

'Is it her, then? The Bloody Baroness?' asked Oughton quietly. 'Even those of us as have met her can't swear to it.'

It was true that Henrietta did not look herself, and I knelt down next to her to get a better view. In an inexplicable flash of morbid curiosity, I could not resist reaching out and touching the clammy skin of her forehead. It felt more like putty than flesh, and I withdrew my finger sharply. I had struggled to recognise her the previous week, and the severe cut of her hair had changed the shape of her face, yet even in the ghastly rictus there remained enough of Henrietta. I found myself transfixed by her odd stare. After a few moments I nodded and rose.

'It's her. What happened to her?'

'Stabbed. A lot. Six or seven times, all in the heart and lungs, by the look of it. Must have just stuffed the hanky in her mouth to keep her quiet while she bled out. It wouldn't have taken long. Seems as if she tried to defend herself, but she didn't stand a chance.' He poked a broken stoneware pint mug with the toe of his boot. 'Landlord found her back here, sharp enough to realise he was looking at the body of a woman rather than a man. That's how we got to her so quickly. We knew we were looking for a principal boy with a straight razor, then this came in. Looks like Burlington Bertie has taken his last little supper at the Savoy, eh?'

No doubt he considered himself rather witty with his reference to Vesta Tilley's celebrated drag act. I thought it ghoulish.

'No-one heard anything?'

'Not a thing. It's a busy pub, and no-one comes out here until they dump the empty bottles at the end of the evening.' I felt sick as I considered that the poor woman in front of me had met her death with help only a matter of feet away. I could not help glancing back at her wide eyes.

Oughton steered me back into the half-empty public house, where his officers had finished taking statements and were sitting around in the warm, waiting to remove the body. He sat me down at a table.

'I'm going to bring Dukanwalla in,' he said abruptly.

'Duke? Why?'

'Lady cut him up, so he cut her back. With his connections it wouldn't have taken him long to find her if he wanted to.'

'Duke's a bit shady but he's no cold-blooded murderer.' I realised as I spoke that I did not know this for a fact. 'And his business is all over in the east. I'll stake you anything he's got a dozen people who'll swear they've seen him in Limehouse tonight.'

Oughton shook his head. 'Doesn't matter. He could just have easily sent someone else to do the job for him. I've been making some enquiries of my own since you first came to me with his information. Seems like Dukanwalla has all the wrong connections. He's a career criminal, Mr Catcliffe. Not to be trusted. And his sort aren't the forgiving kind – it's not in their nature.'

'Criminals, you mean?'

'Indians. I told you, I know the type. Lady Halsingham knifed him, and he's returned the favour. That's the way they do it. "An eye for an eye", isn't that what they say?'

Duke's progress in tracking Henrietta had embarrassed the inspector, and he was not about to let an opportunity for retribution slip away.

'But can you not see, man?' I snapped back, staggered by his obtuseness. 'Whoever did this was connected to Lord Halsingham's murder. I don't know how, but they must have been. Lady Halsingham knew something that was keeping her on the run, and now someone's silenced her for good. It proves there was more to it!'

'Oh, come now, Mr Catcliffe! If someone wanted to get rid of her, why go to all the trouble of shipping her off to Calais with the lad then bringing her back in secret? They could have just done for her the same morning she escaped from the clinic. I'll tell you what's happened: lady kills her husband, then enlists help somehow to get herself out of Rochester's guesthouse; same bloke spirits her and the boy out of the country; she hands the boy off to some trusted friend in Calais, then returns in disguise herself.'

'Why?'

'Oh, who knows why, for God's sake? Just look at her! She was prancing around in men's clothes. Maybe she just fancied the thrill of it.'

'Inspector, you surprise me.'

'You just watch yourself. Come up with a better solution and I'll listen. Actually, come to think of it, don't, and I won't. Go home.'

'I can't. I must go immediately to Miss Cleveley's house and tell her what's happened.'

'Must you indeed? Well there's no need. I'm going there now myself, and it's best if you don't join me. You can stop round in the morning, offer the lady a comforting shoulder to cry on. I'm sure you'll enjoy that.'

I resented his insinuation, and I pleaded with him to let me speak with Agnes alone first. I didn't know what I would say, but I knew no decent friend would let a stranger deliver news like this. However, the inspector's patience with me, ever a brief candle, had well and truly expired, and I was escorted once more back to my own residence by a constable.

....

I did at least follow Oughton's suggestion of calling upon Agnes first thing the following morning, as early as could possibly be considered decent. For in the spirit of honesty I had two urgent admissions to make.

I had expected to find her in a condition of some considerable hysteria at the tidings conveyed to her during the night, but in truth I can't think why, for her past conduct had given me no cause to. Probably I had enjoyed too many novels and operas and was trying to shoehorn Agnes into one. If anything, in the aftermath of Lord Halsingham's murder, Agnes had manifested an odd appearance of disorientated detachment, and it was in this state that I discovered her on the morning after Henrietta's murder. I sensed also that she was keen to apportion blame, and that I might find myself in the firing line if I wasn't careful.

Upon my arrival, I found Agnes standing in her drawing room, and she didn't sit, as if she expected our encounter to be a brief one. She had made little attempt to mask her grief or her fatigue, and she wore an ostentatious black mourning dress with jet buttons and a great deal of crape about it. It appeared old-fashioned and rather ill-fitting, and the crape was distinctly wilted. Seeing me observe this, she permitted herself just the faintest shade of a wan smile.

'It's rude to stare, but if you must know, I find I possess no appropriate mourning clothes. The items I was wearing out of deference to poor George were not nearly formal enough for one so close as a sister. My maid, Eve, has gone to Robinson's on Regent Street to find something better, but in the meantime this dress was all we could unearth upstairs. I think my mother left it here after Granny died. Don't get too close – I'm bristling with pins.'

'If only you'd been born a man. A gentleman of our era always looks ready for a funeral.' I realised as soon as I had spoken how untimely she would find quips about wearing male attire, so I pressed on with haste.

'Agnes, before we say anything else to each other, I've got to tell you something without delay. I pray only that you'll hear me out before you question or doubt me.'

She nodded coldly.

'Very well. Then let me say to start with that I'm convinced the woman I saw, both last night and last week, was not your sister...'

She interrupted me instantly, as I had known she would.

'Harry, please. What are you doing? I know you've got a good heart, but can't you see how... appalling it is to come out with something like that? It was George's double you encountered last week, not Henrietta's. To offer such mad hope when none exists is simply the cruellest.'

Her voice was steady, belying the gloss on her eyes.

'Agnes,' I ploughed on, 'listen to me. There's no lie in this. Believe me, I realise how unlikely it sounds, but it's the truth. I knew something wasn't right the moment I saw that woman step off the gangway of the *Jeanne*, but it wasn't until last night that I had the opportunity to see the wretched girl up close. Her eyes, Agnes – they were brown, like yours. Henrietta's are blue.'

This time she was silent, and I could see her trying to wrestle with the implications of my words. When she spoke, it was with the most inevitable of questions.

'Harry, are you absolutely sure? The light...'

'...Was enough to tell. They were brown, I'm telling you. Eyes don't change colour, do they?'

'If you're playing some sort of game...'

'Why would I do that?'

'...It will be more than I can bear. I will never see or speak to you ever again.'

'I promise. I'll promise on whatever you want me to. I'm certain, Agnes.'

Before I knew what was happening, Agnes stepped suddenly forward, wrapped her arms around me and sank her face into my shirt front. She didn't shake or cry as my operatic sensibilities would have preferred her to, just clung on and breathed slowly in and out. Close up her dress smelled of mildew. I stood there stupidly like a scarecrow, arms sticking out to the sides. A curl of hair tickled my chin and I smoothed it down then left my hand there.

In the street outside, a carriage clacked by. Agnes stepped back, smoothed her dress, and held my gaze for a moment. And then it passed, and we did not refer to it again.

'But if you truly thought this,' she asked quietly, 'then why didn't you tell the inspector?'

'I've been turning it over all night. Don't you see? If this woman wasn't Henrietta, but was somehow connected with her, then it changes everything. Quite how, I don't understand yet, and I don't even know whether the murderer was after the impostor or the real Henrietta... but if it's the latter then keeping the victim's real identity a secret might just keep your sister alive.

'You know Inspector Oughton – he's shrewd enough in some ways, but he doesn't have any imagination, and his prejudices blind him. If he suspects that this woman isn't your sister then he'll just cry deviancy and close the case. He won't use this clue the way we will.'

She sat, now, finally. A heavy slump into the chair, immediately followed by a hiss of discomfort and an adjustment of the pinning round the back of her skirts. I followed suit, my heart thumping ferociously with nerves. Agnes leaned forward and rested her head in her hands. I couldn't tell whether it was thought, indecision or grief. Finally, she looked up at me, her face drawn but not unfriendly.

'I'm going to believe you, Harry. Because I want so desperately to, and because I don't think even you would be such an idiot as to lie about this.

'If you're telling the truth, though, then there are so many new questions that I don't know where to start. This woman's presence in London can't be a coincidence, especially since she ran from you without provocation. But which Henrietta was where? Was it the impostor who left London on the *Tyne Lass*, or my sister? I can't believe a double could have fooled Dr Rochester – so it must have been

Henrietta who broke out of the hospital. And I'm certain it was really her that we discovered in bed on that terrible night...'

'But was it really her who walked past us in the corridor?' I broke in, unwilling in my vanity to let her be first in voicing the most intriguing question of all.

'I don't know. In the darkness I certainly couldn't vouch for the colour of her eyes. She was so altered in attitude... knowing what we know now, it couldn't have been her, could it? Were there any other differences?'

'I fancied that the murdered woman's face was a trifle rounder than Henrietta's, though it might just have been the way her hair was cropped.' Then, because I could already see where Agnes's mind was running, I felt bound to add, 'Please, Agnes, don't jump to conclusions just yet. I'm as keen as you are to clear Henrietta, but we have to go looking for the actual truth, not the one we want to find. Remember that the deaths of two men, and now this woman, are bound up in this business. They deserve justice as much as your sister does.'

'Surely you cannot say that of this impostor? It seems beyond doubt that she was involved in it all, and perhaps she has got her just deserts?'

'You would not say that if you had seen her, Agnes,' I replied with a hint of sharpness. She looked at me, and I saw remorse pass across her face as she realised the hardness of her words.

'I'm sorry, Harry. That was vile of me. I find myself so frightfully at sixes and sevens this morning. I hope you won't blame me for it.'

A thought suddenly occurred to her.

'Mr Dukanwalla! Our first impulse must be to protect our allies. I shall head at once to Inspector Oughton to plead his innocence. I daresay it will sound better coming from me than you.'

'I daresay it would. That said, I'm hoping most fervently that Dawoojee hasn't yet found himself in the inspector's clutches.'

Agnes looked at me with surprise.

'And why might you think that? Have you found it in you to actively interfere with the business of Scotland Yard, Harry?'

'I have. And perhaps it was a bad idea, but it's done now. That's why I didn't come directly to you last night. Believe me, Agnes, I would have spared you these hours of despair, but I couldn't be in two places at once – and Dawoojee's liberty had to come first. I hope you won't hold it against me?' A remark flippantly made, but earnestly meant.

'After Oughton's constable dropped me home and went on his way, I headed straight out again and took a late-night cab to Jabez Potter's lodgings in Vauxhall. I'd have gone to the Saracen's Head myself, but I don't exactly blend in over in Limehouse. If Oughton and his officers had discovered me in the neighbourhood then I'd have ended up in a cell for meddling with police business, and I needed to be here this morning to talk to you.'

I recounted to Agnes how I had endured a stern dressing-down about the lateness of the hour from Potter's landlady – a frightening old crone in an unravelling woollen bed jacket – before her tenant himself had descended groggily from his room and sent her back to bed with uncharacteristic gentleness. While the driver waited, I explained quickly how matters stood, then put both the cab and all the money I had on my person at Potter's disposal. As the cab driver hopped back up and prepared to pull away, Jabez had turned to me from where he sat in the hansom.

'Suppose this means you're back in it then?'

'I suppose it does.'

'Good lad.'

'In this exact moment, Jabez, you look almost friendly.'

'Just a mask,' and he shot me a grin that was pure malice.

The little man dashed off in his cab, and I was left with empty pockets and a long walk home from Vauxhall to Great Portland Street.

'You must promise me, Agnes, that you won't breathe a word of what has passed between us to another soul until I can work out what to do next.'

'But what of my mother and father? Surely you wouldn't put them through the anguish of believing their oldest daughter murdered under such horrendous circumstances? Not when it's in your power to spare them that?'

'All right. I can't argue with you on that score. But just them, no-one else. And please, they can't tell anyone, however much they feel compelled to. Can you impress that upon them?'

'I'll make them understand, I promise. But what about Robert? I expect him within the hour, and I'm sure he will want to do something for Mr Dukanwalla. They haven't met yet, but he will surely not be insensible to the plight of a man who has helped us so much. And knowing that he loved Henrietta once, wouldn't it be a sort of cruelty to have him believe in her death when she may yet be alive?'

'No-one else, not even Robert. Please, Agnes,' I entreated her. 'Duke may be innocent, but my own crime is real. I've helped a wanted man escape, and Oughton is a suspicious old bird. The more people know the truth, the more likely I am to end up at His Majesty's pleasure.'

She gave in reluctantly, which was a great relief to me – since there was more bravado in my version of events than I cared to admit. In truth, it had been a long and almost sleepless night, and fatigue amplified my confused state of nervousness and guilt. I had obstructed the police, and my fear about this mingled with the nagging knowledge that it was through my poor decisions that Dawoojee Dukanwalla found himself under suspicion of murder.

I had undertaken my dead-of-night mission to Jabez Potter without, I think, any clear notion of whether Dukanwalla might indeed have perpetrated the terrible crime in the pub yard, but my long walk home had given me plenty of time to ponder it. I am not the best judge of character, but in Duke's case I felt fairly confident that he was innocent.

He was thoroughly crooked, certainly, and I knew that the gregarious landlord holding forth across the table at the Saracen's Head was only one aspect of a man who had risen high and fast in a dangerous world. I knew him to be a killer – Liza had told me as much – but I did not believe him to be a fool. It was inconceivable to me that such a canny fellow would be rash enough to risk life and liberty by taking such savage revenge upon a stranger who had, in truth, injured him only in self-defence. His innocence would vindicate my own more modest crimes, and so I clung to it in my confusion.

TWENTY-FIVE

—•—

I have never believed in fate. There is a sense of hopelessness in the concept which frightens me. Luck, however, is a different matter, even if the distinction between the two is just a question of semantics. Luck always feels to me like a prevailing wind, buffeting you around as you sit at the tiller of a dinghy on open water. Depending on the direction of the wind, there are certain courses upon which it is very difficult to sail, and others which are much easier and faster – though if a fellow is bloody-minded enough then there is nothing to stop him tacking laboriously back and forth, expending a great deal of effort to make very slow progress into a gusty headwind.

Thus far, our amateurish investigations into Lord Halsingham's murder had belonged decidedly in this latter category of journey. I felt like we had expended a great deal of legwork to accomplish very little. But on that grisly December night of spilled blood, the wind had shifted stealthily to our back, and it now began to howl and fill our sails, taking us rather by surprise and driving us forward at breakneck speed onto a squally sea.

The harbinger of this storm came, appropriately enough, in the form of a fury from the old world, who marched into Agnes Cleveley's drawing room as we were considering our next step, swore at me in

Italian, and struck me hard about the head, to the alarm of Drew, who had not yet finished announcing her.

There was a long silence, as Lucilla Fornasini turned from me to Agnes, and the two women regarded each other with a modicum of surprise. For neither had expected to see the other attired in black crape. When they spoke, it was at once.

'Mrs Fornasini...'

'Miss Cleveley...'

'...this is most irregular...'

'...forgive me...'

'...forgive me...'

'...your dress...'

'...Mrs Fornasini, please...'

'...Who has died? I demand to know!'

Agnes motioned to a chair.

'Please, Mrs Fornasini. If you will sit, and refrain from hitting Mr Catcliffe again – tempting as it may be sometimes – perhaps you might explain yourself.' Her tone was gentle, and the fire in Lucilla's eyes seemed to abate somewhat as she sat. My cheeks burned, both with the force of her blow and with embarrassment. Agnes turned to her footman.

'Thank you, Drew, that will be all. Please close the door and see that we aren't disturbed.'

He withdrew, and as the door clicked closed, Lucilla turned to me and glared.

'I knew you were bad news for us. I knew it the moment you came into our house, but my Frank thought he knew best. He was always so confident – always thought he could sort everything out. Well he couldn't, and now he is dead, and you are to blame.'

A tear rolled down her cheek, but her teeth were gritted and her barely contained rage was marvellous to behold. I decided that if I opened my mouth it might be the straw that broke the camel's back, especially if I opened it to ask why she was referring to her husband as Frank. I remained silent, allowing Agnes to speak for me.

'I'm so terribly sorry to hear of your husband's death, Mrs Fornasini – we both are – but you must believe me that this is the first we've heard of it. You find me in mourning at the loss of my elder sister, Henrietta, who was killed last night in the most distressing of circumstances. Terrible events have befallen us both, and perhaps we can deal gently with one another.'

She made no mention, of course, of the fact that an impostor had been murdered in place of her sister, but she was a fine actress, and she presented the very picture of restrained English grief. Lucilla, however, was an altogether different case. She wept now without reserve, and there was something rather noble in the way she let the tide of despair well up within her, as if it were no less than her husband had deserved.

Mutely I proffered her a handkerchief, and she took it without looking at me. When the wave of sadness had passed, she raised her red eyes to Agnes, and spoke.

'I am sorry to hear of your sister. It must be terrible for you, and you have my sympathy. But you are wrong about your part in Frank's death. The two of you came round, asking all those questions with your angry little man, and days later my husband was dead. Murdered last night as he returned from the theatre. We found him on the front steps, his key in his hand and his… his throat cut. The police say it was a robbery, but I cannot believe it.'

'I assure you, Mrs Fornasini,' began Agnes, perceiving the widow's inference, 'our acquaintance Mr Potter is many things, but he is not a murderer, and he had no reason to go near your husband again. Giovanni's part – Frank's, I mean – in the matter we were investigating was a small one, and he had told us all he knew.'

'No, he had not,' said Lucilla, sighing. 'My husband's attitude to truth was always flexible – it was what made his tales on the stage so convincing – but I have always been able to see when he is telling lies. When you left that night, I asked him if the matter was at an end. He said that it was, and I knew right then that it was not. He was nervous in the days that followed, preoccupied in his mind, checking out of the windows as if it were a compulsion. The things you asked him, they must have driven him to put himself in danger, to try and resolve the matter by himself. You and your friends may not have committed the crime, but whatever your business with him was, it killed him.'

How could either of us respond to that? For unless it were the most extraordinary coincidence, we could see that the woman must be right. She had spent first her anger and then her tears, and now she appeared merely drained. She rose stiffly.

'There is nothing more to say. My poor Frank is gone. Know that whether or not his murderer is found, you will always hold a share of the blame. You will carry it with you until your dying day.'

At that, she left, leaving behind her a faint fragrance of patchouli and a crushing sense of remorse. As we heard the front door close, Agnes hid her face. Apparently her stoicism could withstand every emotion except guilt. I felt much the same way.

....

I was applying myself rather half-heartedly to a late lunch of a sandwich and a pint in the saloon bar at the White Bear when Jabez Potter plumped himself down heavily on the stool across the table. His exaggerated sense of weariness mirrored my own inward exhaustion, and notwithstanding the busy night which he had undoubtedly spent, his attitude filled me with dread. He peered into my expectant face for a few moments, then leaned forward, placed his chin on his fist and broke into a wide grin.

'The bird is on the wing, mate.'

I closed my eyes with relief. Dukanwalla was not in Oughton's hands – at least not yet. Potter slid across what remained of the money I had given him the previous evening, and continued: 'Of course, it was all a bit of a rush. I only got to the Saracen's ten minutes before the police did, but as luck would have it, Duke was in the pub doing a bit of after-hours business with some Irish lads. By the time I'd told him and Liza what'd gone on, the coppers were banging on the front door. Liza took her time letting 'em in and the Donegal boys made a right old racket while Duke and I slunk out through a connecting door into the next building. They'd covered the back route out of the pub, but we came out on the next lane across. Bolted round the corner and up Three Colts Street before they had a chance to close off the area.'

He reached over and took a swig of my beer.

'Duke's hiding out with someone he trusts. Some old widow whose husband he did a good turn for back in the day. There's a copper watching my place, but I reckon it's more of a hopeful punt than anything else. So long as that cabbie who dropped me off doesn't get wind of what went on and decide to squeal – and he'd be a fool to, after what we paid him – they've got nothing to connect me to Duke being on the run.'

Potter could be a gruff soul, but he was a good friend, and I could tell he was relieved at Dukanwalla's successful flight. Reassuring as it was, however, it was only a temporary solution to the problem. Dawoojee could not stay concealed forever, and unless we could prove in the meantime that he had not been responsible for the murder of Lady Halsingham's double, then the fact that he had deliberately evaded the police would make him appear guilty as sin.

Potter refilled my pint jug and furnished himself with a drink, as I set out all those developments with which I had not yet had the opportunity to regale him. The haste of the previous evening had prevented me from relaying my conversation with Rowland Renwick, and I continued by recounting my visit to Agnes that morning, and our startling encounter with Lucilla Fornasini. There was no love lost between Jabez Potter and Giovanni Fornasini, but all the same he appeared sorry at the news, and at the part he himself might have played in the showman's demise.

'He was a pompous bugger,' Potter grunted, 'but no-one deserves to run into a blade like that. Specially not so close to their own front door.'

'Someone is tying up loose ends, Jabez.'

'Suppose they are. Who's next then?'

I permitted myself an uneasy smile as I pushed a piece of paper across the table to him.

'I am.'

Mr Catcliffe,

The woman killed last night was not me, but one who looked like me. I cannot write more here, but please meet me tonight, seven o'clock sharp, at 23 Kirkcald Gardens, Somers Town. The house appears empty, but the door will be unlocked. I will explain everything. Come alone, for my sake. Please, I beg of you, above all do not breathe a word of this to my sister. However distraught she is at the present moment, the truth would be infinitely harder for her to bear.

Yours,

H

Lady Halsingham. Back from the dead. A boy had delivered the note to my residence just a few minutes before I left to meet Jabez. Edie had answered the door, and the lad had made himself scarce by the time I realised the letter's contents.

I will admit that in those first moments after reading it I had been almost jubilant at the thought of finally getting to the bottom of it all. But then it had occurred to me that if something seemed too good to be true then it usually was. Though ineffectual and incompetent, I was nonetheless at the centre of our investigation into the deaths of Lord Halsingham and Matthew Grayling. Both Agnes and Jabez, in their different ways, lacked the connections and the uncertain social standing necessary to flit between worlds as I did, and if I were to meet an untimely end in an abandoned house in Somers Town, it would mark an end to the connection between two separate killings.

And then there was the very fact that such a note should have found its way to me at all. Henrietta barely knew me, and it would take a remarkably well-informed fugitive to have discovered that I was taking any active interest in her disappearance. Perhaps through monitoring my visits to her sister at the Cleveley family residence in South Kensington, she might have construed some attachment to Agnes, but it was almost inconceivable that this would be enough for her to adopt me as a confidante.

No, a trap it had to be. And I had not yet voiced it to Agnes, but I had a distinct idea about who was cleaning up in the aftermath of the Halsingham affair. I just did not know why.

'All right then, smart bastard,' muttered Jabez through his pipe smoke. 'Out with it.'

'Think about it, Jabez. Who knew we had met with Fornasini? Aside from us, his wife and his maid?'

'Well, you told that inspector.'

'And the valet. I told the valet.'

'But you told the valet because you said you could trust him. You reckoned it was the butler fitted the description of the man who went to Fornasini in the first place.'

'No, I thought that the description Fornasini gave did not match Brown, the valet. Then we shoehorned Inman, the butler, into the role instead. But that was our mistake, you see? We let ourselves believe just because Fornasini was finally telling us something, that what he was telling us was the truth.'

Realisation crept across Potter's stubbly features.

'The bugger. He was keeping his end of the deal after all – throwing us off the scent by giving us the wrong description.'

'Apparently he was a man of his word when you greased his palm. Except then I went straight to Brown and told him everything Fornasini had told us.'

I felt rather foolish. Not only that, but after Lucilla's tirade earlier that morning I had the horrible feeling that I had directly brought about Fornasini's demise.

'He realised we were onto Fornasini, and that he might cave sooner or later. So he dealt with him. It can only have been Brown.'

'It could have been the inspector, though I can't see why.'

'No. Fornasini was killed late last night on his way home from the theatre. By then Inspector Oughton was investigating the death in the pub. Besides, Oughton's a blinkered imbecile, but he's not a killer and he doesn't have any connection to the family.'

'Brown's hardly a killer either. He's a valet. Cufflinks and starched collars.'

'I forget you haven't met him. Brown was a soldier. Don't you remember me saying in the car on the way back from Fornasini's? Rhodesian Police.'

Potter nodded in considered approval.

'Takes a leap of imagination, all that, but then you're an imaginative lad. Chances are you'll get your head popped open for it one of these days. So what will you do, then?'

It was precisely this question which had been spoiling my appetite. I knew of course that it was silly and suicidal to attend a meeting which was almost certainly a trap, but I had no other cards to play. Together we had followed each line of enquiry to its end: Fornasini was dead; Lady Halsingham's impersonator was dead; Grieve was a fit-up if ever there was; Oughton's investigation had turned up nothing, and Robert Edlington could not confirm Grayling's presence out in Surrey – a fact which meant there were no more clues to be gained from the direction of Halsingham House.

Nor could the matter now simply be abandoned. The boy was still missing, Dawoojee was on the run, and there was no guarantee that the murders would stop with me. Things had gone too far. I knew there was no other option than to turn up in Somers Town that evening and hope that curiosity did not always kill the cat.

As I sketched out my thoughts to Jabez, I found him uncharacteristically gentle. I think even he had a notion that such a course of action was not really in my nature.

'I have to ask, mate,' he said, when I had finished. 'Those... well, you know?' He jerked his forefinger up and down his cheek.

'The scars?'

'The scars.'

I gave him a wan smile.

'Unlike many of my fellows, who attended Oxford, Cambridge or the London colleges, I undertook my university schooling in Leipzig, where they followed the tradition of the "mensur".'

He looked baffled.

'German academic fencing – though thankfully the days of hot-blooded university students skewering each other in the open street over some petty insult are long past. It's a less hazardous affair these days. You fight with special basket-hilted swords, and thrusting is strictly forbidden. All the vulnerable parts like your arm, neck, nose, eyes and mouth are protected by masks and chainmail, so only your temples and cheeks are exposed to the cuts.'

'What's the point, then?'

'Mainly just to endure a couple of slashes with gritted teeth. Sounds ridiculous, I know. Over there a good set of mensur scars are the badge of a bold young rake. Practically a requirement if you want to be an army officer. Students find the flimsiest of excuses for a bout. In my own case, a good friend and I contrived to exchange a few tentative swipes while a gang of howling inebriates egged us on.'

'So that's why the marks are so clean and well-healed.'

'Try telling my mother that.'

He took a breath to speak, then paused for thought.

'Just to be clear, you've never in your life raised a weapon in anger?'

'I pointed a gun at you once.'

Jabez couldn't help the sly grin spreading across his face. 'Fair play, then,' he said. 'It's half two now, so we'll have to move quickly. Let's get to working out how you're going to survive this.'

TWENTY-SIX

—·—

Number 23 Kirkcald Gardens, Somers Town, was a wretched place. It was Christmas Eve, and though gas lamps shone warmly out through the curtains of the narrow terraced houses that lined the street, number 23 was dark. The fabric of the building seemed sound enough, but the paint on the door and railings was flaking off, and the faded curtains that hung in the dark windows were ancient and disintegrating, falling gently to ribbons that sat among the dust on the sills. There had formerly been a modest front garden, but the area was now choked with high, yellowed weeds, dense brambles, and rotting heaps of windblown leaves and newspapers.

Somewhere on a neighbouring street, a group of carol singers were abroad, but Kirkcald Gardens was deserted save for a single elderly Jew who nodded cautiously as he hurried past us, his coat pulled tightly around him against the chill.

I did my best to subdue the blaring crescendo of apprehension deep in my innards and climbed the steps to the front door, with Jabez at my heels. I had not asked him to accompany me, but he had insisted, and my resistance had not been particularly strenuous.

'This whole thing reeks,' he had reasoned. 'Only a total simpleton would have come alone, and whoever asked you here would know that.'

We had made other preparations too. I had sent a note to Agnes, telling her everything (except the address of the meeting, for I was not so foolish as to think she wouldn't leap straight in her car and put a stop to it), and Jabez had visited the Saracen's Head for a talk with Liza Dukanwalla. My little derringer sat comfortingly in my pocket, more like a lucky charm than a real weapon.

I pushed gingerly at the front door. For a moment I thought it might have been locked despite the promises of our mysterious correspondent, for it did not give under my hand, but the wood was merely swollen with damp and lack of use. At a firm shove with my shoulder, it swung open, revealing a dank hallway. In the parlour at the other end of the hall I could see a faint light. Anyone in the house must have heard me barging the door open, but we crept in spite of ourselves down the short passageway to the parlour entrance. The smell was of rot and mould, mice and paraffin.

Inside, a smoky lamp on the heavy kitchen bench threw a yellow light over the stained walls and the cold range. And seated at a table, as I had predicted, was Brown. He stood with a sort of deference that seemed entirely out of place in the circumstances, but was perhaps instinctive.

'Mr Catcliffe, sir. And Mr Potter, we haven't met, but I knew we would eventually.' His manner managed to be both respectful and unpleasant at the same time.

'If you would be so good as to place your weapons on the table here, then we can have a little talk.'

Jabez took a heavy military revolver from his coat pocket, but did not give it up.

'I don't think we need to be surrendering these, do we?'

Brown did not smile, but cleared his throat, and we were suddenly aware of footsteps on the stair. I spun round in alarm to see a man in shabby clothes standing between us and the front door. As I turned back, I saw that two more had entered the kitchen from the back passageway. All were armed.

'I have taken the precaution of hiring these three gentlemen. All former military men in need of a shilling or two and not altogether fussy about how they get it.' Brown gestured first towards Jabez's pistol, and then to the table. The little marine glanced steadily from one fellow to the next, sizing them up like livestock at market, before returning his attention to Brown.

'We're done either way?' my friend asked cautiously.

'That's it.'

'Well, how about I cut you a deal then? If it comes to shooting then you'll win, but some of you will get hurt along the way, maybe worse. And I'll make sure you personally get at least one bullet in you. But when all's said and done, I'm the sort who has to know. Will you swap us the truth for our guns?'

Brown shrugged.

'Fair enough. I'll give you three questions. That's the best offer you'll get.'

Jabez laid his revolver on the table sullenly and sat down on one of the two kitchen stools opposite Brown's chair.

'I'd rather take my chances,' I mumbled weakly.

Jabez smirked at me in what appeared to be a rare moment of genuine friendly affection.

'Good lad! Look at you! Probably a bit late to make a fighter of you though. Think about it, mate. This only ends one way for us, but we might as well take what we can get before the end. Else coming here was for nothing.'

His chin twitched fractionally upwards in a manner I had not seen before, and in that moment I saw what Jabez was. My friend didn't feel fear the same way I did. I was paralysed with fright at the abstract violence to come, but physical suffering was a known quantity to Jabez. He'd been beaten, cut, torn and sawn, and had emerged alive. It was simply death that scared him, and in this his fear was infinitely more acute than mine because he knew what it truly meant and had fought so much harder and longer to escape it.

When I still did not sit down, it was Brown who spoke.

'You have my word, Mr Catcliffe, you can ask me whatever questions you like. But first, that Remington from your pocket, on the table if you please. You forget that I have dressed you.'

I reluctantly obliged and seated myself. He too sat back down, while his three fellows remained standing, wordless.

'So what was Matthew doing at Halsingham House, then?' asked Jabez without preamble. Brown smiled at his directness.

'You're on the wrong track. He was making a mask for my wife, Frances. Hide her poor wrecked face. Gift from the Halsinghams.'

'Then why did you kill him?'

'He got to know something he shouldn't have.'

'That's not a complete answer,' I ventured cautiously.

Brown glanced at the indifferent countenances of his hired men. The money they would be paid to dispose of us represented the extent of their interest in the matter. For all they were concerned, we might have been discussing George Bernard Shaw's latest offering at the Royal Court Theatre.

'Fair enough – I suppose it can't hurt now.' He pulled his coat closer around him in the cold of the dead house.

'Grayling visited our cottage several times in the early spring, to take measurements for my wife's mask and carry out fittings. My duties at the house meant I could not always be present, but he was a gentle fellow, and Frances became confident enough to meet him without me. It seems they developed something of a rapport, and she told him things she should not have done. She didn't mean any harm by it. Tongue just ran away with her.

'I love my Frances dearly, but ours is not a conventional relationship. We are companions, but since her illness I have had to fulfil certain desires elsewhere. I wasn't lying when I told you before that Frances and I have no secrets. I've always been frank with her about my dealings with other women, and Halsingham House was no different.'

He let the sentence hang, daring us to use our third question, but I had no need, for I knew the name he would give us.

'George told me that Lady Halsingham's depressed spirits had improved noticeably in the early spring,' I said hastily, before Potter's impatience could get the better of him. 'He thought it was the promise of their holiday in France, but actually it more or less corresponds with your arrival at Halsingham House, Mr Brown.' He drummed his fingers on the table approvingly.

'It is not a difficult thing to understand,' I went on, thinking aloud. 'A neglected, sensitive woman trapped in a marriage she never cared for in the first place, far from her family and friends, and desperate for love. Then along comes the handsome soldier-servant with an easy smile and a confidential manner.'

'Don't forget that Henrietta was a very beautiful woman,' Brown interjected. It was odd to hear him use her Christian name when he was always so correct about his manner of address. 'And you shouldn't be fooled by that demure exterior. She knew exactly what she was doing. There was a time when I felt I might have made a terrible mistake getting involved with her – particularly when Frances let slip she had tattled about the affair to Grayling – but I think it's all going to work out well.'

Thinking aloud, I followed the events that were now emerging so clearly.

'You knew Grayling was a discreet man, but that he might feel compelled to tell the police about your relationship with Lady Halsingham in the event of her husband's murder. So before the latter could be accomplished, Grayling had to be disposed of.'

He nodded approvingly.

'It was much easier than I expected. You may recall my saying I was formerly assistant to a regimental surgeon in the Rhodesian Police. I frequently assisted him in the preparation of various medicines and became quite proficient myself. So, one afternoon while Lord Halsingham was out at the Lords, I drugged a bottle of brandy and took it to Grayling's workshop in Limehouse. I thanked him most graciously for his wonderful work on Frances's mask, and proposed a toast to his skill.'

Outwardly, Potter was impassive, yet I could sense the desperate ferocity boiling a fraction of an inch below his skin. I felt certain that when the time came to move, Jabez would be fastest off the mark.

'What I still don't understand,' I said slowly, 'is why anyone had to die at all. If you were in the habit of visiting Lady Halsingham – and furthermore of getting away with it – then you had nothing to gain from Halsingham's death. Moreover, you had a great deal to lose by it. Not just your mistress, but even perhaps your livelihood.'

'Why do you think it was done, sir? You must have some notion.' His tone was playful.

'Something to do with Henrietta's sleepwalking?' I ventured, tentatively. 'Did the risks become too great, I wonder? Did she begin to unnerve you? Did you fear her nocturnal exploits would lead her husband into her bedchamber at an inopportune moment? The night terrors only began after the affair. Did you worry that they were the outward signs of a guilty conscience – one that would lead her to confess everything to her husband if you did not act?'

'Is that your third question?'

'No,' I said hastily, and I paused. Did I want motive or mechanics?

'The blood,' I said finally. 'She may have been abroad in the house that night, but she didn't kill George. You did that. So how did Lady Halsingham end up in bed with his blood all over her?'

'Oh come on!' Brown railed at me, full of scorn. 'You have one last question and that's all you can think of? It wasn't sophisticated. I had the key that opened the adjoining door between her room and his. I let myself into his room, killed him in his sleep, then when she walked in I smeared the blood all over her. After that I made a quick escape back through her rooms and down the servants' staircase, same way I always got in and out after dark. By the time she gave you such a fright banging her bedroom door, I was already creeping back downstairs, ready to slip back to the cottage for a clean-up.'

'No. You couldn't have known she would come in. And even if she did, you would have woken her up when you put the blood on her. She would have known it was you.'

'Of course she knew it was me!' he cried, exasperated. 'She was awake the whole time! Are the two of you such imbeciles? I can understand the sister not wanting to believe it, but you should know better.'

I felt cold.

'She was in on it?'

'Finally! Put yourself in Henrietta's shoes. You hate your husband with a passion – a passion, by the way, which none but I saw – and every moment in his company reminds you of what your life could have been, but now is not. The sleepwalking started as a joke between the two of us. It was just a way to have a bit of fun at his expense after dark, but she started to get a taste for it. Before I knew what was going on, it had become a sort of addiction.

'She loved the business of tormenting him, and she was starting to get reckless about it, sneaking off to scratch at his door while I was still in bed. She thought she was showing me what a daredevil she was, but can you imagine if he had rushed in and found me there?

'She was out of control, and I realised I'd made a huge mistake getting involved with her. My only way out was to somehow remove both of them before the secret was exposed and it ruined me. Because rest assured, Mr Catcliffe, it would not have ruined them.'

He was right, of course. If Henrietta's affair had been exposed then Halsingham would have hushed it up and the marriage would have

275

endured, however unhappily. He was that sort of a fellow. But Brown would have been out on his ear without a hint of a reference.

'She was so filled with hate for him – and obsession with me – that she readily agreed to my plan to do him in, so long as I would be the one to carry out the actual deed. Can you imagine anyone agreeing to shoulder the entire responsibility for another's crime, simply through love? The woman was quite unhinged. I sold her this mad scheme that I would spirit her out of the country, and together with young Thomas we would run away and live happily ever after on the continent. There was enough in her jewellery box to give us a comfortable run for a good few years, and she let me take it without a moment's hesitation. It couldn't possibly have worked, of course, but she didn't know that. She'd never lived in the real world. She trusted me, and that was that.

'Once she'd been arrested, I was true to my word, as far as it went. I snuck into the Rochester Clinic – went in right through the front door in the small hours. They only keep a couple of nurses on during the night, and they spend most of their time huddled by the fire in the dispensary. Henrietta was drugged to her eyeballs when I found her, but I popped the window from the inside to make it look like she'd escaped on her own, and helped her out. Then I forced the back door of the Kelverton place and waited till she'd got enough strength back to go in and slip that pasty lad of hers out of the house. Came quietly as a mouse at first, but he started to ask a lot of questions once we were in the cab, so I got her to give him a bit of medicine to quieten him down. The idea was that we'd get them out of the country, then I'd go and join them in Calais when it all blew over. Then you cottoned on to her departure on that Geordie steamer, and I realised you and the sister were never going to let it lie without a body.'

'The lookalike.'

'Exactly. It's a pity I'm eventually going to have to do something about Henrietta, since I'm quite impressed she managed to track down quite such an excellent match so soon after getting off the boat at Calais. I gave her the name of a good man there – an old colleague from the Rhodesian Police – so perhaps she used him. I think the woman was an out-of-work governess or something. The resemblance wasn't perfect, but with a bit of misdirection it was close enough to convince the coppers, and that's what matters.

'She was paid handsomely to take the boat across and meet a man in a public house. My mate told her there was a bonus if she managed to avoid the police and some other men who might be looking out for her. Don't suppose she saw what was coming until the last moment.'

'I suppose you did that cocky rich lad too,' grunted Potter. 'And planted a few shiny bits to fool the inspector.'

'I suppose I did.'

'So what next, then?' I asked. Part of me genuinely wanted to know, but part of me also knew what must occur when Brown stopped talking.

'Well, there's the thing.' He looked a trifle regretful. 'The trouble is, for all her charms, Henrietta is a liability. She's the only one left who can get me into trouble – now that Fornasini's no longer around to identify me and you two gentlemen are soon to have played your parts – so I'm afraid she will have to go. I'll send word in the next couple of days to my former colleague in Calais, and he'll take care of it. Stick the boy in an orphanage or something – I'm not a complete savage. Then, finally, all will be well. Mr Grieve can take the blame for the gems, and they can pin the murder on Henrietta. Her own death can remain one of life's little mysteries, unless with luck they put it on the lascar, which I hear they might. I'll be working for my old friend Robert again, at least until I can find a decent excuse to take my jewels and set up somewhere warm with Frances, and no harm will have been done. At least not to me. And that, I think, is probably enough for you to be going on with.'

I thought for a moment.

'No. There are more questions that need answering. More things I don't understand.'

'Bad luck for you, Mr Catcliffe, sir. Consider yourself fortunate I told you anything. I offered you three questions and you've had more than I can count. And after all, I could have made up any old story. Perhaps I did. You'll never know.'

He was interrupted by a brisk, impatient hammering at the old front door. Brown glared angrily first at me and then at Potter.

'Who is this?' he snapped. 'Have you been foolish enough to walk someone else into your own grave with you?'

'I honestly don't know,' I replied truthfully, glancing across at Jabez. He looked similarly bewildered.

Wordlessly, Brown jutted his chin at the man in the corridor, who went to the front door and jerked it open. Our visitor followed him down the hallway with a strange clacking sound, and when they reached the kitchen, we saw in the lamplight the red-gold hair of Liza Dukanwalla. At her heel waddled Captain, the stately bull terrier, and it was his claws tapping on the mouldering floorboards that had been the origin of the odd noise. He was a grizzly looking beast, and I hoped no-one else in the room realised that he was about as dangerous as a dowager's Pomeranian.

'I've come for my husband,' she announced briskly. Brown looked confused, then turned to Potter with an expression of amusement.

'Is this your good lady, Mr Potter?' He looked her up and down in an appreciative manner. 'I must say, you've done rather well for yourself.'

Liza looked at him haughtily.

'This is certainly not his good lady, and you mind your manners, whoever you are. Sorry, Jabez, love. I've always been fond of you. And Mr Catcliffe, I've no quarrel with you – you seem decent enough. But whatever the both of you have got Duke into, I'm afraid I'm not letting him go down with you. I've my family to think of.'

She turned to Brown.

'I just want Duke. Whatever your business is with these two men, it doesn't concern him.'

Comprehension sprang into Brown's face.

'You're the Indian's woman! I'm very sorry, Mrs Dukanwalla, but you've made a terrible mistake. I had no interest in you, or your husband. If you hadn't turned up here, you would have been left well alone. But I can't now, I'm afraid.'

He sighed, not to signal remorse, but just to let us know that the conversation was at an end and the next part was about to begin.

'Worse luck for you,' he added, 'your husband isn't even here.'

'Yes he is,' said a voice from the darkness of the back passageway.

....

I find that when I try to remember the events immediately following, I am not afflicted by the same gaping blind spot that obscures my recollections of George's murdered body. Rather, my overview of what exactly happened – and when – is muddled by the vivid, minute detail of small things. Still wet paint, even all these years later.

I recall, for example, the first movement in the shadows that indicated Dawoojee's presence, and the stomach-wrenching thump and bright muzzle flash of his shotgun going off in the confined space. I can see Liza's face as she fired her concealed pistol upwards through her skirt pocket into the man next to her, contrasting with the panic in Brown's wide eyes as he realised how quickly his odds were lengthening. The tension that had hummed unbearably about the room exploded in a roar of gunfire and motion.

Potter's unlikely speed was as remarkable as ever, and as Brown snatched for my derringer where it lay on the table, the little marine ignored the firearms and launched himself savagely into the valet's long body, smashing both of them headlong into the kitchen range and overturning the table.

One of Brown's men was already gasping and dying on the slick floor, his companion emptying his revolver wildly as Duke's second barrel went wide, the shot whipping around the walls in a storm of rattling lead grains. I felt a sharp sting in my hand as I finally moved, long after everyone else, diving after my little pistol as it clattered across the floor. There was noise all around me, and as I came up with the weapon in my hand, Dukanwalla flew past me, blade out, towards the man still firing from the other end of the room. Before I could find my feet, I felt a finger hook inside my cheek and drag me backwards by my lower jaw. A brawny, bloodied arm closed roughly around my throat.

In front of me, Brown rose up, seized the other gun from the floor, and fired it mercilessly into Potter as he tried to get up. Despite being gripped from behind, my hands were still free, and I emptied both barrels of the Remington in Brown's direction. I can confirm that it is substantially more difficult to hold a steady aim in the chaos of conflict than it is when one is taking leisurely pot shots at a swede on a stick, but the range cannot have been above four feet. One bullet, at least, must have hit him, for he stumbled, and Potter was back on him, fierce and desperate. Behind me, there was a piercing scream, which for a terrible moment I thought might have been Liza Dukanwalla, until I realised it was coming from directly by my ear. The man holding me let go his grip, and to my surprise, I whirled round to see the geriatric pit dog latched firmly to his neck, worrying the flesh like a horrid giant rat. I could see my assailant was already injured by Liza's derringer, but as I fumbled in my pocket for two more of the little .41 rimfire cartridges, a deafening thud slammed through my head, and I fell, stunned. Black dots spattered in like spreading ink blots at the edge of my vision, and I thought I was going to faint, but they began to recede again, and I saw Brown staggering down the corridor and out of the front door.

I followed in a daze, pushing my way out of the grisly kitchen and shambling unsteadily down the hallway like a drunk. My face felt wet and I could taste blood and dirt. As I went, I pushed a cartridge into the breech of the Remington with shaking hands. I was slow, but Brown was slower, and as I came out of the front door, he was dragging himself laboriously along the wall at the front of the garden. He had lost his gun and was obviously badly hurt.

He tumbled out of the gate and fell headlong into the street with the finality of a man who had lost his legs and would not get them back. Rising to his knees, he looked up to find his way blocked by a smartly dressed man. For a moment, recognition sprang into his eyes, and he began to smile. A wide, dopey smile of relief and acceptance.

Afterwards I wondered if, in those closing moments of his life, he saw the face of his old commanding officer or that of the man he had murdered.

In Robert Edlington's hand was a blue-black revolver, and as I watched, Brown wrapped his shaking fingers around the barrel and pressed it to his forehead. For a moment, Robert hesitated, and I remembered Halsingham's words on that cold morning in the woods.

'I do believe my brother owed his life to Brown's actions...'

Then he fired, and stalked past me without a backward glance, close enough that I could see the tears streaking his cheek.

....

Two more shots barked out at the back of the house, then silence.

Without exchanging a word, I followed Robert shakily back into the hallway. After the commotion, all was suddenly very quiet.

The first thing I saw was Potter lying propped up against the range, gory and heavy-eyed. The second thing I saw was Dawoojee Dukan-walla. In a room full of bloodshed, he was, incredibly, completely unscathed, yet he was the saddest thing in it. A pistol lay discarded nearby, as he sat silently on the floor, his arms full of skirts and red hair. The old dog waited patiently by their side.

We never discovered who fired the shot that took Liza Dukanwalla. No-one remained breathing that could say, though at least I could be certain that it was not one of mine. We had misjudged the odds and it was unlikely that we would have survived without her intervention, but all the same, she should not have been there. I cursed our naivety. We had used her to set up a meeting with Duke, without ever considering that she might take matters into her own hands.

I could see now that Liza had watched the three of us discreetly as we had sat scheming in the White Bear. That she had followed us north into the quiet streets of Somers Town. She must have seen Duke part ways from us a couple of streets away from Kirkcald Gardens, slipping over the high wall into the maze of darkened back gardens as he made his way to the rear entrance of number 23. And somewhere along the way, Liza had decided that enough was enough.

Robert looked ashen and desperately sad, and in that moment there was an unmistakeable look of George – or even Thomas – about him. I wondered how he had found us. It could wait.

'I shall get help. Don't move, anyone,' he said, and rushed out.

I slumped miserably next to Potter. He turned his head weakly.

'You all right, mate?'

I felt my shirt sticking across my shoulders, soaked through with blood from my battered head. My hand throbbed where the piece of shot had caught it, and a dirty fingernail had raked the inside of my mouth. I could have come off a lot worse.

'I'm all right, Jabez. You?'

'Been better.' He gave a nasty, damp cough and gazed woozily across at Duke, still motionless and mute.

The dog shuffled and made an odd whistling noise.

TWENTY-SEVEN

—.—

Kirkcald Gardens was not the end of Jabez Potter. At half past nine on Christmas Eve, as I sat closeted with Inspector Oughton at New Scotland Yard, Robert Edlington called in a favour from a half-drunk surgeon, and remarkably Jabez survived the operating table. Infection took hold all the same, but his constitution was as unyielding as the rest of him, and after several weeks in a convalescent home in Epping, he was declared out of danger.

Oughton listened to my account of the violence in Somers Town silently and impassively, wreathed in the noxious bluish fumes of his evil-smelling pipe. Despite his expressionless exterior, he gave an impression of deep scepticism at my story, but it was a trick that had worn thin on me by now.

For my part, I no longer cared much for the truth of things. I genuinely had no idea how much of Brown's story had been fact, and his final words had been as good as an admission that some of it was fiction. So I mentioned only the affair and the associated murders of Matthew Grayling, Lord Halsingham and Albert Grieve. I omitted all mention of Henrietta's complicity in her husband's killing, and left Oughton to draw his own conclusions.

At any rate, he sent me home with the understanding that he was satisfied to draw a line under the case, loose ends and all. As far as he was concerned, only the whereabouts of young Thomas Edlington remained unresolved, and he undertook to contact his opposite number in Paris with the object of tracking the lad down.

'And if I find that you have been looking into his whereabouts yourself, Mr Catcliffe, then I promise you I'll finish what Mr Brown started in that empty house.' It must have been plain to him that any enthusiasm for detective work was quite out of me, but doubtless he felt no encounter between us was complete unless he had threatened me at least once.

As I sat shivering and aching in a hansom on the way home, a cloth clamped to my broken temple, I considered that somewhere, Henrietta and Thomas were still alive. She was possibly the last person living who knew the whole of what had happened at Halsingham House and why. As far as I was concerned, she could keep it, for the answer was not worth the lives lost in its pursuit.

....

That Christmas Day of 1907 I spent alone. After all that had occurred the previous evening, I could not face the prospect of festivities, even with my own family. Following breakfast and a good deal of fussing and prodding from an uncharacteristically sympathetic Edie, I presented my maid with a paper parcel containing some gloves and chocolate, and told her to take the rest of the day off. For my own part, I embraced a day of solitude. I put on my millwright's clothes and took a modest luncheon in a quiet corner of a working men's dining room where no-one gave me a second look, then retired to my rooms to stare absently into the fireplace with an open book unread in my lap, an untouched glass of brandy on the side table and an unlit cigar hanging in my limp fingers. My fine hat sat conspicuously on the side table, its brim split and stained.

I think I knew that I would not remain alone all day, despite my best efforts, and I answered my own front door late in the afternoon to find Agnes Cleveley standing there. She still wore her elaborate mourning black to keep up appearances, but the sadness in her eyes was genuine enough. I had attempted to clean myself up a little, but I had evidently not done a terribly good job. She spent a moment taking in my pale face, the bruising that was already beginning to creep across my forehead, the blood-crusted hair above my swollen ear, and my bandaged hand.

'May I come in, Harry?'

'Honestly, Agnes, I do not want to talk about it. Any of it. Not today.'

'And we don't have to. The questions can wait, although I've got such a lot of them. I just wanted to see if you were all right. Poor Harry – more scars for your collection.'

She reached up to touch my bandage with icy fingers. I flinched slightly, and she dropped them again.

'Are you terribly hurt?'

I made an effort to smile.

'Of course I'm not. My hat took the worst of it. I'm all right. I'm always all right. Poor Liza, and poor Duke. And things do not look good for Jabez.'

At that point I knew only that Potter had survived his surgery, but no more. As for Dukanwalla, he had said not a word, only relinquishing his hold on Liza's body when the police arrived to arrest him. He had gone meekly, but I understood from Oughton that they would not hold him long. They intended to place the murders of Matthew Grayling, Albert Grieve and both Lord and Lady Halsingham (for Oughton still believed the impostor lying in the pub yard in Soho to have been Henrietta herself) at Brown's door, and Dawoojee faced little more than a slap on the wrist for avoiding arrest. He would doubtless be home in Limehouse by now, and it would be a bleak Christmas in those rooms above the Saracen's Head.

'I don't suppose you'll believe me,' said Agnes, 'but I should be most upset if anything happened to Mr Potter. He is... well, he is what he is, but he has been a good friend to both of us. At least Robert turned up when he did.'

I had no heart to laud Robert Edlington just at that moment, despite his conspicuous gallantry in Somers Town, but I knew what she was trying to admit to, so I let her continue.

'I hope you won't hold it against me,' she went on. 'I contacted him the moment I got your letter, told him all that was occurring – including the bit about Henrietta not being dead – and asked him to do everything he could to find you as quickly as he could. I couldn't bear the thought that anything might happen to you, after all you have been through on my family's account and that of the Edlingtons. I saw Robert this morning, and he is desperately sad that he should have planted such a pernicious seed in that household. He blames himself for everything.'

'The blame isn't his,' I said, sighing. 'I don't hold it against you that you went to him. I'm glad you did it. And I didn't do all this for your family, or Robert's.'

'Why, then?'

'I have no idea,' I answered, truthfully. 'I think I just followed my imagination too far.'

I realised that we were still standing on the threshold, with the cold draught blowing up the stairs behind me.

'Can I give you a cup of tea? I'm afraid I've given my housekeeper the day off, but I'm a very modern man, and making tea is within my capabilities.'

It was a half-hearted invitation and she knew it. She smiled sadly.

'No, thank you, Harry. I can tell you want to be alone, and not to think about George or Henrietta or Matthew Grayling or Robert or me. As you say, not today. Besides, my mother and father are arriving from Kelverton tomorrow lunchtime. I've tried through my letters to explain to them in the strictest of confidence that the woman they have come to bury is not their daughter, but I'm going to have to steel myself for a thousand and one questions – and I don't have any answers.'

Agnes sniffed briskly and glanced over her shoulder at the elegant motor car waiting in the road behind her.

'I should go. You can demonstrate what a modern man you are another time. But I'm relieved to see that you're not too badly hurt, really I am.'

As she left, I had an uncomfortable sensation of having rejected a hand held out to me, however gently. All the same, I had spoken the truth, albeit a partial one.

You see, the reason I wished to put the case entirely out of mind was not simply the tragic loss of life of the previous evening, but the incomplete story that Brown had fed me. I knew, to my nagging dismay, that there was more to discover, and despite her best efforts to steer clear of the subject, something Agnes had said had started up the engine of my thoughts once again. Only now the unwilling jumble seemed to order itself without effort, and I saw what nerves, hot blood and distraction had henceforth blinded me to.

I closed the door, returned to my sitting room, and took a warming slurp of the brandy. It tasted sweet and silky. I discarded my Galsworthy novel, lit the cigar with the table lighter, and subsided loosely into my armchair, unwilling to admit, even to myself, that something had lifted my mood. What a cold creature I was becoming.

....

The week that followed – that empty period between Christmas and the New Year – was a dead time in more ways than one. In the space of a few days, they buried Lady Halsingham, Joseph Brown (for that indeed was his forename), Liza Dukanwalla and Giovanni Fornasini (or plain old Frank). I attended none of the ceremonies.

With Fornasini's end came that of the Tin Face Parade too. His performers vanished into quieter lives – perhaps with some degree of relief – and I daresay Sergeant McCarthy drank where he pleased from then on. A popular magician's act took over the top spot at the varieties, and when presented with a man who could drop white mice through a mincer then produce them whole again, audiences forgot all about Fornasini's much more real miracles of man and metal until the hospital ships started returning from the front a decade later.

Despite some unease around the matter, Henrietta was laid to rest in the graveyard at Halsingham village, though not in the same mausoleum as her husband, as was the usual custom. While the detail of Brown's confession had not been made public, a shadow lingered upon on her character, and there remained the unspoken but widely acknowledged supposition that somehow Henrietta had brought about the destruction of her own family. The murder was now pinned on another, but she would remain for all time the Bloody Baroness. Not that I suppose it mattered when all was said and done, but I could not help feeling a small, irrational flicker of relief that George was not sharing his eternal resting place with a stranger.

More controversially, Agnes told me that Brown, too, had finished up in the same churchyard. A brief and discreet ceremony had taken place at first light, and the murderer was in the ground before the first villagers emerged from their cottages for the morning.

'Poor Robert,' she said thoughtfully, as we sat in my sitting room, drinking the cup of tea I had promised her five days earlier. 'I gather he owed the wretched man his life from their days in Africa, but then he had to reckon that up against the murder of his own brother. In the end they buried him in an unmarked grave at the back of the churchyard. Robert was the only mourner.'

'His wife didn't make the trip from Tunbridge Wells, then?'

'She did not. Robert sent Inman to inform her of the terrible news – I don't suppose he felt he could face her himself, though of course he didn't exactly say as much. Apparently she was distraught, torn as Robert himself was between affection and horror. Her state of mind is, I gather, not the steadiest even without the added burden of such knowledge, and her uncle and aunt felt it best that she remained with them in Tunbridge Wells rather than making the trip to Halsingham.'

'Her uncle and aunt?'

'Indeed.' She looked perplexed. 'She has resided in their care since she left Brown's cottage on the Halsingham estate. Don't you remember?'

'Yes, of course, I recall now.'

'You know, I saw her once,' said Agnes. 'In May, not long after George and Henrietta returned from France. It was my last time at Halsingham before our awful weekend in November. It was a fine day and we went for a picnic on the hill with Thomas – the views out towards the Downs from there are quite wonderful. I've no idea where she was going, but she passed quite close to us. Thomas pointed her out. She wore a hat and veil, of course, but I could see her face all the same...'

She drew breath to describe it, then paused, perhaps considering how such a countenance could be sketched with sensitivity. I saved her the trouble.

'I've seen Mrs Brown too, Agnes – in the garden of her cottage, that weekend. I know the face and why you hesitate.'

'Odd that she chose not to wear Mr Grayling's mask when out-doors, do you not think?' she remarked. 'After all the time and effort it must have taken to fit it. Somehow it makes his death seem even more of a waste.'

If I appeared contemplative for a moment, her impatience was such that she did not notice.

'And now, Harry,' she began, leaning forward, 'we need to talk about those things we have not yet discussed.' She handled her teacup nervously. 'Are you... able to? I feel like I might burst if I don't, and dear Robert finds the whole matter too distressing.'

I studied her, trying to read her intent hazel eyes, to divine which of the various facets of her personality and loyalties were currently uppermost. I don't wish to suggest that my friend was a fickle creature, for in many ways she was far more constant than I was, but we are all of us at the mercy of our own conflicting motivations. At this precise moment in time, a lot depended on my ability to parse Agnes correctly.

'Go on, Agnes,' I replied simply, and the effect was that of uncorking a champagne bottle. The questions bubbled forth.

'What did Brown say? How did he kill George and frame Henrietta? Because the story Robert told me, albeit briefly, simply can't be true. And what part did Henrietta's impersonator play in all this?' She took a breath, then said quietly, 'And where are my sister and my nephew?'

She was daring to hope, and I felt I could almost dare with her. But she was not going to like my plan.

I recounted to her the exact content of Brown's patchy confession. She was appalled that he should have tried to implicate Henrietta at the last, and the close of my story saw her as frustrated and full of questions as she had been at the start.

'What can we do, Harry?' she cried out, more in exclamation than in query. 'This simply can't be the end of it all. Henrietta didn't conspire to kill George! She disliked him, no doubt, but not enough to wish him dead! However often I try to tell you all that Henrietta was a gentle, peaceful soul, it doesn't make it any less true. This evil man wished to send you to your graves believing a lie, just because he could.'

Agnes was flushed with exasperation.

'I'll go to Robert, and to Inspector Oughton, and to Mr Dukanwalla. We've got to go back over everything. Why is everyone else content with this rotten, half-baked explanation? All these people dead, and we're supposed to leave it like this?'

I waited until she had finished.

'There's a way, Agnes. I think I may be able to play one last card, but I need your help.'

'Anything!' exclaimed Agnes, her face bright and full of hope. 'What can I do?'

'You can agree not to go to Robert, Duke or Oughton, not to ask me what I'm doing until it's done, and not to demand why.'

Her expression clouded over instantly, and she sat back in her chair for the first time since our conversation had begun. She peered at me, critically, as I had measured her only a few minutes earlier. I simply sat in silence, arms folded, and stared her down. I felt like we might have been the captains of two opposing battleships, trying to divine each other's intentions from a great distance through telescopes.

There was sadness in the feeling too. Really, what it all came down to was that there was one thing we could never say to each other, and it compromised everything else.

'You know what I think, Harrison?' she said at last, tight-lipped. 'I think your opinion of me is unfair. You value my character, but not my judgement. You consider me irrational and short-tempered.'

'You'll admit, Agnes,' I ventured warily, 'that you have occasionally given me a hard time during the course of our acquaintance.'

She exhaled wearily, and rubbed her eye in much the same way as she had done weeks earlier when we sat on the steps together outside Halsingham House.

'Save for that one occasion in this room – and I've apologised for that – I have only been cross when people have deliberately kept things from me. Surely you can see my frustration? Why am I alone considered so unreliable? Dukanwalla is a criminal; Oughton is a bigot;

Potter is a psychopath; and you, Harry, are an impostor in every world you inhabit. I have let none of you down since this all began.'

There was no arguing with any of it.

'I'm sorry, Agnes. You're right, but I must still ask you to do this. Either I can explain things to you, or I can act, but I can't do both.'

The feeling of betrayal in her face was heartbreakingly plain.

'Fine. But there had better be more to this than some simple dramatic desire to keep me in the dark.'

'There is, I promise.'

'And it had better work. Now, if you'll excuse me, I will agree to do as you wish, but I won't tolerate sitting opposite you while you deliberately stick a bag over my head. Good day, Mr Catcliffe.'

After she had left, I opened the fancy box Agnes had set down by her chair when she arrived. Inside was a smart grey homburg, of the modern sort, in fine beaver felt. Tucked in the grosgrain band was a card.

You need a new hat. You can wear it to Maxim's. A

Twenty-Eight

— · —

I f Robert Edlington was surprised to find me waiting for him in the
drawing room at Halsingham House, he did not show it.

I heard the motor car draw up outside, and the clip of his boots on
the stone steps, then the murmured conversation as Inman informed
his master of my presence. Though I could not catch the words, I fancied I caught a hint of nervousness in the timbre of the butler's voice,
and it would have been understandable. While Robert had returned
from London on the mid-morning train, I, on the other hand, had
been in the village since the previous evening. And my time had not
been wasted.

He entered with a wide, sympathetic smile, and shook my hand
warmly. We had not seen each other since Oughton had bundled me
into the back of a carriage outside number 23, Kirkcald Gardens.

'Harry. Good to see you. Forgive my absence when you arrived. I
wasn't aware you were planning to visit.'

'I'm the one who should apologise for turning up unannounced,
but there were some matters I needed to discuss with you, and with
your servants.'

'Of course,' he said, glancing across to where Inman stood in the
doorway. 'I'll have some tea sent in. And will you stay the night?

I'm having a modest dinner party later to ring in the New Year. A small party of friends are coming down on the afternoon train, and you'd be most welcome to join us. Unless you already have plans, of course. Agnes, her parents and her brother will all be there. They came south for the funeral, you know, and I'm trying hard to rebuild relations between our two families, after all that's happened. Old Lord Kelverton enjoys ill health, of course, but between you and I, "enjoys" seems to be the operative word, and he enjoys a good bottle of wine almost as much.'

His hospitality was admirable, but I declined politely and suggested it might be best that we were left alone during our conversation.

'Very well,' he said gravely. 'I suppose it concerns what happened the other night. And... before. Well, naturally we must talk about it, however painful it might be.' He turned to his butler. 'Inman, would you be so good as to see we are not disturbed?'

With Inman's departure came a sudden welling up of nervousness deep in my chest. I did my best to remain as externally impassive as I could manage, but I wondered if Robert could sense it.

'Now then, Harry, before you say anything, please let me speak for a moment. You have no idea the guilt I feel for bringing Brown into this house. It's something that will live with me until my dying day – the knowledge that I introduced the instrument of my own brother's murder. So please, if we must speak of what happened, let it be with that in mind.'

I drew breath to speak, then exhaled again, not certain how to begin. Then I said simply: 'There is no Mrs Brown.'

He looked perplexed, but there was just a flicker of something else in there too.

'I beg your pardon?'

I repeated myself.

'There is no Mrs Brown. Frances Brown. The valet's wife. There never was. You told Agnes that you sent Inman to speak to her in Tunbridge Wells. But you didn't.'

'You spoke to Inman earlier, I suppose?'

'I did. I turned up on the doorstep and reminded him that you and I were friends, and that you had agreed to do everything in your power to solve the mystery surrounding your brother's death. Perhaps I also reminded him how he had once before been manipulated into withholding information from me. He told me he'd taken no trip to Tunbridge Wells.'

'Listen, Harry,' Robert rejoined earnestly. 'The woman is very sick. Terribly fragile in her mind. The derangement would be too much for her. I sent a telegram to her uncle and aunt about what happened, and the old man agrees with me that she can't be told. At least, not yet.'

It was a good response to my ambush, but I shook my head.

'No. That isn't it. You slipped up again. You've just said that Frances is living with her uncle, and that's the same thing you told Agnes, but Brown himself told me that his wife had gone to stay with a maiden aunt. Not the sort of thing he would have got wrong, I wouldn't have thought. The two of you should have been more careful about matching up your stories.'

'Are you sure you remember right, old chap? It was definitely her uncle I communicated with. I will say it's rather ill-mannered of you to come in here and start accusing me of lying. But you've had a rough week and perhaps you've got confused.'

'No, Robert, I haven't,' I said, sighing. 'Because there's more. I'm fairly sure how things happened, but I'm still not certain I understand why.'

He maintained his expression of indulgence, as if he were talking to a fellow afflicted by the most fantastic lunacy, so I ploughed on. There was nowhere to go now but through with it all.

'Back on the night George was murdered, it was your sister-in-law we found blood-soaked and disorientated in bed, but the woman in the corridor – the woman who was killed in Soho last week, and who fled London on the *Tyne Lass* – was not Henrietta. No doubt Henrietta thought she was proving her innocence by sending Agnes to wait behind that cupboard, just as George thought he was proving her guilt by sending me. But in my case I saw what I was supposed to see. I'd wager if we asked George where the idea of setting me up as a spy in my nightshirt came from, he'd say it was Brown's. And if we could ask Brown, we'd find it was yours.'

Robert made no attempt to protest, or even to interrupt me. He merely sat and regarded me, waiting patiently for me to finish. But all the warmth had drained out of his appearance, and his mouth was set in a fashion I had not seen before.

'The story Brown told me was riddled with lies. Henrietta had never sleepwalked at all in this house, either unconsciously or with the intentional object of tormenting her husband. She did when she was younger – a fact which was well known to you and your brother – but not for many years, until Brown appeared on the scene. It was Agnes who first put the idea into my mind when she turned up at my rooms on Christmas Day. She talked about how you'd planted a bad seed in the household, and I realised that was exactly what you'd done. You had placed your most trusted ally at Halsingham House.

'His story that he had seduced Henrietta and that they had plotted the murder together was a good one, but I don't think it could have happened that way. Considerable as Brown's charms might have been, you couldn't have founded a whole plan upon the certainty that Henrietta would be unfaithful. However, she was in ill health, and had for years taken regular medicine at morning and night. Brown boasted that he'd used his experience as a military surgeon's assistant to dope Matthew Grayling, and it wouldn't have been difficult to tamper with Henrietta's evening tonic.

'George told me that his wife was always discovered back in bed after her nocturnal wanderings, and that when awoken she was frequently found to be unnaturally groggy and disorientated. I witnessed her in just such a state on that terrible night, and it was no clever simulation on her part. She was drugged – unwittingly administering the sedative herself each evening. And while Henrietta slept like the dead, another woman roamed the corridors causing her mischief and using the servants' staircase to get in and out.

'Perhaps the idea came originally from your own close resemblance to George. At any rate, I'm impressed you managed to find someone who bore such a close resemblance to Lady Halsingham. Brown's story that Henrietta had unearthed her own double within a day of arriving in an unfamiliar city was wildly unlikely, and the woman who cut Dukanwalla open with a razor was no out-of-work governess. But I suppose Brown was having so much fun with his tall tale that he didn't think it would matter. The true scheme was much longer in the making. Though it's a shame you couldn't find a girl with blue eyes. When I saw her lying behind that pub, I knew it wasn't the real Henrietta.'

'Agnes told me, you know,' Robert suddenly interrupted. 'She said her sister was still alive. That you'd spotted the difference. I said you must have been mistaken, but I knew then you would have to go.' His manner was almost casual, and it was clear that he had decided to waste no more effort on deception.

'It was an extraordinary spot of luck finding her in the first place, especially all the way over in Africa,' he mused. 'If I hadn't run into pretty Maria, I don't suppose any of this would have happened.'

'The books in her trunk,' I remembered, 'were in Dutch. She was an Afrikaner.'

He nodded.

'Resourceful little thing. Her father was a Boer commando. Got his pardon during all that magnanimous handshaking after the war, licensed his rifle as a sporting gun, raised his daughters tough and stealthy. And as you're no doubt about to tell me, Maria spent most of her day dressed up like a beekeeper out at the old gamekeeper's cottage, posing as poor, disfigured Frances Brown and trying in vain to get her skin as pale as Henrietta's.'

'And there you have the reason for Matthew Grayling's death.'
'Oh?'

'For such a supposedly reclusive creature, Frances Brown did seem to run into a lot of visitors. I crossed paths with her, as did Agnes. Even old Fletcher. It was almost like she went out of her way to let people see her. And when they did, she was never wearing the mask Grayling had made her.'

'Only she was.' He smiled and his top teeth sat on his lower lip in an unappealing manner.

'Only she was,' I repeated. 'Grayling's mask wasn't meant to turn a damaged face into a whole one, but to accomplish the opposite. To make an otherwise attractive woman appear disfigured – in combination with a little stagecraft. She was always seen from a distance, and never for long, with her heavy hat brim and veil shading her mask. Lighting, stance and perspective – just like Fornasini's Tin Face Parade.'

'Excellent. Now what else do you think you know?'

'That Brown slit George's throat, silently, while Agnes and I were just yards away in the corridor. That he crept through the adjoining door into Henrietta's room, where she lay doped, and smeared her with George's blood, ready to be the centrepiece in his accomplice's imminent bit of theatre. That he slipped out through the bathroom and the servants' staircase, just as Maria did moments later, leaving Henrietta to face the law.'

'Go on.'

'That Brown was telling the truth when he admitted to breaking Henrietta out of the Rochester Clinic. You knew Henrietta had spent time there before, and were banking on the fact that her wealth and status would see her transferred there after the tragedy. It was a gamble, but a small one. A Kelverton daughter wouldn't end up in a common jail if her family could help it. Rochester might have been able to prove her innocence – given time – but his security was lax enough that she didn't need to remain there long.

'Awaking in the night to find Brown there, she would have been confused, and slow-witted with Dr Rochester's opiates. He urged her to flee with him, spiriting Thomas out of the Cleveley mansion on the way. I can only guess what story he might have told her – that he'd been sent by you, perhaps? That the police would let her hang for a murder she knew she hadn't committed, and escape was her only option? I can't say.

'What I also can't say is what happened to Henrietta. Only that in between sedating Thomas to keep him calm and the two of them getting on the boat, Henrietta was once again switched for Mrs Brown – this Maria. Was it Brown who put them on the boat? People saw a man with a beard, but a decent costume version is easy enough to come by. Whatever the case, I don't think Henrietta ever left London.

'There are other things I don't know, but perhaps you can tell me, Robert? I don't know where Thomas is, or why Maria came back to London.'

He shook his head wistfully.

'Silly girl. She came to blackmail us. Brown and I had a long and involved past together, and Maria possessed details not just of our present scheme, but of our previous history as well. Armed with this information, she sought to increase her already substantial fee. She bundled the child into a poorhouse in Calais then surprised everyone concerned by altering her appearance and getting right back on the next boat to London.'

Robert looked momentarily regretful.

'I don't suppose you'll believe me – and in all honesty it doesn't much matter – but the plan was to let her live. She was to take her payment, return to Africa by a circuitous route, and to be left alone. Then she turned up back in London again, encountered you the moment she stepped off that ship, and like a startled dog she ran straight back to her master. If you'd been a bit subtler at the wharves, she'd have led you right to Brown. It was a stroke of luck that she gave you the slip.

'Apart from that, it is in the fundamental nature of a blackmailer to return again and again, and that simply couldn't be allowed to happen. Surely you can see that?'

'I'm not sure I believe you,' I answered frostily. 'Perhaps she was supposed to end up skewered behind a Calais café rather than a London pub, but you killed everyone else. Why leave her alive?'

He pursed his lips reprovingly.

'Believe what you like. We mostly only killed the people who threatened us, and you yourself bear some blame in that, Harry. Grayling, I'll admit, we planned to remove from the outset. He knew well enough not to ask questions about Frances's mask, but George's murder was always going to hit the front pages, and Grayling couldn't be relied on to keep quiet when that happened.

'He was a rather devil-may-care chap who didn't always do as he was told. Brown and Maria insisted he kept away from the house when he visited, but on his last visit he just breezed into the servants' hall and took lunch with the builders on his way home. Brown thought it was funny the way no-one asked any questions – I think he quite liked the man. And no-one would have given Grayling a second thought until that wretched Potter connected him to Halsingham House and drew you into it.

'As for Fornasini, he was yours. Brown was sure of the man's confidentiality, but then you turned up at his cottage that night and more or less told him Fornasini was going to give him up. So he had to deal with it.'

'But he didn't tell us anything,' I protested weakly, feeling a nause-ating sense of remorse. 'In fact, he told us a lie to cover up Brown's identity. He stuck to his end of the bargain.'

Robert shook his head.

'You told a seasoned killer that a man who knew his secrets had revealed a small portion of them, then you said that you were con-vinced he had more to tell. That's how Brown recounted it to me, and you can see why he would have felt it necessary to silence Fornasini. You brought the fellow back into it, then you arranged his death. Your ignorance in the matter is neither here nor there.'

I did not protest. Guilt is not a rational emotion, and I knew that however much I justified what I had done, deep down some part of me would always feel blame for Giovanni's death – would feel the sting of Lucilla's slap upon my cheek.

'And Grieve? Surely you can't pretend he was any sort of threat.'

'Grieve I will give you too. Like Grayling, he was a necessary casu-alty. Maria had to be paid – and paid very well – before she departed England, and Henrietta's jewellery was a good source of ready pay-ment. Jewels, after all, can easily be exchanged for cash in any country, and come with none of the attendant paperwork and nosey human functionaries required to transfer large amounts of money from one person to another.

'We knew the jewels would be missed sooner or later – many of them were Kelverton heirlooms, after all. If any of them were recog-nised down the line by some jeweller or other, tugging on the thread might eventually lead to Maria. Obviously that couldn't happen. By leaving a small number of trinkets in Grieve's possession, we could imply that he had disposed of the rest. Anything that turned up later would just be linked back to him without the need for further enquiries. He was supposed to put an end to the whole business. The neat suicide of an opportunistic thief racked by guilt.'

'Why Grieve in particular?'

'Joe Brown's poor judgement, mainly. You can consider yourself very fortunate on that score. Brown had to pick someone from George's dinner party to fit up for the theft, and in his position I would have picked you. It would have had the added bonus of removing a witness who might later come to question what he had seen. But poor Joe was only human. He took a dislike to Grieve and regarded you as a likeable incompetent, at least until you turned up on his doorstep full of questions.

'Anyway, Maria sank the plan by turning up like a bad penny. The timing was unfortunate. Brown killed Grieve first thing in the morning, then got back to Belgravia to find a note from Maria waiting for him. I wonder what she did with all that jewellery we gave her? Perhaps some boarding house owner in Calais will take up their floorboards in a decade's time and discover an unexpected windfall.'

He sat back, waiting for me to challenge him over one more death, and the playfulness in his attitude melted away as I spoke.

'You yourself killed Brown.'

'Only because he told me to. Joe was supposed to grow old here at Halsingham with me. We two conspirators could have had a happy life together. That night in Somers Town I knew you would have made some plan to try and get round his ambush, and I meant to hang back and head off whatever scheme you had dreamed up. But Dukanwalla was a sly one. I didn't realise he was there until it was too late. I saw that wife of his go in, of course, and when the shooting started I realised I'd missed something crucial.

'You owe Joe your life, you know. When I saw you following my friend out of that house with your little gun, I was ready to shoot you down, but Joe had other ideas. The final act of his life was to put me completely in the clear. Captain Edlington, hero of the hour, with you as my witness, and no-one left alive to say different.'

Robert's tone was measured, but there was a gloss on his eyes. His fingertips pressed into the low coffee table in front of him with such force that it seemed to me his prints would be impressed upon the grain when he let go.

'Joe Brown was more to me than you can know. He was the only person in life I have ever trusted, and the only one I ever will. There's no other like him, and I will feel his loss as long as I live. Rest assured, Harry, I bear you unending hate over Joe. I would kill you if I could. I still might, one day.'

We measured each other up for an instant, neither sure what the next few minutes would bring.

'May I ask you a question, Robert?'

'Only if I may then ask one of my own.'

'Agreed.'

'Very well then.'

'Why? I know you loved Henrietta – Agnes found one of your letters among her sister's possessions. Was that the reason? For all of this? All these deaths?'

He almost laughed.

'My dear chap, do you think youthful heartbreak is at the root of the matter? After what I've just told you about my particular regard for Joe Brown? I fear you've spent too much time at the opera. It's much more profound than that.

'You, of all men, should appreciate my motives. I've seen the way you and Agnes are in each other's company. You think yourself so subtle and urbane, yet the bond between you is painfully obvious, whether or not you see it yourselves.'

'Agnes and I are friends. Nothing more,' I interjected stiffly. 'And what has any of that got to do with anything?'

'Just as you say. All the same, if Lady Kelverton were to see you together at my party later, I daresay the old bird would make sure you and young Miss Cleveley saw fewer opportunities to encounter one another. But she would be mistaken in that, for you are both conscious of your place. You and Agnes occupy different shelves, and you accept without question the notion that some things are forbidden to you. She is a lady of breeding, and you are a glorified blacksmith got up in a nice suit. How does that song go? The "latest young jay" with his brandy and cheroots, splashing his pater's riches on singers and sweet little barmaids. Agnes will make the good match that everyone expects of her, and one of these days you will seek out some Gaiety Girl at the stage door and make her your wife. You are as you were made, and you're happy to stay there.'

'You, Harry, think yourself a modern man because your people turn a coin making parts for motor cars, and because your money lets you flit like a tourist between the lives of different sets. But all you are is a symptom of other men's dynamism – a follower, clinging to their shirt tails and gathering rich crumbs. You haven't made your own luck, and you never will.

'Me? I was supposed to be a follower too. I was born a second son. I was destined to stand dutifully aside simply because George tumbled into the world a quarter of an hour before I did. Yet I was the brother with the imagination, the energy and the intellect. I am no follower.'

I looked at him in horror.

'But he was your brother...'

'...And judging from the way you say that, you did not know him very well,' he interrupted. 'What if I were to tell you that George's greatest crime, beyond being unimaginative, timorous and dull, was that he was almost completely incapable of love?'

'Are you really going to talk to me of love, after everything you have done?'

At this, he sat suddenly forward in anger.

'Yes, I am!' he snapped. 'Since you're so quick to judge. Do you have brothers of your own?'

'Yes.'

'And I suppose you're close?'

'I suppose so,' I said cautiously. I felt instinctively that Robert was not a man to allow near one's family, given what he had done to his own.

'Well my brother and I were twins. Ours should have been the closest of bonds, and yet where I felt great affection for him, he apparently felt little for me. No doubt he thought he loved me, but he did so in a spirit of cold rationality which was completely at odds with the word. At school, as my own preferences in the matter of love became apparent, I yearned for someone I could trust with my confidences. I thought I could talk to my brother, and yet when I did so, to him my feelings were simply not to be countenanced. He immediately told our father, whose cruelty towards me in his last years was so overwhelming that I resolved to do whatever I was supposed to. There was no malice in George's betrayal, and that made it all the more heartless.

'It was typical of George that when he decided to marry, he did so based on a book of genealogy and the advice of old ladies, as if he were investing in a good horse. Poor girl, she never stood a chance. And inevitably, when we found an opportunity to make the acquaintance of the Kelverton girls, she fell for me rather than him. I wonder, is it hard for you to believe that I liked Henrietta? I enjoyed her company, and in my own mind she was well above my own allotted degree as second son, so I thought nothing of our good-natured flirtation until her letters began to arrive. Letters that could get a young woman in her position into a lot of trouble. I tried to discourage her without being cruel, but it was no good, so I made the great mistake of trusting my brother a second time.

'The odd thing is that George wasn't angry about it. I could have taken that. But he was just practical. He explained to me that not only was I going to bring Henrietta into disrepute, but our own family too. The situation was compounded by my harmless habit at the time of visiting a place off Oxford Street where I could enjoy the company of other like-minded gentlemen. An acquaintance of ours from school had seen me go in and had informed my brother. George could see only one sensible course of action to save his upcoming marriage, the names of both families and my own moral character. I was to be packed off to Rhodesia forthwith.

'I refused, of course, and he replied that if I didn't go, he would be forced to expose me, for my own good. That was the worst bit of all – he genuinely believed he was doing his best for me, by blackmailing me into exile. Africa was a dangerous place for a fighting man, and for all he knew it might have been a death sentence. I was consumed with sadness and anger, but I had to accept it. I wrote a last letter to Henrietta, urging her to marry George, then I left.'

He paused, and sighed in a manner that almost made me forget the terrible crimes he had committed.

'And then I was in Africa, and I found I was rather good at being a cavalry officer. Men respected me, valued me. I met Joe Brown. Life was full of possibilities, and I began to be more open to them. One day I took a patrol out to visit a Boer farmer suspected of stockpiling rifles, and when his daughter opened the door she was the very image of Henrietta.'

So that was how it had begun. A seed of a plan based on years of heartache and a chance encounter. Robert's scheme had not been about revenge or envy, greed or lust, though perhaps elements of all those things lurked in there somewhere. He had simply decided to alter a world that did not fit.

'Agnes is beyond you, Harry, but why? Personally, you're well-suited. From my own limited observations, you may even love each other a little. Practically, you're probably rich enough to support her lifestyle. There's no decent reason in the world why you shouldn't be together, save the decaying customs of this corrupted old country. I resolved in Africa that I would not live my life confined to my allotted place. That world over there is built on men like me, and in time this one will be too.'

'And Thomas? You can't be Lord Halsingham until he is confirmed dead. Surely you have not...'

'I'm not an absolute barbarian, Harry. Even I would baulk under most circumstances at butchering a small boy. And fortunately I don't need to. I have no wish to squander my days listening to dreary old men in the House of Lords, especially not with these bloody Liberals in government. As it is, I have control of all the money and the property – everything except the title, and there is no rush on that score. In a few years I'll simply have him declared dead. It may well be true by then anyway, for the orphanage in which he currently resides is, according to dear departed Maria, a most squalid institution, and Thomas's health is far from robust.'

No words would come to me. Robert was persuasive and appalling in equal measure. The things he had brought about were nothing short of monstrous, yet it occurred to me that if George could have listened to his brother's whole speech from beyond the grave, he might still have struggled to understand what he had ever done wrong.

When I was growing up, there had been a whimsical old volume of American essays on Grandpa Catcliffe's bookshelves, and one of these tracts had claimed that when two men meet there are in fact at least six distinct personalities present: each man's ideal of himself; his ideal of the other, and the two men as they really are – known only to their maker. I had once likened my own character to that of adventurers such as Captain Edlington and Joseph Brown, but I now saw how mistaken I had been. I was a toothless house cat by comparison, lacking their most essential characteristics: their daring, their ruthlessness, their energy. Even my imagination was of an inferior kind.

Robert broke into my thoughts.

'May I ask my question now?'

'Certainly.' Then I added coldly, 'You've earned it with your tale.'

'What do you want, Harry? I can't believe that, having so lately walked into a trap, you would repeat the mistake so readily, so you must have taken measures to safeguard yourself. On the other hand, you haven't exposed me. Which means you've come here to bargain.'

'You are correct. I haven't told a soul of my suspicions, but everything I've just recounted to you is written down in sealed envelopes. I don't need to tell you how many copies there are, only that you won't find them all, and that various trusted people will place the information in the public domain if anything happens to me. One, for example, is in a packet in the company safe at Catcliffe's, and I've amended my will to the effect that if anything occurs to end my life prematurely, it is to be widely distributed.

'You ask what I propose. In short, I propose that I allow you to live this life which you've bought for yourself with the blood of your own. In return, you give me Henrietta and Thomas, for I don't believe they will ever be discovered otherwise. I find them a place to live well out of the public eye, and you undertake to pay a modest annual sum towards their upkeep, and to guarantee their safety and mine.'

'And when Thomas grows up?'

'Let's cross that bridge when we come to it. As you say, his health is weak.'

'It's my turn to ask why.'

'And I agreed to answer only one question. Which I've done.' I felt powerful, and confident in my plan.

'Suppose an accident befalls you which has nothing to do with me?'

I smiled for the first time since Inman had left the room.

'I rather think you'd better hope that does not happen.'

312

He thought for a moment. There was no rancour in his face, just simple indecision as he weighed up options and risks. Though outwardly calm, I prayed inwardly that he came down on the side of letting me live. I knew enough of Robert Edlington now to realise that if he decided on the other option then there were few powers on earth that would save me.

Finally, he spoke.

'I can give you Thomas. He's in Calais and can be retrieved. But Henrietta is out of reach.'

'How so?'

'I shouldn't need to spell it out to you.'

And indeed he did not, but the sadness was no less piercing. I wondered where Henrietta lay, and whether she would ever be found. I imagined her, disorientated in the small hours, hurrying to the Rotherhithe wharves in a four-wheeler, with Thomas doped and asleep in her lap, and Brown sat opposite. The carriage would have stopped somewhere quiet. Brown might perhaps have told her to leave Thomas inside and to follow him down an alleyway on some spurious errand or other. The cabman would have seen the two of them disappear, and sometime later, two would have emerged once more. He would not have noticed the difference in the woman. I hoped fervently that she had not seen it coming.

Robert continued.

'You can have Thomas. It will take me a week or so to arrange, and I want two things in return.'

'I cannot see what else you could possibly want.'

'An undertaking from you, and one more question. If you refuse these things then the whole deal is off.'

'Go on.'

He gave me a winning smile.

'When a suitable opportunity arises, I'm going to ask Agnes to marry me. You will do nothing to hinder this, including telling her a single word of what has passed between us today.'

'Not a chance,' I replied curtly.

'I shall add another incentive. If you don't agree to this, I'll have both Thomas and Agnes herself murdered. There are plenty more men in London like the ones who fought alongside Brown on Christmas Eve, and I know how to get word to them. You will think to try and prevent this by getting me arrested, but I shall make sure my instructions are clear – that Agnes and Thomas are to be killed either on my command, or immediately upon my being taken into police custody. I'll hang, no doubt, but they'll be dead, and you care more about the latter than the former.'

I felt sick.

'What's to stop me going to the police immediately?'

'Can you guarantee that from where we sit at this moment on my family's fine furnishings, you can summon Inspector Oughton faster than I can contact the men I've mentioned? Would you stake Agnes's life on your ability to get through that door before I can knock you down?'

'So my choices are either to let Agnes die or to let her spend the rest of her life married to the man who had her sister murdered?'

'Not quite. I'll give you a third option.'

I waited, my mind racing through possibilities, but he took his time. When he spoke, his proposal was unexpected.

'I will make it explicit in my instructions that, in the event of my death – however it comes about – Agnes and Thomas should not be harmed. So if you really want to save her, then you can just kill me.'

'Why? Why add that?'

'Because you won't do it. You will endure watching me take Agnes as my wife, and though it will be within your power to stop it, you won't be brave enough. You'll choose to sacrifice Agnes's future rather than your own, and I will enjoy that thought. Joe Brown would have enjoyed it too.'

The surety I had felt moments earlier had vanished, replaced by the crushing enormity of what I had just brought about in that room. What my recklessness and cowardice had done to that young woman who I esteemed so highly.

'She may not accept your offer of marriage,' I said weakly.

He appeared not to hear this, continuing breezily, 'If I'm to assume your agreement with my condition, may I now ask my question?'

'Very well, but when I've answered it, our bargain is set.'

'Agreed. In that case, why didn't you tell Agnes any of what you've just told me?'

I glowered across at him, more fascinated than ever by his cruelty.

'You know why.'

'Of course I do, but I want to hear you say it.'

'Damn you, Robert,' I snapped, getting up to leave. He remained seated, only remarking mildly.

'No answer, no deal. I may swing, but I promise you that Thomas and Agnes will be cold before the week is out.'

'Very well.' I remained standing. 'I didn't tell her because I decided that if I forced Agnes to choose between us, she would probably choose you. I thought if I confided in her, she wouldn't believe me, and there was a good chance she would tell you everything.'

'So you can't trust her? I call that a poor sort of friendship. I don't mind saying that I remain optimistic about my marriage proposal.'

I ignored him, turning on my heel.

'One week. I shall expect to have Thomas within one week.'

As I opened the door to leave, I heard him calling after me,

'Happy New Year, Harry!'

Twenty-Nine

— · —

Jabez Potter shuffled his feet irritably and pulled his coat closer around him. It was a couple of weeks since he had returned to his job at the brewery – or at least the business of roaming around London in a dray for which someone seemed generous or naïve enough to pay him – and yet he was still not quite his robust former self. His limp appeared heavier, and the February cold seemed to cut him deeper. He leaned upon a hazel root stick, and though this was not especially remarkable in a man with a wooden leg, I had never seen him use one before.

We stood on the half-empty platform at St Pancras station, watching as the early-morning travellers clambered on board the hissing Midland Railway train, bound for the north.

I nudged Jabez and indicated the far end of the platform, where a smartly attired group of five all in black were making their way towards us, their breath steaming in the air. There was an older couple – the gentleman rather bowed and placing some weight upon his cane – a bright-looking fellow of around twenty, and a graceful young woman on the arm of a tall, well-built man.

It was her I had spotted. Picked out unconsciously from the crowd when she was still a stick figure.

'Your capacity for torturing yourself is a thing to behold. Honestly, mate.' Jabez whistled to himself, then needled my arm with his forefinger in what I imagine he considered a reassuring gesture. 'I'm off to get a cup of tea. Find me in the buffet when you're done.'

The young woman caught sight of me as she drew closer, and I removed my hat in mute signal. She turned and held a brief exchange with the rest of her family, pointing at me as she did so, then she came towards me, leaving the others to board the train. The older lady looked suspiciously over her shoulder as she was helped up into the carriage. The tall man loitered on the platform, chatting to a couple of porters who were loading the family's luggage. I avoided his eye.

'Hello, Harry,' said Agnes, kissing me stiffly on the cheek. 'I wondered if I might see you here.'

'I came to say goodbye.'

'There's really no need,' she said briskly. 'I'll be living at Halsingham House permanently after the summer.'

'Yes. Congratulations.' I smiled awkwardly.

'Thank you. I'm sorry you couldn't attend the engagement party. I hope we'll see you at the wedding?'

I could think of few things more hateful than sitting in the church where they'd held George's funeral, watching as his Borgia of a brother married Agnes Cleveley with my unspoken complicity, but I nodded vaguely. As traitors went, I was unsurpassed. I noticed Henrietta's little star brooch glittering on the lapel of her jacket.

'Harry, I don't really understand why you're here.'

'Because I wanted us to part as friends, and last time we didn't.'

This was something of an understatement, but my deal with Robert had been very specific that Agnes was to be left in the dark. I had begun

1908 by enduring a piece of invective that had turned several heads in the refined surroundings of the Cordovan.

Agnes shook her head. Today she was not angry, though this cold resignation was not really much better.

'I don't think you understand what friendship is. It's just a face you wear rather than something real. If you were a friend, you would give me the truth. You could tell me everything right here and now, and we could find a way out together, you and I. Only you won't. All you'll tell me is that Henrietta is dead but Thomas is safe, and you refuse to say a word more.'

She motioned towards the train carriage.

'Needless to say, I've fed Mother and Father a fabrication. That Henrietta lied to protect Brown because she loved him, that he arranged to make it look as if she were dead – a secret which they will keep for her sake – and that she was last seen on the Calais docks. As far as they know, she's living abroad in hiding with Thomas, and will be for evermore. They would rather imagine her a happy fugitive than a corpse. So would I.

'Only I know it's not true, and you won't say what happened to her or how you know. How are we supposed to go on with such lies hanging over us?'

I turned the smart grey homburg nervously in my hands.

'I suppose it won't help my case to start mumbling about the difference between a lie and an omission?'

She gave me a half-smile.

'You've been lying to me about one thing or another since the weekend we met. You justify it with nonsense about ends and means,

319

but I think you just keep me in the dark so I can't question your choices. What if I'm better at making decisions than you are?'

Agnes raised her eyebrows at me expectantly, but it didn't matter that she was right. I still couldn't give in. I had gambled on a decision not to place my trust in her, and had lost. I felt doubly ashamed because I knew she was not the only sister I had underestimated. Henrietta had been an innocent. She had never hurt anyone and had never been unfaithful despite her unhappiness. Yet there we had all been, trying to persuade Agnes into doubting her.

Behind her, the guards began whistling and shouting as the last passengers hurried along the platform. Agnes was still waiting for me to reply.

'I wish there had been someone better,' I said simply.

'But there was just you, Harrison.'

She put a hand on my arm and kissed me again on the cheek, this time with just a flicker of frost-laden affection. It must have been barely a second, but it stretched out longer than it ought to have.

'Bye, Harry.'

'Goodbye, Agnes.'

She began to walk briskly away, and the world recommenced falling in on me. Then she turned back.

'You think this is goodbye, but it isn't. Because I'm not giving up. Sooner or later I'm going to find out everything. And then you'll have to account for yourself.'

She did not look back at me again. I watched as Robert escorted her on board the train, realising after a moment or two that Jabez had reappeared at my elbow.

'I thought you were getting a cup of tea.'

'Queue was too long. Let's get a pint instead.'

'It's eight in the morning, Jabez.'

'Market pubs'll be open.'

Robert alighted from the train, then stood and waved as it drew slowly along the platform, a sunny smile on his face. The man was incredible. I was so busy watching him that I forgot to scan the windows of the train for the Cleveley family.

When the full length of the great steel beast had slithered noisily out of the station, Robert paid the two porters and offered them each a cigarette, cupping a match for them as they leaned gratefully in. Looking past them, he gave me a knowing nod, the flame still alight in his fingers. He lit his own cigarette, flicked the end of the match onto the tracks, and marched off jauntily towards the station doors.

'Think you can get him from here with that ladies' gun of yours?' asked Potter, barely moving his lips. 'Because from a distance of two feet you can hit a man half the time. I can vouch for that.'

He knew full well that the Remington had languished in a desk drawer since Christmas Eve.

'I don't understand why you're so calm about all this. You know what he did. And what he's doing.'

Potter considered the question for a moment as he rummaged for his smoking apparatus.

'It was always about the truth for me. It was the not knowing that was the worst. The idea that no-one could be bothered to find out what happened to Matthew. And anyway, the man who did the killing is gone.'

'But the man who orchestrated it all is right there,' I pointed, exasperated.

'And he's not going anywhere,' said Jabez, calmly. 'His time will come, mark my words.'

He could see I was in high dudgeon.

'Listen, mate. I said it was about the truth for me, but for you it should be about life. What about that pasty little lad, over there in Ireland with Liza's people? At this very moment, Maggie Duke and the boys are probably teaching him how to give himself a tattoo with a penknife and a lump of coal. We might have cocked it up all along the way, but that little boy's alive and safe because of you. Isn't that worth something? Now, what about that pint?'

'All right then.'

Potter and I floated ourselves out onto the human tide of Euston Road, beneath the overblown façade of the Midland Grand Hotel, its orange jumble of colonnades and spires like the crackpot lunacy of some Bavarian prince. As I stepped out to hail a cab, I saw Jabez glance down the road towards the Great Northern Railway Station at King's Cross. It was just a momentary twitch of the head, but in that instant I followed his gaze to where a familiar lean figure lounged against the base of a lamp post, camouflaging himself behind a pinkish copy of *The Sporting Times*. At his feet, on the end of a short length of frayed rope, an overweight bull terrier lay inelegantly on his side, displaying his nether regions prominently to the passing pedestrians.

We rattled off eastwards, the puffs of Potter's tobacco smoke making our cab appear like a sort of elaborately disguised steam engine as we overtook a procession of omnibuses bearing adverts for Fry's Cocoa and Nestle's Milk. I had begun to comprehend my friend's uncharacteristically phlegmatic demeanour. Quietly, I asked him, 'Jabez, why was Duke following us?'

He stroked the curves of his pornographic little pipe thoughtfully.

'Duke's business is his own, mate. But between you, me and the cabbie, it's not us he's stalking. And that right there is something worth raising a pint pot to at eight in the morning.'

For all the world, I would not have been Captain Robert Edlington just then.

Acknowledgements

I'm grateful to an awful lot of people for getting Harry Catcliffe and his cronies this far. To everyone at the Bridport Prize, where *The Tin Face Parade* was shortlisted for the Peggy Chapman-Andrews First Novel Award in 2018, and to Aki and Joe at TLC, who have been generous with their help and encouragement ever since. I owe a great debt to Imogen Robertson, who comprehensively butchered an early draft and inspired me to do better, and also to my brilliant editor, Richard Sheehan. The mistakes that remain, of course, are mine.

Self-publishing has been quite an adventure in itself, and I'm very thankful to crime writer and indie publishing expert Debbie Young for guiding me through it. The wonderful cover is the work of Jessica Bell.

J L Carr once said that novel-writing is a cold-blooded business, and a lot of what lies in these pages is pilfered. Thank you to everyone who has lent me snippets of information, whether or not they knew they were doing it. Among many others, I tip my homburg to Shelock

Pearson for giving me Dawoojee, to Edward Crangle for his advice on late-Victorian jewellery, and to Ruthie Knight for Jabez's leg. I've also shamelessly cannibalised my own family history. Braime boys have run the real-life equivalent of Catcliffe Steel since the 1880s (and still do) – and I feel honour-bound to point out that none of them have been so work-shy and incompetent as Harrison Catcliffe.

Finally, there are my friends and family – especially Gwubba, Ian and Popy. And PF, the industrious father faced with wayward sons. Much missed, he would not have cared for the violence and bad language, but might have been quietly proud all the same.

Joly Braime

Joly Braime is a writer, editor, illustrator and occasional adventurer. He's written on everything from Sherlock Holmes, moorland dialect and home-brewing to international hiking trips and bee-related etiquette. He lives in a cottage by the sea with a lurcher and a tortoise. *The Tin Face Parade* is his first novel.

jolybraime.co.uk

If you enjoyed this book...

Harrison Catcliffe and his friends will return in *The Porcelain Poet*, due out in winter 2023.

For updates, please do pop along to **jolybraime.co.uk** and sign up to my mailing list.

www.ingramcontent.com/pod-product-compliance
Lightning Source LLC
Chambersburg PA
CBHW050926220726
48290CB00018B/1603